PRAISE FOR GWENDA BOND

"The book was different to anything else I've read in recent months and Gwenda Bond is certainly an author I'll be keeping my eye on."
A Dream of Books

"If you enjoy supernatural teen dramas like *Teen Wolf* or *The Vampire Diaries* then I think that Blackwood may be the book for you."
The Eloquent Page

"An excellent debut where the author has taken a true story and completely made it her own by adding elements of magic and paranormal activity."
Serendipity Reviews

"If you're looking for a story that brings history to life and then puts a supernatural spin on it, a story that will keep you gripped and make you desperate to uncover the mystery then look no further."
Feeling Fictional

"With whip-smart, instantly likable characters and a gothic small-town setting, Bond weaves a dark and gorgeous tapestry from America's oldest mystery."
Scott Westerfeld, New York Times bestselling author of the Leviathan *series*

"Weird, wise and witty, *Blackwood* is great fun."
Marcus Sedgwick

"Miranda Blackwood's battle against her own history is utterly modern – and utterly marvelous. She's truly a heroine all readers can rally behind."
  Micol Ostow, author of Family *and* So Punk Rock

"This haunting, romantic mystery intrigues, chills, and captivates."
  New York Times bestselling author Cynthia Leitich Smith

"A deft and clever debut! Bond takes some reliably great elements – a family curse, the mark of Cain, the old and endlessly fascinating mystery of the Roanoke Colony – and makes them into something delightfully, surprisingly new. How does she do that? I suspect witchcraft."
  Karen Joy Fowler, New York Times bestselling author of The Jane Austen Book Club

"*Blackwood* is an impressive debut novel for Ms. Bond and is hopefully just the first of many novels she plans to write."
  SFF World

"With two endearing and lovable main characters and a creative supernatural spin on a very real historical mystery, *Blackwood* is a well-crafted and intriguing paranormal explanation of the events surrounding the lost colony of Roanoke."
  Refracted Light Reviews

"I liked Miranda and Phillips. Both are intelligent, realistic portrayed teens not burdened by the emo angst that sometimes overwhelms a YA storyline."
Smexybooks

"I enjoyed *Blackwood* because it had a brilliant lead character and some unique and interesting ideas which kept me guessing throughout the book."
The Overflowing Library

"Offbeat and imaginative, *Blackwood* mingles past and present, dark forces with a hint of pulp SF, along with many kinds of drama – from Shakespearean revenge to an amphitheater show where the island's legend is just an entertainment for passing tourists. Whether viewed as young adult, genre mix, or a first novel, it belongs with the year's best."
Locus

"*Blackwood* has several notable strengths, and its intense pacing and likeable protagonists make it a quick and satisfying read."
Strange Horizons

"*Blackwood* sends chills down your spine, keeps you on the edge of your seat, all while unfolding a clever storyline."
A Journey Through Pages

GWENDA BOND

The Woken Gods

STRANGE CHEMISTRY
An Angry Robot imprint
and a member of the Osprey Group

Lace Market House	Angry Robot USA
54-56 High Pavement	Osprey Publishing
Nottingham	PO Box 3985
NG1 1HW	New York NY 10185-3985
UK	USA

www.strangechemistrybooks.com
Strange Chemistry #16

A Strange Chemistry paperback original 2013
1

ISBN: 978 1 90884 425 5
eBook ISBN: 978 1 90884 426 2

Printed in the United States of America

9 8 7 6 5 4 3 2 1

To my Grandmother, who gave up everything to raise me as her own. I miss her every day.

And to my mom and dad, for making the years we had together filled with joy and dreaming.

THE CITY ASLEEP

Night enfolds the sleeping city, shadows unfurling like wings across deserted streets and empty parks. Many of the painted townhouses stand vacant. In others, people succumb to the insomnia of ordinary worries – misbehaving children, unpaid bills, stressful jobs – or dream of the extraordinary that has become commonplace: blazes caused by gods, friends vanished into cults, the Society's reassurances that everything is fine. Everything will be just fine, so long as everyone listens. So long as everyone believes them.

Across the city, in a nearly abandoned neighborhood that used to belong to politicians and lobbyists, the gods are awake. In the strange embassies of the seven tricksters willing to live in this place, to risk everything that they are, the inhabitants never sleep. They slept for thousands of years, after all.

The pyramid of Set House rises from a jungle. Milk-white columns front the temple of Hermes House. The black fortress of Loki House juts into a night as dark as its walls. Rough hide slants into the massive teepee of

Coyote House. The bright tiers of Tezcatlipoca House stand on barren sand. A sacred grove of thick trees surrounds the ornate shrine of Legba House, situated at the convergence of two wide red-and-black paths. And at the end of the property, the ziggurat of Enki House towers over a marsh.

Broad steps ascend the base and two long ramps extend from the flat surface at the top, where a towering stone temple soars. A man climbs the ramp, deliberately, a small lantern held in one hand to light the way. He has not been invited here. But when he reaches the temple's arched entrance, a god with two faces is waiting. He is taken inside, where he shares a secret and asks for help.

He leaves before long. He does not focus on what lies ahead. Instead the past replays itself. He remembers five years ago, the day of the Awakening, when the gods rose from the earth. He remembers the plan the Society put into motion. The gods' own magic turned against them, the relics men had gathered while they lay sleeping the only thing that could allow humanity a chance to survive. The doors were sealed, one on this side of the world and the other far away. The Society held its breath.

He is one of them. He held his.

The god they captured was one of the most powerful. She had a lion's head, and a warrior's heart. They marched her from the Library out onto the green mall of the United States capital, torches blazing along each side. The relic that slew her was a blade, a curving scimitar collected from beneath the ruins of a Babylonian palace. It had been a gift from a god to a king during the first time. The time before the gods vanished, when they ruled over humanity.

The cameras broadcast Sekhmet's death around the world, giving humans hope. Gods swarmed the city and watched, some with eyes like many-faceted insects, others with wings and tongues sharp as knives, with glimmering scales and skin hard as armor. They watched Sekhmet, her lion's head and warrior's heart both still as she lay on the bed of green, green grass. Black blood spilled from the wound at her neck. The torches burned until the oil inside ran dry. She did not move again.

And they knew it was true, gods and men alike. The world above and the world below are denied the gods now. Closed off by the Society. Stuck here in the world between, so long as those doors are shut, gods can be killed. Gods can die.

So the treaty. So this city became the Society's stronghold and the home of the seven tricksters most sympathetic to the humans, the ones who volunteered to deal with the murderers of gods. This is the city where deals are cut. Sometimes in the light, more often in the shadows.

There should be billowing black clouds, the man thinks, thunder and lightning to shatter the silence. The world deserves some sign that the peace is fraying. His hand grips the lantern's handle tightly, as though if he can hold onto the light he might keep it all from unraveling.

He alone sees the storm approaching. He alone knows what tomorrow will bring.

He walks back into the city holding onto the hope he can at least save his daughter.

CHAPTER ONE

At the window, I watch rain that gives every impression it will never ever stop – probably because I need it to. Otherwise, I'm going to get soaked on my walk home.

My best friend Bree snores softly (which she claims she doesn't do) across the room. I pace and admire her latest sketches, taped around the walls. In them, gods loom like horrors, ghost wings and horns traced inside with hieroglyph shapes. Bree draws them like monsters, and maybe they are.

They're inescapable, but we avoid getting up close and personal with them. Sure, we see them in photographs and on TV, even occasionally out and about. But the closest I've been to a real-life, in-the-weird-flesh god is the length of a city block, traveling up to the Library of Congress for a Tricksters' Council meeting. Looking at Bree's drawings, knowing what they're capable of, that suits me fine.

I go back to the window, drum my fingers against the sill. Rain still sluices down in sheets. Finally, *finally*, it slacks to a minor downpour and the gray light of early morning becomes visible. It'll have to be good enough. I sift through Bree's colored grease pencils and select a nice red one with a fat tip. Her corkscrew black curls sprawl messily across her pillow, and one of her hands dangles off the bed.

She's a deep sleeper, so there's a fair chance she won't wake as I start to write on the pale skin inside her arm: *See you at...*

Her other hand flies up and catches mine. "Kyra, you better not have drawn something on my face again," she says.

"One time. I did that one time," I say. "*And* you thought it was funny."

That was on the last Day of the Dead. We stayed up late, raiding Bree's mom's bar. I sketched a skeleton over her passed-out features, and the result was a worthy effort, if far less scary than she could have done on me.

"After it came off, I thought it was hilarious," Bree admits, blinking in a half-hearted attempt to shake off sleep. She's small, curvy, and frequently looks like a work of art herself. This morning, she's in rumpled PJs, a little smear of mascara beneath one eye. "You leaving?"

"Yeah. Better get home." The whole point of staying over was to allow a grand entrance this morning – and not to have been alone in our big empty townhouse all night. These days I'm never sure when Dad will bother coming home from work and when he won't. He could let me know, but the idea never seems to occur to him.

Turnabout is more than fair play.

Bree holds her arm up and squints. "See you at... school?"

"It's like you're a mind reader."

Bree's head thuds back onto the pillow. "You are predictable."

"Take that back." I pull on the cracked brown leather jacket I scored on our shopping expedition at the outdoor market the night before. Dad is guaranteed to hate it.

Bree grunts, tugging the blanket over her head. I slip downstairs and unlatch the door quietly to avoid waking her mom. Heading into the only-slightly-less-insistent rain, I'm grateful my new-old jacket is thick. By the time I make it home, the rain has ended but my long brown hair drips, the ends curled into tips like twin question marks. My jeans are soaked.

I shiver as I fumble out my key and fit it in the lock. With great feeling, I slam the door shut behind me. If Dad's home, he won't be asleep anymore.

But then I see he's right here, not upstairs in bed.

He sits on the leather couch, a coffee cup in front of him. He wears sweats, but manages to look, as ever, like a scholarly librarian. Which he is. What he cares about most in the world is finding the facts the Society of the Sun needs. He's more at home at the Library working for them than here.

He pushes his round glasses up his nose. "Up for a run?" he asks.

My sneakers are beside him, and he tosses them over. I sidestep, and the shoes clunk to the floor.

Running was something we used to do together before... everything. I try to remember the last one we went for together and come up empty. All I can think of are too-bright memories, untethered from a specific time. All my memories from before the Awakening are like that – too light, lighter than they really were, like overexposed film. I also can't remember the last time he *wanted* me to go for a run with him.

"Aren't you going to ask me where I was?" I counter.

"No." He frowns. "You should change into something dry."

"I'm fine." So maybe my prickling goosebumps and the puddle growing around my feet make it less than convincing. "I don't really have time for a run."

He nods toward the chair beside the couch. "Please, have a seat," he says, and the oddity of a request instead of an order throws me off. I flick the light switch beside the door, but nothing happens. The electricity is out again. The gods' magic tends to fritz it periodically, so not a huge surprise. I cross the still-dim room and sink onto the leather chair opposite him.

"Kyra," he starts. But then he says nothing else.

"Present." I drag a hand through my wet hair. "Look, if there's nothing, I should get ready for–"

"There is something," he says.

The chill from the rain turns to ice. I swallow and barely manage to get out the question: "Is it Mom?"

In the next moment, he's on his feet and kneeling in front of me. He takes my cold hands in his warm ones. I let him.

"She's fine," he says. I notice the dark circles under his eyes for the first time. He hasn't been sleeping much.

He amends his description to reflect reality. "She's the same, I mean. It's not her... I need to talk to you about something else."

Relief at the news Mom is OK – as OK as she ever is – makes me willing to hear out whatever this is. Having his attention, undivided and on me and not angry, doesn't happen often.

"Kyra, if anything ever..." But he breaks off again.

"You're starting to freak me out."

He nods. "I'm sorry. It's just... if anything were to happen to me. If I ever... get hurt or disappear or am suddenly not around, you have to promise me that you'll leave the city. There's enough money hidden away here in the house to get you far away." He waits for a response.

I have trouble figuring out what to say. I settle on, "What would happen to you?"

When he speaks, he seems to choose the words with such care that it becomes clear he's leaving out as much as he's saying. "This is a dangerous city. A dangerous world. You know that. Anything could happen."

"Anything could happen to me, too."

It's the truth. Gods may be anywhere and everywhere now, but D.C. is different. They come and go from here constantly. Most don't linger after they bring whatever petition to their trickster of choice. But occasionally they decide to make a statement, calling up an epic storm or sending a wave of holy fire along a street, whatever they feel like to thumb their divine noses at the Society's authority. And then there are the crazies who come to protest or pledge fealty to gods or men or to neither.

There are the oracles at the Circle, where Mom has spent the last five years.

That's why we stay here. We can't leave, not without her. And it's not as if Dad would give up his job at the Library.

I lift one of my hands from his to push my wet hair over my shoulder so it won't drip on his arm. He releases my other one to adjust his glasses again, and moves back to the couch.

"Nothing's going to happen to you." He says it fiercely, as if his insistence can make it true. "But I want you to promise me. I *need* you to promise that if I ever don't come home, you'll leave the city."

I stand. "You don't come home all the time. Three times last week, actually. So that's a lot of leaving the city. Why don't you just send me away, if that's what you want?"

He rises again, and we face off. This, *this* is more familiar. This is how we talk now. We argue.

"That's not what I want," he says. "And you know I'm talking about something besides working late."

Right. "So this theoretical time you really never come home, should I take Mom with me or just leave her over in oracle central? Wait. Never mind. We leave her there now, so I guess I have the answer."

"You know she wouldn't go with you. I'm sorry about having to bring this up. I hope none of this is ever necessary. But I need you to promise me."

"I won't." I shrug one shoulder. "If you're gone, I'll be on my own. I'll do whatever I want."

When he responds, it's with something less exasperation, more admiration. "You always do."

I can't trust my interpretation of that tone. "Like father, like daughter." I head to the stairs, but his last words stop me.

"I wish you would promise, Kyra. But remember this. Remember what I asked of you. That'll have to be enough. I love you, you know that."

I close my eyes, unable to look at him. *I love you, you know that.* "I'm going to be late." Then I open them and pound up the stairs, leaving wet footprints in my wake.

I *am* going to be late. When I come back downstairs dressed in blissfully dry jeans and a strategically ripped T-shirt over a tank carrying my new (still wet) jacket and my backpack, Dad is gone. Presumably to work. I eat some bread with butter, then pause at the door.

Bending, I pick up my sneakers. They've been neglected lately. I choose a dry spot and sit, swap my thick-soled boots for them. I strap on my backpack, and keep my jacket with me in case I want it later.

Getting to school more quickly isn't why I decide to run. Dad's out-of-nowhere request unsettled me. If I ever had to leave this whacked-out city, where would I go? There's nowhere, no one. He knows that. He knows it's just the two of us, and Mom across town surrounded by her delusions, peering into a future only she sees.

My feet slap the sidewalk as I run faster, not caring how sweaty I get. In the morning light, the streets and sidewalks that front our neighborhood's tall Victorians are streaked with the dull red of overripe cherries. The trees used to be ornamental, cherry *blossom* trees. My too-bright childhood was frosted with the pretty pink petals of their blossoms, and never a single fat cherry. Not until the gods set up house.

Now the bottoms of my shoes get gummy with the residue. The damp fruit smell clogs my nose. I pass an empty house with graffiti slashing across the front that proclaims *The End Is Here*. Must have been wishful thinking.

A herd of revelers appears up the street, and, finally, I slow. The tourists descended on town a few days ago, here for the weekend's solstice celebration. They meander all over in the meantime, indulging in obnoxiously loud drumming in extremely tacky costumes inspired by their favorite deities. They sport wooden necklaces of skulls, belts made of plastic snakes. They are, without a doubt, the worst visitors we get.

I turn into an alley to avoid them, and realize I feel almost calm beneath the thin layer of sweat. Stopping, I cursorily smooth my hair and put on the leather jacket. I walk the rest of the way, so that by the time I reach school I'm positive no one – not even Bree – will be able to tell I was upset. No one will know that I raced here like hungry ghosts chased me. There are always ghosts at my heels, anyway. Not real ones, the ones that everyone has.

The lurking past, reminding us of everything we lost and will never ever get back.

CHAPTER TWO

Oz Spencer has no clue why he's been summoned, but he waits patiently in the office of the Society's director – and his guardian – William Bronson, deep within the Library of Congress. A few feet away, Bronson is engaged in an intense conversation with two senior operatives clad in navy field uniforms with gold piping.

Oz can never quite get over how odd it is that the "Bill Bronson" he grew up knowing as an old family friend has become one of the most famous faces in the world. Even with the Society out in the open, it's hard to believe how little outsiders acknowledge the live ammo – in the form of relics and politics and secret history – that the man is juggling at any given time. His poker-face is composed of half polished businessman and half silver-haired grandfather, comfortingly familiar. He wears suits instead of the uniform, saying when people see him on the news looking like any leader from any time and any place, it helps put them at ease.

Their ease is more important than ever.

Oz doesn't mind waiting. This is one of his boring days, devoted to thumbing through dusty records and texts in the archives to learn the history of various relics, rather than using them for something fun like combat training. It's his best friend Justin's favorite thing, which he'll never understand.

He catches the name "Henry Locke" from one of the men. Locke has been his instructor now and again, and is at the top of the food chain, along with Rose Greene, the next in seniority to Bronson. The two men nod their agreement with whatever Bronson has said and leave. Oz clears his throat, "You called for me, sir?"

An operative Oz doesn't know bursts in before Bronson can answer.

"Since when does my office not require a knock?" Bronson asks, frowning.

The chagrined operative squares his shoulders. "I'm sorry, Director, but the Pythias wanted to send word again that they are waiting. They said they need to see you immediately."

Oz hides his surprise. The Pythias get sent *for*. The most powerful of sibyls and oracles, they rarely insert themselves into any situation willingly – at least that's what he's always been told. And no one chastises Bronson. But all his guardian says is: "Come with me, Osborne. They asked for you too."

Bronson's already heading for the door, and Oz follows, certain he misheard.

"What's this all about?" Oz asks, as they make their way down a dark hallway in the lower levels that house most of the main Society offices. Carved insets cradle statues of famous figures from the organization's history. Heroes the world had known nothing about before. "Did something happen to Mr Locke?"

"You could say Mr Locke happened to something else," Bronson says.

He doesn't elaborate, intent on their destination. Oz has heard many stories about the legendary oracles they are about to visit – about traitors uncovered and the locations of powerful relics disclosed – but as an operative who's barely earned his stripes he has never seen them. Nor would he expect them to know he exists. He keeps quiet in case Bronson realizes that he's probably been included in error and sends him away.

Down and down they go, until they reach a tall door covered in small pieces of glass. They reflect the soft blue glow of the sconce light, so that the door appears to be moving, flowing. Bronson presses it open.

The long room is lit by glowing candles in pale bowls. On the wall, a mural depicts a green mountain surrounded by wispy white clouds. Three high-backed black chairs sit at the chamber's center, a pool of water in front of them. Both the Pythias have long white hair, despite the difference in their ages. One is elderly and the other not that much older than Oz's eighteen. The old woman occupies the far left chair, the younger woman the far right. The middle chair is empty.

The oracle meant to be in the vacant chair left after the Awakening. She went mad, even according to the values of oracles and sanity. She was the director's daughter *and*

Henry Locke's wife. Oz came here after that, after he lost his own parents, so he never met her. But he knows the orders. She was allowed to leave and now lives across town as a street oracle. Henry's and her daughter – Kyra – is and always has been off limits. Society operatives are never to approach her. Her mother's wish that she never be involved in its business was granted because, seemingly, it was in her father's power to do it.

Oz has seen Kyra Locke three times. Once, not long after he moved here, when she was out running with her father. The second time was upstairs in the Great Hall, two and a half years ago, being told she wasn't allowed in, not even if her father worked for them. He could tell she'd been crying. The third was a few months ago, when he and Justin were sent to collect a report from an informant at a Skeptics meeting. She was not only attending, but sitting on the lap of the son of the group's founders. He left both of these facts out of his report, for what reason he still isn't sure.

She'd gotten taller, long honey hair a messy tangle around her heart-shaped face. There was an almost feral intensity about her. As if, in the past few years, she'd gone wild.

The director stops opposite the Pythias, staying on this side of the pool and sinking to one knee. Behind him, Oz follows his lead.

"Rise," the old woman says.

Oz waits until Bronson stands before he does. He spots a small black cup at the edge of the pool. In other times, these women would have been Apollo's to command, the oracles at Delphi, decoders of mysterious visions. The Pythias still drink from Apollo's cup, but in service to the Society.

"You have news for me," Bronson says.

"We have a request," the elderly woman counters.

The younger woman adds, "Our sister's daughter is in danger. You know this, and have done nothing to protect her."

They don't mean sister in the familial sense, but the oracle one. Which means the person they're concerned about is Kyra Locke. Oz's interest, already high, spikes.

Bronson raises a hand to his cheek and scrubs at it. "I hadn't even thought about her."

"We know," the old woman says. "You will send a force immediately to protect her."

"Of course," he agrees, bowing his head. "And your... sister. Hannah. She is safe?"

The old woman's head tilts to one side. Oz wants to look away when her pale eyes land on him. They are white as milk from thick cataracts. "Bring me the cup," she says. The younger woman rises, but the old woman says, "No, the boy. We will want a look at him."

Bronson nods once. Oz has no choice but to obey. Though he's curious about the oracles, being across the room was more than close enough. It seems they really *did* summon him too. His boots clomp against the stone floor as he strides to the other side of the pool and lifts the cup.

"Fill it," the old woman says.

He dips the cup into the pool. The water chills his hand to the bone, but he gives no sign of it. When he rises, the woman beckons him and he goes to her, wishing for a monstrous god to fight instead. Those milky eyes never look away from him.

He has heard she's blind, but he can't believe it. She studies his every move. He extends the cup to her, gently touching her hand with it.

Her fingers clasp the cup, and he drops his. "Brave boy," she says.

"High praise," the younger woman chimes in.

"Thank you," Oz says, hiding his discomfort as best he can.

The old woman sips from the cup, then presses it back into his hand. Her papery eyelids drift closed, quivering with the motion of her eyes behind them. He waits beside her, not sure if he's dismissed or if he should take the cup to the younger woman. When he looks to her, her eyes are a near-solid black, her pupils enormous. She winks at him.

Yikes. But he stands, unflinching, like the good operative he's trained to be.

The old woman says, "She will be down the street, at the statue of Einstein. You will find her there. Go quickly, or it will be too late to offer her protection."

"It will be done." Bronson hesitates, then asks, "Henry Locke, do you know where he is?"

A smile curves the old woman's thin lips. "Yes. But I don't think we will tell you. Not quite yet. Our sister would not want us to."

Bronson opens his mouth, and Oz expects him to order her to tell him what he wants to know. Is Henry

Locke missing? And, if so, why would his wife not want him found? Oz braces, wishing he was back on the other side of the room. But all Bronson says is, "Thank you, ladies who look upon darkness and light."

"The boy," the old Pythia says, her supposedly unseeing eyes on him heavy as a touch. "Send the boy for her."

"It will be done." Bronson backs toward the door with a bow.

Oz sets the cup down and joins him. "You'll need relics," says Bronson, beginning to outline the deployment. "If someone's going after her, it's likely to be the Egyptians. Set won't be happy with what Henry's done."

"Of course, sir." Oz will take Justin too. He'll know which relics to bring.

When they reach the hallway, Bronson puts his hand on Oz's shoulder. "This is my granddaughter, Oz. Bring her in safely. It's past time she found out who she is."

Oz nods, sure of only two things. One, that there will be no more dusty papers to worry about today, and two, that he's about to see Kyra Locke for the fourth time.

CHAPTER THREE

The school day *finally* ends. As Bree and I cut across the lobby, we have to navigate around parents picking up little kids. "We should hurry," I say, because I have a feeling. My ex-boyfriend Tam has been trying to catch my eye all day.

Bree doesn't respond, but she stays with me when I speed up.

The entire building exists in a state of disheveled grandeur. The murals on the vaulted ceiling feature angels so dusty and faded they look sickly instead of sacred. This used to be the kind of school that only heirs to agribusiness or underwear fortunes, president's daughters and senator's sons, could afford to attend. Now that so many people have left the city, it's the only school here, period, with a couple hundred students and a handful of teachers. What we're taught is periodically interesting, but mostly irrelevant.

Take physics. Given that the gods' magic has introduced chaos into everything, there are way more variables than math can account for. More mythology instead would be useful, but they maintain it's important that humanity "hold onto our wisdom." As if *that's* what gives us protection, and not the fact the Society killed a god and the others don't want to die so they agree to (mostly) play nice.

Outside, the day hovers just shy of too hot. We make it down the stairs and to the sidewalk and I'm sure we're home free... until a hand lands on my shoulder, and another one on Bree's.

"Wait up," Tam says, suddenly between us. His arms prevent our escape.

My chest tightens. A month ago, I'd have turned into Tam's touch. I'd have spun to face him, stepping lightly onto his heavy boots and touching my lips to his, and Bree would've quipped, "Cough cough," or something else vaguely chastising to remind us she was still there. We would've laughed, my hand in his as we walked home.

None of that is going to happen today.

"We can still hang out, right?" he asks.

My response is careful. I'm honestly not sure of the answer. "Can we?"

Tam is half-Vietnamese with overgrown black hair that's always a mess. The three of us used to hang out all the time. Bree misses having him around, and so do I. *I* messed up our group dynamic. The breakup was my fault.

He drops his arms, and my sense of constriction eases. His answer for now must be that we can, because when Bree and I set off up the sidewalk, so does he. He lives in a different part of town than us, but in the same general direction.

"There's a Skeptics meeting tonight," he says.

"We know," Bree agrees.

"Are you coming?" he asks.

Tam's parents run the group, the most vocal and organized of the Society's critics. Dad hates that I go to the meetings, which, of course, only makes them more attractive.

"I forgot about it," I say. A lie. "I think maybe I have to be home tonight."

Bree frowns at me. "Since when?"

I give her a look that I hope communicates something along the lines of: *What are you doing, please go along with me, OK?* In answer, Bree shrugs one shoulder. She's ready to pretend mine and Tam's relationship never existed. If only I was ready for the same.

Tam says, "There's no reason this has to be weird."

"Please both of you stop," I say. "This is not normal. You're supposed to repress this stuff, not talk about it. For my sake, repress."

Tam and Bree exchange grins that that make me want to run again.

"*You're* telling *us* to repress?" Bree asks.

She's still curious about why we broke up. I haven't given her a reason.

Tam adds, "Since when do you care about normal?"

He wears that smile, the one that lured me into bad decisions in the first place. I don't respond.

Bree and Tam stop prodding me and turn back to the topic of the Skeptics meeting, what's on the agenda, who's supposed to be there. I count the seconds until

I can break off from the two of them. For once, being alone at home seems infinitely desirable. I will put a record on the turntable – vinyl forever, now that most digital stuff's spazzy when it works at all – and crank the volume way too loud and stare at my bedroom ceiling and pretend this awkwardness never took place. Iggy Pop, maybe? Or Patti Smith? The old punk stuff is easy to dig out at the market, and I've amassed a decent collection.

We reach the back of the National Academy of Sciences campus, the main building a hulking stone rectangle. The street next to it is our usual path to the Mall, the quickest and prettiest way home. Shade trees dot the grounds. Their leafy canopies sway in a light breeze.

Wanting some distance from Bree and Tam's too-easy conversation, I brace on the low concrete wall and jump up into the yard. Tam extends a hand to Bree to help her follow. He leaps up behind her.

So much for distance.

I reach the platform that houses the Academy's enormous bronze statue of Albert Einstein. He sits on a trio of steps, a sheaf of papers in one hand, looking a little thoughtful, a little sad. This was always the spot where Dad and I stopped to rest on runs. It's one of my favorite spots in the city.

I climb the steps and put a hand on Albert's arm with the intent of clambering over him, just like I used to when I was younger. Instead, I fall backward in mute shock.

Tam is close enough to lunge in and catch me. He holds me with my back pressed against his chest. My heart pounds, but not because he's touching me. Because of what caused me to lose my balance.

An impossibly tall god perches on Albert's ragged halo of hair. His shadow falls over us, blocking the heat of the sun completely. I realize that the god is at least the same height as the statue.

The statue is twelve feet tall. Dad told me that once.

A cobra-like hood flares on both sides of his terrifying snake's face. His long, scaled arms slither over the sheaf of papers grasped in Einstein's giant brass hands.

Outside the Tricksters' Council and other gods with big followings, knowing every one of them would be like memorizing the name of every plant and flower, every rock and river. I wish I had done it anyway. I have no clue which god this is.

My breathing gets shallower by the second, and my heart beats so hard the god *must* be able to hear it.

Tam speaks, low. "It'll be alright. Don't move."

The god's eyes aren't like an *actual* snake's. Red lids lie heavy over globes set deep. I'm pretty sure Tam's wrong, that none of this will be anything close to alright. Because I am almost certain that the god is looking at *me*. Not at Tam *and* me, just at me.

I can't quite get my breath. I feel weak. I'm like a leaf in a strong wind, about to be carried off for good.

But I force myself to take a step away from Tam.

"Kyra," he says.

"Tam," I murmur, "stay back."

The god's red globe eyes follow me. Unmistakably.

"Kyra," Tam says again.

"Stay put," I say.

I'm the furthest thing from a hero, but maybe I can keep his attention long enough for them to get out of here. Bree must be even more scared than I am. Her sketches alone are proof that this is her worst nightmare. If the god wants me, for whatever reason, there's nothing any of us can do about that.

I shift to the side... and he jumps down. He lands a few feet away from me, his scaly skin like wet black glass. He reaches out to rest a misshapen hand against my cheek, and his touch is cold enough to burn. His mouth opens, red tongue flickering out. Words pour into my mind: *He took it, and now we will take you.*

The strap of my backpack falls off my shoulder because I'm shaking so hard. I shrug it the rest of the way loose, and it drops into my waiting hand. This is the only weapon I have, and so I sling it at the god as hard as I can.

He knocks the bag away with a motion so fast it blurs.

If I don't get out of here somehow, I'm done for. But my legs won't move.

A deep voice says, "Now, now, Mehen. Calm down. We can't have that. Your master's not even here yet."

I recognize the god who interrupts. West African, and he goes by more names than some others. Eshu, Elegua, but mostly known as Legba. He has on a black suit, but there is nothing else that seems human about him. He slowly approaches me, his brilliant red pupils surrounded by uniform black.

He's one of the Council. Supposed protectors of humanity, though now I wish I'd never been to a Skeptics meeting, never heard their theories. The Skeptics claim the gods would gladly wipe out humanity if they could do it without risking death. The tricksters included.

I turn my head to find Bree mostly hidden behind Einstein, and Tam out in the open halfway between the two of us. He must be considering doing something stupid.

No, I think at him, *I'm not worth it. Stay where you are.*

"I want a word with the Locke girl before he gets here, if you don't mind," Legba says.

I blink. Shocked. Confused.

The snake god stays put.

"Have it your way." Legba comes closer to me. His teeth when he grins are sharp and pointed like a shark's. He grips a cane in one hand, though he doesn't lean on it. He twirls it in his fingers.

It's made of metal and bone, and I'd bet anything the bone is of the human variety.

He follows my attention. "The old and the new. I like them both." He extends the cane out to one side, pointing it at Tam. "No need for that, boy. Stay where you are. You should trust me. Your father does."

The whole time Legba never takes his red pupils off me. "Your life is about to get very interesting. But remember, Locke girl, it's *your* life. For better, or for worse. You do like to run, but something tells me you won't go far, not this time," and he leans in, his lips far too close to my ear. My terror is cold and blind and fixes me to the spot.

I can't even flinch. "You might try Enki House for him. Though I wouldn't share that fact. Not if I were you." Shark teeth flash as he backs away, grinning.

For him *who?* I think.

Legba says, "Look, Mehen, here he is now."

Another trickster appears on the lawn not far from us. Dust rises around him in a cloud, despite there being only grass beneath our feet.

It's Set, the Egyptian who is the strangest of all the city's gods. He has a jackal's elongated head with a sharp curved snout, his body a blend of canine and human. His square ears lift to attention, and his long forked tail writhes through the air behind him. He raises his arms and more dust appears from nowhere. Flecks of it hit my skin.

A whirlwind of... not dust, *sand* surrounds us, particles rotating slowly under Set's control.

"That's my cue," Legba says, and is gone.

In the next moment, the sand builds and descends over all of us in a wave, and we're caught in a dry, roiling ocean. I squeeze my eyes shut. I hear Tam call my name. Bree screams. I make a noise, but the whistling shriek of the sand swallows it. I drop, burying my face between my knees, curling into a ball.

Through the stinging fury of the sand, Mehen's snake-cold hands touch my neck, my arms, and then lift me off the ground. I struggle, but I can't open my eyes. Mehen carries me as if I weigh no more than my backpack.

In the sandstorm, no one will see. He can take me anywhere. All Tam and Bree will know is that I'm not here anymore.

I struggle harder, but when the god releases me, the drop is so unexpected it knocks my breath away. I hit the ground hard.

The sand swirls once more before it settles. Mehen steps over me.

Spitting out grains of sand, I sit up and see my saviors.

Society field operatives fan out into the yard in their familiar navy uniforms. I scan for him but, like laughing Legba, sandstorm-causing Set is already gone.

The snake god stands in front of me as if I'm a prize he has to protect. The operatives approach him warily.

Most of them are adults. But a skinny blond boy not much older than me pages through some kind of small black notebook and mutters to himself as he gets closer to Mehen. He has something else in one of his hands too, a green cuff of some kind, and he looks from it to the god, his dismay clear... He frowns at the book, and Mehen glides toward him.

I consider shouting a warning, but the boy glances up and finds the god coming at him before I can. He backs away, his panic reminding me of my own.

He doesn't see the other boy running up behind him. This one is taller, all lean muscle and speed, with angular features and dark brown hair clipped short. He's like a human knife slicing through the air. He draws back the string of his bow, and lets a quarrel fly. It pierces one side of the snake god's hood, drawing a hiss of pain.

The boy-like-a-knife tosses the bow aside so he can shove the backpedaling blond boy out of the way. He says, "Move it, Justin!"

He leaps into the space the other boy occupied. The god flings his arm out hard and fast. The blow will knock the boy out, maybe even kill him – except that it doesn't connect.

Despite his successful dodge, the boy curses, first in English, which I understand, and then speaking what I think might be Ancient Greek. Definitely ancient something. He dips in close enough to… touch the god's face. Not that different from how the god touched mine. His hand rests against one scaly cheek for a breath, before he steps back.

I wait for the god to go after him, but he doesn't budge. At all. His red globe eyes are open and fixed on the brown-haired boy.

"Quick," the boy waves the other operatives forward, "it won't hold him long."

Two men advance and sling a loop of golden rope over the god, a more visible binding than whatever the boy did. I have never seen a relic this close, but everyone knows the theory of how they work. The Society collected all of them that it could find and spent hundreds of years figuring out how to activate the gods' magic that remains within them. Each produces a different effect.

The hero of the moment offers a hand to the other boy and helps him up. The blond's cheeks are pink with what can only be embarrassment.

Dude, I want to say, *that was a snake god. You and I, we understand each other. I can't believe you tried to get close to him in the first place.* But I'm still trying to clear my throat so I can speak.

Tam leads Bree over, supporting her with an arm. They are both coated in a fine layer of sand, and I check my clothes to confirm I am too.

When they reach me, I finally manage to choke out my question, "Is it over? We're safe?"

The brown-haired boy stops in front of us. "Yes, it is," he says. "Yes, you are." His British accent is a surprise. He takes in Bree and Tam, but focuses on me.

"How did you know to come here?" Tam asks.

"Thank you, is what he means," I say. They did save us. But it's possible Tam doesn't know the snake god tried to take me. I shiver.

"We just did," the boy answers Tam. He extends his hand to me. I take it, a reflex without really thinking, to shake. But he puts his other one over the top of mine instead, and the touch helps steady me after the shock of the last few minutes. His pupils are small in the sun, irises the gray-blue of the Potomac River.

It's nice to look into eyes that are *normal* eyes, and not those of threatening gods.

"Sandstorm, I take it?" he asks.

I nod.

"Set *was* here," he says. "Interesting."

I don't take my hand back, not yet. "Who are you?"

"Oh," the boy says, as if he's forgotten to introduce himself and this is any given situation. I notice my breath comes easier. I'm already having trouble believing what just happened, well, *just happened*. He goes on, "I'm Osborne Spencer. You can call me Oz, though. I'm here to take you to your grandfather."

The confusion on Tam and Bree's faces is a mirror to my own. I look back to the boy, still holding my hand in both of his, and I point out the obvious problem: "But I don't have a grandfather."

CHAPTER FOUR

The other operatives bundle a still-bound Mehen into their big black carriage to deliver him back to Set House. Oz has clarified that he's supposed to escort me to headquarters at the Library, and he waves a hand toward the Mall to indicate our route. "We'll walk it," he says.

There's no way Bree, Tam, or I will abandon each other after being attacked by gods, so we're all going. But as we start heading that way, Oz stops and scans us. He frowns, holds up a finger. "Wait."

We do. He jogs across the lawn, and disappears behind Einstein's statue.

A strange, frazzled euphoria hums through me. I recognize it from times Bree and I snuck into the Black Cat club, from the first time Tam and I made out, from six months ago when my mom saw me from a distance and waved like everything was OK… The last memory drowns out the hum, which is too bad. Surely I deserve a little high for surviving.

Bree catches my arm. "Grandfather?"

I shrug. "Both dead. Long time ago. Never met either of them."

She nods, the purple swirls of her earrings shaking with the movement. "That's what I thought."

I feel a momentary twinge of guilt, because Bree believes my mom's dead too. She only moved here post-Awakening, when her perfectly-coiffed, TV reporter mother divorced her father and accepted an assignment at the network's D.C. bureau. I wasn't ready to talk about Mom when we met, and so when she assumed I didn't correct her.

Anyway, I'm positive that Society boy Oz has the wrong girl, like the gods did, and that this is a mix-up of epic proportions. I'll play along for now. I haven't mentioned that my dad works at the Library yet, figuring I can surprise Oz. And the rest of the Society, *and* my dad, once we get there. I haven't been allowed in since I was a kid and the general public was welcome. I miss the place.

The embarrassed boy with the notebook stands near us. He was introduced as Justin. I tilt my head toward Oz as he emerges from behind the statue, holding something I can't see from this angle. "Justin, what's he doing?"

Justin shrugs. "I wouldn't want to speculate."

I feel a laugh bubble up at the formality of his answer, but worry he'll think I'm making fun of him. In truth, I can't help liking him. I can see the appeal of hiding your nose in a notebook in a situation like a god attack. Translating the impulse into a smile, I end up directing it at Oz as he returns. He holds out my backpack to me. "Yours?"

"How did you know?" I figure it's the skull-and-crossbones decal, and if not that then the fact Bree's still wearing hers. But he hesitates like he has to come up with a response. I let him off the hook, "Thanks," I say, taking it and swinging my arms through the straps. "You found my favorite weapon. I threw it at Mehen's head. You could say it was a swing and a miss."

"That's not much of a weapon," Oz agrees.

We cross the street in a pack. Traffic is light today, just a few riders on horseback and a commercial carriage headed along the broad street. In some cities, cars work fine, but we seem to have just the right amount of magic to stop a car engine flat about ninety percent of the time. Horses and bikes are popular.

"Speaking of weapons, what happened with your relic?" Bree directs the question to Justin, whose pale cheeks flame again.

"I'm curious about that too," Oz says.

"I don't know," Justin says, and I can tell he means it. "The notes were right. It should have worked, but when I tried to fling it, the cuff stayed locked."

"It's probably just something in the wrist, or a missing word in the command," Oz says. "You'll figure it out."

"What relic was it?" I put in, riveted at an insider convo like this, even a vague one.

Justin hesitates, looking over at Oz, who shrugs, "You can tell her."

I'm not the only one who catches the way they both glance at Tam and Bree. Bree tosses dust-coated black curls over her shoulder. "Don't take this the wrong way, because you seem nice. But you're not going to try to disappear us or something? My mom will go nuclear and his parents are–"

"We know who they are," Oz interrupts. "And we don't disappear people. Only conspiracy crazies think that. We save people, like we saved you." He says it like he shouldn't have to.

This back and forth clearly makes Justin uncomfortable. He holds the cuffs of his uniform sleeves, fidgeting while he explains. "It's the Monkey King's jade cuff. It was used to hold him captive briefly. We recovered it from a crime syndicate in Hong Kong sixty years ago. It should've worked."

"And so what did *you* do?" I ask Oz.

Oz brushes the gold bars pinned to the left breast of his uniform. They're slightly wavy to invoke rays from the sun. "When we get our stripes, they include a piece of the chains Hephaestus forged to hold Prometheus. Only a small piece, so we can't use it all the time and it doesn't work that long, but it'll freeze someone – human, non-human – in a pinch. You've never heard this before?"

"We're not Society groupies," Tam says.

Justin ignores Tam. He touches the bars on his shirt, and says, "I forgot all about mine."

Oz claps him on the shoulder. "Next one's all you."

"Right," Justin says.

I hope he does get the best of whatever god behaving badly they come up against next. *And* also that Oz's there in case he has another relic malfunction. It's a weird thing to hope when it's likely I'll never see either

of them again after we get to the Library. One more
Weird Thing to add to today's list of them. I'd almost
forgotten mine and Dad's argument, which would be
the first item. Remembering now brings that hum back,
but instead of euphoria it's a hint of worry. I'll be glad
to get to the Library and see him. He won't be able to
blame me for this. Maybe he'll give me some sympathy
for once.

"Osborne, you never did say how you knew we were
in trouble," Tam says.

That he's not dropping this question and refuses to
use the shorter form of Oz's name could be added to a
list called Unsurprising Things. Luckily, I'm not the type
who actually keeps lists.

"It's not a conspiracy," Oz counters. "I promise."

His smile is sharp, like a razor, like him. He's been nice
– witness the backpack retrieval – but there's an edge
beneath it. Justin seems like a normal kid who somehow
ended up in the wrong place at the wrong time, but Oz
couldn't have been more comfortable going up against
that god. I wonder what his story is.

"Give it up, Tam. He's got your number," I say.

But Tam isn't done. "Do you think it's possible they
were there because of my mom and dad... Maybe
they...?"

"No," Oz says, "they weren't there for you."

The certainty in Oz's expression makes the hum kick
up when he turns it on me.

"You think they were really there for me?" I ask. "I'm
nobody. They just fixated for some reason. Sometimes

gods do crazy things. You should know better than anybody."

Oz says, "Yes, sometimes they do."

I sense he's humoring me. "Let's just get there, so we can go home." The hum is turning into full-fledged worry, and I don't know why.

Bree and Tam must be freaked too, because we stay quiet as we make our way up the rest of the Mall – passing a clump of camped-out revelers – and around the vacant white-domed Capitol. Congress only meets here twice a year. The rest of their increasingly pointless work gets done in some underground hideaway where the president is stashed. We stop across the street, in front of the Library's main building.

The front fountain is off, but water pools around the dark statue of Neptune. He's flanked by Tritons blowing into conch shells, calling the court of the sea. The Jefferson Building looms above us, covered in statues and busts and stone flourishes. Three arched entrances wait like dark mouths at the top of the stairs.

There had been a Society outpost here since it was built apparently, and when they announced they were taking over, that made sense. All those painted and sculpted gods everywhere, all those books full of hidden logic and forgotten knowledge. Conspiracy theorists had a field day.

I pull my jacket on as we walk up the steps. "It's always cold in there," I explain. "Well, it used to be."

Oz only nods, intent on our destination. A line of Society guards waits at the top. Taking in Oz, the one in front of the only open entrance says, "The director is waiting in his office," and steps aside to admit us. Bree slips her arm through mine, and asks, "Your dad's working today, right?"

I nod as we go through the door and pass into the deserted Great Hall. It hasn't changed.

Stained glass squares of blue and gold stretch high overhead. Rows of electric lights shine around windows on the upper levels. Marble stairways curve opposite one another, bronze ladies thrusting globe lights into the air at their bottoms. There's the great brass sun in the middle of the floor. I used to lay on it right before closing sometimes, Dad calling out the astrological signs marked out around me, telling me I was at the center of the universe. When he got to mine, he'd always shout out, "Crabby!" and Mom or I would correct him, "No, Cancer, silly!"

Nice as it is to see the inside of the Library again, I've let this go far enough. I start, "Look, it's been fun…"

"It has?" Bree interrupts.

I correct, "OK, *not* fun, not fun at all, but we're glad you showed when you did. I think you should know my dad works here. For you guys. Can you get him? His name's Henry Locke. He's a research librarian."

Oz speaks to Bree and Tam, and only them. "The first operatives back will have already gotten messages to your parents. You can wait in the gallery over there. Justin will take you."

Tam steps forward. "And Kyra will come with us while you go get her dad."

Oz says, "She needs to come with me."

"Where?" Tam prods.

I step in. "I'm sure he's just taking me to Dad. Tam, it's fine. You probably can't go because you might see 'secret Society business' or something."

"Then why would they let you?" Bree asks. "I'm sure your dad'll come to you if you don't want to go off alone with…" She swallows Oz's name, realizing he's right there.

"Oz doesn't scare me. Besides, I can't wait to see the look on Dad's face when I show up in front of him. Promise I'll call you later."

"I really don't like this," Tam says.

But when Oz prompts, "Justin?" and the blond boy says, "This way," Bree and Tam go with him.

Oz leads me through the Great Hall, turning the corner to steps that go down. Tam's paranoia must have rubbed off. I stop. "Doesn't Dad work in the upstairs libraries?"

"Not today," Oz says.

I frown, but follow him down, and down again, to a long hallway with regularly spaced doors and paintings. He leads me to… a marble wall. Featureless gray and white, except for a curving gold gas lamp. The backup lighting system, I assume. "Oz, where *are* you taking me?"

He doesn't look at me. "You'll find out what you want to know when we get there."

"Nice non-answer."

He reaches out and takes the unlit lamp like a handle, turning it like one too. The wall grinds open, creating a seam big enough for a person to go through.

"OK, that's cool," I admit.

"After you," he says, and I walk through the wall. So to speak. The hall behind it is lit by flickering gas lights. Oz comes through, but stops. He doesn't move for a long moment. Which is weird since he's been in such a hurry to steer me down here.

"What is it?" I ask.

He hesitates, and I can't help but admire the line of his jaw in profile, the rounded muscle of his shoulder under the navy uniform.

He says, "I'm taking you to your grandfather, but I don't know exactly what he's going to tell you. It's just... Be prepared for anything. It may not be good."

I am always prepared for the worst, I want to say. *And usually it happens*. But I go with, "I already told you I don't have a grandfather. This is a huge mistake."

"If that's true," he says, as if he's unconvinced, "then all this will be cleared up soon. But if it's not..."

"Got it. Prepare for apocalypse." He cuts me a surprised look, and I add, "Not a real one, sorry. Forgot who I was talking to. The metaphorical kind."

Oz shakes his head, having no doubt decided I'm a lunatic, and presses something on the wall so it closes behind us with a decisive thud.

For a second I feel as if I've been sealed in a tomb, the hall airless and dim. As bravely as I can manage, I say, "Lead on, gallant helper of girls in distress."

"You mean gallant *warrior*," he corrects, but he starts walking.

I do too. "I think I said what I mean. Gallant warrior of girls in distress doesn't even make sense."

He half-laughs, but, besides that, the only sound is our feet on the marble. His clomping boots, my squishy sneakers. Carved insets hold statues between the doors. Based on the names carved below or above, and the fact they're of humans, I guess they're Society members. I don't bother asking, because I want to see my dad already. I want to be proved right.

We stop before a door covered in carvings of angels and devils, weeping and laughing. Oz knocks. "Come," says a man's voice.

Something about the voice is familiar-ish.

Oz turns the knob, pauses, "This is where I leave you. I hope everything works out how you want it to."

"Actually... would you mind waiting out here?" I want someone I know – even if it's someone I just met – out here. In case of what, I don't know, but I do.

"Sure, I'll stay."

"Come," the man's voice says again.

"You better get in there," Oz says, and opens the door for me.

"OK, OK," I say, and take a few steps into the room.

Oz closes the door behind me. The office is cavernous but well-lit, filled with expensive-looking art and furniture. There are two people in the room. Neither is my father.

"Where's my dad?" I ask them. "I want to see him now."

When the man behind the desk stands, I recognize him. And know why his voice was familiar. He's William Bronson, the director of the Society. The dark-skinned, freckled woman sitting across from him is one of their spokespeople, I think. She wears a suit, her Society bars pinned to the breast.

"I wish that were possible," Bronson says. He's looking at me in a way that makes me even more uncomfortable. Like I'm his long-lost daughter. "Please sit." He gestures to the empty chair beside the woman.

"I'm Rose Greene," the woman says, "and I'm pleased to meet you, Kyra."

I can smell the lie in the words from a mile away. "Where is my dad?" I ask again.

Bronson sits, and I notice the portrait on the wall behind him. Without meaning to, I take a few slow steps toward it. The woman in the painting has glossy brownish-black hair and wears a safari jacket. She looks like she's a few seconds from laughter. Her skin is the same olive as my mother's. I've seen her before – in a photo my mother was holding the day before she left us. She was drinking, a short glass filled with brown liquor, a picture clutched in her hand of her as a teenager with this woman. Their arms were around each other, and they were in long flowered sundresses, smiling. There was a man behind them, but his face had been shadowed. *Who's that?* I asked, and she said through tears, *It's my parents. My mother.*

If William Bronson has the woman's portrait in his office... in such a place of prominence... and Oz said he was bringing me to... Stumbling back a few steps, I don't shrug Rose off when she takes my arm and guides me into the empty chair. I practically fall into it.

"They *weren't* wrong. You really are my grandfather, aren't you? And that's my grandmother... Is she..."

"I am," he says, "but I'm sorry. Gabrielle passed away when your mother was sixteen. An accident."

So my parents hadn't lied about that. Only that my grandfather was dead. "I'm sorry."

"Me too. Every day. But that's not why you're here."

I have a million questions, but only one that's pressing. "Where is my dad? I know he works for you."

Bronson folds his hands over each other and leans forward. "You do, but you don't know exactly what he does."

"He's a librarian."

He shakes his head. "Please know it was never my idea to keep any of this from you. It was their wish – your mother and father's. He's not a librarian. He's a senior operative in the Society, from one of our oldest and most decorated families. And he's missing."

I don't where to start with my disbelief. But I look at the painting of the woman with the dancing eyes. This apparently *is* my grandfather, this man who's telling me my father is missing. My father who told me this morning that he loved me and to leave the city if he ever didn't come home.

I drag in a breath, hating that they'll be able to hear how close I am to crying. "What happened?"

"I know this is too much to take in, especially after the attack, but it's important you know. In case you can help us find him." Bronson's manner is so kindly, so grandfatherly.

We just met. "What do you want from me?"

The wording surprises him. He sits back in his fancy leather chair. His tone stays sympathetic as he goes on. "Earlier today, your father stole a powerful relic."

"How can he steal it if he's one of you? He'd be allowed to take it." I don't know why I'm defending Dad. He's been lying to me since forever. And so has Mom.

"If he'd logged it out, that would have been fine. In theory. But this particular relic is not one we'd ever allow in the field. It's too dangerous. He took it and now we can't find him. Has he said anything to you that was strange in the past few days? We want to bring him in before it's too late for him to come back from this."

Isn't it already too late when you steal a dangerous relic? So I say, "Nothing."

"Kyra," Rose puts in, "wanting to protect him is only natural. But you should know, you're risking *everything* by doing it. If he said something, *anything*, tell us."

Dad may be a liar, but no way am I selling him out this quick. All he said was for me to leave. Anger starts to flicker inside me. The burn of it feels better than being so thrown, than feeling like everything *ever* is a lie. "What does the relic do?"

Bronson and Rose don't respond. They look at each other like parents who've agreed to keep a secret.

"If you want me to help you, I need details."

Bronson opens his hands, and starts to talk. "That's fair. I don't see how it will hurt for you to know, as long as you promise to keep this confidential."

I don't cross my fingers, but I also don't make the promise out loud. I nod.

"The relic is called the Solstice Was," he says. "It's a Was scepter – a walking stick with an elaborate headpiece and a forked tail, used in Egyptian funerary customs."

"Like in *Indiana Jones*?" It just slips out.

Bronson comes close to smiling, openly amused. "Yes, like in *Indiana Jones*. Only real." When he continues, he's serious again. "This one was made by Set and smuggled onto a coffin during the summer solstice thousands of years ago. He had planned to use it to open his own door to the Afterlife, and usurp Osiris' command. The relic worked, but Osiris outwitted Set."

A door to the Afterlife. "Oh."

"Yes," Rose says. "Oh."

"But why would Set attack me?"

"We're not sure. But we believe your father is working with one or more gods," Bronson says. "Until we find him, we won't know which ones for sure."

I want to make sure my assumption about why the relic would be dangerous is right. "They'd be able to resurrect then, wouldn't they? If that door reopens? You wouldn't have any control over them."

"We don't have control of them now," Bronson says. "We have weapons. That's all. The only thing gods fear is real, permanent death. If the Solstice Was is used successfully in a ritual on the solstice, then…"

"But solstice is in a few days," I say.

"Four. You see our problem," Rose says. "Now, Kyra,

think hard. Is there anything your father might have said? Anything that didn't make sense at the time?"

I do think, but about what my next move is. What do I do with all this? This is the one place my dad definitely *isn't*.

"I'd like to see my friends," I say, finally.

Bronson frowns, and during his moment of confusion, I stand. "Wait–" But I'm already at the door and pulling it open. Bronson says, "Osborne, she's not leaving."

Oz plants himself in the doorway. I start to worry. "I just want to see Bree and Tam," I say.

There's a commotion in the hallway. Tam appears behind Oz, and with him are Bree and his dad. Ben Nguyen may be a few inches shorter than his son and soft-spoken, but he has an undeniable presence. One the Society is all too familiar with. A handful of operatives trail them, and one starts: "I tried to stop him, sir, but he said he'd go to the media and they insisted–"

Ben holds up a hand to silence the man. "Bill, what's going on here?"

I say, "Ben, I'm so glad to see you. I was just telling them I want to leave."

Tam ducks around Oz, who stands, waiting, presumably for his orders. I take Tam's hand when he offers it, and he pulls me forward with him. Oz doesn't move out of the way.

"Kyra," Bronson says. "Please wait."

The please makes me hold up.

"I'd rather you stayed here, where we can protect you," he says.

I do turn to him, then. I feel better with my friends at my back. There's no way Tam's dad won't enjoy showing up William Bronson.

"My dad *may* be a Society operative, but he clearly didn't want me to know anything about it. He didn't want me anywhere near you guys. So I'm leaving with them." Bronson's mouth drops open. Rose's eyes have narrowed, and maybe what I see there is respect. I turn to Ben and say, "Please don't leave me here. They claim my father is missing. He wouldn't want me left here."

Ben considers briefly, and informs Bronson, "You've already bugged our phone, so you'll know where to find her." He waves Tam and I forward, and we go toward him. "Let them," Bronson says, and Oz shifts so he's only half in the doorway.

I have to pass close to him, and there's a question on his face. He did try to warn me, and maybe that's why I feel the urge to explain. "I can't stay here, gallant warrior," I say, low. "I'm no damsel in distress."

He doesn't respond. He joins Rose and Bronson in the office, like a good operative. I pause in the hall and look back at a still-astonished Bronson. "It's really nothing personal. It was nice meeting you."

"Remember, the more people who know about your father, the worse it will go for him," Bronson says, no doubt to remind me about the "confidential information", but being careful because of Ben. He studies me for a long moment. "You can come back here anytime. You *are* my granddaughter, Kyra, and you will always have sanctuary here. I'll do my best to protect our family."

"Good to know," I say.

But I leave without looking back.

CHAPTER FIVE

I'm squished between Tam and Bree on one side of the rickety commercial coach Ben has hired, with him occupying the bench across from us solo. Earlier, I might have worried about being so close to Tam, asked him to move, but it feels nice to have friends on either side of me. It keeps me from feeling so untethered, like I might as well float away, not much left to anchor me here.

And that's what Dad wants, for me to go.

The coach jostles along the street toward my house. I turn what Legba said about my dad being at Enki House – he had to mean Dad, didn't he? – over and over in my mind, but first I need to be sure he's *not* at home. That this is really happening.

"So sorry about this, Ben," I say.

"It's OK. I'd need to see that he was gone for myself, too. We can also check if they file the right paperwork for a missing person with the police. And you'll need to pack a bag... Only if he's not there, of course."

Tam's parents, Ben and Maya, may get distracted by their work with the Skeptics, but they're *always* there for

Tam when needed. Maya's out of town visiting the Chicago chapter, and, according to Ben, will be sad she missed the excitement. Your son being in a god-caused sandstorm probably shouldn't be considered "excitement". But at least Ben's not a secret Society agent.

Bree lays her head on my shoulder. On her lap, her fingernails are painted with tiny yellow daisies, in sharp contrast to the darkness of her art. Her mom was on shift at the station, but Ben knows her too, and gave her a call. She's working late, so Bree's staying with Ben and Tam tonight as well.

Bree says, "So your dad's a super-librarian."

"I guess," I say. "I have a suggestion for your art."

"Yeah?"

"Your gods need to be scarier."

She snorts. "Noted and agreed. That was... But your dad is a bigger shock."

"The biggest." I haven't told them about the Was yet. I don't want to do it in front of Ben.

Tam has been staring out the window, but he angles toward us. "You really had no idea about your dad?"

He seems so intense, as if the truth about my dad matters to him as much as it does to me. I can't imagine why. "None. I'm an idiot."

"No," Bree says, and I use it as an excuse to turn from Tam, though I can still feel him watching me. "We all believe lies from people we love. And, hey, he stuck around. My dad doesn't even bother to visit."

"Or send you birthday bribes out of guilt. Agreed, your dad sucks. But mine... Well, I just hope I get a chance to yell at him." I'm trying to keep it together. Part of me wants to curl into a ball, like I did during the attack. All of me wants to shower off the remnants of the sandstorm.

The carriage pulls to a stop in front of the townhouse.

"You want company?" Tam asks.

"No. If you don't mind, I'd like to go alone."

"Are you sure it's safe?" Tam persists.

"Son, she'll be fine," Ben says. "Bronson assured me there will be no more attacks against her and, for once, I believe him. We'll wait right here, Kyra."

I climb out, digging the key from my backpack, and let myself inside. My boots sit right next to the door, where I left them when I changed into my sneakers. Nothing has moved. Dad hasn't been home.

I close my eyes and stand in the dark listening to the house. Hoping I'll hear him. Hoping I'm wrong. Finally, I flip on the lights. *I love you, you know that.* Lies or no lies, I can't stand the idea of a fight where I disappointed him being our last conversation.

Instead of my room, I climb the stairs and go to his. The bed is neatly made, as usual, and not a thing is out of place. Mine is a disaster area. Or that's what he always calls it.

The hiding place where we used to stash notes for each other as a game is behind his desk in the corner. There's a picture of Mom there, beaming up at the camera with her hands in the dirt of our long-gone backyard flower garden. I press aside the wish that she could be here to help me deal with this, before I lay the frame down flat and push the desk out from the wall.

An upside of finding out about Bronson is that I believe he'll do his best to watch out for her. That's something.

I crouch and peel up the cream-and-maroon striped wallpaper from the baseboard, exactly six inches from the corner. There's a brick-sized hole behind it, and I stick my hand in sideways. The notes we left for each other when I was little were a back and forth of funny meaningless nothings. I know this is where he'd hide the money he mentioned.

My hand touches a wrapped bundle. I pull it out and lay it on my lap. The cloth is a worn-soft Ramones T-shirt that I have never seen before. I like it, but no clue there. I unfold the fabric and gasp.

Though I was expecting money, I wasn't expecting this much. Several stacks of hundreds and fifties and twenties spill out. In the middle of them, there's a plastic ID card with my picture. I squint to read the name on it. Amelia Jones. Amelia is from Ohio, and two years older than me. There is also a note, disappointingly short, written in Dad's handwriting: *If you're reading this, it better mean I'm no longer here. This is not party money and a fake ID for no reason. It's too late for me to explain now, but you probably know some of the truth already. There are other things you can't know. Shouldn't know. Please, leave the city. Go far. Be as careful as you can. Know that we love you. Dad.*

Only after some unknown amount of time has passed do I realize that I'm rocking back and forth over the contents of the T-shirt. It feels as if someone has reached into my chest and squeezed my heart until there should be nothing left, but instead my heart is so full it *hurts*.

I get up and stagger like I'm drunk. Bracing one hand on the desk, I fix on Mom's smiling face in the picture frame, a captive piece of the past, and wait until my breathing evens out. I can get through this. I can deal. I have to.

"Kyra?" Ben calls from downstairs.

"Be out in a minute."

I put the cash and the ID in my backpack, though I have no plans to be Amelia Jones anytime soon. Not on my own.

Legba told me where Dad is. I just have to figure out how to get to him.

The driver lets us out in front of Tam's single-story white clapboard. The neighborhood is nowhere near as swanky as mine and Bree's Capitol Hill. A skinny TV tower is rigged to the roof, its thin rusted metal poles joined at crooked angles that branch into a receiver at the top. It's like a – slightly – more modern version of a weather vane, only trapping broadcast signals instead of gauging wind currents. Most stations use old-school transmitters, since they're more reliable here.

Ben tips the driver, making a joke about the "in God we trust" phrase still being on the bill. The driver laughs, and the horses clip-clop the carriage away.

Tam unlocks the door and we go inside, stopping in the alcove. "I'd really love a shower," I say, rubbing a gritty arm.

Bree has been subdued since we left my place, and we didn't bother with hers. I tossed some clothes she'd left at my house in with my stuff. But she shakes her head. "I'll fight you to the death to go first."

I hold up my hands. "It's all you."

"I'm last then." Tam rolls his eyes. "Come on, I'll get you towels."

Ben clears his throat. "Tam, you'll sleep out here on the couch tonight. The girls can take your bed. Understood?"

Tam says, "Duh."

I can see he's embarrassed. Maybe his dad doesn't know we're not on again, off again, but only off. "Towels," I prompt.

"Right this way," he says.

"Going to catch the news. I'll be right out here," Ben reminds us.

"*Dad*," Tam says.

Ben goes into the living room and flips on the TV. I hear Bree's Mom's voice emerge. She's on screen, anchoring a report.

We make our way back to Tam's room, which looks the same as ever. Map of the world on the wall with Skeptics chapters marked by stars. A bookcase filled with reference and school stuff. An ancient poster with a guy and a lady on it that says "The Truth Is Out There" he took from his dad's office.

I toss my backpack down and flop onto his bed without even considering that it might turn out awkward. I need to not be on my feet anymore. He has a little bathroom and shower of his own, and he shakes his head at me, goes to get Bree her towel. I turn on my side and dig out a long T-shirt from my backpack, toss it to him to give her when he starts to come back in.

He does, then closes the door. The shower starts up nearly immediately.

And Tam and I are alone. He walks around to the other side of the bed and sits back against the headboard. I flip around to face him, staying on my side. "I need to tell you guys some things, but we should wait for Bree," I say, nervous and wanting to buy time.

Looking at him in such close quarters is like staring my own failures in the face. But he has something on his mind. "You really had no idea about your dad?"

I sit up, even though I'd rather close my eyes and sleep forever. It's the same whenever I think about Dad, all his lies, what comes next...

"I don't know why you find it so hard to believe. Do you really think I wouldn't have told you?" I try to drag a hand through my hair and find it's too stiff with sandy residue. "I guess I wouldn't have been allowed to, but that would have been the only reason."

"Would it?" On Tam, the grime manages to be attractive. Like it's the next big fashion. His eyes flash. "Are you sure you didn't go out with me just to get to your dad? If he *was* Society, that'd be even more rebel points, wouldn't it?"

At least some of my anger is because he's not completely wrong. Dad hated that we went out. I liked that. "Look, don't use my crappy relationship with my dad. Not right now. Please."

"I'm sorry." He reaches down and takes my hand in his. He cradles it and is quiet. I don't take it back, because this whole mini-truce between us feels fragile. He lifts his hand and touches my cheek, gentle. He slides it down until he cups my chin. "You're going to make it through this. And so's your dad."

I want to lighten the moment. "Where's the doom and gloom Tam I know?" He doesn't smile. "I'm going to need your help, Tam. I know I have no right to ask…"

Tam leans in closer. "You're not alone. You've got me and Bree. We're not going to abandon you."

"I know. But I think it's going to come down to me getting to Dad."

"Then I'm not worried."

His eyes hold mine, and for a breath I worry he's going to kiss me. Then he *is* kissing me. His lips are soft, his hand sliding to the back of my neck. It's comfortable, like I've gone back in time. This part of us was always easy. But it isn't fair to him.

I push back. "I'm sorry. But nothing's changed." Everything else, maybe, but not us. "You deserve someone else…"

He lifts his hand from my neck. We look at each other, faces still close.

"I'm sorry about that," he says. Then, "I should be honest with you."

I scoot back against the headboard to put some space between us. "What do you mean?"

The shower stops and we both look at the door. Bree will be out any minute.

"When I told you... you know..." he says, and I fill in silently, *I love you.* He said it and I froze. I broke up with him the next day. "...it wasn't true. Not yet. You weren't in this as much as I was and I could tell. So it was a test. I wanted to see if you'd lose it. I know it wasn't fair."

When Tam said those three words to me I couldn't imagine saying them back to him. I couldn't imagine saying them to *anyone.* I panicked just thinking about being *in* love with someone, having to worry about losing them too. I can't be that girl, that starry-eyed girl who falls in love. Anyone I ever love will leave.

The stacks of cash hidden two feet away confirm it as the truth. No one I love will *ever* stay.

"You didn't break my heart," he says. "You could've though."

I am beyond glad I didn't. Because I *do* care about Tam, which means we can only be... "Friends, though?"

"Friends. Definitely."

The bathroom door swings open, the T-shirt nearly hitting Bree's knees because she's so tiny. She raises her eyebrows at us, a silent question about whether she's interrupting.

"Good," I say to Tam, and I mean it. I need all the friends I have to get through this. "Legba told me Dad's at Enki House. I have to get in there tomorrow, without anyone knowing. *Including* your dad. Cash is not an issue. Possible?"

Their expressions of shock almost make me laugh. Almost.

CHAPTER SIX

The next morning, the three of us skip school and hire a commercial carriage to take us over to S Street, as close as it will go to the Houses of the Gods (of the gods who live here, anyway). We lurk behind a boarded up mansion at the back edge of the huge overgrown gardens and park, waiting. Right in front of us is the tall stone fence marking the border to the back edge of the property claimed for the Houses. But there are no guards, not back here.

Going in the front loghouse way was out of the question, but Tam had come up with an alternative by the time I was done showering. Bree handed me a photocopied sheet he'd gotten from his dad's study with the solstice week schedule of blessings. "Not revelers, please not revelers," I'd said when I understood, but Bree and Tam insisted it was the best idea. I had to agree they were right.

Blessings are a shadow tradition, not done out in the open. No one's sure exactly what they are, and if or how they work. But at the big seasonal shifts, they're popular with tourists and acolytes and people desperate for a divine encounter for whatever reasons of their own. A lost job, a sick kid, a broken heart. You wouldn't want your name registered on a log if you showed up at a House to get one, and so in the week before each solstice or equinox, revelers gather and climb the back fences to visit the trickster of the day.

We're lucky. Today they're heading to Enki House. The plan is to blend right in and hope for the best.

I'm not used to doing either of those things.

"You really think this isn't a trap?" Tam asks. "Legba usually stays out of the gods' games with each other."

"It's all I've got," I counter. "I need to find Dad, and Legba said to try Enki House."

Tam sits against the brick wall. His boots and jeans and T-shirt are the usual, but, like us, he's sporting elaborate face paint. Our cheeks and foreheads are covered with shining suns, random dots and swirls and bone shapes. A pretty smart disguise.

The paint isn't *so* bad. I forget it's there, but I can't say the same for the leftover solstice junk jewelry Bree and I are wearing. A strand of black plastic skulls hangs around my neck, over the random Ramones T-shirt from Dad. Bree has on an outrageously tacky snake motif necklace done in a hot green shade. Tam was able to beg off the jewelry, but he has extra paint swirling across his forearms and hands to make up the difference.

We look like goofy tourists playing with divine fire. That's the point.

I'm serious when I tell them: "You guys don't have to come in. After yesterday, you really shouldn't. I can meet you after."

Bree shakes her head. "I already told you, no. No, no, no. It's not that I'm looking forward to seeing gods up close again, but you said that Mehen tried to take you. Someone needs to be there."

"To report me missing like my dad, you mean? But you won't be able to if you're with me."

She says, "K. We're going to get through this. You are not disappearing. And neither are we."

I pretend to be convinced. "Sure, and if we don't make it, then there's a Big Bad Relic for everyone to worry about. It still doesn't make sense to me why Dad would have taken it. Operative or not. No one wants gods stalking the skies and streets doing whatever they feel like."

"Someone probably does," Tam says, ever the conspiracy-lover.

Bree twists the snake necklace in her hand and frowns at him. "I sure don't."

"If your dad's at Enki House, he'll be explaining it to you soon enough." Tam climbs to his feet, pointing. "Here they come. We're on."

The quietest bunch of revelers I've seen, thanks to no drumming, shamble along the street toward the wall. The lack of noise is probably a nod to the semi-secrecy of this tradition. A guard back here's all it would take to kill it. So they climb over the wall, get blessed, and then leave, as silently as possible.

Tam hesitates for a second. "Look, guys, I told you I've heard stories about blessings. This is probably going to get intense."

Bree is not happy. "You're telling us this now, because?"

"Because there's no time to get into the rumors and freak you guys out more," Tam says.

He's right. I don't know about Bree, but I'd rather be in the dark. I take off to join the pack of revelers, waving. "Wait up!" I call.

A middle-aged woman in an impractical-for-climbing-over-walls flowing dress beams at us. Her flushed cheeks round into apples as she welcomes us. "Stragglers," she says, "you're just in time. Don't want to miss today's blessing."

By the time I reach her, Tam and Bree catch up with me. I don't point out to her that we were here waiting, not late. There are about ten people total, a ragtag assemblage. Most look like the typical worshipful hippies – our face paint blends right in – but there are a few with a harder edge. I'd expected more, in numbers and character. Then again, even though the Houses are technically open, most humans avoid them. Other gods visit only when they have to. From all reports, it's just the chief trickster of each House and a handful of others from their pantheons who got relocated to D.C.

Most gods stay where they woke. And most humans are smart enough not to go visiting.

Tam makes a scoop of his hands to help us over the ten-foot wall. "Here goes nothing," I say, stepping in first. I fit my fingers and then the toes of my boot into the grooves between stones, copying the reveler to my left. When I reach the top, the view steals my breath.

I've seen pictures, but they're flat, static, easily faked. Seeing this for real is something else. Like stepping out of our world – or it will be once I land on the other side.

This area used to be a sprawling park beside a private estate with formal English gardens, before it got annexed and transformed. Now the whole place feels strangely ageless, out of time. It's hard to imagine it ever having been different, and even harder to accept that it exists in its current state.

Plants and trees grow wild. Trunks and limbs bend into strange shapes, making the lush, green forest more like something you'd wander into in a dream than reality. Within the overgrown wildlands are the seven Houses. I see the top of Set House's pyramid and fight the urge to shiver because he's probably in there. There's a majestic temple beyond it that belongs to ladies' choice god, Hermes. Opposite, the black castle of Loki. Then the grove of massive trees surrounding Legba's home. The slanting sides of Coyote House. The bright flat-topped pyramid of Tezcatlipoca House. But once I fix on our destination, the rest fade into the background.

Enki House is to our right. The forest gives way to marshland around the enormous ziggurat, its angles sharp, golden. What look like birds wheel through the clear sky above the temple at the top of it, but they're so large they must be gods.

"You OK?" Tam asks, and I glance down at the not-crazy side of the wall. Bree clambers up and swings a leg over at the top, joining me. She's as silenced by the sight as I am.

Not the revelers, though. They whisper and giggle and are generally obnoxious. "Hurry up, slowpokes!" the lady who greeted me says, as she launches herself off the wall and into the waiting arms of her companions.

Tam reaches the top of the wall, climbing up on my other side. The three of us stand at the same time, without agreement, and jump down together. We land in a messy tangle of arms that keeps any of us from falling.

With Tam's hand gripping my arm, it's hard to believe we were kissing last night – and coming to terms with the end of the kissing. Bizarrely, I feel more comfortable around him knowing he was never really in love with me. We can safely return to the status quo.

"This way," the lady hisses.

We stumble around bendy trees and jagged-edge vines that look so sharp I'm afraid to touch them. No one speaks. There's something about sneaking through this odd, shadowed wood that feels unbelievably stupid. If someone told me we were being hunted, I wouldn't doubt it.

At that thought, I make sure I have Bree's arm and that Tam follows as I get us to the front, right behind flowing dress lady. She's clearly done this before. She weaves through the trees, turning sideways when she needs to keep from touching blooms like hungry mouths. We mimic her as closely as we can. The aroma is of earth, breathing and living. The feeling of unseen eyes that consider us prey never goes away.

Finally, our feet hit mud, and we're out of the forest. I'm relieved until I look up, where Enki House towers over us. But we aren't quite there yet. There's a paved path broad enough for the three of us to walk beside each other nearby, and the apple-cheeked hippy makes for it.

So do we.

"Stay on the yellow brick road," Bree says.

"We're off to meet the wizard," and I wince at how grim my tone is.

"Off to meet something," Tam says. "But seriously, let's try to stay on it. I've heard stories…"

"Keep them to yourself," Bree says. "Those stories are warnings. We're ignoring them."

She's right. Even I can't believe we're doing this. But there's no choice. Dad may well be in there. *He doesn't want to see you.* I'm sure that's the truth, not just the little voice inside me being evil. It doesn't matter. He's going to have to deal with me. He can't vanish and expect that to be fine, that I'll take the money and go. We owe each other something more than that.

I want us to, anyway.

The way the path curves reminds me of a twisting snake, and not the harmless plastic kind around Bree's neck. We are careful to stay on it, winding through muddy river delta swampland, all the way to the foot of the ziggurat. The stone and sand sparkle, like the sun itself is inside the bricks.

"Up we go!" Apple-cheek announces, a greedy hunger beneath her cheer.

Her excitement is as troubling as anything else.

The long ramp that extends down the front like a tongue is our new path. To the sides are wide steps carved out of the pyramid-shaped base. Maybe talking will help distract us.

"Tam," I ask quietly, as we climb, "tell me about Enki."

"You already know the Sumerians were among the first, the oldest, gods that we know of."

"Tell me something I don't know, I mean." We all have a working knowledge of the tricksters and the major pantheons. Public schools scrambled to add better no-longer-mythology units after the gods woke up. "And let's drop back. More time to see what the deal is up there."

The three of us slow to let the revelers pass us.

Tam goes on. "I guess you remember that there are a lot of them? More than most other pantheons combined – one scholar estimated almost four thousand. And in that number are chaos monsters, sentient ancient darknesses, demons with animal heads. Enki has always been one of their leaders, sometimes *the* leader. He's the lord of the watery deep, the abzu. Think of it as the mysterious water that yielded creation. For what it's worth, Enki was always supposed to be one of the good guys. Even before."

"How good?" I ask.

There are pictures of bearded priests and winged creatures and ornate inscriptions in long forgotten languages carved into the ziggurat alongside the ramp.

"One of the most famous stories about him involves the creation of humankind."

Bree says, "Hang on… I thought that, yes, they're older than people, but they didn't create us. We're just different species, different evolutionary tracks."

"Listen to you, evolutionary tracks," I tease. "Someone's been doing their science homework. Fancy."

Bree pulls a face at me.

Tam shrugs. "So the Society claims. Who knows for sure? But we do know that gods exist and what they're like. They don't care about right and wrong, not like we do. A lot of them view us as…"

"Cows?" I supply. "That they can kill and eat and… do whatever else they want with? And my dad may be giving them carte blanche to do just that *and* we're walking in the front door of one of their houses. OK. This is making me feel so much better. Please, go on."

"So, there are lots of versions of this story. In the one I like the best, Abzu is still a being – a god himself – in addition to being the mysterious water. The older, more powerful gods are basically using the newer, less powerful ones as slave labor. And the new ones start complaining. It's loud, because Abzu starts making noise of his own, about how he's going to flood the entire world, drown everything out. Enki's mother decides her son can take care of Abzu, so she goes to wake him up."

"But supposedly the new gods were being so loud – how's he asleep?" Bree asks.

"Chalk that up to story blur." Story blur is the part of myths that don't make any kind of sense. "Or maybe he's just a really deep sleeper. Enki does finally wake up for his mother, and he then magically puts Abzu to sleep and confines him below his city."

"Where do the people come in?" I ask.

"Oh," Tam says, "right. Well, everyone agrees that gods shouldn't be doing all this hard labor, so Enki makes people, to do the work for them."

"Cows," I say. "Labor cows. I'm not getting the part where he's a good guy."

"Later there are tons of myths about him helping humans out, giving us knowledge. Art. Water for crops."

"Don't all the tricksters have stories about them like that?" I press him. "Isn't that why the Society knew they'd be willing to do the go-between thing? I thought it doesn't mean they're really that friendly."

"*I* took you to those meetings." Tam rakes a hand through his messy hair. "All I know is Dad thinks Enki's one of the more sympathetic to us."

That might explain why my dad would come here. If he needs help.

Whatever I was going to say next is stolen by the appearance of the winged creature. It launches out of the temple's entrance and into the air. Brown and black wings spread wide as it circles above us in lazy swipes. The body belongs to a giant eagle but the head… That's all lion.

"Holy crap," Bree says.

"Tam," I say, "would that be a chaos monster?"

Tam lifts a hand to shade his eyes. "Nah. Anzu. He's the son of a bird goddess. Part eagle. Enki likes to keep him close. He's not supposed to be one of the good guys."

"Great."

The revelers in front of us point and cheer and speed up. Not that they need to. We're nearly to the top already. With each step closer, I become less ready to face whatever lies ahead. *My* stuffed shirt of a dad's been hanging out with part eagles? Then Anzu roars like this is a circus and one of us stuck our hand in his cage, and I have to rethink. *My* cranky, rule-obsessed dad's been hanging out with part eagles, part mad lions?

We finally arrive at the top, where the temple sits. Straight ahead is a long hallway with arched entrances that I assume leads to the interior where Enki and company are. The revelers walk in without a hitch. But I stop on the flat stone, still open to the sky.

Anzu the giant lion-eagle swoops. Close. Closer. I feel wind from his wings in my hair.

Bree and Tam rush toward the first arch, but I'm afraid to go with them. Afraid Anzu will take notice of them, like he has of me.

I peer up at Anzu, wishing for him to fly off or up or anywhere away. But he's so near I can see the precise edge where his feathers shift from brown to black. He lands in front of me and his enormous lion nose twitches. He's sniffing the air.

"Nice monster," I say, and my voice only shakes a little bit. Hardly any. Dad would be proud, if he could see me.

Anzu roars loud enough to wake a god.

I step back once, then again. He stalks forward, claws scraping the stone.

We are locked in a terrible dance. His giant teeth are knife-sharp and on full display as he bares them at me, roaring.

My heart threatens to stop. I'm shaking, and it's like yesterday all over again. Death is staring me in the face. Maybe if Dad can't see me, he'll hear me. I suck in a breath and go for volume. "Dad! Dad, I could use some help!" I shout.

Behind me, Tam says, "Kyra, no sudden moves."

Tell that to the monster.

Anzu claws toward me, his mouth stretching wide enough to swallow the world. He's close enough that I can see the clumped mats in the fur of his mane. I have *nowhere* to go to get away. Sheer panic kicks in. I cringe, lifting my backpack in front of me. But it's a too-weak reaction behind a too-small shield.

After Oz's observation that my backpack isn't much of a weapon, I am keenly aware that I don't have *any* way to defend myself.

"Tam, go inside," I manage. It doesn't matter that my voice shakes, since Dad's not showing up to be proud. I couldn't shout for him again now, even if I thought he'd show. "Make sure Bree gets out of here. OK?"

It's only then that I notice Anzu is no longer coming *at* me. He's stopped. In that brief reprieve, Tam grabs me and tugs me backward. I turn and we lunge for the first arch. I expect to feel the back of my T-shirt ripping, claws and teeth tearing into me. I wait for that roar to sound too near to survive it.

But no flesh-rending pain or ear-scorching warning comes. We're through the arch, and another, and the rest, tripping forward as fast as we can over the mosaic floor.

Bree is waiting for us at the end of the hall. The temple entrance is visible from here, and so is Anzu, pacing in front of it. But he stays outside.

"You are not going to believe this," Bree says, pointing up an adjoining passage. Beyond it is another broad archway.

"Oh, I don't know," I say, fighting to catch my breath. "At this point I'd believe anything, except that I'm getting out of here past that thing."

CHAPTER SEVEN

Now that we're not evading a monster, I take in the place. The walls have changed from the glimmering gold of the sand outside to a blue deep as a night sky or the bottom of the ocean. The floor's mosaic patterns are wavy lines that must indicate water and curving ones that might be Enki's horns. Yes, horns.

"The only way out is in, then," Tam says.

Bree whirls on him, green eyes wide and afraid. "How are you keeping your shit together like this?"

"One of us has to." Tam is trying to be funny.

But I punch his arm. "Excuse me. We all are." I put my backpack on so I don't have to carry it. "Bree, what's unbelievable?"

"The blessings. This way." She waves at the passage, frowning, and we start up it.

Tam ignores Bree, somehow not getting that she's worried. He says to *me*, "He couldn't hear you. That's all. He would have come."

Sure, Dad not showing up to rescue me stings. But that doesn't mean I'm surprised by it.

I exaggerate my shrug. "Sure. He would've."

Bree stops at the arch, and when we join her, it turns out she might be right. I do have trouble believing the scene in front of us.

Several of the revelers writhe, moaning, on the tiled floor of a large rounded chamber with those same seamless blue walls. The woman with the flowing dress tips her head back and opens her mouth. A bright-red fishtail slowly lowers until it touches the woman's extended tongue. She pulls back with a blissed-out smile and spins around in joy. The revelers aren't what defies belief, though, it's the *things* doing the "blessing."

Long tanks form a border around the edges of the room. The glass is smudged with grime, not the spotless clean of the temple. The water within is so deep and dark that it appears black, as if they're swimming in ink.

Oh, yeah. The *they*.

They're not quite as big as Anzu, but still larger than any man-fish thing should be. They're not mermen or anything ridiculous like that. They're nothing you'd put in a child's storybook, unless you wanted to mess that kid up for life.

They are the size of small whales, the oversized tanks hardly big enough for them to do more than turn around in, and there's enough of them that the water ebbs in endless swells. Their heads end in disconcerting fish lips that contain giant jaws with rows of razor teeth. (The teeth make me think of Legba. I don't want to think of Legba.) Their bodies are a mix of scaled hues, the tails sharp-finned as they swipe from the tank to touch the tongues of the revelers.

The head reveler lady says to us, "Don't be shy! Get yours! You'll see…"

What I see is her being pulled down to the floor by one of her companions, a guy whose intentions are not anything I want to witness.

"Where would my dad be? Tam, any ideas?" I ask.

He shakes his head no. "You'll have to ask them. The seven sages. Minor gods Enki made. They're his attendants."

I count the weird fish-men. There *are* seven. "These are sages?"

Bree says, "I'm not letting them touch me."

"Smart." But Tam's right about no way through. There's a shadowed opening, door-sized, that goes further into the temple, but it's on the other side of the tanks. There's no going anywhere but back the way we came – blocked by lion-eagle – without help from these sages. Dad had better be here.

I choose the nearest tank, averting my eyes as I skirt around the revelers' disturbing activities on the floor. "Yes," I hear the woman say, and she adds, "get your blessing."

Every muscle in my body wants out of here, to do anything besides take another step closer to the tank. Black water sloshes over the top, and a head three times the size of mine emerges. "*Cooome* close to me," the sage says, in a voice thin as liquid. He has to push back when another sage forces up beside him. "Let us show you *truuuth*," the new one says, and the voice is more feminine. So there are fish-*women* sages, too.

I am the center of attention of the revelers, angry at the fact their blessings have stopped, as all seven of the sages mass at this end of the tank. They hiss, coaxing me to come to them and be shown truth.

"Stop it." I can't think of anything else to say.

They don't stop. If anything, the order amuses them. Well, maybe it's amusement. Their reactions are hard to read, their eyes fathomless flat discs in their half-human, half-marine faces.

"I'm here about my father," I say.

"You want to know why he attacked *youuu*," the first sage says, pressed into the corner of the tank by his fellows. "Our cousin Anzu was told to protect your father. You are a threat. He saw *youuu* as a threat."

I swallow. That monster attacked me on Dad's behalf? "Is my father here?"

"*Youuu* are." They chant it.

The reveler lady pokes my shoulder. "They don't talk to us. Who are you?" she asks.

"No one for you to worry about. You can leave me here."

The moment I turn from the tank, one of the sages' tails caresses the bare skin of my neck. Cold, wet, scaly. I dart away, and the hiss-chatter-maybe-laughter gets louder. Bree and Tam are stuck between the rest of the revelers and me. I look at them, and tick my head toward the reveler lady. "You guys go with them. I'll stay."

"She *loooves* us."

"She'll *stayyy...*"

"The threat will stay *foreeever.*"

"Blessed ones *leeeave* her..."

The sing-song hiss makes me nauseous.

I expect giggles and protests from the dismissed revelers, but the woman bows her head to the sages. The others steeple their hands in a semi-universal gesture of respect as they shuffle back out. The wish of the seven sages is their command.

But Tam and Bree aren't going. Of course.

"All three will see truth. We will show *youuu.*"

"I just want to see my dad," I tell them.

More hissing and, "There's a price. Truth is the price. *Cooome* to us. You three. Then we *miiight* tell."

I refuse to ask anyone to do *this* for me. The pictures Bree made without anything like the sages in front of her are enough to make me regret bringing her here forever. The nightmares she'll have... And Tam, he doesn't owe me this.

But they exchange a look with each other and move to the front of the tank before I can step in. "Don't–" I start, already too late.

The laugh-hiss of the sages fills the chamber, two tails swiping down to Bree and Tam's open mouths, their tongues extended – if not with the abandon of the departed revelers, at least with determination. Both of them close their lips and step back as soon as the tails retract. They clutch each other's hands.

"You too or it's for nothing. *Cooome* here, daughter." I don't know which ones beckon for me, and it doesn't matter. Now that Bree and Tam have gone this far, I have no choice.

The water sloshes as I approach the tank, open my mouth and put out my tongue like when I was tiny and had a sore throat and Mom would use a flashlight to say strep spots or no strep spots. As a tail delicately deposits a drop of foul black water onto my tongue, I hang onto that memory of Mom. I step back and close my eyes. My plan is to try my best to resist whatever the droplet's supposed to *do*.

But the room I'm in… suddenly it's home. I'm in Dad's room. I remember coming to myself over the shirt and the money and the ID, his note in my hands as I rocked back and forth. I hear a sob and the room is dark and so I'm sure it's *me* from the night before that I see and I get so angry at the seven sages, with their clever game, their empty promises of truth, that I almost don't realize.

It's not me, it's *Dad*. The shirt's open on his lap, and he slips in the note. He folds the T-shirt around everything. He is crying. His head shakes back and forth, *No,* as he folds the fabric with such care. So deliberate, he rises and pushes back the desk, hides the bundle in the wall. I lean in and hear him whisper, "I'm sorry." I want to forgive him everything. I reach out, saying, "Dad, it's OK. Dad, I'm here. It's Kyra."

That's when the cool hand touches mine, and brings me back to the seven sages' chamber.

I resist for a blink, two blinks. But, no, this is where I am. The tanks, sages watching instead of hissing, the blue ocean walls.

Tam and Bree stare at me. The god touching my hand obviously pulled them both out of their sage visions – or whatever that was – first. His skin is composed of blue and white scales, alternating, so I know better than to feel relief. When I look up, I discover he has two faces. Each is perfect beside the other, one blue and the other white. The foreheads and the planes of his jaws curve like twin moons of a single planet. He wears a long pale robe.

Tam says, "This is Isimud, Enki's messenger." He can't hide how shaken he is. Not from me. The droplets must have taken them somewhere too. "Now we're getting somewhere," he says. "Ask him."

Tam's bravado strikes me as false, but the suggestion he makes is genuine.

The two-faced man waves his free hand. "Our apologies for the greeting you received. Anzu is an overzealous creature." The last word is soaked with disdain. "But he has his uses."

I force myself not to shy from his dual gaze. "Did he really attack me because I'm a threat to my dad?"

His blue face frowns, and the white one speaks. "I believe you are familiar with complicated situations. This is one. Come. Enki will allow your audience now."

He releases my hand and gestures to an opening in the floor in front of the tanks. I'm certain it wasn't there before. Steps descend into cool blackness. The sages' silence is almost worse than their gibbering.

I hesitate. "My friends? They'll be safe."

"They have nothing to fear from us," Isimud answers, though I don't see which mouth says the words.

"What about Kyra?" Tam asks, and I have to admire him even while I want to tell him to keep quiet and worry about getting out of here in one piece. Not about me.

"She is a guest," Isimud's blue mouth says. "As is her father."

That's all I need to hear, that Dad *is* here. As I start down the steps, the black water of the tank sloshes, and the last thing I see before there's only darkness in front of me is one of the fish-men's faces, as he swims to the bottom of his glass cage to watch us disappear. He's showing me his teeth.

We walk down and down, and the black is like being inside a permanent night. There is no soft candle glow, no faint hint of light. Wherever we're going, it's the deeps. I find each step with care, glad they are regular and steady. Stone, I guess, from the sound of our shoes.

Bree has her hand on my shoulder, the only sign of her fear the tightness of the grip. I don't complain. It's only right I'm the one in front. I should have been strong enough not to bring them, to come here alone in the first place. We *are* in danger, no matter what assurances my grandfather Bronson made to Ben, no matter what the two-faced god claims.

Anything might happen to us. Of that, I'm certain.

I assume Tam's following Bree, and that Isimud needs no guidance. We do not talk. We might be descending into an ancient cavern, winding far below the surface of the earth. Or we might be beneath the ocean by now. There is no sound except the heaviness of our feet and our breathing as we travel down, and down, and down.

I know the destination is close when the smell changes. The air holds nothing, no light, no air, no smell, until it does. Like a memory of visiting the harbor and getting a snort of water up my nose by accident, there's a sting to it. The scent *is* water, its nature, as pure as possible. I don't know how else to explain it. One moment we're inside living darkness, the next we're inside living water.

The steps end, and there is light.

"Wow," the word escapes Bree, a soft exhalation.

The wall of water stretches higher than I can follow. It's a solid sheet of blue, not held there by glass or by *anything*. It simply is. We stand on a scant few feet of sandy soil with the night stairs behind us, and a subterranean magic ocean in front of us. I'm trembling, and it's hard to imagine how anyone could *not*. I grip the straps of my backpack to help disguise it.

This is where my father is. I have to keep going.

"No harm will come to you in the abzu," Isimud says.

"What does he mean?" Bree asks. "He can't expect us–"

Tam puts a hand on her arm. "I believe we can trust him on this."

Bree bites her lip, but nods. I extend my hand, and she takes it. Tam takes her other one. Bree's trembling too, which makes me feel better and worse.

Isimud angles toward the water. "He awaits."

Walking into the mass of water feels wrong, but necessary. So we move forward. I pause at the edge of it… "Should we hold our breath?" I ask Isimud, and both faces say, "There is no breath in the abzu. It is life itself."

"So that's a no?" I mutter, and Tam snorts. I want to hug him for the normalcy of it. I look at Bree and Tam, and ask them, "Ready?"

Bree swallows. Tam raises his eyebrows.

"Yeah," I say, "me neither. Here we go."

Forgetting what Isimud said, I suck in a breath, and we step together into the deep blue.

CHAPTER EIGHT

It's not just water, of course. There are more *things* swimming in it. Monstrous gods, large and small, and fish – magical or regular, I can't say. I keep holding my breath. I glance over and see Bree and Tam doing the same, cheeks puffing. We discover almost immediately that we don't have to swim. No waving our arms and legs around required. We release hands because it's easier to move with them free.

We walk *through* the water, the endless water that is not warm and not cold, not dark and not light. Isimud stays to our left, and I suppose he's leading us somewhere, though he's not forceful about it.

Finally, I have to release my breath. For a long moment, I can't move. I feel my lungs empty and start to burn. The lining of my nose stings. My mouth fills and fills again with water that tastes of nothing – not salt, not sweet. Life has no taste, it turns out. I want to laugh, and the word *hysterical* floats through my mind.

Bree and Tam are flailing too, inhaling water. Have the gods tricked us down here to drown? We could go back, except behind us is only water. In front of us, water. On our sides, surrounding us completely, water. I'm not even sure which way is back anymore.

We've been allowed into the abzu to die. Lucky us.

I shout for my Dad again, but the endless water absorbs the sound. Then comes a voice that is everywhere and nowhere, inside our heads and outside them:

Enough. Finish the journey.

My lungs calm. I breathe in... water. And I breathe it out again.

"This is weird," Tam says.

The sound comes to me muffled, but I can hear well enough to understand him. I clear my throat, which is such a ridiculous thing to do *underwater* in the freaking *abzu* that I almost revisit hysterical. I ask, "That voice, was it...?"

"Enki. He awaits," Isimud says. Both his faces seem impatient with us.

Bree has her mouth open, letting water come in and out of it. She closes it when she catches us watching her. "At least there's no head trip from this stuff," she says.

So they *did* see something too. I'll have to ask her what later. Except I can't, because I don't want to have to talk about seeing Dad crying in his room. But it has made me more eager to get to him. He didn't want to leave me. He was sad. I *saw* him being sad.

"If Enki awaits, we'd better get going," I say.

Able to breathe without trouble, we make better progress. Massive bodies curve past us from time to time, but we keep moving. The shift in environment at the end of the stairs was clear enough that I recognize when we hit the next one.

There's light, though it's not bright and doesn't seem to have a source. The blue water around us lightens, suffused with the glow. We pass into the heart of the deeps. The glow pulses, and my not-breathing grows deeper. My body likes this water.

"Life itself," Tam repeats, beside me. He's shaking his head in amazement. Bree wears an expression that's somewhere between overwhelmed and in love.

This part of the underground freshwater ocean, the part where Enki apparently receives visitors, continues to brighten. We have to squint.

"Um," Bree says.

"I know."

The everywhere and nowhere voice comes again.

Approach.

We all hear it. That much is certain, because we do what he says. The light begins to dim. When I have the guts to look up, I understand why. We're standing in a shadow.

Enki's shadow.

He's not this big out there in the world. I've seen him on TV, only a little taller than the tallest basketball players. He wouldn't fit through the doors of the Jefferson otherwise. But down here in the abzu, his height is the depth of the ocean. He towers over us like, well, a tower on some enormous castle. Like an underwater mountain. I can make out the curving white bone of his horns far above, the scaled ink-blue flesh that covers his body, not so different than a human's in theory. He has arms and legs. But he also has flowing rivers that spring from his shoulders, constantly refreshing the water around him.

We might as well be an inch high down here. But he's receiving us, so that's a good sign, right? I'm still trembling. In fact, I'm not sure I've stopped since we came down the stairs.

I look to Isimud for guidance, but he's as hard to read as ancient Sumerian.

So I address Enki, "Great lord of the watery deeps." I wait, hoping it's a decent beginning.

"Good move," Tam says low, encouraging. "They like flattery."

ENOUGH.

Bree and Tam jump back, but Enki's sonic boom of a voice isn't what knocks into me with such force. It's the accusatory question that comes after.

"Kyra Locke, what do you think you're doing?"

"Dad?" I rush toward him before I can stop myself.

He's marching toward us from the general direction of Enki, dressed not like usual but in a Society uniform. The gold sun bars of his stripes are pinned at his breast, and his posture is as stiff as a soldier heading off to war. I can read him well enough to see that he's angry.

I stop short and cross my arms in front of me. "You could at least *pretend* to be happy to see me. That I'm not dead. Killed by Set or one of your other enemies. Who I'm sure are legion by now."

Dad is close enough for me to take in his face. Grim. Dark as the true night we endured to get here. I can't believe what I've put my friends through only to find out Dad is mad that I came to him.

My own anger flares to life.

But I'm caught off guard when he keeps marching until he's right in front of me. He hugs me. In the watery deeps, I stand with my arms crossed as my dad presses me against him.

"Kyra," he says, "I can't believe you'd be so stupid."

But he holds me as if he can't bear to let go.

"Sometimes I surprise myself. I'm just stupid enough to not be ready to let you off this hook."

"Kyra," and he sighs. I can *hear* the exasperation in it, even through the abzu's waters.

"Why?" I ask. "Why didn't you ever tell me you were one of them?"

He releases me. Steps back, but not too far. He nods to Tam and Bree. "I'll make sure you all get out of here. Safely."

"Dad, you and me, we're talking about this. I'm not going anywhere until you tell me why. I'm your daughter."

He raises one of his hands and I catch the flinch before I give into it. I guess this situation is even more uncomfortable than I want it to be. He gives me a wounded look. "I would never hurt you."

It's true. He would never lift a hand to harm me. Traveling through Enki House has left me skittish. But I'm not ready to back down. "Really? Because it hurt when I found out you were a liar. It hurt when I found out you were gone. It hurt because I knew you wanted me to leave without a goodbye."

"I'm sorry," he says. "I don't know how else to say it. You *are* my daughter. But I'm your father. And I have my reasons."

"Which are?" I slam a hand out through the water.

"I can't share them."

"You're going to end the world. Isn't that the reason?"

His eyebrows go up.

"When the gods attacked me yesterday because you stole that relic, Bronson took me in. Told me what you'd done. I didn't believe it. I still don't. Why would you want to set them free?"

There's a disturbance in the water around us, and one massive scaled leg advances in our direction.

"Peace," my father says.

Enki stops.

Then to me, he says, "They are free. I'm doing what's right. You have to trust me." His lips quirk like he realizes the ridiculousness of what just passed his lips. "You can trust me to do the right thing. Even if it doesn't feel like I'm doing it by you. I promise... I am."

"Then let's just leave." Here it is, the real idea that's been in the back of my mind this whole time. "If you have this money, you must have more. Let's just leave. All of us. Me, you..." I glance over to Tam and Bree. They still don't know about Mom, and so I swallow the word. He'll know who I mean.

"My sweet fierce girl, that can't happen. I wish it could. More than you know. I wish none of this was happening. I wish there was nothing for you to find out about. That there were no lies to tell. I wish I could remake the world so it's exactly what you want it to be, exactly what you need it to be. So you can have ice cream sundaes every day and yell at me and play your music as loud as you want. I wish I could do that for you, but..." Dad throws out his hands in frustration. "Instead all I can do is this. And hope you will understand one day that I'm doing it for you."

TIME IS SHORT.

Dad gazes up through the water at the towering god. "What do you mean?"

"Is this guy your *friend*?" I ask him, incredulous.

"No, an ally. Maybe. A friend to you, I hope."

THERE ARE OTHERS ABOVE. ARRIVING.

Dad frowns at me. "Did anyone know you were coming here? Bronson?"

"You mean my *grandfather*."

"I would remake the world..."

"But you can't." He waits for my answer. "No, I didn't tell anyone. I may be stupid, but I'm not that stupid."

"I shouldn't have said that. I just can't believe... You shouldn't be here." He takes my shoulders. "Our time's almost up. You need to go. As far as you can. This is not for you to be a part of. I might as well die if I can't keep you safe."

"Dad, you're the one being stupid."

He keeps one hand on my shoulder and I let it stay there. He peers up at Enki. "OK," he says, "I guess now I fight and lose. You'll watch out for her?"

SHE WILL HAVE A GUARD. THAT IS ALL I PROMISE.

"What if she doesn't *want* one?" I ask.

"Don't challenge him," Dad says. "He's not that much of an ally. Still a god."

WE MUST MEET THEM NOW.

Isimud appears beside us, and offers me his arm. His other one he holds out to Bree and Tam. "Take it," the pale face nearest me says, and the blue one says to them, "take it now. It will steady you."

My dad squeezes me into one last hug and bounds away, back to Enki. "What's happening?" I ask, and when I start to pull away to go after Dad, Isimud's hand fastens on my arm.

"We're going to the surface," he says, "to receive uninvited guests."

The water around us transforms into a shaft of moving light, like we're in a movie spaceship hitting warp speed. I hear Bree scream, and I might be screaming too. It's hard to say. I can't believe we came all this way for Dad to blow me off.

Except for that speech. You can hardly ever get good ice cream these days. Between subsidies and delayed shipments, ultra-pasteurized soy is pretty much it in our part of the country. Caramel topping's just not the same without full fat vanilla. I love sundaes in a way no one else knows. Back then, we had secrets that we shared. Not from each other, with each other.

I can't believe he remembers.

The tunnel of water vanishes and we are no longer in the abzu. We aren't wet from our trip below either. We stand dry as sun-bleached bone in a large chamber with that curvy-horned and wavy-lined tile, those deep blue walls curving into a rounded ceiling. There is a small pool of sky blue water in front of us, with a visible bottom I suspect is not really there.

This must be where the door behind the sages goes to. I can hear them hissing and calling. This time, there's no mistaking it for laughter. It isn't. They're making threats. And why wouldn't they?

Society operatives are invading Enki House. They pour through the door in uniforms that include masks covering their heads, so all we can see is a navy flood of them, narrowed eyes, weapons lifted. Some have relics, others more traditional bows and swords and knives. One of them is trigger happy. A shaft of sun comes through the top of the chamber and glints off a bolt that's winging its way right at my father.

Dad doesn't see it and I jump to intercept its path, but Isimud raises his hand and catches it without a spare motion. He drops it to the floor with a clatter.

"Hold fire," a male operative calls out.

It's not just us and the Society operatives. Enki is here.

He's not the ocean size he was below, but he still towers over us from a throne covered in elaborate shell-like crenellations that match his sharp, curving horns. His face is a mix of planes and curves sharp as the ziggurat we're inside. His deep blue skin is so finely scaled it looks smooth until the light hits a certain way. He's wearing a thick breastplate of shell armor.

The operatives fill the space. They don't speak or call out, which is disconcerting. As I slowly rotate, backing up toward Tam and Bree – staying behind Isimud, because that arrow maneuver was both timely and impressive – I scan for Oz or Justin. Not that I'd have any way to recognize them, or any reason to believe they're here. But it turns out the operatives are not the only warriors present.

There are Sumerian gods and goddesses spread throughout the room, maybe ten in total. Some of them must have been the swimming *things* below in the abzu, risen to the surface when we did. There are beings with crab-clawed hands and webbed legs, with sharp fins and spear-point tails, skins of green, blue, red. To a one, they look offended by the presence of the humans.

The whole room is still, waiting to see what will happen next.

Finally, there is motion. One last trio of operatives breezes through the door at the far end of the chamber. Bronson leads them, unhooded, and so instantly recognizable. I'd bet anything the two operatives with him are Oz and Justin.

Bronson is wearing a flashy silver breastplate over his uniform that *has* to be a relic. He makes his way through the assembled humans and gods like he's visiting royalty. When he reaches the edge of the round pool, he bows his head and says, "Enki of the first time, our apologies for the unannounced visit. But you threaten the peace by harboring a fugitive."

My father is standing beside Enki's throne, his shoulders back and chin raised in defiance. He hefts the Solstice Was in his right hand. The headpiece has a face eerily reminiscent of Set's. That same elongated head, its unseeing eyes painted black and mouth snarling in a vicious grin. Beneath it is a thin metal rod that forks into two sharp points.

Even from here, I can sense that it is powerful. The same way I can feel waves of energy rolling off Enki. The god is pissed off.

Bronson speaks again, "All we want is our operative and the relic. I'm sure he told you a grand story and we'll get to the bottom of his plans – which I hope we won't find implicate you in any way – but you don't want to be on the wrong side of us. Not on this."

Enki rises. I want him to stick up for Dad, to tell them there's no way they're taking him.

"You are in my house," Enki says.

It's a minor shock that he speaks to them through his mouth. Some part of me knows that the actual sounds are gibberish, no language I know, but can understand anyway through some trick of godhood.

I have to give it to Bronson. If he's intimidated, I can't see it.

He says, "Not like I had a choice, and you know it. All we want is what belongs to us. We will take him by force if we must."

The tension in the chamber ratchets up a notch. Arms holding bows ready themselves, stances shift.

"You told me you were going to try to help him. To protect our family," I say to Bronson, accusing. I leave Isimud behind and make my way to Dad's side.

"Kyra, stay out of this," Dad says, and then prompts. "Isimud?"

But when the two-faced god starts toward us, I slip behind Dad to his other side. Bree and Tam watch me from their vantage surrounded by operatives and gods. Their concern is plain, but they stay put. "Isimud, stay with my friends?" I ask him.

Almost imperceptibly Dad nods, and Isimud returns to them.

"He's endangered you with this treason," Bronson says to me. And to Dad, "That's the hardest part for me to believe. How could you put her in the way of such harm? Family should come first."

"You don't get to say that," Dad says. "Not after Hannah. Not after... You know I could end this in a moment."

Bronson absorbs the meaning of that – a meaning that's lost to me, but which I'd give anything to know. If Dad can end this, why on earth wouldn't he?

"But you won't," Bronson says, "because you would have already. I wonder what you think is going to happen. You may be a great operative, but you can't stand against the entire organization."

Enki stares down at Bronson with eyes hard as diamonds. *"You risk the wrath of my house."*

The warning is spoken without emotion, like some serial killer calmly confessing where he's hidden bodies.

"Apologies," Bronson says, "no disrespect is meant."

"And yet it is given."

There's a scuffle on the other side of the chamber. An operative and a pale green goddess with a long ridged fin over her scalp grapple with each other. She lowers her head and knocks him to the ground with her fin, but he slashes at her legs with a long knife. He goes still as her spiny foot hovers over his vulnerable throat. The operatives around them slide into flanking position.

We're about to be caught in the middle of an attack in a trickster's seat of power. This will not end well.

"Dad, how do we get out of here?" I ask, softly.

He turns his head, and gives me the saddest look I've ever seen. "You can't stop this. But I can. Remember what I asked. Do it this time. Please." His hand comes up to my shoulder, and he says strangely familiar words in an ancient unfamiliar language.

I want to talk back, to say, "Oh no, don't you dare." But I can't, because I'm frozen. Unable to move. I remember where I first heard the words he said. Oz used them on Mehen, to access the power of his stripes.

Dad has bound me.

I'm forced to stand, helpless, as Dad heads around the pool to Bronson. The entire chamber is quiet, waiting on the verdict. Try to kill each other or go in peace?

But I am certain Dad means to turn himself in, and there's not one blessed or cursed thing I can do about it.

He extends the Solstice Was to Bronson. "This is what you came for," Dad says. "So have your moment. I couldn't beat you in that armor anyway. Believe me, I would enjoy nothing more than making the attempt."

I can't reconcile the scholarly Dad who nags me about homework and staying out too late with this one who's in league with gods. But trapping me here, leaving me unable to do anything? That's so very him. It's the relic equivalent of being grounded.

Bronson takes the scepter, a reverence in the way he accepts it. Another operative slaps handcuffs onto Dad's wrists. "We will be leaving now," Bronson says, bowing again to Enki. "No hard feelings, old one."

The old one in question doesn't acknowledge him. But I glimpse a flash of movement as the green goddess removes her foot from the operative's throat. He climbs to his feet.

Bronson frowns at me. "Kyra, you can come with us. And the other two, your friends."

"No," Dad speaks up. "I don't want her to see any more of this. Leave her out of Society business. That's a promise you made long ago and not just to me. It's one promise you'd better keep, for *her* good."

Bronson's response is an annoyed look, but he huddles with the two operatives who came in with him. He's ordering them to stay behind. With me. I'm certain it's Oz and Justin, and so, weirdly, I'm grateful. They may be useful.

Dad meets my eyes. He lifts his cuffed hands to push his glasses up on his nose, and that familiar motion is what gets me.

I think at him as hard as I can: *This isn't over. I'm not giving up.*

But all I can do is continue to stand here like a stupid statue, as they lead him from the chamber. All I can do is listen to Bree and Tam telling me it's going to be OK as I watch the back of my dad's head and wonder if I'll ever see him again.

All I can do is stand right here. Unable to scream. Unable to cry.

CHAPTER NINE

I can't even ask how long it takes for the effect of Hephaestus' chains to wear off. Though I remember Oz saying it wouldn't last too long yesterday, it might as well be an era, an age, an epoch. Dad's getting further away with every passing second, and I become more and more convinced that I am the only person who cares if he makes it back out.

He may not want my help, but he's going to get it anyway. I can't cope with a world in which he disappears for good.

Oz peels back his mask, as does Justin, and both of them bow low to Enki. I'm not surprised when Oz ends up right in front of me. He even slouches, so we can make eye contact. Which is nice of him, really.

"It won't last too much longer," he says.

His short brown hair is ruffled from the mask, his pupils huge from the relative dimness of the chamber. I would look away, but there's the problem of not being able to.

I hear Justin's voice off to my side, greeting Bree and Tam, "Hello again," he says, while Oz looks at me like he's the one unable to move. "You OK?" Justin asks, and Bree mumbles something that's probably a lie about being alright. I wish I could turn my head to see her face. Is Justin her type? It's always so hard to get her to admit she likes anyone, but the shy way she answers makes me wonder.

I figure Tam will interrupt Oz and me, but he doesn't. He must be curious about Bree's reaction to Justin too. He can be my source of intel there. Once I can ask him.

Oz bites his lip. I can tell he's thinking of what he can possibly say next to me, probably some comforting line of bull. Maybe something that my grandfather told him to say. I am spectacularly unimpressed with Bronson, and how he strode in here as if he owned the place. How he talked about family while he broke mine apart, without showing any remorse.

Spit it out, I want to tell Oz. But he says, "I bet you hate us all right about now."

Do I? I should, but it's hard to blame Oz and Justin. They're following orders. Except I've never had that problem, so why am I cutting them slack for it?

"But," Oz says, "think of it this way. Your father is safer in custody than out running around with that relic. And now that we have it back, the crisis is averted. He will get a hearing, a chance to make his case. If a god encouraged him, well, then the outcome's not certain. His best chance was to be brought in quickly and he has been."

Excuse me if I don't trust the Society on that.

But I do appreciate that Oz is trying to make me feel better. He's not giving me a line of complete bull like I expected.

"Oh, look at that," he says. He raises a hand and it comes so near my cheek I'd stop breathing or swallow, if I could. I'm sure he's about to touch my face. But he doesn't, just brushes a hair that's in front of my left eye away. "You blinked. It's wearing off."

I test his theory, blinking again. Then blinking up a storm. He grins, but apologizes for it. "Sorry. It's not funny," he says. But he blinks at me, and I roll my eyes at him. Slowly, my face unfreezes, and, finally, my limbs. I shake them out, relieved, and then bend to brace my hands above my knees like I've finished a run.

When I tilt my head up, I'm surrounded by concerned faces – Bree, Tam, Justin, and a no longer grinning Oz.

"You OK?" he asks.

"Getting there," I say.

This next part, telling them where I want to go, won't be easy. So I put it off, for a little while longer, anyway. I turn to face Enki.

"Thanks," I start, but my confidence ebbs under the weight of his gaze. Why on earth I thought it'd be easier to look a god in the face than my friends I don't know. It isn't. He's blue and scary and *examining* me. The green goddess with the sharp fin and Isimud take positions so they are behind and to either side of the throne.

I have a feeling if I stepped a foot out of line – and if Oz and Justin stepped a toe over it – they'd be on us, and no apologies.

After a long pause, Enki speaks. *"I would not have let them take your father had he not wished it. He was a guest here. You will have the guard I promised him."*

Oz weighs in on that, doing his best to sound respectful. "Great lord, that's really not necessary."

Enki gets to his feet. The shell armor scrapes against the chair.

"She will have my guard."

Oz clears his throat, about to say *more*. Is he kidding me?

"Oz," I say, "shut up."

Justin mumbles, "Listen to her."

We should leave before this escalates again. But I hesitate. There's something I want to know, maybe even *need* to know. "Enki..." There's no reaction, so I add, "...great lord of the watery deeps... I just wanted to ask a question. Can I?"

He lifts a hand, palm up. The armor has cracks and chips and from the shape I'm keenly aware it used to be the shell of a living thing. He says, *"Proceed."*

This is unwise, but I can't help asking. "Why are you helping my dad?"

He studies me, and I'm a specimen. A speck. He could do away with me between one breath of mine and no breath of his. My bones could be formed into armor too. I am absolutely certain the pause is to make sure *that* knowledge sinks in.

"PERHAPS I AM HELPING YOU."

"Oh." I'm smart enough not to tell him that seems unlikely. Like Bronson and the others did, I bow and start to back around the pool. "We'll just be going, then." I grab Bree and Tam when I reach them, and pull them along with me. They're as eager as I am to get out of here. "Thanks for the... hospitality, great lord of the watery deeps," I say.

His response is inside my head this time.

You are always welcome here.

The others don't react, and I'm sure it's because they didn't hear it. I wasn't looking for a permanent open sign to flick on. If I have to visit here again, things will have gone south, *way* down south.

We make it to the opening along the back wall. In the next room, the seven are hissing like a nest of giant snakes.

"How did you get past the sages?" I ask Oz.

"Easy," he says, and we pass back into their chamber. We're in back of the tank this time, but the sages are ready for us.

"*Youuu* said you'd stay, threat," one of the female sages sings to me.

"We used that," Oz answers, ignoring the sages to gesture at a black tactical bridge that arches over the tank. "Ladies first," he says.

"No splashing," I tell the sages, as I start toward it. I channel Dad, trying to make it sound like I'm the boss of them. They aren't fooled.

"*Nooo,*" says one. And another, "Not for *youuu*. Wouldn't want your guard to notice." That creepy not-laughter ensues.

"Bree?" I check to see if she's coming.

"I'd rather have an escort," she says, and I note that she already has her hand looped through Justin's arm. He looks surprised, and Tam disapproving.

Oz offers me his arm, like he's a courtly gentleman, and I take it despite the ridiculous thought. I don't know what a courtly gentleman even *is*.

We only make it a few steps before one of the sages leaps above the water. She hooks scaly flippers over the edge of the bridge. Black water slops over onto its surface, and Oz slides me behind him. "Get back," he says, and then adds, "Please." Justin lets go of Bree to join Oz, holding some sort of small green knife that might be a relic.

"Put away your fin-splitter, *boooy*," she says, and the other sages hiss and clamor. "We *exxxist* only to give knowledge."

The sage releases the side of the bridge, but her tail flips up and out of the tank to spray water across Oz and Justin's faces. This opportunity is exactly what she wanted all along. I barely have time to tuck my nose into my elbow to avoid another vision of my own.

I grab Oz's uniform to lead him across. "Been there," I say, loud enough for Justin to hear too, "it's just a vision. It'll be over before you know it."

The sage fish-woman slides back into the water with the others. "You never know what you need to know, but *weee* do," one says.

Oz's eyes are closed as I lead him onto the tile, his lids moving slightly in a mimic of dream state. Surprisingly, Tam tows Justin across, leaving Bree to follow last. I'm not sure what's going on with Tam. He's never this quiet.

"Tam, everything alright?" I ask.

"Why wouldn't it be?" he counters, his irritation plain and, again, not like him.

"I can think of about a thousand reasons," I say, but let it go.

We get the Society boys out into the hallway, empty of humans *and* gods, and wait out whatever gift the sage decided to give them. Oz slumps against the wall, and I have to force myself to stop watching his eyelids flutter. I want to know what he sees. From his scowl, it's not anything good.

I'd love to ask if the visions the sages gave us were true or false. I can't believe Dad was crying like that, not over me. But I don't want to know, not if it wasn't the truth.

Bree is near Justin, keeping an eye on him. His expression is blank.

"What about you?" I ask her. "Everything alright?"

She shrugs one shoulder. Her mascara has run down her cheek, blending in with the face paint. I'd forgotten we had it on. "No," she says. "You?"

I shake my head. We exchange a half-smile. It makes what I know is coming harder. So I focus on Oz and Justin, waiting for them to come out of the visions.

Finally, they do. Oz reenters the waking world first, dazed. "So sorry," is the first thing out of his mouth, "that was a rookie error."

Beside him, Justin says, "We are rookies."

Oz's scowl has not gone with the vision.

"Hey," I say, wanting to distract him. He was kind to me back there. Why not be the same? These are the only people I can ask about Society stuff for now. "How did you find us here?"

Oz straightens. "One of the revelers recognized him." Oz nods to Tam. "She passed on the news to his dad."

"My dad would never tell you," Tam says.

Oz smiles. "He would if he was worried for his son, it turns out. And so he was. Something about your mom killing him if you got hurt while she's out of town. He's not happy with you."

"Where is he then?" Tam asks, suspicious.

"We told him we'd bring you right to your front door as soon as we were done here."

"No," I say.

Oz asks, "What do you mean?"

"I need to go somewhere else first."

I don't relish the next part, but it's time. Past time. This is my only next move. "If you're willing to come with me, that is." So maybe I want to delay a few more seconds.

Bree and Tam stand beside each other, unified. She says, "I'm not backing out after that. Whatever you need. But your dad... He confessed, Kyra."

"No," I say. "He didn't. He turned himself in. That's different. I need to figure out what to do about it."

Oz says, "We can't let you do anything about it."

"Not your call," I say, sweetly.

"Where do you want to go?" Bree asks.

The question is simple and the answer oh-so-complicated.

"To Oracle Circle." I have always known the day would come when Bree and Tam find out about Mom.

Dread of their reactions has kept me from telling them. They know I keep my walls high, if not why, not the reason I'm like this. But necessity is a devil, and I can't stomach lying to them anymore. Not after the way I feel about my dad lying to me. "I need to go there to see my mom."

Bree's head cocks back in surprise. "Come again?"

Tam says nothing.

"My mom," I say. "I need to see her."

Bree shakes her head. "First a grandfather, then your dad's a super-librarian hiding out with Sumerian gods, and now *this*? A mom?"

"I've always had the mom."

Bree doesn't respond.

"You don't have to come with me," I say. "I had reasons, but... I know I should have told you sooner."

I look down, study my boots. Oz and Justin stay out of this. It isn't their business. I wait for Bree or Tam to tell me off, to start talking about what a lost cause I am. I dragged them all this way, put them through *that*, and without even being honest.

Finally, I can't stand it any longer. I have to look up.

Bree must have been waiting for that. "We're coming," she says. She nudges Tam with an elbow. "Right?"

"Of course," he says, and then, "I think I get why you didn't want us to know."

"No, you really don't." Because it's not just that Mom's an oracle at the Circle. That's not the worst part.

When I start walking, they do too. We go back out the main hallway, where it becomes clear that twilight is coming on outside. We must have been in the abzu far longer than it felt like we were.

As we exit onto the top of the ziggurat, the sun sinks below the horizon of the strange view. That's also where the monster meets us with a roar. Two beats of Anzu's wings brings him to me. Make that in front of me, separating me from the others.

Oh no. This can only mean one thing.

"Guys," I say, "meet my new guard. Anzu."

CHAPTER TEN

"Anzu," I say, in the careful tone I'd use on a stray dog, which may prove unwise, "these are not threats. These are..." I hesitate, considering what category Justin and Oz should go into. Bree gives me a meaningful eyebrow raise. "...friends. All friends." But I amend to, "At least unless I say they're something else."

The lion head cocks to one side, but otherwise there's no indication he understands. Or wants to. Until he launches back into the sky.

"We *are* friends," Oz says. "Or, if you can't believe that, we're not your enemies."

"I like your dad," Justin adds. When Oz gives him a look, he clarifies, "Of course, not if he's a traitor. Which it seems like he is. There's never been anyone accused of treason who's been cleared before..." He stops talking. "I shouldn't say anymore, should I? I'll just be quiet now."

"There's never been anyone cleared before? Ever? In the history of the Society?" The thought makes my head swim.

If that's the case, I may have even less time to figure out how to get Dad back than I was planning on. Not to mention I'd rather make it out of here before darkness falls. So I start down the front ramp, and the others do too. It's wide enough for us to walk abreast. Yes, Anzu continues to circle above.

"But, Justin, I bet it's not much of a pool size, is it?" Oz says. "It's a rare charge."

"True," Justin says, "only sixteen I can think of."

Tam sniffs. "Technicality to the rescue. You were born to be a bureaucrat, Osborne. No wonder you're Bronson's pet."

I expect Oz to counter him, but Justin does. "You mean the director's ward. Oz is a model operative and that's nothing to be ashamed of... not unless you're sympathetic to traitors."

"I'm sympathetic to Kyra," Tam says.

Bree puts a hand on his arm. "We all are," she says, "despite her keeping secrets from us."

I can't come up with a word to say to that. But Oz, again, to the rescue. "Cut her some slack. Her mom was a Pythia. That's got to be hard."

I stumble on the stone, and Oz catches me. His hand is warm on my elbow, and when he removes it, there's multi-colored paint on his palm. "Sorry," I say, "but *what*?"

"I know you didn't know about your dad," he says. "But they didn't tell you about your mom?"

"What's a Pythia?" Bree asks, and I notice she directs it to Justin. He checks with Oz before he answers. Oz nods.

"They were the oracles at Delphi, once upon a time," Justin says. "Women conscripted by Apollo into divine mysteries, able to look into the future. Now the Society has Apollo's cup and they work for us. The mother, maiden, and crone configuration is best, but two will do. That's all we have now, since…"

I need to sit down. But all I can do is keep walking. "Since my mom left. What does it mean?"

Oz offers me his arm again, apparently not caring if I smear paint on the sleeve of his uniform. I take it, because we still have quite a ways to go before we reach the bottom. If the surprises keep coming at this rate, I'm bound to stumble again. I've already learned I have no clue who *either* of my parents is. And if I don't know about them, what does that mean for me? Am I someone or no one? I honestly don't know the answer.

"Oz," I prompt. "What does it mean?"

"It means she's probably had a hard time of it, on her own," he says. "They do better in groups, when they can share the visions. The Pythias, they're–"

"Oz saw them, yesterday. I never have," Justin puts in.

"Then let him finish," Tam says.

I don't know if Tam's working on some problem with Justin beyond his general dislike of operatives or not, but I also couldn't care less at the moment. What Oz is saying matters to me.

"What were you going to say?" I ask. "Did they say anything about her? My mom?"

Oz stares into the distance at the tops of the Houses visible over the crazy forest. "They sent me to you. They were looking out for you, because of her."

I gaze out over that same horizon, though I hardly see it. My thoughts are on my mom and our past. "That's funny," I say.

I don't explain what I mean. They'll see soon enough.

"They also refused to tell Bronson where your dad was," Oz says. "They said your mom wouldn't want them to."

"What if he isn't guilty?" I ask. "What would you do then?"

Oz frowns as if he's not sure what I'm asking. Justin says, "We would do whatever we were told. That's the way the organization works. Your dad would have agreed, before he went rogue."

"So there's nothing that could convince you not to do something they told you? You follow orders, no matter what." I'm genuinely curious.

"Hypotheticals are meaningless," Justin says, "without specifics. Your father hasn't claimed to be motivated by any noble cause."

But he had – not specifically, but he asked me to trust him, claimed that he's doing the right thing. Tam and Bree exchange a look with me, and I give a slight shake of my head. I'm not confiding that in these boys. I wanted to see if they would be open to a truth different than the one they're told to believe. The answer seems to be no. For Justin, anyway.

"About treason," I say. "What's the penalty?"

There's an uncomfortable silence. Justin obviously knows – at this point it's clear he knows just about everything, off the top of his head. But it's Oz who answers. "It hasn't been levied yet."

"But you know what it is. So tell me," I say.

"It's death," he says, with regret.

I drop my arm from where it's linked with his. I can't bear to be touching him – or anyone – with that word echoing in my head. Instead, I speed up. The sooner we get out of here, the sooner I can find out what the future holds.

When we pass the turnoff to Set House twenty minutes later, I brush my cheek at the memory of the Egyptian hench-god's cold touch and check to see if Anzu's still above us. He is and, if I'm right, he lowers his flight path so he's nearer. But his protection skills aren't put to the test, and neither are Oz and Justin's.

We don't meet a soul on the path as we make our way out, and we don't talk much either. Dark continues to descend by degrees. Oz and Justin acknowledged that it's better if we're out of here before night falls. The only people who make a habit of visiting the Houses of the Gods then are other gods, and that alone is reason enough to hurry.

We reach the grand sprawl of the mansion that serves as the loghouse as dark takes hold. I pretend the calls that start up behind us in the forest and overgrown greenery aren't happening. It was bad enough in there during the daylight. I'd rather not consider what might have been sleeping.

There are a couple of Society guards posted at the main loghouse, sitting at their posts as we enter a long tiled and windowed salon. They salute Oz and Justin, rake their eyes over the rest of us in disbelief. "I just want to wash my face," I say.

Before they can argue, Oz moves in to talk quietly with them. Their respect for their fellow operatives – and maybe for my grandfather – gets us leave to use the loghouse bathroom to scrub our faces and arms clean. It's not vanity. I don't want to give my mother any reason to be more thrown than seeing my regular unadorned face will make her. That's always been enough.

Tam heads into the men's room, leaving me and Bree alone in this small wallpapered one that's been converted for visitors by the addition of stall doors and two polished white sinks. I meet her eyes in the mirror. The one degree of remove makes it easier than actually facing her.

"I am sorry I never told you. I wanted to. So many times, I almost did."

Her attention stays on me in the mirror. "I don't doubt it, K. I really don't. That you were sorry that time you drew on my face? That I doubt." Her voice is artificially breezy, but I think she means it. She waves me in front of her, having freed the small make-up case she brought along from my backpack. "At least let me freshen you up for your mom. Do you see her much?"

I shake my head.

"Not ready to talk about that yet?"

"I guess not," I say. "You going to take it out on my face?"

"No," she says. "Not this time."

I scoot up onto the sink, perching there and hunching so my face is easy for her to reach.

"You'll have to soon enough, you know," she says. "And you'll find out nothing terrible happens. I'm not going to judge you based on her."

"I won't blame you." Because I can't imagine how anyone couldn't. Whose mother feels about them the way mine does about me?

"Maybe a little, but we'll still be friends. That's a promise."

I consent to let her comb my tangles, and swipe some neutral shadow over my eyelids. I even hold still while she applies heavy liner that tilts up at the end. Bree offers me a lipstick tube and starts on her own makeup, twice as elaborate as anything I wear. I hop down and smooth the red over my lips. "Better," she says, "right?"

Undeniably. I put on my leather jacket, and feel almost ready for what's ahead. Mom. I don't rush Bree.

Sure, we're killing time. I know we are. But it comforts us both, this chance to take a breath – and not of water. This is the same thing we do when we're going out to the market or planning to try and sneak into a club. Sometimes before school. Here and now, it's hard to believe we'll ever do those things again.

When we emerge, Oz is talking to the guard again. He glances over and doesn't look away as he watches us cross the room.

"Tell me we don't still look like crazy messes?" I ask.

"You never did," he says.

Bree says, "Good try."

I point out, "We were coated in sand yesterday, and painted into hippies today. This is the first time you've ever seen what we look like."

He hesitates. "You look nice," he says.

Bree and I laugh.

"What?" Oz asks.

"We always say anyone who tells us we look nice is off the list," I explain. "No girl is ever trying to look nice."

"Well," Bree says, "some of them probably are. Just not us."

I expect Oz to be embarrassed by this, but instead he leans in. Solemnly, he says, "You look bad, then. Very, *very* bad."

Bree drops her wrist, a parody of southern belle flirting. "Don't you say the *nicest* things?"

Oz smiles. I can't help but catch it and return one.

"Ready?" Tam asks, as he and Justin come back out, apparently not noticing the effort we put into our appearance. Justin, however, might be admiring Bree. Surreptitiously. If he is, this is something that I approve of. She deserves admiration.

In answer to Tam, I say, "For whatever's next." I mean it not even a little.

There's a big black Society coach waiting for us on the street when we get outside. Oz unlatches the coach door and holds it open for me, like a knight in some fairy tale.

I remind myself that Oz is not on my side. But he might not be entirely on the opposite one.

We rattle our way toward the Circle, and I assume Anzu drifts above the carriage like the world's most fearsome kite. The carriage slows when we hit the neighborhood's heavily trafficked outskirts, and we decide to go the rest of the way on foot.

Tall buildings wear tattered remnants of bright paint, and lush green trees dot the sidewalk. The street is wide, with plenty of other people traveling the same way on business of their own. Every third streetlight or so works, and a few trash can blazes help... if not so much with lighting, then with conjuring a dangerous ambience.

Here's what I couldn't say to Bree.

I *see* Mom at least once a week. I wait across the street from the market, hoping to catch sight of her. On those rare occasions when I can catch her working a table, I quietly observe from a distance. I sneak, because Dad doesn't approve. I'm not supposed to approach her. Dad has tried to explain that her reaction to me has nothing to do *with* me, that it's part of the vision-brought madness that took her over after the Awakening, the thing that led her to leave us and live here in the first place. Logically, I understand he's probably right. For the most part.

But I'm also the *only* person who sets her off by existing. I make her worse. That's a fact. So I haven't spoken to my mom in over a year, and that last time was a mistake. She saw me when she shouldn't have. It destroyed her equilibrium. Dad yelled at me afterward.

It was a bad scene, which sent me back to hovering at the edge of her life. Dad brings bags filled with each week's crop of subsidy groceries to whatever squat she's living in, takes her to the doctor when she needs it, helps keep her semi-stable. Unlike Bree's absentee dad, I always get a birthday card from her. Dad brings it to her, has her sign, leaves it under my bedroom door. I have all five of them in a drawer in my room. I look at them an embarrassing amount.

These are the things I can't bring myself to say out loud. The street opens up on the abandoned traffic roundabout and circular park that gave first Dupont Circle and now Oracle Circle their names.

"What now?" Oz asks.

Bree examines the crush in front of us. "Do you know where she'll be?"

I, too, take in the throng of people in the tree-covered space. Stalls and tents and tables are arranged one after the other in a jumble of noise. Candles and strings of fairy lights illuminate the market, which I've never seen at night. Besides fortunes, people come here to get charms to stave off the evil eye, amulets to hide someone from the attention of the gods. The effects are probably make-believe, but I wouldn't say no to one of each to loop around my neck, pin to my sleeve, hide in my pocket.

This isn't normally the time that I come here, but given the brisk trade I assume she'll be working. Dad being in custody means I don't have to be sneaky. Not this time. He's not around to yell at me.

"I guess we'll have to look around," I say. "Ask if anyone knows where she is?"

"OK," Bree says. "What's her name?"

Oz answers, "Hannah Locke."

I nod.

Tam finally speaks. "We'll split up and ask for Hannah, then."

"You split up," Bree says, and ignores Tam's hurt look. "If you get a lead, then come find us. Otherwise, we'll meet you guys at the fountain in the middle in twenty minutes."

"I don't know–" Oz says.

But Bree shakes her head. "Twenty minutes."

It's hard to argue with Bree when she's in command mode. Spending chunks of her childhood in a TV studio has given her a well-developed talent for bossiness. I can't help smiling at her as the boys head into the mix together. Tam isn't the only one scowling.

"Thanks," I say, "for not bolting or abandoning me. You may regret it, though."

Bree dips her head in acknowledgment. "I figured you might not want them there... if we find her first," she says. "Now, come on."

We walk toward the market. "How'd you know about the fountain? Have you been here before?"

"Once. Remember Mark?"

I do. He was one of her mother's boyfriends.

"He thought I'd love to get my fortune told for a birthday present. I was thirteen."

The pavement beneath our feet is cracked, and I go wide to avoid the worst of the split. "Did you love it?"

"A creepy lady told me I was going to die alone," Bree says. "Not the best birthday fortune ever."

"That sucks. Con artist."

"Mark was a tool. I think she did it to make him look bad. It worked. Mom dumped him. I have no issues with oracles."

A bent woman stands at the edge of the market stalls. Her arm crooks, urging people inside. I suspect her stoop is for effect. The hat at her feet overflows with bills.

Now that we're closer, the tall fountain at the center is visible. It spews water from a bowl lifted by three carved beauties. The city leaves it on so the oracles will have a ready source of clean water. Something about the Circle feels different tonight, and I don't think it's the time of day or my nerves. I never come here calm.

The Society's position on street oracles is that the average person can't wield relics with such skill and so they're not legit. Dad has always disagreed and claimed that an innate gift and a found relic – even a rock with the tiniest smidgen of divine energy – is enough to give people visions of *something* real. He doesn't want me to think of Mom as a phony. I assume most of the oracles are charlatans, a few genuine. I've never been sure about Mom, but *she* believes she's one of the few. If she was an oracle of Delphi, I guess she's right.

An old woman at one table shakes a teacup in her hand, reading the leaves for a tourist on break from the revels. The woman beams, happy with her fate. I don't want to interrupt, so I wait until we reach two women who are clearly mother and daughter, with painted Tarot decks laid on their table. They beckon me forward.

"Hannah Locke?" I ask. "Do you know where she is?"

"If you're not buying, get out of here," the mother says, and the daughter cackles.

"Charming," I say.

We move on. The next stall houses two Yoruba diviners at a low table. A small shrine to Legba sits at the back of the tent, a cane wound with green beads propped against it. The women consult with a client in a Hawaiian shirt, leaning over a round tray where a handful of the small brown nuts they use for divination form a pattern.

Bree notes my pause. "Here?"

"No," I say.

One of the women tilts her head at me in what might be recognition. The tray with the nuts has a face impressed on the rich brown wood. A bloodless imitation of Legba's.

The woman shrugs one shoulder and reaches out to gather the nuts. She rattles them in her palm and tosses them again. We keep going.

"Hey, did you and Tam say anything about Legba showing up yesterday?"

Bree thinks for a moment. "No. They never really asked. Did you?"

I shake my head no. "And I don't think we should in front of them."

"Wonder what he wants with you," she says.

"He's destined to be disappointed, whatever it is. But I'd rather keep any info we have that they don't, just in case."

"He could be the one, you know," Bree says.

I don't know who she means for a moment, until she says, "Your dad. The one who beats the odds. Who gets off clean."

"He has to." But I feel less sure than I sound. He's not even fighting for his freedom, but *I'm* going to win it somehow? The unlikelihood isn't going to stop me from trying.

A pale woman in a flowing white top and a crimson headdress catches my eye. She sits beneath a small tent, a lone card chair beside her. She holds a bowl in her lap, and water laps the sides. But so does fire. Or maybe that's a trick, some reflection on the water. Whichever, her fingers stroke the fire in the bowl, pulling it through the air like taffy.

She smiles at me. Her hand hovers over the bowl, and flames cling to her skin as she waves to us.

"Let's go," Bree whispers.

But I'm not sure. "Wait."

The woman keeps smiling. "She is waiting for you. Next street over, fourth door. The red one."

Of course Mom knows I'm coming. She's an oracle. Maybe this message means she isn't going to turn me away. I dig in my backpack for a large-ish bill, place it on the ground beside the oracle. "For your trouble."

"Be careful, girl," the woman says, her hands dipping back into the water, the fire dying. The thin coating of liquid on her skin that allows the trick is visible with the flame extinguished. She picks up the money. "Secrets are like wolves. They have sharp teeth."

Bree steers me away. "She's probably just messing with you."

I don't respond.

The boys are waiting for us at the fountain, not talking, with their backs to the naked stone goddesses.

Leery children with smudged cheeks race around them. I'd bet anything they're thinking, *Should we try to jump these guys or just pick their pockets?*

"We struck out. You guys have better luck?" Tam asks.

"Think so," I say, hooking my thumb in the direction of the street that burning-hands lady told us. "Sounds like one of her regular spots."

"Let's get going then," Tam says.

I start to shake my head, but Bree holds up her hand. "I'm going to save us an awkward conversation. We're walking you there, but we'll wait outside."

Acceptable. I nod, but I should prepare them. "She may not let me come in."

"I bet she does," Oz says.

I shrug a shoulder. In mutual silent agreement, we head toward the street. Usually people try to sell charms or predictions nonstop, but there are no interruptions on our way. At the corner, we can see the buildings ahead. They're rundown, mainly squats, because who wants to live in the middle of Oracle Circle otherwise? But this was pricey territory once upon a time.

Graffiti is everywhere, but not the same type as in other parts of town. An ankh sprayed on a two-story townhouse marks it as a place for Egyptian divination, three slashing runes for the Norse on the blue house next door, a knotted symbol for the Celts on red brick, blocky Aztec symbols on the front of a dirty cream apartment building. The graffiti here is advertising.

The red door is about halfway down the block. Mom moves around, which is why I started looking in the market. I rarely tail her to the same place twice. This house is three dilapidated stories of faded maroon, with no pantheon markings. Wide alleys on each side are colonized by thick, curling vines of ivy.

The red paint on the door bleeds onto the edges of the wood frame, sloshed on carelessly.

"She's your mom," Tam says, an attempt at kindness. "She'll be happy to see you."

I wonder what he sees on my face. "You guys have to stay outside. No matter what."

Bree squeezes my upper arm. "Promise."

Oz looks at Justin, then me, and says, "As long as it's safe."

We continue down the block. Across the street, the door to the house with the Norse runes on it swings open. A man with a bushy beard stands in the doorframe and watches us. Down the line of marked houses, the doors open, one by one. A woman with kohled eyes and looping golden chains around her neck stares at me from the Egyptian squat, a robed woman with wild curls in the Celtic one, a man with tangled hair in the next…

They track our progress. I focus on the red door until all I see is it, the color of a fresh nosebleed. Everything else fades. And then I'm right in front of it. I check over my shoulder. The others wait, uncertainly, a few feet away. Anzu lands on the street beside them. His claws scrape the pavement as he turns and roars at the gawking oracles. They don't move.

"Don't kill anyone, Anzu," I say.

I turn back to the door, but before I can knock, it swings open. The hand that holds the door has short, ragged fingernails. I assume it's her. There may only be seconds to make my case. "I'm so sorry to show up like this. But I need to see you, if it's you, Mom, and if it's someone else, look, I need to see my–"

"Come inside," a woman's scratchy voice says.

The door conceals her, but it's Mom. I know it the way I know who I am when I wake up in the morning. Without question, without thinking.

Looking behind me, I find the other oracles watching from their thresholds. Bree and Tam frown at me. Or toward me, at least. Oz and Justin watch, neutral. Well, Oz is watching me. Justin has his eyes trained on Anzu.

Beyond the door is darkness, and my mother. I take a breath and go inside.

CHAPTER ELEVEN

Bree Norville's best friend disappears inside one of the shadiest places she's ever seen. The line of creepy oracles lingers across the street, attention trained on the closed red door. That red is the shade of her dreams last night, mixed with ever-lengthening black shadows and stinging clouds of golden sand. She'll paint the images soon. She wants to get them out of her head. Today's visit to Enki House will be lined up right behind them.

Her forearms have tiny abrasions from the sand yesterday, from when she lifted them to protect herself. She absently touches a tender place beneath her right elbow. The monster the Sumerians have sent to guard Kyra tracks the movement, and Bree hopes she doesn't look tasty.

"How can you be so calm about this?" Tam presses her. "She's been keeping this from us for years."

Bree is amazed by how little Tam seems to know her sometimes. They were friends, the three of them, since way before Kyra and Tam started dating. She knows a shocking amount about him. There's a sketchbook hidden in her closet with nothing but drawings of Tam. Long lines to capture his lean body and messy black hair. She draws him in motion, usually advancing some argument at a Skeptics meeting. That's the best place she has to study him without anyone noticing.

Tam has no way of knowing any of that. Neither does Kyra. He was drawn to Kyra. Case closed. It's not you, it's me. It's not me, it's you. Friends. Fine.

Except she thought he and Kyra were over, until those scaled nightmares in the tank showed her the two of them. It had only taken a heartbeat to realize *when* she was seeing – the night before. The light coating of sand on both their clothes gave it away. They were kissing. Again. Not that it matters.

But, still, it bugs Bree that Tam can't see she's reeling from everything that's happened. Including the news that Kyra has a Mom. An *oracle* Mom. A *Delphic* oracle Mom. Bree says, "You're just mad she didn't tell you. I'm worried about *her*. She's barely keeping it together – can't you tell?"

Tam hangs his head, and she regrets being so harsh. Part of his charm is how intense he is.

"I know this is hard," she goes on. "This whole situation is crazy. You know Kyra – she'll believe it's all on her shoulders. She keeps secrets, but I don't think she likes to."

Tam runs a hand through his hair.

Bree has considered doing the same, many times. "You know, there's this miraculous invention known as the comb and you can use it on your hair. It doesn't even need batteries."

Tam ignores her needling. She holds back a sigh.

"Did you hear Kyra ask him to leave? Just leave here," Tam says.

Oz clears his throat. Tam frowns at him, and maybe that's why Bree cares what he has to say. It doesn't hurt to hear him out, that's for sure. "What is it?" she asks.

He and Justin are in their navy uniforms like yesterday, shaped by light protective body armor underneath. Those golden wavy-line sun rays are pinned on their shirts.

"I don't know everything about you guys, but you seem to be close," Oz says. "So how can you blame her for anything she does right now? She's alone. All alone. And she will be forever if this goes down the way it's looking."

"No," Bree says, "that's the thing. We have to make sure she knows she's not."

Oz shakes his head. "It's not the same and you know it. She's losing her family."

Tam is angry, probably because what Oz says is right. Somewhat. "How would you know? You've probably never been alone in your life. Surrounded by a squadron who tells you exactly what to think. Exactly what to do so you never *have* to think."

Bree moves back out of the way, as Justin steps in and pushes Tam's shoulder. "You don't know what you're talking about," Justin says.

Justin might be as surprised as she is, from his expression.

"It's alright, Justin. I don't care what he thinks." Oz keeps his tone neutral.

The last thing she expects is Justin to shove Tam again, but he does. "You've got the most stable family of anyone here, so stop pretending you know what it's like." Justin adds, "For her."

Too late, Bree wants to tell him. Now she wonders about Oz's family *and* about his. Her own? Well, he's right about that.

Tam continues to frown. "How would you know about my family? Oh, right, you're spying."

Justin sighs.

Bree says, "Don't worry. He loves being spied on."

"Bree," Tam says, and he gives her a look as if she's betraying him. That's rich enough that it makes her need to sit down. She decides the low wall of the flowerbed on the squat next door will work.

Justin joins her, and so does Tam – on the other side. He's close, but not close enough. A respectable friend distance. For that matter, so is Justin. Though he at least noticed when she put on makeup. He might notice when she's freaked out. Oz paces in front of them, always keeping one eye on Anzu.

The monster might as well be napping with his eyes open. He does nothing except sit on the sidewalk, mouth slightly open to bare his teeth at the oracles across the street.

"Why do you think her dad did it?" Bree asks.

"No one has a clue," Oz answers. "Bronson doesn't like him, but his record is clear."

"Spotless," Justin says. Then, "He's one of the only scholars that also did successful field time."

"He was your hero," Bree says quietly.

Justin's blond hair is shorter even than Oz's, his eyelashes just as pale. "No," Justin says, "a legend, which makes him interesting. He's not my hero."

Oz is whirling on his bootheel to make another circuit and doesn't see what Bree does. The way Justin's eyes flick to his friend. It makes her like them both more, if she's honest.

"Do you think Kyra knows anything about what he's doing?" This question comes from Oz, but he's still turned away and she can't read anything into why he asks. She considers.

Bree's known Kyra for four and a half years. They've been tight the whole time. Kyra's never been able to win the competition for her dad's attention. The fact he's a super-spy sort of makes sense of that, but if he was so committed why would he go rogue? It doesn't add up. One thing she's certain of, Kyra was *shocked* yesterday about Bronson being her grandfather and about her dad being a Society guy. And she didn't want him to turn himself in.

"I don't think he tells her anything important," Bree says, finally.

"She could talk to us and then we wouldn't have to sit out here guessing what she knows or doesn't." Tam sifts a few shed leaves from the wildly overgrown plants in the bed. "Couldn't she?"

"Her dad just got taken into Society jail and we just found out her mom took off for Oracle Circle at some point. Don't you get it?" Bree pauses, but Tam shrugs one shoulder. "She thinks we'll abandon her."

Tam freezes, something he does when he has a strong reaction to a new piece of information. "Of course."

Bree takes in the tense set of Oz's shoulders. He could be her mom on a big story, not having stopped working for twenty hours straight. His eyes are slightly narrowed. He's worried about Kyra. He stops and stares at the red door. "She's been in there too long."

Oz starts toward the door, but Anzu makes a low rumble in his throat. Bree stands. "She wants to be alone with her mother. You're not going in there."

"You couldn't stop me," Oz says, "if I wanted to." He glances back at the lion-bird creature. Who might be able to stop him. Or might not.

A messy situation for Kyra to come out to, whichever.

Tam gets to his feet. "She absolutely could."

Bree can't believe it. Was that a compliment? Is Tam sticking up for her?

But Tam goes on, "I'm sure her mother would *love* to run a story about whether new Society operatives are abusing their power."

Bree's disappointment is quick, familiar.

Oz directs his next questions at Tam. "Why wouldn't you go in with her? Doesn't that make you the world's worst boyfriend?"

Tam hesitates. Bree can't help herself. He might betray what that kiss meant. "They broke up," she says.

This revelation interests Oz, she can tell. Tam clears his throat, "Is there a reason you're worried about her being in there too long?"

Oz nods. "Hannah Locke was one of us. Before. She was a Society oracle. You know I've seen them. They can be... disconcerting."

"Is that why *they're* watching?" Bree asks. She nods her head at the oracles across the street.

"No," Oz says, "I don't know what they're doing besides being supremely creepy." He steps beside Anzu, perhaps to give the impression they're together and calls across to them. "Mind your own. Go inside, or there'll be a raid here. Maybe not today, but soon."

Anzu must approve the message, because he lets out a sidewalk-shaking roar. Bree doesn't notice she's grabbed Tam's shirt until she has to apologize. "Sorry," she says and releases it. He has his arm around her shoulder, and she has to step away to get out from under it. "It's OK," he says.

The oracles' response to Oz's threat is to obey. Door after door is slammed. Bang, bang, bang.

"I bet it feels like she's been in there a million years," Bree says, into the silence that's left in the wake of the symphony of slamming.

"If she's not out in five minutes, I'm going in," Oz says.

He's daring her to challenge him, but she doesn't. His concern for Kyra strikes her as real. So she agrees, "Understood."

CHAPTER TWELVE

If someone told me I just passed over the boundary to the fabled underworld – relic-less – I'd believe them. The darkness of the house's front hall is blinding, and the boards beneath my feet protest each step. I might fall through and into some trap Mom has prepared for me. Stranger things have happened today already.

On that happy thought, the front door shuts with a click.

My eyes adjust, seizing on a slight glow at the end of the hallway. I still can't see Mom. I say, "Sorry to drop in out of the blue, but I didn't have a choice–"

She slips past my shoulder, interrupting my nervous apology. "This way," she says. Her voice sounds too old for her, scratchy as a record.

I follow her creaking footsteps toward the light ahead. Our destination turns out to be a divination room.

Mom keeps her back to me. Her hair is long, darker than mine, and nearly dreaded. She busies herself lighting a few more candles over a boarded-up fireplace. The room smells of must, dirt, sweat. The mingled scents take me back to the day Dad explained to me that I couldn't be around Mom anymore. The last time she came to visit us.

I am thirteen on that day, my birthday, a little more than a year since she left. It's one of those summer days so hot the air boils. Dad and I are in the backyard, lighting candles on a sad saggy cake he made himself (the effort he's made thrills me, though I never admit it to him). When I spot Mom coming out of the alley, my heart soars. I run to meet her. And she starts to talk, an endless stream about me, about how fate has driven us apart, how it's my fault Dad drove her away. Dad tries to get between us, but I cling to Mom's heavy skirts, unable to let her go. Her eyes are rimmed with heavy kohl that melts down her cheeks as she snarls at me. I throw my arms around her, and inhale the smell of sweat and sadness. Dirt and dust. Dad pulls me away.

I blink, coming out of the memory and back to this room, with her so near.

The last candle lit, she turns. "Let me look at you," she says.

I swallow and step forward. I wait for her to start talking about me, like she did that day, but she simply drinks me in. So I do the same.

The dress she wears is black, long enough that it brushes the floor. A few threadbare spots are visible, revealing her shoulders, her arms. I would know her face anywhere. Even with her eyes rimmed in thick kohl, with her lips pale and cracked. Even with all those things, it's her. A stranger who I will always, always know.

Mom says, "He brought me pictures. Of you. Sometimes."

"I hope they weren't school pictures." They make us wear blazers and we generally look like anything but ourselves for those.

She throws her head back and laughs. "My funny girl," she says, as a tear slips from her eye and smears the kohl more. "You're wearing one of Henry's shirts. I remember when he bought it. It was at a music store." She worries at her lip with her finger. "Closed now."

I take the fabric of the Ramones shirt in my hands. "*This is* Dad's?" All he's ever done is yell at me for playing them – or any music – too loud. The possibility he gave this to me for a reason, that maybe there's one thing on earth besides ice cream sundaes we both like and it's the Ramones, makes me feel both closer to and further away from him at the same time.

"Oh yes. He was a bad boy. A bad Society boy who snuck me into dark clubs. When we first met, we were always going out, dancing." She spins in a slow dreamy circle, then jumps up and down once, pogo-style. Her feet thud on the floor. I hold out a hand when she stumbles out of it, but she only smiles, her skirt clutched in her hands as if she's a little girl. "We went dancing like that, not really dancing."

They met at work, is what they always told me. I guess it's the truth. But the idea of them in clubs together rivets me. The image of my dad in some music shop buying a band T-shirt. I can't imagine him doing anything remotely like that now. He's so serious. But that was before he got himself locked up on a charge of treason.

Mom continues to swing her skirt around her legs with that eerily innocent smile.

"Mom," I say, "we need to talk. It's about Dad."

"We are." She winks and says, "I'm only making conversation and..." She lets go of the skirt, troubled by a word she can't find. I brace for the flood of terrible things to start, but she surprises me again. She says, "Please. Sit. You have come for a reason. A need to talk."

The candlelight barely reaches a table and two chairs at the far edge of the room, probably for clients. She sweeps a hand toward them. As I get closer, I can make out what else is in the corner. A third wooden chair sits empty beside a shrine nearly as tall as I am. Seemingly random shiny objects are stuck to it, mostly bottle caps and shards of glass, and several empty liquor bottles rest on the small flat ledge beneath. In the center is an image of Legba with red beads glued on for eyes.

I search for any connection Mom might have to him, especially after what Oz said about her having once been an oracle who used Apollo's cup. Do gods get angry if their oracles change allegiance? Whatever the case, it makes me uneasy. I choose the chair that puts the shrine to my side, because I don't want my back to it.

Mom takes the one opposite. She lifts her skirt out as she lowers into the chair. Once she's seated, she tilts her head back, mouth open like she drinks this stale air.

Divine madness. It's permanent. You know that.

"You probably noticed Dad didn't bring you groceries yesterday," I say.

"Was that just yesterday he was here?"

"No," I say, "he didn't come by yesterday."

"Oh, but he did. He wanted me to know he might be going away for a while. It was time." She stops and taps her fingers against her chin, like we're discussing the weather. "You're supposed to be going away too. But here you are. That's not good, Kyra, not good at all…"

I can't believe he told her he was leaving. But no warning for me except an unexplained request and that bundle. I pull my backpack into my lap and unzip it. Before I can change my mind, I pull out handfuls of money and the ID, and place them on the table between us.

"He left me this and he told me to go. But I can't just leave. Mom, he's in trouble. The Society. They have him. I know, about you, about him. They told me. Why didn't you guys ever let me know who you were?"

She is quiet for a long moment. Then one of her hands darts forward, pushes the money toward me. "No. No, no, no. You are the one who has to go."

It could be worse than us talking in circles, I remind myself. She's not screaming at me. Yet.

"Mom, I'll go… soon. Just… *Your* father believes Dad committed treason. They're going to try him. He took a relic."

"So he was able to get it?" Mom asks.

"Wait. You know what he did. But why…?"

When she glances to the side, her gaze locks on the shrine. I have to push down a surge of pain. All these years, and I'm not even the most important thing in the room. I don't know why I came here.

OK, I do. I need guidance from someone who knows more about this situation than me. And Dad wasn't around to stop me. Painful or not, every time I see Mom there's a brief period in which it makes me feel better. That's more important than the after, when it makes me feel worse. I turn my head to see what's captured her attention and flinch.

Legba is in the chair beside the shrine. His hand grips the head of the cane, with its shiny metal and dull white bones woven tight as a strand of DNA. His grin reveals those jagged black-pearl teeth.

Secrets are like wolves, the oracle in the market said. *They have sharp teeth.*

"I can see you're surprised to find me here. I admit, I am surprised as well," Legba says, with a quiet menace that might be intention or just the way he is. I worry, though, that I am looking at a god I have displeased, without even meaning to. "I hear the missing relic was recovered, along with your father."

He stands and strides to the table. His hand hovers over the money. "You won't need that, not today, but you'd best put it back where it belongs."

The money and the fake ID float from the table into the open backpack on my lap. As I sit, unmoving, the zipper closes on its own. I can't quite breathe.

"Don't be too impressed," Legba says. "Parlor tricks. I have more... rarified talents."

Mom says, "Stop scaring her."

"I can't. Look at me. Only *you* wouldn't be afraid of *me*, Hannah."

Mom shakes her head. "I am afraid *for* her, and you know this. She has to–"

"Shhh," Legba says, and Mom stops talking. "You know the rules of this game. There are things she needs to know."

"I'm right here. What things do you mean?" I butt in, without thinking. When his red and black eyes settle on me, I wish I'd bitten my tongue.

"I like you, Kyra Locke," he says. Those shark teeth gleam. "A key in a lock, indeed. And so spirited. That's good. Your father needs your help. The world needs it."

"*Eshu Elegua*," Mom says.

He ignores her. "She didn't tell you what the relic will cause, did she?"

I breathe in, out, muster the courage to answer. "I know what it does. Bronson told me. But they have it back now, so that doesn't matter. I just want to help Dad."

His grin widens. "The old man told you. Did he now? But, no, that's not what I mean. And I'm afraid you're mistaken about it no longer mattering. Because what it causes is your father's death on Saturday night. He's not going to die for treason. He's going to be the sacrifice in the solstice ritual."

I hope I misheard. My heart sets up a fiercer rhythm.

"I hear the beautiful music of a girl understanding. In her gut. In her veins," Legba says.

"Mom – is it true?" I ask her, but she ignores me.

"Only a few gods can walk through all time," Legba interrupts before she can answer. "I am one of them. I was tracing threads back – not with my feet, but with my essence – and I encountered your mother, trapped in a moment. Looking at a terrible thing that had been done, and seeing its ripples. The past is that butterfly halfway around the world, always flapping its wings and causing what happens in front of our faces, Kyra. The past and the present are linked. Sometimes the link is weak, other times strong. When the link is strong enough, when it's trouble, well, that's what prophecy is." Mom hasn't taken her eyes off Legba. He says, "Tell her what you can. Give her a glimpse of why you left. She'll never ask it."

Mom's eyes are wide and black, wild. She says, "No, no, I won't do it."

Legba leans one hand on the table in front of her. "Yes, you will. Now." He waves that hand in front of her face, like you might do to see if someone's pupils are reactive. I don't know if hers are or not, because her eyes drift closed. Her eyelids flutter, and the flames of the candles leap.

"Mom?" I try.

But she begins to speak. I press against the back of my chair, wishing I wasn't witness to this. Legba's grin stretches wider.

"When the gods woke," Mom says, wetting her lips with a nervous dart of her tongue, "I knew it was not meant to happen. I had a mother too, that I had lost some years before. My *father* had lost her in the field. It's why he forced me to become an oracle. We are not usually made quite so young. I was sixteen, but he did not want me to have a choice. He wanted me confined, safe, and so I was named a Pythia and free only when I looked into the pool. It is a great honor to be one... or it was, before." Mom shakes her head, remembering. The ghost of a smile returns. "Your father and I met. We went dancing. When Dad found out, he was furious, but I was eighteen by then. The Lockes are a family as old as ours, a suitable match. He could not object to a marriage. And so he watched as we wed. He made the cuts on our palms and held the cup as we joined our blood together. I love your father, still. I dance with him in the dreamtime."

I look over at Legba, who is seemingly enjoying the happy story about weddings involving blood. He's still showing his teeth, anyway. "Don't just listen," he says. "*Hear*. You need to know all this."

Mom stops, uncertain. Her eyes pop open. "Am I hurting you?"

What a question. There's no way to answer. "Not anymore. You can go on."

Her lids flutter shut again. "We were happy, and we had you and we were even happier. I remember you, racing through the Great Hall, up and down the staircase at home. The shadows of the past had not yet reached you, and they were never going to be allowed to. My father had agreed to leave you free. It seemed like you might live in the light." She purses her lips. "But then the gods awoke. And it was as if I had felt it coming. Felt all our happiness coming to an end. I did not believe it was chance. I went alone to the pool, and I looked. My father had woken the gods, but the ripples of it were worse. I saw what it had done to you. To us. The gods were awakened and it changed everything. But I could tell no one."

"You told me," Legba says.

"Hush," Mom says, looking at him. "Not until much later, and you already knew."

"But how could Bronson do that, wake them?" I ask.

"I could not see that, only his triumph," she says. "Only the ripples. The use of a relic, its power can cloud our visions…"

Legba nods. "And I'm not inclined to divulge the specifics. The problem is not what he did, but what it caused. The tragedy of a prophetic vision is that you can't just pull the person at the center aside and say, 'Don't do that or the world will end.' Attempts have been made with very bad results. There aren't many laws *I* observe faithfully, but that's one."

"Who's the subject? Of the prophecy?"

"It's why he asked you to go," Mom says. "Why you should. He knows something dark is coming. The end of our happiness. Again."

But we don't have any, I want to say. *There's none left.* This time, I do bite my tongue.

Legba vigorously disagrees, shaking his head. "She's the only one who might be able to stop it, to save her father. She's the only one I see who might prevent this. He knows that there's fire and brimstone coming. I told your father, Kyra, that the ritual was planned, that you, that all of us, the peace and everything preserved by it, are in danger, and it's true. Someone wants that door open, and there are others who would like that access to the Afterlife restored. I warned him, and suggested he take the Was to Enki House, should he be able to liberate it. They are inclined to friendliness in these matters. Peacekeepers." Legba shrugs. "But despite the fact I didn't break the rule, that didn't work out. So your dad's onto plan B. He intends to sacrifice himself."

I try to take it all in. "But why would Dad do that?"

Legba shrugs. "Humans are foolish. He's doing it for you."

Mom makes a noise.

"For you, for her," he says. "For the foolish world. He's a fool, and he doesn't know what he risks. He can't know. He thinks he's saving you all, but if that ritual happens... Hannah, tell the girl what she's won if that ritual happens."

Mom doesn't want to, that's clear. But she speaks in a flood, closing her eyes again. I assume what she describes is visible to her, and I wish I could keep her from having to watch it. No one should have to bear such visions. "There will be war among the gods, and between the gods and men. The end won't come so fast this way. Blood and fire, doom and death, blood and fire, doom and death... blood on the marble like a river... It will be worse than the end of the world."

Legba snaps his fingers, and Mom blinks. "I think she gets the picture," he says. Then to me, "Your grandfather just wants that door open. It was closed too quickly after we awakened for him to get what he wanted. He doesn't care about any of this, or we'd be talking to him."

"Bronson is behind this," I say. "That's what you're telling me."

"You're a smart girl. He woke us up. You have to ask why? You'll figure it out. You've heard the story," Legba says. "And you *can* save your father."

"No," Mom says. "No, no, no. That was not to be the plan." She shakes her head. "That's not what I told Henry. Not what he told me."

Legba swings his cane in a circle, props it against the table. He towers over her, forcing her to peer up at him. "That's because of the rule. This is a better plan. The only way it can be changed. Trust me, Hannah. You do, don't you?"

He gazes down at her, steadily, waiting.

"Yes." Mom finally nods. Two quick dips of her chin. "You have been a friend. I trust you. But I wish I didn't have to."

It's the most lucid statement she's made in years.

Legba takes his walking stick. He knocks it against the floor, and speaks to me. "Not all gods believe fate is changeable, but I am a god of divination… among other things… and I do. The future is never fully set until it becomes the past. Ripples are in motion, which means they aren't fixed. It's up to you, Kyra Locke, to find the path that stops the ripples by stopping the ritual. You might stop the blood and fire, too. I would say there's no pressure, but you know better. If it helps, I'm rooting for you." His grin returns. "I find the Lockes endlessly fascinating. You understand what you have to do?"

I can't manage to speak. Dad will die unless *I* save him? There has to be someone else. Someone who can actually do this.

"You are it. The only option. Do you understand?" Legba prods.

My heart hammers in my chest. I have to force my response out. "No problem. Got it. Stop the ritual. Done."

I'm not as confident as I sound.

"You got it. The game is on. I am officially no longer bored." Legba's fingers caress the top of the walking stick. His head cocks, as if he's listening to something. "I'll be going. But, dear girl, should you need to, you can always find me at the crossroads."

"Wait!" My chair clatters to one side as I get to my feet. "How much time do I have?"

His voice lowers. He's right next to me, speaking into my ear. "Hardly any from my view, but enough in yours. The ritual must take place when, as they say, the stars align."

I struggle not to move away. I barely breathe.

"The moment of solstice. Saturday night at the witching hour. My favorite. Midnight. Get cracking." With that, Legba vanishes.

The candles gutter and die, leaving Mom and me in the dark. The stale smell comes back.

"Kyra?" someone calls.

I'm pretty sure the voice belongs to Oz.

"The switch is inside the door," my mother calls back.

A bare bulb overhead flicks on, revealing that it *is* Oz joining us. *Better than another god.*

That makes me wonder if Legba's departure and arrival tipped him off. "Why'd you come in?" I ask.

"What are you guys doing in the dark?" he counters.

"We weren't, it was..." I shouldn't mention Legba or what he told us. I'm not certain of much, but that is plain.

My madwoman mother is in league with a god to try to save my doomed father. My doomed father who apparently doesn't know he's doomed but wanted me out of here before the fire and blood. And my grandfather has plans to do a ritual to kick off the end of the world by killing my father. But why?

Legba said I should know, that it was in the story... I think back, searching it.

Then I grasp it.

The woman in the painting. My grandmother. Mom's mother. She died. Bronson lost her in the field. He wants to bring her back. First he woke the gods, and now he's going to open the door to death.

All this for *that*? It seems like nonsense. Except look at what I'm considering doing for Dad.

I might as well die if I can't keep you safe. That's what he said to me, below Enki House. He knows the ritual is going down, and he's agreeing. But he doesn't know the full stakes. He doesn't know why he shouldn't, because the prophecy rule means he can't. Which *does* make sense.

What a mess this is.

Oz frowns at my silence, and I try to step out of the flood of thoughts. Act natural.

But Mom starts babbling, inventing a completely new story I wouldn't expect her to have the presence of mind to spin. "I was giving my daughter some advice. Do you see, my heart?" She waits until she has my attention. "No matter what he says, you should still go."

"I won't let you down." She has to know I won't abandon Dad. In case, I add, "Or him."

"My sweet Kyra, we have done what we have done, and now it must all play out, and I find I'm not ready for the future. Not ready in the least." Her words slur and her eyelids droop, and I realize she's bone weary. Legba and the blood and doom have taken her energy.

Oz stops beside the table. "Like I said before, it's harder on oracles when they forecast alone," he says, for me to hear only.

I rise and go around Oz to her side. "Mom?"

"Tired," she murmurs. "So tired." She peers at Oz over my shoulder, though, and points a lazy finger at him. "This is a good boy. Good Society boy. All the mothers must love him." Her head bobs with fatigue.

"I think you'd better lie down," I say.

"She seems sharp enough to me," Oz says. "I *am* a good boy and all the mothers *do* love me."

I roll my eyes at him.

When I slide my arm under one of hers to get it around my shoulder, he's there on the other side to help me lift her without a word from me. She leans into me as we take her to a long, low sofa that's seen better days. Sinking onto the worn brown fabric, she pulls a pillow to her chest and hugs it, like a child with a stuffed animal.

"I hope I see you again," she says, "my daughter."

I hold onto those words, ones I never thought I'd hear. "You will. I promise."

Mom's last words drift out, take away that warmth, "Only if I've been alone all this time for nothing. Only if there is no fate." Her eyes close, her breathing steadies. Her features become peaceful. I smooth a twisted lock of hair back from her face, and find a soft quilt on the back of the couch. We have one like it at home. A gift from Dad, then. I settle it over her. I smooth her hair back one last time, careful not to wake her.

"I hope your sleep is dreamless," I whisper. Mine rarely is.

When I look up, Oz is watching me. "Are *you* OK?" he asks. I find that I don't want to lie to him, either, even though he's not really my friend. Not like Bree and Tam. Even though I know I'll have to. And soon. For now, I stick with a harmless truth.

"No," I say, "but I'll live."

I lead the way up the dark hallway and to the door. I swim around in the new information from Legba as if it's the river he mentioned. I consider what I have to do next. I let it rush over me like the waters of the abzu, as I lock the door behind us.

Bree rushes to me, Tam behind her. "Is everything alright?" she asks.

Justin's there too, and he and Oz close ranks. Shoulder to shoulder, watching and listening. Legba left right before Oz came in, almost as if he knew Oz was about to show. That can't be a coincidence. I'll have to be careful with them.

"Fine," I say.

Tam takes too much pleasure in saying, "She can't talk in front of you guys."

"I don't see why not," Oz protests. But he must get it, because the protest is weak. "Kyra, you should come back with us. Your grandfather's worried about you."

"I know he is," I say. The words flow out so smoothly I almost feel bad – except I don't have time to feel bad. "We need to get these guys home first, and then I'm coming with you. Back to the Jefferson. I'm sick of doing what my dad says, and my mom can't take me in. So I want to join. When can I get my stripes?"

CHAPTER THIRTEEN

On the way to Tam's house in the big black Society carriage, Tam and Bree try their best to talk me out of going with Oz and Justin. I'm ready for them, though. I have a purpose now, and my first objective is to get them out of harm's way and myself further into it.

"Look," I say, "Mom didn't brainwash me in a half-hour. If I'm losing the parts of my family I've always known, I should find out more about where I came from. Bronson can give me that. I can't stay at Tam's forever."

Bree *almost* buys that. "But tonight? So soon?"

"I don't want to wait."

"OK," she says. "But we'll talk tomorrow. Promise me. You can change your mind about this."

"I hope you know what you're doing," Tam says. He shoots a meaningful look at Oz and Justin.

I want to tell him they're the last thing I'm worried about.

We stop at Tam's, and the distraction I need is waiting on a silver platter. A carriage is parked there and it has a splashy TV station decal painted on the side. This means

Bree's mom Nalini left work early. That's a big deal. Nalini is even more of a workaholic than Dad.

"Crap," Bree says. "She's going to kill me."

"Let me take the blame," I tell her. "I deserve it."

Oz narrows his eyes like he's suspicious of my motives. I shrug and ask, "What's my dad going to do – ground me?"

Tam and Bree might feel guilty, but they don't argue for me to let them take a noble fall on my behalf. I'm sure they *would*, but I don't want them to and it's not necessary. I'm glad they don't press it.

No one arrives quietly in a giant carriage. So Nalini and Ben are out the front door and on top of us as soon as we climb out. They're clearly upset. Nalini's as perfectly coiffed and made-up as ever, but she's scowling. It's something that causes frown lines, so she usually avoids it. Nalini's like an older version of Bree – with all the interesting artistic edge taken away and replaced with slickness and a business suit.

Oz and Justin stand off to one side, as if they know they don't belong here, witnessing this.

"It was all me. Don't punish them." I purposely avoid sounding contrite. I want them to think of me as the bad influence with the winged eyeliner and leather jacket who marched their precious children into harm's way, into a *god's* House.

My years of practice with Dad pay off. It works.

Ben demands, "What were you thinking?"

"I wasn't." I shrug. "It was beyond amazing, though. Did you know about blessings?"

Nalini's scowl cedes to horror. "You *didn't* get blessed?"

"Only me," I say, quickly. Maybe mentioning that was too far.

Bree's cheeks go pink, and Tam's studying his feet. I really do want to know what they saw.

Oz gives his head the slightest tilt backward and off to the side. I look fake-casually over my shoulder in that direction... and spot Anzu at the end of the driveway, beyond the mailbox. The golden brown ruff of his mane flares above it in the night.

That's something I don't want to explain. It's not as if I can communicate with him telepathically or start waving him away without the parents noticing.

"We'd better get going," I say. "Mr Bronson will be worried. You shouldn't be, Ben," I add, when I see he's considering an objection, "I'm the granddaughter he never wanted. I promise to make him a little bit crazy. For you."

Nalini examines her perfect coral nails, ready to get out of here and not in the mood to argue with me. "Sorry about your dad," she says. "If he's in trouble, I may have to cover it. No hard feelings. I always liked him."

I raise my eyebrows at that.

"No," she says. "Really. He always knew when you were staying over. He told me not to tell you that he'd call to ask. But, now, you may as well know."

I assumed he didn't care, since he bothered to come home only about half the time lately. Since no matter how I tried to get his attention by staying out, he refused to take the bait.

"Guess we never really know anybody," I say.

"We do," Bree says, pointedly. "I will talk to you tomorrow."

I nod, and check to make sure Anzu's still relatively out of sight, before climbing back into the carriage with Oz and Justin.

My bones feel tired. My blood. My everything.

But as soon as Oz gives the driver the destination and we take off, I jostle back to nervousness. There's no guarantee, after all, that my grandfather will greet me kindly. I may have to win him over.

Exhaustion still lurks beneath the nerves. I rest my cheek against the cool leather seat.

What a day. What a life. What a mess.

"Sleep," Oz says. "We'll wake you when we get there."

I begin to tell him I don't think that's possible, but why not let them think I am? They might talk if I give the appearance of conking out. "I'll give it a shot, but I don't know…" My voice dies to a mumble, and I close my eyes, dropping my head back and letting out the world's heaviest sigh.

The clomping hooves outside and the quiet inside conspire to make me drowsy. The bounce of the carriage puts me in mind of the flowing abzu, and, in minutes, I actually am almost asleep. But not quite. I hear when Justin asks, barely above a whisper, "Do you think they would allow her?"

My impulse is to sit up and say, "Allow me to do what?" but I simply shift a little on the seat to sell the sleeping more. It's only after I've settled that Oz says, "She's got the bloodline."

"Pedigree might not be enough. No training."

"She went in a House and came back out again unharmed. And with a guard."

"Fair point," Justin says, a cringe hidden in the words. I wonder if today was the first time they've ever visited a House. I get the impression it isn't.

"And," Oz says, "she has nowhere else to go. He won't turn her away."

That he's right about the first part isn't the best feeling, but he seems confident about the second and that's a relief. The carriage slows, then stops. I contemplate yawning, coming slowly to, but before I do Justin asks, "How do we wake her?"

There's a long moment in which Oz says nothing. Then I feel his arms gingerly slide under my knees and around my shoulders. He picks me up, and I do my best not to tense up. My head tucks in against the fabric of his uniform and I feel muscles everywhere. He's crouching in the carriage, and carries me out of it, easily, like I weigh nothing. And carefully, like he's smuggling precious cargo.

I'm far too aware of every place he's touching me. Of how warm he is. Of how nice he smells. Not that I can describe it as anything except *boy*. The smart thing to do would be to open my eyes, see where we are at least. But I can't bring myself to. Not just now. I'm afraid of what my face might show.

I hear a door open and footsteps. "She fell asleep," Oz whispers.

A hand smooths the hair back from my face. I recognize Bronson's voice, low. "Long day," he says.

"Her mother could sleep through an earthquake at that age. She can use the rest. Take her to the guest room. I'll bring up some Hypnos tea in case she wakes up."

I'm carried over a threshold. I make a little noise, because otherwise it seems too unbelievable that I wouldn't stir at all, despite my mother's long-ago sleep patterns, and they are quiet for a moment.

My eyes stay closed. I swear I can hear Oz's heart pounding through the fabric of his uniform, but I know it's only my imagination. His grip tightens around me the slightest bit.

"How'd you convince her to come?" Bronson asks.

"We didn't," Justin says. "She asked us to bring her. She said she wants to join." He half-snorts. I don't frown, but I'd like to. "She asked when she could get her stripes."

Given the tone he's using, I expect scoffing agreement that it's a ludicrous idea.

"You won't regret this," Bronson says, and I believe he addresses it to me. There's an emotion I can't read in his voice. Is this really the man who woke the gods? The man plotting to kill my father? He sounds so... human. Like me. Like Dad. Like anyone.

It'd be easier if he wore a sign around his neck that said Monster. But nothing is ever easy. Is it?

Oz carries me up a long flight of stairs, and he's strong enough that I hardly move in his arms on the way. He deposits me on a bed in a dark room, and someone pulls a blanket over me. I don't want to be dosed with Hypnos tea, whatever that is – a nasty brew in some relic from the sleep god is my guess – so I keep mimicking sleep. Until at some point, I'm no longer pretending.

The last thing I think before I give in to it is that I hope Bronson's right. I hope I don't regret coming here.

I wake from a nightmare – the usual, about Mom, with bonus laughing Legba and snarling Set, and sloshing black tanks of seven sages' water – breathing hard, sitting up in the bed. I can't recall where I am right away, but I know it's not home. The bed feels different, and so does the darkness.

There's a streetlight outside our brownstone that shines in my room at night. I can make out the shapes of furniture in its glow, except when the power's down. Here, the curtains must be heavy enough to block any light that might come in from outside. That or I'm in a windowless room.

Joy.

I push off the blanket and walk with my hands extended in front of me, feeling my way to the door. My fingers graze a light switch beside it, but I worry turning it on will bring someone. I want a look around.

So I ease the doorknob around slow-oh-so-slow, and open it as quietly as I can. I'm rewarded with a long, dim hallway, a lamp left on at the end of it. I stand in the doorway, ready to duck back inside if I need to, but no one's making noise in the house. They must be sleeping.

I close the door behind me with care and head into the hall, passing the doors to other rooms upstairs that I assume are bedrooms – wondering idly which is Oz's, which my grandfather's. Whether Justin's still here or stays somewhere else? None of the doors up here are open, and I don't investigate to find out. I keep moving.

The house is impressively big and well-appointed. Clean as if someone tidies it daily. Of course, I'm sure there's a staff that does. Bronson's an important man. Expensive art dots the walls, but there's something impersonal about it. As if he paid a decorator to make this look like the image he needs to project, should anyone come to check and make sure he's a real person.

I don't see a single portrait of my grandmother. I think back to Bronson's office and remember her name. Gabrielle. She's nowhere in evidence here.

It goes without saying that neither are Mom or me.

The staircase down to the main floor is at the end of the hall, and I give thanks that the boards are too dignified to squeak as I make my way down. Or the thick carpet laid over them mutes the sound. Whatever, gratitude.

The front door's right there. I could leave.

But, come on, I'm not going to. I glide past it, discover the kitchen, but keep fishing for what I want. At the very back of the house, a door is cracked, and – score – there it is. Home office.

The lamp on the large, tidy desk is on, but nobody's in here. There are glassed-in shelves along one whole wall, holding ledgers and old leather books that seem to be journals of some sort. They have names and years, but affixed on small gold plates, not printed on the spines. Mental note, made. Grandfather prefers some records to live here. The back window of the office looks out over a sprawling backyard with a high fence. Other, similarly fancy properties adjoin. No surprise there.

The surprise is Anzu sitting in the middle of the yard, gazing up at the window like he's my Romeo instead of my scary assigned stalker. I'm going to have to figure out if there's any way to lose him. Later.

The grass itself could use mowing. I don't get the sense that Bronson entertains much. The house feels solemn, like it hasn't seen a party in a long time. I recognize it, because it's the same feeling mine and Dad's townhouse has.

What I came in here for is right on the desk, practically inviting me over. I slide into Bronson's high-backed cushy leather seat, which dwarfs me, and pick up the telephone receiver. The dial tone is crisp. It probably never goes out. The phone is black, but should be red like in those old movies where the president gives orders in emergencies. Bronson's practically that guy now.

And you're going to trick him. Right. Good luck.

I peck out the number on the buttons, and wait for the ring. I'm ready to hang up if needed, but after four rings, a sleepy voice says, "Hello?"

It's Bree. I figured her mom would head back to work, that she'd be home alone. I want to hear a friendly voice, after waking up in this strange place. Maybe I need confirmation I was someone before this started. I consider hanging up, but she says, "Kyra? Is that you?"

"How did you know?"

"Where are you? How are you? Do you need me to–"

"I'm at my grandfather's mansion. And I'm fine. I just... I woke up. Wanted to make sure the rest of the world still exists."

"Of course it does." But she's silent for a troublingly long moment.

"What?" I prompt.

"Did they tell you anything when you got there?"

"I was asleep."

"You wake up when a pin drops."

"A pin has never dropped in my presence so I don't know how you'd know that."

"You know what I mean."

"I was pretending. It was easier," I admit. "Now, what?"

Another silence. I check out the papers on the desk in front of me. But they seem boring, though some of them are covered with languages I don't recognize. I'm pretty sure Bronson's too meticulous to leave a piece of paper headed with the words My Nefarious Plan laying around anyway, even in ancient something or other.

"Mom only heard this through a source, so it might not be true... But your dad's supposed to be on trial soon. Day after tomorrow."

The treason isn't the problem, I think. But it is still *a* problem. "Hm. Quick." But it has to be, so it's over by solstice. "Anything else?"

"Just that the full Council's expected to be on the jury. If he's convicted... well, you know already. Kyra, what are you doing there?"

"What I have to," I say. "Thanks for the intel. I'll call again when I can. Bree?"

"Yes, person who is making me crazy with worry."

"You're a better friend than I deserve."

"No, I'm not. Listen–"

I would, but Oz appears in the doorway. He leans against it, like someone in a commercial cast for the specific purpose of leaning attractively. By which I mean, he's shirtless, wearing only baggy pajama pants.

"Bye," and I hang up.

"Are you a spy?" he asks, tone teasing.

"Are you?" I ask.

"I got up to get a snack and heard your voice," he says. "Anyone I know?"

"It was Bree. I wanted her to know I was alright."

"You guys seem tight," he observes.

"So do you and Justin. How best friends work, right?"

He saunters toward me. "I guess. Hungry?"

It is really hard to concentrate with that bare torso in front of me. It's... defined. Not that Tam's wasn't, but we're over. *This* is a dangerously handsome boy. Maybe he *is* a spy. Which is a silly thing to think, because I already know he can't be on my side.

Get your head, not your hormones, in the game, Locke.

"Starving." I get up, and slip past him. "Can't afford a shirt?"

"Sorry," he says, and oh-my-god I can't believe it, his cheeks color. He's blushing. "I didn't think about it. There's not usually..."

"A strange girl roaming around at night."

"Exactly. Though I don't know if I'd call you strange."

I give him a *Really? Nice try* look. "Where's this magical food you speak of?"

He leads the way to the kitchen, where he opens a wooden box with a pulldown closure. Inside is a plate of perfectly round cookies. I can smell them from where I'm standing, a few feet away.

My stomach growls. "I haven't eaten since breakfast," I say defensively. "Yesterday."

"You like chocolate chip?" he asks, extending the plate toward me. "We could make you something else too, a sandwich?"

"You have got to be kidding me. Chocolate chip is my favorite. I live for it. Give me all of them. Now please."

He smiles as I pick up two – make that three – off the plate.

Mom used to be a baker. A gardener, a homebody, someone who liked making stuff. She was constantly putting out plates of cookies for a pre-bedtime snack. The first cookie I bite into tastes *exactly* like the chocolate chip ones she used to make. More cake than chocolate, balanced between crispy and chewy.

"This is oh-my-god good," I say, with my mouth full.

"Bronson's family recipe. His wife used to make these. The cook, Ann, does them every week."

Oz is leaning against the counter this time, and again looks like someone paid him to be here and do just that. His short hair sticks up in messily random spikes, and the nightlight plugged into the kitchen wall seems to have been placed to highlight the angles of his cheekbones, his jaw.

I have to focus on his face, right? So I don't get distracted by his torso again.

I chew and try my best not to sound like Bree's mom interrogating a hostile interviewee. "Does he talk about her a lot? Gabrielle?"

"Not really," he says. "But you can tell he misses her. You saw the portrait of her in his other office?"

"What about Mom? Does he talk about her?"

"Never," Oz says. "Your mysterious family is something of a favorite topic of gossip though. You should be prepared. You're a celebrity. Like royalty, if the Society had royals. It's not going to be like British tabloids or anything, but we were banned from talking to you before. You'll be noticed."

The cookie tastes like sand in my mouth. "You knew about me?"

"We all did. Strict orders not to make contact. Your mom and dad's wishes. Your mom's mostly, I think." He shakes his head. "I upset you."

I wave it off. "Nah," I say, "finding out your parents basically conspired to keep you in the dark your whole life... it's nothing. Happens to everyone."

I can tell I fool him not at all. "Well, if it were me, I'd be pretty thrown."

I wonder again what his story is. Where are his parents? Why is he Bronson's ward? But I can't ask those questions. I don't have the right. In this moment, I'm keenly aware that the pretenses I'm here under are false.

It bothers me that I want to *not* have to trick Oz, to confide in him. Because there's not going to be any way around it and I can't. "Will you show me around tomorrow?" I ask.

"I'm sure your grandfather will. He was really happy you came. Maybe... I know this is a tragedy for you. What's happening with your dad. But maybe it won't all turn out to be one?"

I think of blood and doom and death. Of that snarling Was scepter at the center of everything. "Do you trust Bronson?"

Oz does me the favor of considering. "He took me in. He's demanding, but kind when it counts. Yes," he says, and it seems like he had to talk himself into it. "Yes, I do."

"Good," I say. "I better get back upstairs. Sleep. Another long day tomorrow."

I move to breeze past, but he touches my upper arm right where the T-shirt stops. I try to recall if I ever had this many nerve endings before, if it felt like this when Tam casually touched me. The reaction could be because Oz is an impossibility.

"Maybe tomorrow won't be so bad," he says. "We'll help get you through it. I promise you that, Kyra Locke."

The sound of my name on his lips is almost as strange as knowing he was aware of my existence for years. Years that I didn't know about any of this.

The fact is, though, he'll hate me before this is all over. That's a given, and something I *do* already regret. Thinking about tomorrow, I find my appetite's gone. So I say, "Good night," and put the dead woman's cookie back on the plate as I leave.

CHAPTER FOURTEEN

The next time I wake the room is light, so I can see what I missed the night before. Which isn't much, except wallpaper with cotton candy pink stripes and curtains with an over-the-top prissy flower print. The curtains have also been tied back. Perhaps it's a subtle nudge to get out of bed.

Between the color scheme and the flowers, I realize... This could have been my mom's room.

I'm almost afraid to find out if it is. The room is so stuffy compared to our house, which she decorated in old maps and photos and watercolors and warm shades. I can't imagine her growing up with all this heavy wood furniture and cold classiness. Conflicted about whether I want to know, I climb out of bed and check the dresser for evidence. The drawers are empty of anything but spare sheets. The closet door is open and it's empty too – except for a lone outfit on a hanger.

I walk over to get a better look, disbelieving.

When I came back up the night before, I took off my boots and tossed them on the floor. They're neatly arranged below the clothes. Which means the ensemble *is* for me.

It isn't a *uniform*. Not exactly. But it's close. Maybe this is what operatives wear when they're training? Or studying? It's almost too good to be true. They left me a costume that will show precisely what I want them to see. That I'm here to become one of them. Bronson's granddaughter, operative.

More like "traitor's freak daughter we all already knew about", but I have to cling to my illusions to make it through this. I'm well aware that even with them I may be in for major trouble.

The adjoining bathroom has towels waiting and expensive travel-sized bottles of goop in the shower. So I take a quick one, making an attempt to be fresh-faced and scrubbed clean of the last remnants of the face paint. I consider pulling my hair back into a ponytail afterward, but I don't want to go overboard.

Dressing in the clothes is odd. The navy fabric is stretchy, fitted, and *so* not my style. No awful bulky padding, at least. But also no stripes. I was really hoping for stripes.

I dig in my backpack for lipstick, because hello? Despite everything, I would like Oz to remember me as that devil girl who's cute. After I find it and put it on, something clicks. I empty the backpack to confirm what's no longer there. Someone has taken most of the money, leaving me only a hundred bucks. They must know I can't get far with that. The fake ID is gone too. Knowing someone snooped through my stuff is worse than the loss, but I'm not that surprised. I don't trust anyone here, so there's no reason to expect them to trust me.

Stuffing the hundred in my pocket, I repack my stuff – including the Ramones T-shirt. I'll have to leave the backpack here today, but I want everything ready to go. In case.

As soon as I open the door and start into the hall, Bronson greets me. "Good morning. Well, good late morning." He grips a giant coffee mug with both hands. "We wanted to let you sleep in. I see you found the clothes. They're OK?"

Why'd you take the money? But I simply nod. "This is why I'm here. My parents, they took this from me. This life."

"You can have it now." He can't hide how much the idea pleases him. "But are you positive you're not just angry at your dad? He does bring that out in people. From the admittedly little I've seen, this" – he waves his hand at the outfit – "doesn't seem like your style."

I meet his eyes, unflinching. "My dad and I... We've never been close. He's always been too distracted to pay attention to me. When I met you the other day, I was in shock. Then I guess I thought since I knew the lie, since it was out in the open, it would be different. That things between Dad and me would be different. That he'd *care* about being there for me. But you saw what he did. You were there. He left me without a thought. Again."

"I don't think it was that easy for him. And you seemed pretty upset with me."

"I was." I force myself to keep meeting his eyes, to sell every last bit of this as gospel. Besides, it's not so far from being true. "All I've wanted, since Mom left, was my family back."

He starts to speak, but I hold up my hand. "I don't know you. But we *are* family, like you said. And I want to. I want to have a place in the world. Somewhere to go. Dad, he just told me to leave town, and Mom isn't able to be there for me. I know you took the money out of my backpack and I don't care. I don't want to go anywhere. I want a *place* here. I want to know who I am now, after all the lies are gone."

Bronson rakes a hand through graying hair. He really does look like the definition of a kindly grandfather. What I want to ask is: *How did you wake them? How did you do it without getting caught? You really think you can pull this off too?* Instead I add, "You believe me, don't you? I have no reason to lie."

"You remind me of your grandmother," he says, finally. "She would adore how direct you are. You take after her in that. Not me. I'm the politician. But I've wanted to build our family back since your mother left it too. I can help you find that place you want. It would be my honor, in fact."

I reach out and take the cup of coffee he's holding. After a sip, I ask, "Where do we start?"

"Breakfast," he says, "and then we'll visit the family reliquaries."

I hesitate.

"What is it?" he asks.

"I'll probably cry at some point. I can't help it. He's my dad, still. Just warning you."

"I'd expect nothing less," he says. "I hope I'm there when you do, so I can help."

After showing me to the long empty dining room table where I'm to eat breakfast solo, Bronson goes into his office. Ann, the cook and housekeeper, brings me eggs over easy and toast. She's a nice middle-aged woman with curly red hair and a service uniform. I'm betting she's the one who crept into my room for the leaving of things. When she sees I'm alone, she returns to the kitchen and then sneaks two pieces of bacon onto my plate. "Mr Bronson can't have it anymore. But you're a growing girl."

"And bacon is packed with nutrients," I say.

She grins as I take a bite.

"Do you make it for Oz too?"

"Yes. Don't tell." She winks, puts her finger in front of her lips. "You'll be good for the house," she says.

I want to ask if Oz and Justin are around, and if they aren't, where they are. But... I feel shy about it because of my middle of the night confab with Oz.

When I finish eating, I seek out Bronson in his office. He's making notes in a ledger of some kind while talking on the phone. "3.30, sharp," he says, and hangs up. I earn another smile as he rises from the desk. His coat's draped over the back of the leather chair, and he swings it on.

"What's at 3.30?" I ask.

"Nothing you need to worry about," he says. "Ready?"

"More than." Neither of us is going to be fully open with the other, apparently. But I let it pass. For now.

There's a fancy black carriage with the Society's symbol – the wavy-lined sun rays over a book – where an old-school crest would have gone in some other era. Anzu sits on the sidewalk beside it. He sniffs the air, and I do my best to think "this is my grandfather who I love" so he won't attack Bronson, even though he can probably scent the reality of the situation.

"If he's making you uncomfortable, we can get rid of him," Bronson says. "I could send someone to speak with Enki."

Oz must have explained the god's presence as guard already, since otherwise I'd expect a *few* more questions.

"I'm sure he'll go away on his own, once everything's over." Assuming it ever is.

Anzu growls when Bronson puts an arm lightly around my shoulders to steer me into the carriage. I shoot lion-face a *stop that right now* look, and regret it when his liquid gold eyes give me one back that's more than a little bit hungry. But he stays where he is.

For all I know, Bronson's carrying a relic for defense if needed, and Anzu can sense it. I breathe slightly easier once we're inside on the bench seats opposite each other. As we rattle away, I try and figure out where we are. The street's unfamiliar, and most of the other once-grand houses on it are closed up. The pavement and sidewalk are cracked in spots, and the carriage steers wide at one point around a huge sunken patch of asphalt.

"Are we on Capitol Hill?"

"We're just a bit off the Mall. Sometimes the best disguise is a little squalor. No neighbors this way. The director always occupies this address."

"Smart." I drum my fingers on the seat.

I'm having trouble in the light of day believing that Bronson's behind all this, collaborating and maneuvering to put my dad in harm's way, bargaining with gods. But even if Legba isn't telling the truth, Mom is. She trusts him. So his advice remains mine – and Dad's – best bet for now.

"How old are you?" I ask.

"Good thing I'm not a woman."

"Women don't really care about age." But then I realize I have no idea. "Do they? I won't."

"I hope you're right. But some of them do. Some men too," he says, confidingly. "But I'm not fussy like that. I'm sixty-six. I still have all my hair and we Bronsons usually live to a hundred. My whole life is ahead of me." His hands clasp in his lap, his index finger tapping his knuckles. "Just like yours is for you. I've always kept tabs on you, Kyra, even though we weren't allowed to know each other. Now that your heritage is open to you, you can be who you were always meant to be." He unfolds his hands and relaxes the right one to reveal a small object in middle of his palm. "Take a look at it."

I lean forward. It's a blue glass eye, a black dot where a pupil would be.

"What is it?" I ask.

"The key to the Locke family reliquary. That's where we're going first."

"Can I have it?"

"Of course. It now belongs to you. You should know that I won't let anyone judge you because of what Henry did."

I put my hand out and the blue glass drops into it, cold against the skin of my palm.

"You can't keep people from doing that. People will judge no matter what." When he looks skeptical, I say, "Trust me. I'm in high school. I know these things."

He snorts with appreciation. "I have a confession to make."

Don't get your hopes up. "Spill."

"I didn't expect to like you so much."

I have no idea what to do with that, so I roll with it. "Likewise."

It's sort of true, like everything else I've told him. I don't *want* to like him. I want to hate him. That would make this easier. But it's hard to get there, when he grins as he scoots back in the seat. He really does seem happy that I'm here.

I turn the glass eye over and over in my hand and watch as we pass the familiar sights of the Mall. When we reach the Jefferson, the operatives are told not to worry about Anzu lurking outside. Part of the treaty is gods don't come and go from this building without invitation. The guards and operatives we encounter say, "Morning, director!" or, "Hello, sir!" to Bronson, but nothing to me. They stand at stiff attention. If Oz hadn't warned me, I'd be more than thrown by the way they try to get a look at me, and the way they exchange looks after, careful so

Bronson doesn't see. As if I'm an exotic alien life form arriving from outer space, or an overly pampered pet. Prepared, I'm able to smile brightly at them, to make my grandfather chuckle so they get the message that I'm here to stay, that I'm under his protection and if he did see them gossiping, they'd be sorry.

Bull, in another word. But bull I want them to believe. I enjoy pretending for their benefit, even.

Bronson takes me down one level, then two, on marble staircases wide enough for us to walk beside each other, and then up a long hall with dangling gold light fixtures. Patterned flooring and identical heavy doors flank the hall, making it seem to stretch into infinity. For all I know, it might.

"I'd expect the family relics to be in dusty stone crypts," I admit. "Though these doors could hide anything. Even crypts. Which would make you a crypt keeper."

"Of sorts," he says, dryly. "We're a little more modern than that now. Give us some credit. These are more like archives of family history *and* relics. Most are in other Society headquarters, because moving a reliquary is no small project. But those of us based in D.C. maintain ours here. You'll see."

On closer look, the doors aren't exactly the same. There are sigils beside them that change, each one a different House So-and-So. Wasserman, Dulac, Weisz, Ahmed, Mondor…

"That's mine," Bronson says, indicating a roaring winged lion with the label *House Bronson*. "We'll do it next."

"Funny that the gods have houses too."

"A house is a place of power," Bronson says, pleased. "That's a good observation."

I resist the satisfaction the compliment gives me.

Bronson stops at a door marked *House Locke*. The family sigil is an elaborate rendering of a key, surrounded by flourishes of radiating light. He gestures, says, "Use the key. Your bloodline gives you the right. It'll know you."

"So only me or Dad can open this?"

"Or your mother. These keys are produced with an iron bowl that belonged to Hera. It was a gift from her guard, the hundred-eyed Argus Panoptes. The eyes, like his, don't make errors. They only let in those who they should."

The glass is still cool against my skin, even though my palm should have warmed it by now. I have a thought. "Where did Dad steal that relic from the other day?"

Bronson's jaw tightens. "From my reliquary."

Which means it's probably back there, waiting for the ritual. "But how if...?"

"Your mother gave him her key, and he shares Bronson blood by marriage." He sounds irritated, but then relaxes. "As do you. That's why we're visiting both reliquaries. You're a part of two houses. You'll receive a key to the Bronson reliquary once you complete your vows. Like mine." He pulls out a small blue eye of his own from the front pocket of his suit jacket, then slips it back inside. "I gave you the Locke one earlier than I should've, but that's one benefit of being the boss."

"It'll be our secret," I say, and examine the door.

He may be breaking the rules for *me*, but it just confirms he's a rulebreaker. I wonder if the key I'm holding is Dad's.

I don't see a lock, nothing to fit the blue eye into. The knob and door are smooth gold metal.

"Over there," Bronson says, and taps the brass plate of House Locke. "Touch it with the key."

"You're the expert."

When I touch it and a fingertip to the surface, the nameplate rotates and I jump backward. Bronson laughs.

"Funny," I say.

"It was," he says.

I focus on the backside of the plate. It's a smooth surface, except for a single oblong opening at the bottom. "This time, I got it," I say, and insert the eye inside. As it clicks into place, the glass eye vanishes. The door releases without a sound. My dad has done this who knows how many times? My mom's probably been in here too.

And now me.

I wait for it to spit the key back out.

"You can only get it back when we leave, and close the door," he says.

I have no clue what the reliquary will be like since Bronson shot my crypt concept down. Maybe it'll be like a bank room filled with safety deposit box after safety deposit box. Or a library (since that's what we're in), with drawer after card catalogue drawer, and shelf after shelf of books. Maybe it'll be like a museum, all exhibit-style glass cases. It could be like a really eccentric hoarder's attic.

I take a breath and step inside, and discover the family reliquary is like all of those things. The deep, tall chamber before me is packed with *stuff*, some that's been organized and the rest seemingly not.

I do my best to take it all in. Which is impossible, of course. This collection is far too big to be understood in a glance.

First are a few tables of dark wood carved with scenes of people dancing in clearings or temples, with stiff-backed, mismatched chairs around them. Muted portraits hang along the far wall, in no order I can figure out. Card-catalogue cabinets stretch in a line below those strangers' faces. Oversized books lie open on tables and stands, displaying yellowed pages with tiny type and detailed illustrations of bizarre creatures and objects and places.

I approach one for a closer look and take in a chimera, or at least a chimera's skeleton, on brittle paper. A glass-encased shelf appears to hold nothing but small leather journals, dates marked on the spines. A shelf ladder is propped in front of a full bookcase. A typewriter sits on a stand, a telescope aims at the ceiling, a thing like a coat rack has various sinister-looking antique weapons hanging from it. And dominating the entire left wall is the stretching sprawl of a hand-painted map on what might be some sort of animal hide.

The further in we go, the more relics are set apart – some on pillows atop stands, others in fancy glass cases.

"Tell me what they are?" I ask, stopping in front of a case with four distinct levels. It's rimmed in gold that shines pure enough that it has to be real (and worth a small fortune) and there's only one artifact per shelf. They must be important.

Bronson squints, taking in the items. "Nice eye. These are all significant relics. The top one is Vidarr's shoe."

The shoe is recognizably a shoe, but the riot of colors in the multi-hued leather makes no sense. Some parts are creased or have scuff marks, but there's no stitching. Yet the thick sole and pieces bigger and smaller that curve to form the top of it appear solid despite that.

"Shoe, singular – he couldn't afford two?" I ask. "What's the story?"

"Vidarr is a Norse god of secrets, stealth, and silence. Also known as the god with the thick shoe. One of your Locke ancestors recovered this. It's made of all the discarded pieces of leather from people's shoes, from up to the time this was created. It confers invisibility on the wearer and anyone they're touching. No one can see or hear them. And let's see…" He ticks the glass in front of the next shelf. There's a wooden bow on it that looks relatively plain. "This is Celtic. Brighid of the Forge's. Any arrow it shoots becomes a fiery one. The aim is always true."

"*That* is a weapon I want to learn how to use. Because I'm betting my aim is terrible, given that I've never shot a bow before." When I see how he's looking at me, skeptical, I add, "In my life. City girl. No Society training."

"Right. Of course."

"What about this?" I tap the glass like he did, getting into this.

He grumbles a little. "That's a stone pipe belonging to Red Horn."

I don't see what's so offensive about a clay pipe with some faded paint on it. "Who was?"

"A god of the Winnebago peoples, among others. He was also known as He Who Wears Human Faces on His Ears."

"No. Way." This is fascinating. "Real ones? Of actual people?"

"Oh, no, he made them. They were small human heads that spoke. In some stories they were more like living earrings."

I realize I'm touching my ears unconsciously.

"Don't worry. Someone else collected those. Troublesome things." He sighs. "You'd probably want to know this, so I'll tell you. Your dad collected the pipe and gave it as a gift to your mother. It gives pure visions, unclouded and pleasant only, to the user. Of course, as her father, I did not appreciate finding her lighting up with it."

"But that's nice? To want to give her happy visions. Being an oracle seems..." I shudder.

"It's not for you. Don't worry," he says. "It shouldn't have been for Hannah either. Everything went wrong."

He's quiet, clearly snagged by the past, but there's still one shelf left. So I pull him back by asking, "And the last one?"

The cap is small and not that impressive looking. The fabric is half white and half black, the seamless change of color in the middle.

"Eshu's cap," Bronson says. "Very famous relic tied to Legba."

Ice travels up my spine at the name. "It belonged to him?"

Bronson nods. "He wore it to prove to two friends that they shouldn't honor their relationships with each other above him. They got into a terrible fight, arguing over whether someone they'd seen ride by while they were working was wearing a black hat or a white one. It can be used to sow discord and confusion. The wearer needs only to be in the room to create the effect."

"Does it do anything *good*?"

"Sometimes confusion is necessary. It's not always bad. You know the trickster lore – even in public school they teach it, correct?"

"Yes."

"In stories they give us gifts, show us things, but also sometimes trick us. Or other gods. Hence their reputation. But there's always a purpose to what they do. That's why they are friends to us in a way the rest of the gods can never be. Even some of the Skeptics believe that." He pauses, and it's an ominous one. "Are you involved with that boy? I can't approve."

Tam. He's talking about Tam.

I bristle. "I didn't ask for your approval."

He stares at me, eyebrows raised, for a long moment.

I remember my intention is to play nice. "Sorry. We broke up. It's a touchy subject."

A grin splits his face. "It would never have worked out. You're a Society girl now."

Having a nosy grandfather is going to be a serious pain – for as long as it lasts.

"Let's never discuss this topic again." My cheeks are burning. So I wander away from him, over to the long map on the far wall. The edges are irregular, and it does seem to be made of hide, but there's no way any single animal was big enough. It must be an effect, some material made to look this way. I decide not to ask, because if there are giant monster animals that someone in my family killed to make this, I would seriously rather not find out.

"That," Bronson says, not agreeing or disagreeing that we will never again talk boys, "is the story of the Locke family. Your hunter's map."

CHAPTER FIFTEEN

The map is the kind of thing both Tam and Bree would geek out over. I find I do too – though not because of the secret knowledge reasons that would appeal to Tam or the artistic ones that would entice Bree. It's because Bronson says this is the story of Dad's family.

Of *my* family. A story I wonder about daily, but never ever thought to learn.

The paths between slanting peaks and snaking valleys and strange forests are drawn in heavy black lines. There are renderings of creatures and objects, dates scrawled in irregular intervals. Long ago ones, for the most part, but I spot one twenty years ago. Another only ten. Five. Still, the meaning isn't fully clear to me. I touch what appears to be a unicorn horn, twisting and dangerous, sketched beside a thick stand of trees.

"Do all of you have one of these maps?" I glance over my shoulder. Bronson's clearly enjoying my interest in it.

"All of *us*," he emphasizes the word, gesturing to himself and to me. "Every family has a hunter's map, and each is unique. There are journals that correspond, tell the history more fully. The Bronson map is more traditional, more map-like, you could say. The matriarch is usually responsible for keeping it up to date, if there is one. If not, whoever the senior member is."

Over Bronson's shoulder is a portrait of a woman with deep, tanned skin and a pale green dress. I count and the number of women depicted are roughly equal to the men. He follows my gaze. "Yes," he says, "those are your hunters. Minus your father and mother, whose portraits haven't been done yet."

"And probably never will," I say. He frowns, troubled, and so I rush on, "Why that word – hunter instead of operative?"

"Relic hunter. It's what we used to call active members of the Society instead of operatives. When the gods were asleep our primary job was collecting relics, discovering what they did, keeping them safe. If we hadn't, humanity wouldn't have survived the Awakening."

Which you caused. "Scary."

"It is. But it could have been far worse. We were prepared, at least, because of this work. Your father's family goes way back – to the organization's beginning, the first relics found, Sumerian and Egyptian ones. You've had a long time to hunt. The Lockes are famous for their affinity at teasing out the secrets of where relics are hidden. There were rumors that the gods whispered locations in your ears, but, of course, that's because we thought the gods had gone somewhere else. Not that they were just resting." He pauses. "The map doesn't record *everything*, only particularly important times and places."

I trace one of the lines on the map with a finger, pacing along it. A half-jaguar, half-man in mid-leap and roar is drawn inside a rough outline of a star. The image segues into symbols and sigils and gods' inhuman faces. There are monsters drawn in seas with tails that remind me of the sages. Here and there, names appear as well as dates. I stop when I come to an image that's easy to decode.

A winged lion with an ornate key caught between its teeth, drawn in red and outlined in black. I recognize the date too. My parents' anniversary.

"This is when Mom and Dad got married."

"Yes."

"You didn't approve, did you? Don't lie. It's pretty obvious."

I watch him as he responds. "Hannah was too young. She had only been an oracle for a few years. They stay at Society headquarters – here, in London, in Beijing – wherever they're most needed. They're kept safe."

Examining the map more closely, I backtrack. Before their marriage, there's a line extending from the main one, a river of black that widens as it runs down and down and down. As if traveling to the abzu. I bend to follow it. A long green stroke is painted a foot from the bottom of the wall. And below it are only names. The bottom of the map represents the underworld, the Afterlife. The skeletal bones sketched there make that clear.

The name at the bottom of the black line is Gabrielle Bronson. Even in the thick brushwork I can pick out Mom's neat handwriting. "Mom told me you guys 'lost' her mother when she was young. Was she sick? Did she leave? She wouldn't ever say."

He comes closer, looks down to where my hand rests beside Gabrielle's name. The sadness that takes him over makes him seem older. He didn't know Mom had added her death here. That much is obvious from his reaction.

"She wasn't sick. And she didn't exactly leave. Do you want to know what happened to her?"

I'm almost afraid to say yes. Here he is volunteering to tell me the most painful story of his life. At least, I'm assuming it is. Given that my own parents have never told me much of anything, the offer means more than I want it to.

I stand up so he can see my nod. "Please."

"We were in the field together, Gabrielle and I, in the Iraqi desert. She'd have been willing to go out solo, but I never wanted her to. I always wanted to be there to protect her." He shakes his head, self-deprecating. "No, that's not true. I just wanted to be near her. Always. She was so alive. Like your mother, even now. Like you. Her training was as good as mine. Better. She didn't need me to protect her."

He scans the map, though I have the impression he sees something else entirely. Her, maybe. "We were there to recover an artifact long thought destroyed. Gabrielle was as good in the library as in the field, and she'd researched until she was sure she knew where it was. She'd been working with a young scholar – your father, actually – and his mother, who'd agreed to give her access to some Sumerian records here in the Locke reliquary. The only difficulty we would face was with the locals."

"Dad's Mom?"

"Sorry," he says. "Both of Henry's parents are dead, for a long while now. Cancer for him, an accident for her. Their loss was hard on your dad. He went a little wild, after. No one to stop him. I think it's part of what Hannah liked about him."

"Losing people is hard. It changes you," I say. "What was the relic you were after?"

"Oh, right." He rolls his eyes at himself. "It was a... I guess mirror is the word for it, though it wasn't like we think of them now. It was part of a sacred divination pool in the abzu, at Enki's famed ancient ziggurat. Not the one he's in now, obviously."

"Obviously." Although if he'd told me it *was* the same, I'd believe that too.

"Part of it had been captured inside a glass oval. It's known as the Ocean in the Glass. It could supposedly be used to see the future, even to change it. If only we'd had it, we might have used it... I *would* have used it. I'd have done anything." He stares past me.

"There were oracles then, too? Did you consult them?"

"The Society still had oracles, yes. But they were different then. Consulted only on the most important of matters, not simple field recovery. Gabrielle was convinced that the glass had been buried near a lake said to be in the remote desert. There were rumors among the nomadic tribes that you could see the future in it. I didn't even believe we'd find water, but her theory was that the relic being buried nearby actually did allow people to sometimes look into the water and see the future. And that Enki's power seeping into the ground was what allowed the lake in such an arid place."

"Makes sense." Since sense is relative where magic is concerned.

"Back then, travel was easy. We could just take a plane from here to another country." He skims his hand through the air.

I've been on planes twice, once for a trip to DisneyWorld when I was a kid and another time to visit the Grand Canyon, but now ships and trains are more common for long distance travel. They don't fall out of the sky and it's less of a big deal if they mysteriously stop running.

"The journey once we got there wasn't so easy, but Gabrielle was always good with locals, no matter where we went. By the time we'd made it to the interior, we'd traded them all sorts of baubles and they were giving us a royal escort with a full parade of camels. They had invited her to sit with them at night, despite their not believing it was proper for a woman to be doing what she was. They really disapproved of me for 'letting' her – as if I had a choice. She had a relic called the Babel Stone, a fragment of the famous tower. It was a small chunk of rock, nothing special to look at. She'd dunk it in her tea cup or water glass, drink the liquid, and then be able to understand – and speak – any language. The locals were so impressed that she understood them, they told her their stories, including about the lake where time moved differently. That was how they described it. The lake was sacred to them. It had shown them how to save lives of people they loved, when they might be attacked by rivals. It had saved them, time and again. She changed her mind about recovering the glass."

"Really? You guys worry about that kind of thing?"

"Most of us, no. For better, or for worse," he admits, somewhat sheepish about it. "Gabrielle was special. She'd begun to believe that we shouldn't necessarily have these treasures, that some of them belonged in the world and we didn't have the right to take them. The argument against it was that they could have unintended effects, and that we would need them if the gods ever returned. Little did we know."

There's something in his tone, in the way he studies the map. I can't quite read it. But then I understand. Oh, how I understand. I think of me and Dad facing off against each other a million times before that last morning, and again in the abzu.

"You said *the* argument," I say. "But it was your argument, wasn't it? With her?"

He scrubs a hand over his cheek. "Smart girl, just like Gaby. Yes. I fought with her. And she burned her notes in the fire, so I wouldn't be able to find them. But it was too late... I still don't know what made her do it, but in the middle of the night she left our tent and she swam out into the lake. I slept through the whole thing. So did our guides. I woke up to the mourning screams of the women who found her. They'd pulled her up onto the shore, but she was blue. Her lips were like ice. Her hair was still damp when I touched it. There was no bringing her back."

It could have been suicide. It could have been an accident. He seems so gone in that moment, still grieving, that I am certain he doesn't know which. I want to tell him it doesn't matter. The two of them, Bronson and my mom, they lost her. That's the reason Mom describes it that way.

"I'm so sorry." I mean it.

One of his shoulders rolls. "It was a long time ago. The worst day of my life. After that, everything changed."

I understand why he's so hungry to connect with me, to make things right – even if it's a really effed version of right. "You said you made Mom become an oracle to protect her."

"That was the idea. Oracles are too valuable to risk in the field. She was the youngest in our history. As you can tell, it didn't really work. She didn't want that. She wanted Henry Locke."

I step closer to him. My grandfather.

"Yes," I agree. "But still… I'm sorry."

"I had to do something afterward. Make my life still mean something. It's why I climbed to these heights," Bronson says.

What he means is he did it all to get to the place where he can bring her back. Where he can find out what happened that night, and convince her to stay instead. Stay forever. I realize, looking at my grandfather, just what a dangerous man he is.

Because part of me wants him to succeed. Or, at least, part of me is confused, like I put on Legba's cap. Discord,

I feel it. All I can do is hang on to the knowledge that my dad is locked up somewhere in this building, and that the man in front of me is willing to throw him away to get what he wants.

"You should be proud," I say to him. "She would be."

"I hope you're right," he says.

Oh, I bet you do.

There's a tentative rap on the doorjamb. It's still open, of course. Until we leave, Bronson said. He brushes his hand under his eyes. I touch the arm of his jacket. "Thank you for telling me."

He gives me a nod. "Come in," he says, louder.

The woman who was in Bronson's office the other day, sleek Rose, leads in Oz and Justin. Oz raises his hand in a small wave. "3.30," Rose says. "We went by your reliquary first…"

"Which we didn't even make it to. Good thing we've got all the time we need, right, Kyra?"

Bronson steps out from under my hand, but he pats my shoulder. Any sign of the affected man who was telling me the saddest story of his life is gone like that. In a snap.

He hesitates, says, "Would you like to see your father?"

I picture Dad yelling at me more. I can't tell him anything, so… "No. I don't think I can."

Bronson nods. "I want it to be your decision."

"It is."

"I have to go to a meeting with Rose," he says. "Will you be alright with Oz and Justin? They'll get you back to the house, and I will be home in time for supper."

"Sure," I say. "This is my new life. Weird. See you at supper."

I can tell Oz wants to stay in here and pore over the hunter's map, look at the Locke family's cool stuff. "You can come back sometime," I tell him as I pass. "I might even let you touch my things."

That didn't come out right. He gives me a grin that lets me know he got both my actual meaning and the unintended one. I stare straight ahead, not wanting to blunder into anything as we make our way to the door.

That smile of his is way too good.

Justin says, "I'd love to come go through your books."

"For the record," Oz says, low enough my grandfather doesn't hear and interrupt whatever he and Rose are talking about to disapprove. "I don't care about your books."

I have to be blushing. This is ridiculous. The rest of them exit first, which I take is the usual procedure.

"You can figure out how to seal it," Bronson says, waiting.

I hope so, because they're all watching me and it'll be embarrassing if I don't. I finally decide to try pressing my hand against the pad. The blue eye shoots into my palm and the door zips closed, the plate reversing so it shows House Locke again.

"Like you were born to it," Bronson says.

He shows no sign of worrying that the others know I have the key. I put it back in my pocket and try not to feel as pleased as I do about the compliment.

CHAPTER SIXTEEN

Rose and Bronson disappear up the long marble hallway, leaving me to stand awkwardly with Oz and Justin.

I touch Justin's shoulder with a fingertip. He looks at my finger like I'm in the process of stabbing him. I say, "I know you're thinking, 'Please open your crypt back up so I can check out your magical books.'"

Justin says, "I was not." Though the longing way he glances at the door makes it hard to buy.

Grinning, Oz says, "He's definitely thinking it. If he wasn't before, he is now." But his grin slips away. "Are you sure you don't want to see your dad?"

None of them have told me about the trial. I'm waiting to see if they will.

"No," I say, "but it feels like the right answer. It would be too hard. He won't approve of me being here."

"But wouldn't you enjoy that part, the disapproval?"

"Normally, yes, though it disturbs me that you know that. This time? Not so much." After all, we're talking about me seeing him because we've already established the penalty for treason. And the conviction rate. I happen to know that he's only *not* going to meet that fate because I plan to save him.

Which means it's not at all certain he'll survive.

I will see him again though. I can't imagine not. But I can put it off, a little while longer.

"I want to see your crypt," I say.

Oz rolls his eyes. Attractively, of course. "It's not a crypt," he says.

"Your *reliquary*. The reliquary of House Spencer. I bet it's fancy." The request is a whim. But I do want to find out what it reveals about Society Boy Wonder. He's so comfortable here, in these serious marble halls and outside of them.

"No fancier than House Locke's," he says.

"Let's do it," Justin says. "I can revisit the text on the Apkallu you have."

"Seven sages put something in your head?" Oz asks, and begins to walk. To me, he explains, "That's another name for them."

"I'll never catch up to all the stuff you guys know." *Good thing I won't have to.*

We are the only people down here, now that Bronson and Rose are gone. I'm about fifty thousand worlds more comfortable without gossipy operatives giving us the constant eyeball.

"Sure, you will," Oz says. "If you want to."

"You know they did," Justin says, ignoring our side conversation. "They put stuff in yours too."

"Care to share?" I ask.

"No," they answer in tandem.

"Interesting." If I'm not mistaken Oz shoots Justin a warning look. But Justin doesn't catch it because he's looking guiltily away. "Verrrry interesting."

Of course, I don't volunteer to talk about what I saw either. The vision of Dad crying feels almost as if it was a dream.

Nothing more is said until we're at Oz's reliquary, because it turns out not to be much further. He takes a blue eye from his pocket. "We always keep these on us," he tells me, and opens the door with far less drama than I did ours. The sigil of House Spencer is a sword surrounded in flame.

"Come in," Oz says.

Justin strides through first, like he hardly needs the invite.

"I meant Kyra," Oz says, but Justin doesn't bother with a response.

I have to stop myself from telling Oz to not say my name anymore. Because what could I possibly say that would be weirder? Or that would give away how much I like hearing him say it. This is trouble, and I know it. Luckily, it can go nowhere. The harmless variety of trouble.

"Funny seeing you dressed like this." Oz takes in my Society-esque garb, head to toe. He and Justin are wearing their uniforms, stripes and all.

"Hilarious," I say.

"That's not what I mean. You just look..."

Oh, that hesitation is murder. I can't take it. "Hot? Superhot? Plain navy will be what everyone's wearing next year?"

"You look nice," he says, though if I'm not mistaken he considered other options.

"We already told you, never say nice. I've never looked nice in my life." It isn't the whole truth. Mom used to put me in dainty dresses every now and then. But it's been *years* since I've worn one. Not that someone can't look nice in a Ramones T-shirt or whatever, but I doubt that *I* do. Bree's the one of us who has that angle covered.

"Right, I forgot," he says, in a tone that makes me think he didn't forget *at all*. "Still, that would be easier to believe if you didn't look it right now."

We're lingering in the hallway, which we both seem to notice at the same time. "Ladies first," he says. "Especially nice looking ones."

"That would be me, I'm told." I traipse past him, curious if he's watching. So curious I look back. He is.

He follows me in.

"This *is* fancy," I say.

Dad must not have time to keep things as tidy, because our reliquary is way more mad aunt's attic storage than this one. Oz's family hunter's map isn't even on the wall, but on a long table alongside it. It's a model of a city and various landscapes, progressing through different periods of architecture and kinds of terrain.

"Wow," I say, moving in closer to examine it. "You have to keep this up now by yourself?"

It's a nosy question. I'm basically asking if he's completely alone in the world, if that's why Bronson's his guardian.

"I grew up helping my mother do it, so it's not that hard."

The intricacy of the model makes me doubt that there's anything easy about adding to it. I study a miniature gothic cathedral, every detail perfectly formed.

"Except to get him to focus on doing it," Justin calls, from further back. "That's hard." He's at a table with a book in front of him. He doesn't raise his blond head to look at us.

I didn't even notice in the Locke reliquary that the rooms are set up for the ceiling light fixtures to come on when the doors open. They're regularly spaced and cast soft light so that no corners are too dark. Not far from us, I spot a familiar relic hanging on a headless form. A gleaming silver breastplate.

Moving toward it, I ask, "Didn't Bronson have this on the other day?"

"Yes," Oz says.

I reach out and touch the metal. When I turn, Oz is behind me.

"I loaned it to him," Oz says. "We can do that. It's pretty common, really, since other operatives know the major relics everyone else has."

"Does anyone ever give a relic away to another family?"

"Not often," Oz says. "I wouldn't part with that one. Not permanently."

"He didn't even really like loaning it," Justin puts in, head still buried in the book.

"Stop eavesdropping," Oz says.

But his tone is easy, no bite to it. Yet I've apparently been around him enough to see through that forced easiness.

"What is it?" I ask, and keep my voice low.

He keeps looking at the breastplate when he answers, though he moves closer. I guess so he can talk without Justin inserting any commentary. But Justin seems to have obeyed the order to stop listening – for the moment, at least.

"It saved my life," he says.

My eyes go wide. "How?"

He speaks just above a whisper, like we're trading secrets. "When the gods woke up, I wasn't here. I was still in London. My parents were headquartered there. British Library."

I search my memory of what I know about the Awakening, but I can't remember anything specific about London.

"They were... a lot like your dad, actually," he says.

I freeze up.

"Heroes, I mean. The type who took action when they believed it was necessary."

"Don't you think my dad committed treason?"

"Like he was before this," he says.

I nod, conceding.

"They didn't want to leave me at home, so I was there with them. A thirteen year-old who wasn't close to taking my vows, who had some basic training but was pretty crap at most stuff."

I almost wish Justin *was* still listening in, so he could confirm or deny this. If they even knew each other then.

I can't imagine Oz being bad at anything operative-oriented.

He continues. "My mum stuck me in that armor breastplate. It was almost too heavy for me to stand up in. I didn't know then, but it was a relic of Athena's, one she'd given to a warrior she liked. But once Mum put it on me and said the words, it was weightless. She told me to be careful, to stay behind her and Dad, that it would keep me safe as long as I wore it."

"That was smart of her."

"Nothing was able to touch me," he says. "But that was the last time I saw them. On the streets outside, fighting gods."

"I'm sorry." But it doesn't seem like enough. First, I don't deserve this trust, these people confiding in me like it's a natural thing to do. Second, the Society is depressingly full of tragic death stories, judging by today. It makes me worry that Dad's not just in trouble because he's on the prophecy track. It makes me worry that everyone here is doomed. Including me.

Oz gives me a puzzled look. I'm not sure if it's prompted by my silence or at the inadequacy of my offering such a generic condolence. I feel like I should add something. But all I can come up with is, "I'm truly sorry."

Which still isn't enough.

"I don't talk about it, usually." He shakes his head, as if to clear it. "You just asked the right question, I suppose."

"Or you're distracting me from my own problems,

because *you* are nice and not just a pretty face. So, change of subject." I lay my fingers against his stripes for a moment. Barely any space separates us and I'm aware that his chest – which I've seen in its unclothed glory – is under there. Too aware of it. "Tell me how this Hephaestus' chain business works. What's that thing you say?"

Oz swallows. He says, "You'll learn in time."

"Look. I don't even have any stripes to use, and I'm sure it'll be forever until I do. I'm just curious, since I got Vulcan nerve pinched by Dad."

"That is funny. Since Vulcan is another name for Hephaestus." Justin is back to listening, and not ashamed to let us know it. "It's Ancient Greek, so the command is a single verb form. It means to bind. Καταδήτε."

I wonder if he's heard every word we've said to each other, and decide there's nothing I can do about it if he did. Instead I attempt to repeat what he said, "Kah-ta-mumblemumble."

And mangle it horribly.

Oz can't help but smile, and I'd screw it up at least a dozen more times to keep him from thinking about his parents. He holds his hands up in front of him. "Don't worry. I'm not touching you, so it won't do anything. Καταδήτε. It's kah-tah-DAY-tay," he says it slow, and I watch his lips. "Now you try."

"One more time." Really, I just want to drag this out. It's the lightest I've felt all day.

"Kah-tah-DAY-tay," he says.

"Kah-tah-DAY-tay," I repeat, then once more for

good measure. I bob my head along like it's music, hair swinging in front of my face. "Kah-tah-DAY-tay."

"Perfect." Oz laughs. "You're a prodigy."

"Not bad," Justin says, and claps his book shut. "OK, I'm ready to go now."

Oz and I exchange a look. I regret that we're leaving. This is my only chance to learn about the Spencer family history. Then again, I only care about Oz's part of it.

"Me too. I'm ready to go," I say. "Though I want to know more about the map model."

"Another time," he says.

I agree, far too aware there won't be one.

The rest of the day is weird. Turns out it's rare for Oz and Justin to be home during the day. Justin decides to indulge in library time (not a surprise) in Bronson's office, which he assures us is allowed. Though neither of us questions it.

I worry that means I have to spend more time alone with Oz... not that the idea is *all* bad. But I've upgraded the situation from harmless. I can feel it becoming dangerous. It's going to be hard enough to do what I have to already. None of these facts mutes the disappointment I feel when Oz says he has an errand to take care of, and will be back for dinner. The phone's off limits until Justin leaves the office, so trying to reach Bree is out of the question. She's probably still at school anyway.

Before I can explore, I need to see where Ann is. I head to the kitchen.

"Cookies?" I ask her, hope in my stomach, when I get there. She's busy stuffing a bunch of little raw chickens (or some type of birds) with things, and nods toward the counter where Oz found them the night before. I open the case and grab one.

"I might take a nap." I prepare for a lecture in response.

But Ann merely glances up. "Have you seen your new stuff? If I got the wrong things, don't worry. Mr Bronson said to do my best and that we could add whatever you want. And we can redo your room. But he had me stop at this shop and get a bunch of posters. I'm not sure about those." She frowns at the chicken, or whatever it is, in front of her. "I think the clerk just wanted to get rid of them."

I stand, cookie halfway to my mouth, disbelieving. "What are you talking about?"

Ann's eyes widen. She smiles, and puts her attention on shaking some herbs into a bowl in front of her. "Nothing at all. Definitely not something waiting in your room. Because then it wouldn't be a surprise. Would it? Now, out of here while I'm working." She peeks up and winks. "You're in my way."

Intrigued as I am to see what Bronson and Ann believe I need, I don't go to my room first. With Justin in the office and Ann in the kitchen, I have a location for everyone in the house. So when I go upstairs, I open every door except the one to my guest room. Until I find the room that has to be Bronson's.

Everything neat, everything dark colors. On the chest of drawers is a picture of him and Gabrielle. It's black and white, probably for artfulness. They both gaze into the distance, wearing safari field gear not unlike what she has on in the portrait in his office. He looks the same. Not exactly, of course. There are not quite as many wrinkles on his face in this picture, but he strikes me as just as grave. Maybe he sensed what he had to lose. There's also a color photograph of Mom, maybe nine, face streaked with mud, and Gabrielle beside her with dirt on her hands.

Happy families may be the most fragile kind there are.

On that note, I rummage – but with care, shooting for spy-style exploration – through the drawers, checking out the closet, everything I can to learn the layout. I test the door, closing it and then closing it more slowly.

It's nearly soundless, done the right way. Good to know.

My plan is beginning to come together, though there are still pieces missing. I'm not quite sure how well it will work. But I have to prevent the ritual, and to do that, the relic has to disappear again – and *stay* gone until after solstice. That was Dad's first strategy, and so it must be a solid one. The disappearance of the relic while he's all locked up should be enough to reopen the treason case and keep him alive a while longer. The key will be getting it, then running as fast and far as I can for a few days. I won't make the mistake of going to a god like he did.

I have to figure out how to slip my divine guard. When I check out Bronson's window Anzu's perched in the backyard, where he was the night before. He gazes up at me, and I frown at him, feeling like some president's daughter with inconvenient Secret Service.

At least they would be human.

I will rely on no gods, not even Legba, after the discord revelation. I don't want any confusion. I want a simple postponement. *That* I might be able to pull off. And the beauty is, only I will be in jeopardy.

Well, and Dad, but that can't be helped. Mom's left out of it, Oz and Justin mostly are, and Tam and Bree will be entirely. The rest of the world can't be mine to worry about. Not right now. Not when this is more than enough.

When I make it back into the hallway, shutting Bronson's door the quietest way, I hear footsteps on the stairs. If it's Ann, I'm sunk. She'll know by looking that I haven't been anywhere near the gift-a-palooza in my room. I move as fast as I can, but stop after I get a clear view of the stairs.

It's Justin, so I wait at the banister post. I figure that will be less suspicious than streaking down the hall to my room. I begin to question this choice at the frown he gives me when he reaches the top step.

"Were you looking for me?" he asks.

"No." I aim a finger-gun at my temple. "Just being ditzy. I got a snack and then managed to forget which way my room is."

"Oh." He points to the end of the hall. When I start to leave, he says, "Hey…"

"Yeah?" I wait.

"Did your dad tell you what he's trying to do? Did he mention who he was working with?"

Why is he asking me about this? Carefully, I say, "Bronson says he must be working with a god or gods. Dad doesn't share with me. Not his treason plans."

"But Set attacked you. Why did your dad go to the Sumerians? Are they working together, do you think?"

"Dad and the Sumerians?" Anzu is in the backyard. You do the math. They at least like each other.

"No," Justin says, dismissing that. A lock of hair falls over his pale forehead. "Not them. Enki and Set."

I look at him like he's crazy, and for good reason. "Even I know those two pantheons don't mix. Doesn't the Society have to force them to play nice? Or is that not right?"

"No," he says, "they don't get along."

Something about the way he says it makes me curious about where this is coming from. Especially since he was down in Bronson's office. "Why are you asking me this?"

"I shouldn't be. I just... Oz trusts you and I figured it wouldn't hurt to ask," he says. "Don't worry about it. All the answers will come tomorrow."

Oz trusts me? The situation between us is more than dangerous. "They will?"

He closes his eyes for a moment, sighs. He opens them and steps past me. "I can't tell you. Ask Bronson. Don't tell him I told you."

Still shaking his head, he goes into a room two up from mine. I guess that answers my question about whether he stays here too.

I almost want to hole up somewhere else in the house for a while, but I've put it off long enough. I have to visit my room.

Ann was understating things. There are shopping bags everywhere. Recycled bags mainly, but everything inside them is way too new and neat for my taste. Mostly. I do find a drawer of black T-shirts and regular jeans. I have my leather jacket and boots, so those are acceptable. I add a couple of each to my backpack, which is extra-roomy without the cash. Opening the closet, I find it packed with Society outfits – including a uniform or two. But no stripes on them.

The posters Ann picked up are hilarious. A couple feature manufactured boy bands I've never even heard of. Another is a checkerboard assortment of baby animals (ostrich, tiger, sloth, kitten) that I admit are adorable, though I let the sheet curl back up into a tube and leave it on the floor. But the *piece de resistance* involves a unicorn with rays shooting from her horn to form a day-glo pyramid. Ann even left a roll of tape.

Since I don't want to seem ungrateful, I hang the unicorn on the wall.

I spend the rest of the time until dinner staring at it. Waiting.

CHAPTER SEVENTEEN

Dinner turns out to be nothing worth waiting for. The four of us are gathered around the overly long dining table with its perfect white linen table cloth. Bronson sits at the head and is talking nonstop about, from what I can tell, such vital topics as the weather, what was in the paper today, whether his administrative assistant should be transferred to the UK so he can get a better one.

It's the very definition of meaningless chatter.

The food is fine – or it would be if I knew what these small chicken-shaped things *are*. I'm afraid to offend Ann or reveal myself as some untutored barbarian by asking. (Though I may be just that. Mostly I don't want to hurt Ann's feelings.) There's asparagus. Not my favorite, but identifiable, and thus edible. And bread, though I have a feeling I'll be fighting Oz for the last roll if I want it. He hasn't touched his mini-chicken either.

The strained atmosphere makes being enthusiastic about eating difficult, anyway. Every clink of a fork against a plate or plunk of a water glass being returned to the table seems loud as a full orchestra, interrupting

Bronson's symphonic babble. I begin to worry that something has already happened to Dad. They wouldn't have tried him early, would they?

I can't ask. All I can do is wish I *could* ask.

"And so how was your afternoon?"

I miss the question the first time Bronson asks, judging by the way Oz nudges my shoe with his boot under the table. I shoot him a look. "Great," I say. "I unpacked some new stuff. Put up a poster." I tap Oz's shoe back, pushing it away from mine. He doesn't react.

"Good," Bronson says. "Excellent."

Oz and Justin give every appearance of being as thrown by Bronson's stiff behavior as I am. It's as if this really is a dinner party and he's being forced to entertain us, instead of a quiet "family" dinner at home. I finish the last of my roll and my asparagus as quickly as I can.

"I should go finish my room," I say.

If I can slip out and call Bree later, she'll have heard if something's happened...

When I get up, so does Bronson. He asks, "Kyra, can we talk?"

What have you been doing for the last half-hour? "Of course."

Bronson puts his napkin (cloth too) on the table, and abandons his half-eaten food. I can't help but try and decode whether his lackluster appetite is a guilty conscience or excited nerves for his upcoming treachery. I might be about to find out.

I catch Oz's eye, a question in mine about whether he knows what Bronson wants as I leave the room. He shakes his head no. I follow Bronson out and toward his office, and we pass Ann coming back in with dishes of ice cream for both boys. It looks like real ice cream and I mouth to Oz: *No. Fair.*

He shrugs.

At least he's acting semi-normal again, with the foot nudging and ice cream hogging. When we first sat down to dinner, he was as stiff as Bronson and silent as a ghost. He hasn't said a word to me all night. Maybe he regrets telling me about his parents. We barely know each other.

"Let's go upstairs," Bronson says, which is a surprise because I assume we're going to his office. I have to backtrack, and he lets me go up the stairs first. What could this possibly be about?

I pad up the hall to my room. "It's a work in progress," I caution.

"Don't worry about it," he says. "Ann loves a messy room. It's why she was so happy when Osborne moved in."

He doesn't mention Justin, because I'd bet anything his room is as tidy as his mind.

"When was that?" I ask, curious.

I flip on the light and settle on the bed, awkward. He closes the door and pulls over a chair from the corner I hadn't even noticed. At least I don't have to worry about any contraband. There's nothing for me to hide from him.

"Four and a half years ago. As soon as things settled down enough for him to travel here."

"And Justin?"

"Oh," he says, easing into the chair. "His parents asked if I might get him some extra training… three years ago? I thought it would be nice for Oz to have someone else his own age. It's been good for them both."

Whose parents sent them off to the head of the Society for training? People who were *in* the Society. Obviously.

"What did you want to talk about?"

I can't believe how nervous I am. There's no way he could know why I'm really here, or what I'm thinking of doing. I haven't given myself away to anyone. In theory maybe the oracles could rat me out, but wouldn't they protect me for Mom's sake?

"Your father," Bronson says. "I don't feel right about you being here and not knowing. And you'll find out anyway, so I'd rather it be from me. But I also… I really do like you, Kyra. I like having you here. I want you to stay, and us to be a family. I want that to be for a long time. And I'm afraid once I tell you this you'll change your mind. So… I'm asking you not to make any hasty decisions."

I nod. "Oz and Justin… They already told me no one ever gets off for treason."

"That's true."

"And that the penalty's death."

"Also true," he says. He leans forward, arms on his knees. "One thing they may not have told you is that Society courts aren't like regular ones. There's no long delay. No lawyers. A representative or three of the Board and, in this case, the Tricksters' Council will hear the evidence. Then a decision will be made. A final one."

I know all the important parts of this and yet it still hurts to hear it said out loud. Ironically, that only helps me react how he's expecting. As if this is news. Terrible news. The worst news.

Because it is.

"When?" I whisper.

"Tomorrow," he says. "We could go now. See your father tonight, if you like. I wanted to give you one last chance. There won't be time tomorrow."

I want to say yes. Because what if I screw everything up? What if tomorrow goes sideways? What if he dies and I never get to tell him anything I want to? What if he dies before I get the chance to prove myself to him?

"No," I say. "I can't. I just... I couldn't stand it if he yelled at me."

Bronson nods.

"And," I say, "I couldn't stand it if he didn't. If he cried... I don't want that memory. I have enough pain to last me a lifetime already. He wouldn't want me to see him that way."

Bronson keeps nodding. Slow. He gets it. "Don't we all? But don't give up hope. You never know. You might see him again someday. Anything is possible. Maybe he'll be acquitted."

Sixteen times, Justin says, and no one ever has.

"Don't start lying to me now. You know he won't be."

"So you accept the reason he stole the relic as a fact?"

Since I know more about Dad's reasons now, I am able to look straight at him and say, "Yes."

After a long moment, Bronson reaches into an inside pocket of his suit jacket and pulls something out. He holds his hand so I can't see what it is, unsure.

"You don't have to give me anything else," I say. "All this is enough. And the reliquary key."

"I'm not saying you can keep these," he says. "If Henry is acquitted–"

I shake my head. *Stop lying.*

"He would get them back," he finishes. "And they do have to be our secret for now, regardless. You can't use them until after your vows. But you won't need them until you're a uniformed operative in the field. I'm giving them to you because I have always drawn strength from mine. Even though I no longer wear them often, they're always right here." He pats the breast pocket he took the eye from earlier.

I extend my hand, not daring to hope. Barely breathing. But when he drops the metal into my hand, it's what I think. Stripes. Gold bars that shine like sun rays, and it's as if they're working their magic already. I'm paralyzed.

"You have a place," he says.

I close my fingers around them, unable to speak. Stripes. I have stripes.

One element of the plan just got way easier, but no grin bubbles up. Because every piece that falls into place means I have to do it. This is going to happen. My grandfather and I look at each other, solemn for entirely different reasons.

Bronson rises, then. But he stops in front of the unicorn poster, the question on his face plain. He's perplexed by it. If Mom and Legba hadn't warned me, I'd be completely charmed by him.

"Ann picked it out," I say, and it startles me how weak my voice is. "It's growing on me."

"We'll redo the room. You can paint it black, if you want."

"Like my soul," I say.

"I don't think so." He smiles, a sad one. "Know that I'll do what I can to make this as painless for your father as possible."

No, I think, *you won't.* "Thanks."

When he reaches the door, I stop him. "Wait." I need to play at normal – or something as close as I can sell to it. "Will you send Ann up with some of that ice cream?"

He lowers his voice, confidentially. "My guess is she's waiting in the hallway already. She may not be a genius decorator, but she makes the ice cream herself."

After he opens the door, he steps aside to let her enter. She has a metal tray gripped in both hands with a giant bowl on it. "You hardly touched your Cornish game hen," she says. "And Oz said you were jealous of the boys. We can't have that."

I still don't know if that means dinner was a chicken or not. Somehow, even though it's been years since I've had good ice cream, I know I won't taste that either. Not while I'm thinking about my dad in a cell beneath the Jefferson and picturing the long shadow of tomorrow, looming over us both. Dad must believe I blew town at last, left him to his fate. I hold the stripes in my hand tight, like I'll never let them go.

"No," I say, and muster a weak smile. "We can't have that."

I memorize every shade and angle of the unicorn poster. Really, it's amazingly detailed.

I don't have anything else to do while I wait for the rest of the house to quiet, everyone to visit dreamland. After a while, trying to count the number of points on the prism above the horn makes me pass out. I'm still telling myself I have to stay awake when I nod off.

But my dreams are the usual predictable, unicorn-less dark. I wake, as always, with a light coating of sweat, breathing hard, shaking, my mother's voice in my ears. For once, I'm glad I have an internal nightmare alarm clock. Turns out it's 3am. No one else seems to be stirring when I crack the door and listen. Perfect timing.

I make my way down the stairs, start to go in Bronson's office, but have to scoot past the door. He's not there, but a light is on. Justin is sitting at a table and chairs at the far end of the bookshelves, reading something and making notes.

So I decide to visit the kitchen and wait him out there. On the way, I pass a sliding door that looks out onto the yard. I can't miss the creature right outside it. Anzu sits, staring in. I walk to the door, and press my hand against the glass.

On the small patio, he takes a step closer, and another. Until he's so close his breath fogs the glass above my head. It evaporates immediately in the too-warm D.C. summer night. I peer up at him, glad for the barrier. His eyes are liquid gold and unreadable, and I wish I knew whether he could answer questions for me. Can Anzu talk? I wish I knew if between the two of us, we could get into the Jefferson and get my dad out. But I remember he's a guard, not a conspirator.

Big difference.

I hear soft footsteps behind me. "Don't worry," Oz says. "It's just me."

Anzu... grimaces... if that's the word for it. He doesn't growl or roar, that we can hear through the glass anyway, which I'm assuming means he makes no sound. When he does either, it's not subtle.

"Why shouldn't I worry?" I say.

"Because it's just me," he says, again. "Couldn't sleep?"

He stands at my shoulder, and I can *feel* him there even though he's not touching me. We stare out at Anzu together, and he stares back in at us. Considering us.

"Nightmares."

"Sorry," he says.

"Don't be. I always have them."

"That sounds like something I should say more than sorry for, then."

I turn my head to the side, despite it making me nervous to not be watching Anzu when he's *right there* on the other side of the glass.

"Nah," I say, "nothing to be done about it. History. Ancient. I'm not the only person in the world with nightmares. Not even close."

"Still sucks. I thought maybe you were up because of what's happening with your dad."

"Doesn't help," I agree. "But, hey, shiny new life. Unicorns and tiny Cornish chickens."

"Unicorns aren't real," he says. "Just a few gods that look like them."

"But are they chickens? Those Cornish things?"

"Tiny, more expensive chickens."

"Well, that's one mystery solved."

"And you also had ice cream."

"I did, but I felt too guilty to eat it."

Anzu yawns wide and the motion drags my attention back to him. He turns from us and stalks back into the yard. Oz takes my shoulder with a gentle hand, "I think that's a sign we should go back to bed."

The word bed is another word I need to add to the list of things he should stop saying, along with my name and the word nice.

When I face him, I realize how close we're standing. Closer than we were in his reliquary earlier. He has on a T-shirt, plain and blue, with his pajamas tonight, which is less distracting. I start to ask him what Justin is doing in Bronson's office, but instead I flinch when his fingers find mine. It's not as if he's lacing our hands together in some cheesy pop song way. He's just taking my hand to tug me up the hall toward the kitchen. Casual. No big deal.

Only I know this is dangerous. Not for me, for Oz.

I want to warn him off. Tell him he should have a chat with Tam if he doubts me. But, for now, any interest he has helps. So I feel bad about it, but I don't say a word.

He releases my hand when we get to the kitchen. Relief.

"My dad's on trial tomorrow. Bronson told me."

"I know," he says, looking in the fridge instead of at me.

"Look, I don't need you to be on mopey Kyra duty. You can go to sleep."

"I will," he says, "as soon as I get some water."

"Why's Justin up so late?" I ask.

He whirls from the fridge, shuts it behind him. "What do you mean? Justin sleeps like the dead. Like a baby."

"Well, he's in Bronson's office."

Oz swings back the way we came, and I follow, even though it's none of my business. When we get to the office, the light's out. No one's there.

"He was here. I swear."

Oz moves further into the office. I follow him. There's nothing on the table where Justin was sitting before… Wait. There is. Oz walks over and plucks a pen off. He holds it in the air. "This is his."

He slips it into the pocket of his plaid pajama bottoms. "I'm sure it was just some scholar nerdery that couldn't wait. But you won't say anything?"

It takes me a second to understand what he's asking me. Earlier Justin said Oz trusts me. Oh, Oz, you shouldn't. "To Bronson? Don't worry. Your – his, whoever's – secret is safe with me."

"I'm heading up to bed," Oz says, "after all."

He's going to talk to Justin. I say, "Good night." When I don't make a move to leave, he frowns but leaves me behind. He's on a mission to interrogate his friend.

I slip over to the desk, and punch in Bree's number. I wait through the rings, counting them, and, as I'm about to give up, someone answers.

"Hello?"

It's Tam. Tam answers.

I sit there, thinking of what to say. Then I hang up… not in *shock* exactly. But surprised, and knowing I should call back. There's no reason why he shouldn't be there. I let the receiver stay where it is. If they find out my plan, they'll want to help. That can't happen.

I'm on my own from here on out.

CHAPTER EIGHTEEN

Tam Nguyen replaces the receiver of the phone on Bree's desk. The cord snakes across the floor of her bedroom and out into the upstairs hallway. They had to dig a long extension line out of a closet filled with extra camera pieces and miscellaneous gear and hook it to the phone in her mom's room, to get it to reach all the way in here.

Bree smacks his shoulder for the second time. "I told you," she says. "I told you to let *me* get it. I should never have invited you over here."

"Kyra's my friend too. It might not even have been her."

"This is almost exactly when she called last night. Tam, that might have been our only chance to stop her from doing something stupid. We shouldn't have gone downstairs." Bree sighs, the weight of several worlds in that sigh, and lowers her head onto her crossed arms on the desktop. Not looking at him.

He wants to reach out, run his hand over her black curls. He wants to reassure her it will be OK, though he doesn't believe it will anymore. But he's had a hard time thinking of much else – besides worrying Kyra's going to get herself in deeper than even she can swim out of – since the visit to Enki House. What the sages showed him is why he's here.

Instead of a hair touch, he settles for one on her shoulder. He tries to make it as light as possible. "Hey," he says.

She peers up at him, her hair falling half in front of her face, her eyes so green it nearly hurts. How in the world has he missed this? All these years?

"What?" she asks. Those green eyes drop to his hand.

"Why don't I... I don't know, make you some tea or something?" Tam asks. "You might feel better."

Bree shakes her head, eyes wide with disbelief. She shrugs his hand off her shoulder. "Do you even know how to make tea?"

Tam is quiet. He does know how. He learned how to make it from his dad, one of the few family traditions he brought here with him. Tam's dad has tea when he needs to be calm, to think. That's what made him suggest it.

"Fine," Bree says. "I'll make it. You stay here. I need a minute." She gets up, stops in the door and says, "If she calls again, do not answer. I'll get up here to answer."

He nods.

As soon as she's gone, he strides around the room, idly taking in her art on the walls. He stops in front of a fresh canvas, heavy paint. It's of a murky, water-filled tank with several long sage bodies inside, one head visible above the rim. Is that a black heart in the air above it? Stretching so it's almost unrecognizable, so it fills the air of the chamber? It is. He has no idea what it means.

But when she still isn't back, he checks where he's wanted to all night. This is why he came here, instead of asking her to his house. Not that Bree would have agreed to leave the phone. She faked a fever so she could stay home sick from school today, and wait beside it.

Tam opens the closet door and paws the clothes aside. He knows he shouldn't be doing this. It's a violation of her privacy – the kind of thing the Skeptics would say is a civil rights violation. But they're... friends. And he *has* to find out if the sages were messing with him or if what he saw was real.

Plus, it's not as if Tam, average citizen, is equivalent to a secret Society raid or a Man-in-Black showing up to take hard drives or reams of printouts. He's not going to take anything.

He's just looking. That's what art is for.

What he saw in the vision was Bree drawing, and what she was drawing – him – and then her stashing the sketchbook away in here before Kyra came in the room.

Yahtzee.

There are several sketchbooks propped against the back wall. He takes the first, listens to make sure the coast is clear, and flips it open on his knees. Him. The next page is him too. And on the next one, another image of him. This should be creepy, but it isn't.

Bree draws him how he wishes he could think of himself. How he wants and wishes to be. He tears one sheet out of the sketchbook and folds it, puts it in his pocket. Then he replaces the sketchbook, and shuts the closet.

He sits on the bed, waiting, trying to take in the rest of her art. But he can't look away from the one of the sages in the tank, even though it's clearly unfinished. She's managed to capture how it felt, the sliminess of their touch. Even though the visions they give are gifts. Clearly gifts, though it sure didn't feel like one at the time.

What did *she* see? He's curious. She's been short with him ever since Kyra took off. Concern, he's been telling himself. That's all it is. But what if the sages showed her something of him too? Something that makes her *not* see him that way anymore.

He's such a fool. And Kyra. Her dad's trial is tomorrow. No way she's gone belle of the Society ball. She's up to something, and it'll be unbelievable, and it'll be crazy, and it might get her killed. That's the other thing he's worried about. He doesn't know how he and Bree are supposed to handle that.

Bree comes back, and he can only be happy that she is here. She brings two cups of tea. She could kick him out, but she isn't.

"Do you want to stay?" she asks. "In case she calls again?"

"Sure," Tam says. "I don't care about getting in trouble this week. We have to watch out for her. That's more important."

Bree takes a sip of tea. He can tell from the heat of the cup in his hands that it's too hot. He wants to lift hers away, protect her from burning her tongue. He sits his down on the nightstand beside her bed.

"Did you guys get back together?" Bree blurts the question, tea sloshing onto her fingers.

Tam can't bear to watch that, so he does lift the cup out of her hands. He sets it next to his own.

"No," he says. And then, "No, we should never have been together. It would never have worked."

Bree raises her eyebrows skeptically. "It seemed to work well enough."

"People change."

"They do?" she asks, as if she wants his opinion on this.

"Sometimes people are stupid, and then they wise up," Tam says. When she keeps looking at him that way, he makes his first mistake. Well, not his first. His millionth. "Sometimes they don't see what's right in front of them."

"Maybe what's right in front of them is too easy to see," Bree says. She's studying that raw painting, the unfinished one he is so drawn to. "Maybe no one should care what's right in front of them. Kyra never has."

"And look where it's gotten her."

She scowls. "You can't *really* be blaming her?"

Just like that, he knows he's blowing it. What is he doing?

"Well, she hasn't made the best decisions," he says, though he wants to say anything else.

Bree is on her feet. "Get out if you feel that way. Just get out."

"No," Tam says, "that's not what I meant. I shouldn't have said that. Why are we fighting?"

She sighs again. Picks up her tea, drinks from it with no care for whether it's still too hot.

"Because we're exhausted. And we're worried about her." Bree eases back down. "She's not going to call back. I have no idea what she's up to. The only thing I can do... I'm going to see if I can get Mom to let me go with her. To the press room. Maybe I can see Kyra there. I can try to talk to her..."

"You're a good friend," Tam says. He sits down, bumps his shoulder into hers.

"You too," Bree says. "When you're not a lost cause."

Tam thinks of the vision the sage gave him, of the sketch in his pocket, and he still can't believe Bree made it. That she sees the part of him he wants to believe is real. He has to be that person. He has to prove that he is to himself.

"I'll go with you," he says.

CHAPTER NINETEEN

I leave the curtains open so the light will wake me early. The cue isn't necessary. After a couple of hours, I'm wide awake and filled with nervous energy. I feel almost like I did buzzing from surviving that first encounter with Set. But this time it's on a different frequency. A bandwidth I'm vibrating on, like a tightrope walker on the shakiest of high wires.

I wait for the faintest hint of morning. Shower. Get dressed. Be quiet about all of this. Step out into the hallway and listen. And wait.

When Ann arrives and comes upstairs, I go back in my room and shut the door until she heads back down. She doesn't come in. I'm listening so hard that I hear the *brinnng* of the old-fashioned alarm clock I spotted the day before on Bronson's dresser. Creeping into the hallway, I will Oz and Justin's doors to stay closed, and Ann to stay downstairs, where I can smell the beginnings of breakfast.

I stand with my ear near Bronson's door, and detect the shower running. Slipping inside, I move as fast as I can. His clothes are laid out on the bed, and I search the front pocket, hoping... But there's nothing in it yet.

Darting over to the dresser, the worst is confirmed. The little blue eye and the gold bars of his stripes sit in front of the framed photo of him with Gabrielle. He won't put them in his jacket pocket until after he's dressed. I can't risk taking the key now, because he'll miss it. Right away. And I'll be sunk.

I leave the room, and slump against the wall outside for a second to regroup. This was a possibility I considered, and so I should keep going. I head downstairs.

Ann is beating some eggs in a bowl with a fork, bacon already frying on the stove. "You're up early," she says. "You must have rested better."

"I did," I say, and wonder how the dark circles don't give me away. I pour a cup of coffee. Which she allows, though her frown tells me she doesn't like that I drink it.

"So, do we all eat breakfast together?" I ask.

"Not usually," she says.

"Oh." My disappointment bleeds through.

"But if you want I can make something more substantial? Force the boys to the table."

"And Bronson?"

"You should call him Grandpa," she says. "You're the sun in his sky at the moment, so I'm sure he won't mind."

I go and sit at the table, sucking down the coffee. Funny that Bronson took in Oz and Justin, but that they don't seem to do much family stuff, even fake family stuff. Both of them look confused when they come out of the kitchen and take the same seats from the night before at the dining room table. If anything, they're even stiffer than they were then. It telegraphs that group breakfast really is *way* out of the ordinary.

"Good morning," I offer.

They nod, and Oz studies me for a second as if he's trying to puzzle out what's going on. If anything is.

Bronson joining us saves me from further scrutiny. "Ann informs me we're having breakfast together today," he says, with a glance at me.

"I felt like some company," I say. "I hope it isn't trouble. Big day, you know?"

Bronson shrugs out of his coat, hangs it over the back of the chair at the head of the table. "I thought you'd want your space today. But Oz and Justin can stay here with you, if you don't want to be alone. That would be fine with me."

The kind concern in his words convinces me he's being sincere. Maybe he *does* like having me here. Still, I can't imagine being the sun in anyone's sky. I'm not used to adults indulging my whims because they think it'll make me feel better. Like that, I'm back around to not trusting him again. I'm only going to get one shot at this, and that means there's zero room to slip up.

I stare down at the white circle of the empty plate in front of me. "I wanted to go with you… over to…"

"You can't be there, Kyra," Bronson cuts me off. I look up at him. "It's not a good idea. But I'm sure the boys won't mind staying here."

I figured he'd sentence me to house arrest for the day, but it was worth a shot.

"And miss the only treason trial of our lifetimes?" Justin asks. "Of course we don't mind." Though he doesn't sound *that* put out.

"If here's where we're most needed, of course that's where we'll be, sir," Oz says. He doesn't kick Justin under the table, but he may as well have.

"Fine," Justin mutters.

"Good," Bronson says, and leans back as Ann comes in with breakfast.

Plates of scrambled eggs, toast, and bacon. Which we are all apparently allowed to eat openly today, as part of the special occasion of breakfast together. I have to force down every bite. The moment of truth arrives soon and with little fanfare. Bronson rises, his hand starting for his jacket.

"I'll walk you out," I say.

I hop up and grab his jacket like I'm the world's most thoughtful granddaughter, carrying it for him just because. I struggle to stay casual, as if every part of me isn't screaming: *I have it. Right here in my hands. This is going to work.*

Oz and Justin stay at the table, I suppose to allow us privacy. What I haven't come up with is what to talk to Bronson *about* while I do this. It's not as if my pickpocket skills exist. I need him distracted.

"You'll be home late tonight, then," I say.

"Probably." His concern comes back. "Kyra, what is it?"

I drop his coat over my hands, holding onto it and thinking fast. "Will you tell Dad something for me?"

"The decision will be made today, but the sentence won't be carried out immediately," he says.

Right, I think, *there'll be a whole day between. All the time in the world.*

"You don't have to worry about not having a chance to talk," he continues. "We can arrange for you to see him tomorrow."

"I still want you tell him something. In the meantime." I dip my head. "Turn around, I'll help you into your coat. I used to do this when I was a kid. I had to stand on the stairs and lean forward, and Dad would stand at the bottom. He was so much taller than me."

Bronson frowns.

"Never mind," I say, shaking my head. "It's stupid. Dumb nostalgia. I'm not usually like this. An emotional mess. I promise I won't be like this if you let me stay here." I hold out the coat to him, and pray to all the gods and to none of them.

"Of course, you're staying. You're family. And it's not silly at all." He pivots, showing me his back. He holds his arms out. "Like this?"

"Like that," I say. "Will you tell him...?"

"Yes?"

I pluck the eye out of the front pocket, and stuff it into my pants pocket. "Just a sec," I say.

He glances over his shoulder – and sees nothing he shouldn't.

His stripes are still in his jacket where they should be, and hopefully the weight is near enough to normal he won't check. The key is light, and this should be a busy day for him. That's what I'm banking on, that he'll have no reason to use it or notice it's gone.

I position the first sleeve for him to get his arm into, and then the other. He shrugs the coat up over his shoulders.

"Tell him..." I pause, "...that if we could do things over I know we'd both do them differently. That we can't, not anymore, but that I love him anyway. Tell him that I'll find a way to watch out for Mom."

Bronson faces me again. "I will. I'm sure it will help him to know that."

He leans forward and kisses my forehead, as if we really are family. In our own twisted way, we are. The key in my pocket proves it.

I manage to get out of Oz that the trial starts in the afternoon. After breakfast, we go downstairs to hang out in a basement rec room that has actual dust in its corners and on the cases of its library of VHS tapes (enormous plastic behemoths with rolls of videotape inside; I miss the days of instant streaming). Justin excuses himself instead of joining us, saying he's working on a research project. Oz does not seem to believe this, but he also doesn't try to stop him.

Which means Oz and I are on the not-dusty, but clearly not-often-used couch together. Oz let me choose the movie, and I picked an old action movie that's set in the future. It's about a guy trying to prevent his future self from committing a crime. There's a creepy lady spouting predictions in a tank, and I want to tell the hero that is something that *never* seems to turn out well. The lady makes a prophecy about the guy. Another problem I don't want to think about.

Poor Dad. He doesn't even know as much about his situation as the hero of an old movie would. The other choices would have been just as bad. All the movies Bronson owns are ancient and they're *all* set – or mostly set – in D.C. Again, it feels as if someone else assembled this house, someone besides the person who lives here.

"Where did these movies even come from?" I ask Oz. "Bronson doesn't strike me as a buff who's obsessed with movies filmed in town."

"He had Ann buy a library of movies when I moved here and she found this whole set at a junk sale. My guess is that someone told him people our age like to watch movies."

"Ah," I say. "Ann's shopping skills are legend. You should see the unicorn poster in my room."

He smolders over at me. "Are you trying to get me upstairs?"

"Um," I say. "No. I already have you down here."

"That's true. You do."

With timing that matches her purchasing powers, Ann bounds down the stairs and into the rec room. "Everything OK in here? You guys need snacks?"

"Yes, we're OK, and nope, no snacks," I say.

"I'm going to run out for groceries." She hesitates. "Should you be alone in here?"

"We're just watching this great movie," I say, trying not to sound embarrassed.

Oz snorts, but not loud enough for her to hear.

"Shut up," I mutter.

But Ann closes the door. Once she's gone, we are definitely *not* watching the movie anymore. We look at each other.

"I want to go to the Jefferson," I say.

"You can't."

"Hear me out." This is the part of my plan I'm least certain about. I want it to work, though I feel terrible about it. If Oz refuses, miserable failure will be the result.

"I'll listen, and I get it, but the answer is no," he says.

"You know how we went to my reliquary yesterday?"

He nods.

"There's a relic there that makes someone invisible. No one would even have to know we were there."

"And how were you thinking we'd get there in the first place without being seen?"

I want to see his reaction to this next part, to know whether I'm right. "You can't tell me that the director of the Society doesn't have a secret way to get in there. This is D.C. There are passageways and tunnels everywhere. Isn't this house *always* used by the director, whoever it is? There has to be a reason."

"You've been listening to your boyfriend too much," Oz says.

"Ex," I say. "And not just him. The Skeptics are not crackpots." He gives me a look worthy of any skeptic and I put up my hand. "Not all of them, anyway. This whole city was put together by secretive old men. Paranoids who like escape routes."

He shrugs one shoulder. "*That* is truer than you know. But you can't break your father out, Kyra. It's not possible. The cell he's in was designed by Houdini. It involves a door with a hundred impenetrable locks. They'll take him to the Reading Room straight from there. And it won't be long now. I'm sorry, but there's no point."

This. This is what I'm banking will get him. "I don't want to rescue him. I… I just want to *see* him. I want to see the trial. Can't you understand?"

"I can. I absolutely can. But there's no way."

"Oz, please." I am begging now, and I don't try to hide it. "Please, let me have a chance to say goodbye to him in my own way. I won't say anything to him. Not a word. I just want to see him. If we can get to my reliquary first, no one will even know we're there. Vidarr's shoe. That's what it's called."

"I knew what relic you meant already," he says.

Which is encouragingly not a no.

"Oz, please. I'll owe you forever. I just need to see him. This is part of my family story. I'm going to be the one in charge of that hunter's map now, and have to draw that line to the underworld. *I'm* going to have to write his name there. I'm going to have nightmares on top of the nightmares I already have. Don't I deserve to know the truth? To see him meet his accusers? Please. I've been in the dark for so long." I don't dare look away. I hold his gaze, and I ask, "Is there a way?"

We stare into each other's eyes, ignoring the sounds of the false future coming from the TV. It's as if nothing else exists besides this moment and his decision. I am afraid to breathe.

Finally, he raises his arm and points behind us. Toward a corner that, on closer inspection, is not dusty. There's a door there that I assumed went to a closet. The knob shines.

"There is a way," he says. "It starts right over there."

CHAPTER TWENTY

"Ready?" Oz asks.

"Yes." I am, having gone upstairs to get my backpack with the excuse it has my reliquary key in it. Also, everything I own that's here is in it, which I don't tell Oz. The clothes and unicorn poster belong to Bronson, and he can have the uniform, jeans and T-shirts I'm taking with me back later, if he wants them. It hasn't occurred to me until now to wonder if I'll ever spend another night in my actual room at home.

Oz lays his palm against the unassuming wooden door.

"Is there a reason I don't even want to notice it?" I ask him.

He nods. "Same reason no one really pays that much attention to this house. For that matter, to the street it's on. There are fragments of Amaunet's papyrus staff embedded within the door to the outside, and this one. She was Amen's consort, the hidden one."

"You guys and your toys," I say.

Oz angles his head to look at me, without removing his hand from the door. "None of these things are toys.

If you don't understand that, we should stay here. We shouldn't be anywhere near your reliquary or the Jefferson. Especially not today. The reason your father's in such trouble is because the relic he took could–"

"End the world?"

"Close enough," he says. "Maybe things could have been different before, but we killed one of them. We did that. You think they wouldn't turn on us if they could do it without risk? You've seen them. It would be a whim. Wipe out most of humanity. It would make their day. Relics are not toys."

I can sense that he's about to drop his hand, that this will all be over.

"Oz," I say, "look at me." He does. "It was a bad joke. I know these aren't toys, believe me. No one knows better than me. My life is already ending. You get that, right? It's over, I should throw a wake for it. I get a new one, apparently, but... I won't ever have that one back. You said you'd take me to see Dad, one last time, to say goodbye the only way I can. Are you going back on that?"

I feel like an absolute monster as I hold my breath. I don't release it when he focuses on the door and says two words I don't recognize and couldn't repeat, and steps back and says, "After you."

Then, only then, do I breathe. The knob turns beneath my hand, and the door opens.

There is only cool blackness within. Oz cranks the gas lantern that's his contribution to our expedition and it flares to life. "We'll have to stay close," he says, and I step into the dark. He secures the door behind us.

The low visibility takes a little while to acclimate to. I steady myself by putting a hand against the wall (cold stone, but comfortingly not damp). There is a stray scuffle in front of us. Oz must notice how I tense, because he says, "Mice, most likely. Nothing to worry about."

"Says you." Then I ask, "Will Ann release the hounds when she comes back and discovers we're gone?"

"I left her a note," he says.

If he put too much detail in it, that could be a problem. "You didn't tell her–"

"It says we went for a walk, to get some air, and we'll be back later."

"I apologize," I say.

"For what?" he asks, the lantern light flickering over his skin. "Makes sense you're nervous."

I'm beginning to be able to make out the shape of the passageway in the rough circle of light, though not much of it. Brick walls curve, rounded, and a smooth floor angles slightly downward. The mice must have pell-melled away, because the quiet beyond us is immense, a silent forever.

"For assuming you would suck at being sneaky, I meant," I say. "Should we get going?"

"Yes." He holds the lantern up with his left hand to illuminate our path, and offers me his right arm. I slip mine through, wishing I wasn't so aware we're touching. For gods' sakes, it's only my palm on his lower arm. I shouldn't like that spot so much more than where we *aren't* touching. Stupid body.

After we've gone a few feet, he says, "But I'm *trained* to be sneaky."

"For big flashy operations," I say, "not for sneaking out of a house."

"Sneaky operations are by definition not big and flashy."

I grunt to acknowledge this might be a legitimate point. Still, the Society doesn't seem to do subtle.

"You've had lots of practice at sneaking out, I take it?" he asks.

"Every time I thought Dad might notice. Or anytime something fun was going on late. There are still some excellent bands that swing through here, willing to risk having to go acoustic. But," I emphasize, "I never left a note."

"You wanted to get caught, and you wanted him to worry."

I make the mistake of looking over my shoulder, at the absolute black behind us. I refocus on the small circle of light from the lantern ahead of us. As long as it's burning, the dark doesn't matter. The lantern's glow is dim and fuzzy enough that even if Oz didn't have to pay attention to carrying it and leading us forward, he couldn't read my expressions.

"I made sure I got caught, whenever I could," I say. "Dad... never cared. Or if he did, he hid it from me."

"I don't believe that."

"Doesn't matter. It's true. I think... I think he was relieved not to have to share any of this with me. To have a life that was his, without me in it. I think he's always blamed me for Mom. She could have stayed with us, if I didn't set her off." I anticipate that he's going to feel moved to tell me I'm wrong, so I say preemptively, "Just don't. I'm right about this. Look. You know how you told me yesterday, where you were. Do you want to know where I was, when it happened?"

Oz hesitates, but says, "If you want to tell me."

We glide through an ocean of darkness together, on this tiny island of light. This might be a mistake, but I want to. I've never told anyone the whole story before. Not even Bree and Tam. They got an edited version. I owe this to Oz. Maybe it will help him understand why I'm the way I am. As much as I do, at least.

"I was at school." I half-laugh. "And everyone's parents flocked there to pick them up. Cars didn't go dead here. Not right away. There was gridlock. They brought us all to the lobby to wait. There were parents who ran up, sobbing, terrified, who'd left their vehicles to get there faster. All they were telling us then was that there was some kind of world upheaval. Unrest. We thought maybe it was a terrorist attack. Whatever, I was *positive* my mom and dad would come." I go quiet for a long stretch, stuck back there. The school's front steps and the parking lot might as well stretch in front of us instead of darkness. The chaos of pickups transforming into deserted blacktop as the minutes ticked by. "And there I was, after every single kid was gone, after the teachers and the principal had taken off. Waiting on the steps, thinking it *was* the end of the world. Because if my parents could have gotten to me, they would have.

Everyone else's did. So, I made my way home. I was twelve, and I'd never walked it on my own. I kept getting lost. I saw… this lady, in the distance getting mowed down by some blue god and had no idea what it was. I just started running. And when I got home? No one was there. Neither one of them showed up until late that night. Mom already wasn't herself. Three days later, she left us. Dad might as well have gone with her. Everything changed."

He says, with care, "It did. That day changed *everything*."

"What it changed for me was I knew exactly where I stood after that. If the world was ending, no one cared enough to come for me. No one cared enough to make sure I wasn't alone."

"Does it help, knowing a little bit of why they couldn't be there? Or does that make it worse?"

He sounds legitimately curious. I gaze into the nothing before us, and think about the city who knows how far above us. About everything that's happened, and everything that will.

"I don't know yet," I say. Honest.

That kills the conversation for the long minutes that we spend walking through the Endless Passage Under Creepy Street. But it's not endless. Eventually, we stop in front of an elevator.

"No one staffs this up top?" I ask.

"Not the floor we're going to. It's meant to give the director access and an exit route that isn't strictly monitored. No one will be anywhere near the reliquaries while there's a big event like today's underway. We should be able to get in without seeing anyone. At least, that's what I'm counting on. Because I will be in major trouble if we do."

The elevator stops, and Oz pulls the lattice gate open.

I cross into the old-fashioned cage, saved from acknowledging the serious rules he's breaking to help me out. He presses a button on a glowing panel of them. A symbol like an "A" with extra slashes. I lean against the polished gold railing, holding on with my free hand as the elevator rises. Oz busies himself cranking the lantern to power it down. The light shuts off.

"Look at me," he says.

The elevator shimmies slightly in mid-air, like the cable might come loose. Wouldn't that be my luck? But when I glance over at him, Oz is intent. He says, "They may not have come for you that day, Kyra, but I believe they would've if they could. And I believe they should have, no matter what."

I don't trust myself to respond. I'm not as convinced as he is. I *wish* they had, just like I wish he was right.

The elevator stops, Oz slides up to the gate, pushing it open. He peers out into a shortish hallway, marble and relatively featureless. I'm not sure exactly where we are, but even from the back of the cage, I can see we're alone down here.

Unable to turn off his training, as we exit Oz motions for me to stay close to the left side of the hall. He holds a finger up to his lips. Soon enough, we go through a door and out into a more familiar hallway. It's the one lined with those nearly identical reliquary doors, the golden light fixtures dangling overhead at regularly spaced intervals. We stay quiet as we creep past the House names.

When we pass House Spencer, I know mine's not far.

And here we are. The sigil key radiating light, unlike the one I take from my pocket. I have a moment's fear that I've forgotten which key is which – since they look identical – but I stashed them in different places. Bronson's is in my backpack. I open the door with no fuss this time, enjoying the flip of the nameplate at my touch.

"We'll need to be quick. If anyone does come down here, they'll see the door open right away," Oz says.

"Trust me. I'm the last person who wants to get caught here."

I lead him to the case Bronson showed me yesterday, half-worried I'm misremembering. But there it is. Sure, there are other items in here I *could* use. I might don Legba's cap and sow confusion behind me like planting a garden, or take up the bow and fire perfectly targeted arrows. But I can't take that kind of risk. No flashy operations for me, either. I'm doing what I believe I can accomplish.

So I open the cabinet, and reach up to the top level for Vidarr's shoe with its thick sole and wild riot of colors. The size is impossible to fix at a glance. Whether it will be too tight or big enough to swallow my foot is a mystery. The effect is probably part of its magic.

"I just put it on?" I ask. Even though I've seen relics work several times, part of me thinks: *This? This recovered* shoe *is really going to make me invisible?*

"As far as I know," Oz says.

I bend and slip it over top of my scuffed, heavy boot. A hum of energy passes through me, over me, around me. Or does it? It's not so different than the nerves I woke up with, than the way I feel being here and doing this.

Oz tilts his head, narrows his eyes. His brown hair is in perfect order today.

"I can't see you anymore, if you're wondering," he says. "Not even a hint."

The chance to have one more genuine moment between us is *too* tempting to resist. I can't stand doing exactly what I'm supposed to with *invisibility*. Darting forward, I mess up Oz's hair. I ruffle it quickly, and step back as he swipes out to catch me.

He's laughing. And I am too, even though *that* should be impossible.

"Hilarious," Oz says.

He stays completely still for a second, then lunges toward me. I'd knock into the case if I moved away, and so he catches me. His arms seize me, and I'm laughing again. Looking down at me, he says, "Now I'm invisible too."

"Oh, right," I say, like an idiot checking out his arms lightly around me. We are practically chest to chest. Not quite touching everywhere, but... close. Our eyes catch. He lifts one of his hands and flicks a finger outside the tight frame we currently make.

"See it?" he asks.

"I do." There's a light transparent film between us and the rest of the world – there to keep us safe from detection beyond its borders. No sight or sound can escape. "Wow."

"Better than being frozen?" he asks.

But it's not a real question and I don't answer it. I reach out and watch as the trembling film expands at my touch, keeping my hand inside it.

"Wow," I say again. "I understand every abuse of power by every Society member ever. That is *so* cool."

"Now you really *have* been listening to your boyfriend. Relics are sacred. Used for necessity. Not for–"

"Fun?" I supply.

"Not for personal gain," he replies.

Oh, Oz, if only I could tell you everything I've been told. Not by Tam. By people who know the score, namely my mom and Legba. "Anyway," I say, "to suddenly be able to be invisible... There's no other word for this. It's magic. Maybe it's borrowed, maybe it's limited, but it is still extraordinary."

"Try taking a step," he says.

I lower my hand to take Oz's free one, and do as he suggests. I encounter another spectacular oddity. I'm not hobbling along. The shoe has conformed to ensure both my feet are perfectly balanced and light and soundless. We are in our own tiny world. I'm glad the relic demands my attention, distracts me from Oz. Because he's so near, and there's no pushing him away. Not yet.

"Remember," he stage-whispers, "before you think about running off, I'm the one who knows the back way to the second level of the Reading Room."

"And you're the one who'd shout my name and get me caught," I tell him, not letting go of his hand.

"But I'd feel really bad about it," he says.

"I'm sure." I envy his certainty that the Society is a force for good. I envy that *kind* of certainty about anything and, at the same time, I'd pluck it out of his brain or his heart – whichever place it lives – if I could. "You wouldn't be able to sleep at night."

"You forget," he says, "I already can't."

But I haven't. That's something we *do* have in common.

"I didn't tell you everything yesterday," he says, and his tone makes me stop and listen. "The truth is I dream about them. My parents. The last time I saw them wasn't when they were fighting. They were losing. Mom ordered me to hide, and I did... I should've done something. Anything."

"Oz, you were thirteen and not ready," I point out. "You did what they wanted: you lived."

He nods. "I just wanted you to know you're not the only one. With nightmares. With regrets."

"I already knew that, because the world is full of them." I wait, poised for him to say more, or maybe for me to. For us to get closer. There's an intimacy to being within the circle of the relic together, and I try to blame the impulse on that. I shouldn't want us to get closer, and I definitely shouldn't wait for it.

"We'd better get that door closed," I say.

"Right," he agrees, and lets out a breath in what might be frustration or might be something else entirely.

We silently, magically, make our way back toward the door together, stealthily holding hands. The key spits out into my free hand and I put it back in my pocket. Now for phase two, though all I want is to keep holding on. I've never told anyone the stuff I told Oz.

"Kyra?" Oz asks.

I don't move for a stuttering heartbeat, two. When I turn toward Oz, he's pointing up the hallway, the way I'm praying he wants to go, because it's the way Bronson's reliquary is.

Two ghosts approach us from that direction. The women drift along, long white dresses skirting the marble. They are pale, so pale.

"Is the Jefferson haunted?" I whisper, even though they shouldn't be able to hear us.

"Worse," Oz says. "They're real. They're our oracles. The Pythias."

We watch them, me with a different kind of interest. These women are supposed to be like my mother, but they don't remind me of her. One is far older, stooped and leaning on a younger woman, who walks straight and tall.

"They can't see us," I say.

"They shouldn't be able to. But... They can't *live* in the room where they have visions, but I have never seen them anywhere else. Never heard of them *being* anywhere else."

"I want to get a better look," I say. "We're safe in here."

After all, Mom was one of them before. I think of her kohl-rimmed eyes, her ragged black dress. I can't imagine her given over to such pallor, an eerie purity that's almost like a reflection in water.

"I don't know if this is such a good idea," Oz says.

He doesn't fight when I pull us forward to meet them. "We're invisible," I remind him.

Once we're close enough to reach out and touch them, I move to one side of the hall and stop. I figure we'll let them pass us. Then we'll keep going, on to Bronson's reliquary. But as they amble by us, the old woman stops. She turns so her milky eyes are, by all appearances, fixed on me. Which is impossible.

"Hello?" I try.

She doesn't seem to hear. Neither does the other woman. Of *course*, they don't.

"You are trying to do what you can," she says. "That is good."

Oz's hand tightens on mine. The young woman is looking right at us too.

"Do you think they *can* see us?" I ask.

"It's not possible," Oz says. But he hesitates. "Not with their eyes. I suppose…"

"We saw you in the pool," the young woman says, voice nearly musical, "We needed to tell you something. For your mother and what we owe her. We miss her."

The old woman says, "We are pleased the brave boy is at your side, as he should be."

"I'm so dead," Oz says. "I'll lose my stripes for this. For bringing you here."

But the old woman says, "You have nothing to fear from us, boy. And you, sweet Kyra, have more things to fear than I have time to number."

"I'm not sweet," I counter, forgetting they can't hear me.

The old woman's mouth quirks up at the side. "For now, I will say that you should beware of the crossroads. The crossroads is where bargains are made, deals sealed. Where decisions are done that can't be undone. Not by anyone. Avoid it if you can."

"Run," the young girl says, and it's as if she's staring straight at me. Her eyes are black pools. They *do* remind me of Mom. I am within seconds of doing just that. She adds, "Not now, but soon. Run, and remember."

They continue on their way, drifting off like clouds. I don't suggest we follow. Oz steps in front of me and places his free hand on my upper arm. His thumb moves against my bicep. "Kyra, are you OK?"

"I don't know seems to be my only answer today. But I honestly don't know."

"Do you know what that meant, about the crossroads?"

"No idea." But we all know who the god of the crossroads is. Legba. Good thing my plan is to avoid him.

I shake Oz's hand off my arm. Our linked hands remain clasped together. "We better go," I say, and start us on our journey back up the hallway. I ignore the slight injury on Oz's face. I'm not even sure it's real. It might be what I want to see there.

"The relic that started all this, the Solstice Was," I say, because where we're headed next is House Bronson's reliquary. I have the key in my backpack, and in my other pants pocket, my stripes. I put my hand in to touch the cool metal, making sure. "It's in Bronson's keeping, right?"

I put off mentioning it as long as possible, because this should be an alarm bell for Oz. But he appears to be unconcerned.

"No," he says. "It's evidence. The gods only believe what they see in front of them. It's the subject of the trial, so it's up there." He pauses. "Did you think the oracles were going for that? They don't interfere in our affairs. Other than to talk about them. They couldn't get into a reliquary..." He sounds unsure, and who wouldn't after being tracked down and talked to while supposedly invisible?

I let him go on while I regroup.

That the relic isn't down here means I stole Bronson's key for nothing. It also means I will come face to face with what I engineered all of this to avoid – my dad on trial at the mercy of the gods and my grandfather.

CHAPTER TWENTY-ONE

The one thing I have on my side is that from Oz's perspective nothing has changed in the least.

"Where's this famous back way to the Reading Room?" I ask him.

"We're headed there now," he says.

I glide along beside him, our hands linked as if we're on the same team. For now, I let it stay that way. I can't risk the trial ending before we get there.

We don't go up right away, but instead through an unmarked door to another secret passage that – just when I start to get antsy – connects with a set of stairs that do. Those we take two at a time. There are no more encounters with oracles whose visions allow them to ignore our invisibility, but we pass plenty of operatives. Most go to and fro on guard duty, some gossip together. No one gives any sign of detecting our presence.

I overhear two rangy guys taking bets on Dad's innocence or guilt and want to thank the one taking Dad's side… until I learn what his odds are and that he's only doing it so he can be in the pot, gamble away some money on a colleague's future. Not because he thinks he'll win.

"Jackass," I declare, glad the shoe also hides any sounds we make.

"He is one," Oz says. "Don't let it bother you."

We split off to a hall with no traffic on the second floor, and round a corner. Oz directs me through a door, and from there to a small metal-lined opening in the wall that probably hasn't been used for anything in years. We duck through the empty spot, crouching awkwardly, and come out below a window and behind a marble arch.

Most of the view is blocked from this angle. But the otherworldly voices can't be missed. Across empty air, at the top of a swirling reddish brown marble pillar, I glimpse a tall ivory statue perched high above us. She wears a flowing gown and holds a mirror to look behind her. Above is an inscription in gold, from a poem, I think:

One God, one law, one element, and one far-off divine event, to which the whole creation moves. Tennyson.

Ironic, given the circumstances. By the words and the mirror together, I recognize her. She's History. That plus the voices means we are *finally* in the Reading Room.

There will be other towering goddess-like statues level with her, and more normal-life-sized bronze ones of so-called great men on the one below. We're above the main floor.

The gods are arguing. The sound of it is sharp, hard, fast, confused. They talk over each other – bellowing and booming, raging and raucous. Trying to pick out anything I can decode from the cacophony makes my head hurt, as if a nail sits against my eardrum, a hammer poised on the other side. I tune it out the best I can manage and focus on Oz. I have to deal with him before I can go any further.

He says, "It might not be as bad as it sounds. Let's go see."

Frown lines crease his forehead when I don't move right away.

When I do, it's to raise my hand and rest it against his cheek. "Oz," I say.

His worry transforms into intensity. He looks at me, his eyes blue and gray, gray and blue, and his face descends toward mine by slow degrees... His lips are near enough he could steal what comes next, except I turn my face to the side to prevent that from happening. I pronounce the word like he taught me, "*Kah-tah-DAY-tay.*"

I drop my hand from his cheek. He doesn't move. He can't.

"Bronson gave me my stripes last night," I explain. "You tell him I couldn't let him get away with this. Not if Dad's the cost. I'm leaving his key with you, though. Tell him not to come after me and maybe someday... maybe we *can* be a family."

Unlikely, but maybe it will comfort him. Maybe it will even keep him from pursuing me.

Oz stands in the light coming through the window, but he's hidden from the rest of the room by the columns and arches. He may as well belong here, be in that spot on purpose. Like any of the statues placed just so in this majestic space. He always appears at home in his surroundings, and here, frozen in his navy uniform in the sunlight, is no different.

"Oz," I lean in, close to his ear, lowering my voice. "You can't trust people, not like you do. Not people like me. Tell them whatever you need to. I don't mind." I move so he can see me paste on a fake smile, shrug one falsely carefree shoulder. I want this to strike him as genuine. I don't want him to feel bad about betraying *me*. "It's all probably true, so do your worst."

I don't say I'm sorry, because there is no reason for him to believe I am. Sorry is what people say when they are unwilling to do anything but what they want, or when they can't do anything at all. I might as well ask for forgiveness, and I don't expect that either.

Slowly, I withdraw my hand from Oz's, so at least the sight of me no longer plagues him. I'm alone again within the transparent bubble of Vidarr's stealth. I place Bronson's key at Oz's feet, slide the straps of my backpack over my shoulders. Then I slip from behind the column to get a better look at what lies ahead.

Three levels' worth of flawlessly grand statues and paintings and wide marble columns are crowned by a high dome. I have the benefit of my childhood, allowed – on occasion – to explore even here, off limits to all but researchers then. Off limits to all but gods and Society heads now.

The main floor below is surrounded by inset rows of shelves packed with reference volumes. That the thick books with faded lettering on the spines remain in place is a comfort. The world hasn't changed *that* much, if they're still here.

But maybe it's changed *more*. The desks and central dais that used to be down there have been removed, so that the gods can range freely in a loose circle, too agitated to keep still. I hold onto the rail, dizzied by the attempt to take them in at once.

With a broad furry chest and the head of his namesake, Coyote paces, his tongue lolling to one side in between exchanges with the god lounging against a nearby pillar. Hermes. Twelve feet tall in blinding white robes, a gold wreath atop his head of angelic blond curls, wings fluttering on his thick sandals. His skin is a golden brown, as if the sun reflects off him even here, inside. He wears an expression of faint amusement, as if he's above the fray.

Loki has a fearsome elfish face, red hair and beard curling like flames on every side of his massive shoulders, and he's in deep conversation with Legba. Who is amused, as usual, by the look of his grin. He taps his cane against the carpet, and his suit strikes me as a touch fancier than the ones I've seen him in so far.

I remember the oracle's words, and wish she would have told me something more useful. Anyone who's met Legba would know to avoid him. Anyone who's met any of these gods should be wiser than to desire a repeat experience.

Take the next god in the quorum. He might be mistaken for some alien monster. Tezcatlipoca has a yellow and black striped face over an enormous blocky body that features a gleaming black mirror set square in his chest. There are rumors that occasional human sacrifices present themselves to meet the day on the flat top of Tezcatlipoca House, their hearts offered as food for the gods, but no one is alive who can vouch for it. Despite that, he has a devoted following. He shows interest only in the two gods in greatest conflict.

It's the same two gods I'm most worried about. Jackal-headed Set and horned Enki circle each other, thundering accusations. No, wait. They're circling something else, something in the middle of the floor, and it's not until they move out of the way that I realize it's a *someone*, and who that someone is.

My father.

Thick shackles twist around his ankles. His wrists are bound in cuffs with a heavy chain dangling between them. They must be relics. He's in his uniform, except with no gold stripes since I have them. The fabric where they should be is torn.

For all that, he doesn't look beaten down. Worse, he doesn't give off a hint of fear, even with the two gods looming around him, fighting in languages long dead, if any human ever spoke them.

No, instead, my dad is grinning. A mad grin I've never seen the likes of on him – and never would have wanted to. Even I know that grin is not a good idea. In fact, it's probably what's provoking them to go at each other. I wonder if his expression would change, if he knew I was here. Probably not.

Bronson and Rose are the only other humans in evidence, and they are also the only people relying on podiums to make them more impressive. Or they could be using them as a protective buffer. Finally, Bronson decides to intercede. "Order." His voice is amplified by a microphone on the lectern in front of him. "Order," he repeats once more, and waits until the noise dies to a duller roar.

Set and Enki back away from each other, wary. My impression is that either of them might lunge for the other at any moment.

Bronson continues. "We are here to let Henry Locke make his defense if he chooses. There will be plenty of time for accusations *and* for punishment."

As he finishes, I spot the Solstice Was. It lies across a small table directly in front of Bronson's lectern. Rose's is on the other side of him. Dad's back is to them and it. This isn't going to be easy. I'd better make my way down.

After confirming Oz is still frozen (he is), I wind down the spiral staircase to the main floor. When I reach the bottom, I listen as my father states his name for the record and that he's a senior operative in the Society for the Sun, the head of House Locke. The tricksters are subdued – as much as they can be, which means quieter but throwing off enormous force fields of energy. They ring my father at the center of the room.

"You attacked my daughter. You should be glad I'm here in chains," Dad says. He spits toward where Set stands, with his tail lashing the air.

Set growls and his tail whips at Dad, leaving three cuts on his cheek. Dad doesn't even flinch. His grin stays put as blood streams down his face.

Bronson interrupts. "Civility, please."

"You'd let him take your granddaughter without protest," Dad says. "Swallow her up in sand and do nothing? Why was he attacking her anyway, I wonder?"

Dad's back is to Bronson and Rose. Bronson's reaction isn't visible to him, but it is to me. The older man's eyes narrow, but he doesn't dispute it. Not quite. "Henry, don't say anything you can't unsay. I'm her guardian now. Unless you make your case for innocence."

At that, Dad gives a wry laugh. "You know I can't."

"Won't, because there isn't one," Bronson says. "You're guilty."

"Which god was *I* colluding with, do you think? Was it Set? But then why would he attack my daughter...? Enki did harbor me, but he also gave me up easily, and has no interest in Egyptian relics, even such valuable ones as a key to the Afterlife." Dad pauses, stagily pretending to think. "Let me think who else might be willing to engage in such a scheme and I'll point a finger." He rattles his chains. "If I can. Undo these?"

Loud conversation breaks out again among them as they debate the request, and Bronson wheels to exchange words with Rose.

Thanks, Dad. You bought me exactly the distraction I need.

I start across the thick carpet. With purpose, I resist the urge to check and make sure no one has spotted me, that the gods' superior senses haven't given me up despite the bubble. I don't look anywhere but at my father, at the wounds on his cheek, until I'm nearly to him. Then I head toward the table with the Solstice Was on it.

The snarling face at the top of the scepter might be staring back at me. I hesitate with my hand over the metal of the staff. The moment I lay a finger on it, *bam*, it'll disappear. But the doors *out* of the Reading Room are heavy and closed. I'll need time to get over there and out, and suddenly everyone has gone quiet again.

"*Were* you working with anyone, Henry?" Rose asks, calmly.

But before Dad can answer, Set lets out another growl. He speaks in a way I can understand, and which I can hardly bear to hear. "I would never risk my house for such a specimen. He could not even protect his own kin, let alone wield the scepter."

I want to tell him how wrong he is, to defend Dad. Against being called a specimen, at least. He's doing this *for* us, for this whole stupid world, and he shouldn't be.

But Dad shakes his head, and says, "Prove that I can't protect her."

"I can," Bronson says, tone hushed. "If I choose. I can ensure her safety."

Dad drops his head. The first time he's given any sign that he didn't walk in here and sign up for this trial.

Enki cranes his head skyward, toward the dome, and the motion catches my eye. I'm afraid I'll see Oz moving around on the second floor. But he's not.

Who knows why a god lifts his head? Or why he lowers it? Enki's gaze swings from the second floor back down to Set. Enki thunders, "Is the *human* offering the Set *animal* a challenge?"

Legba chimes in. "If he is, I want to start the betting at two cities razed. Including this one."

Loki's responding laugh makes the floor tremble under my feet. They are off again, all talking, Set and Enki stalking closer to one another. Dad shaking his head again.

This is it. The best chance I'll get.

I wait until Bronson is talking to Rose again, both of them paying more attention to each other than the chaos in front of them. And I grab the staff.

Whirling, I dart across the space, hefting the surprisingly heavy metal scepter. I make it to the double doors, and pray they aren't as weighty as they look. I don't dare risk going back up to the way we came in.

I need to get *out* of the building before Oz can raise the alarm. But when I hit the doors where they join, nothing happens. Nothing. Happens. They don't even begin to budge. The sound of the impact is swallowed by the bubble around me. I try again, but the doors are as unmoving as stone, like I'm pushing against a fortress wall. To show myself is certain failure. Maybe even certain death. If not mine, then Dad's.

Think.

But I have. I thought my way right to this moment, and I have no good way to get out.

That's when they notice the Solstice Was is gone.

"*WHERE IS IT?*" booms Enki. He levels an accusatory glare that would cow a lesser being at Set.

Set, whose head tilts at an odd angle, and who whines. It's the angry whine of a hurt dog that's had enough and is about to fight back and take a bite out of someone.

Bronson stalks out from behind the podium, bashes the table with an open palm. "It was right here. You all saw it. No one has come or gone."

Rose steps out from behind her lectern. "We have to lock down the building." She strides across the floor toward me, no-nonsense in her business suit, as if the gods are nothing more than furniture. I step aside before she collides with me.

She knocks three times, *rap rap rap,* on the heavy wood. The doors lever open. They admit one operative, two. As she gives the order to seal the exits and post guards, Bronson tries to calm the arguing tricksters. But the shout is loud enough to stop everyone. "Shut the doors!"

It's Oz.

He's poised on a low wall within an arch on the other side of the staircase. He hurls himself into the air and lands on the main floor in a ridiculously graceful crouch, flanked by suspicious gods.

"Shut the doors!" he calls again.

Bronson starts toward him, and I hope he gets there in time to keep Oz from being the target of divine fury. But I can't stay and find out. I slip out before Oz can shout again at the gaping operatives to close the doors. Before he can tell them anything. Here's hoping he's too late to catch me or to get me caught by others.

The oracle's advice comes back to me, and it seems better this time. I bolt through the hallways, my only thought to keep on running. I hit the Great Hall at top speed. Navigating through the guards rushing toward the meeting, I can tell they don't know what's going on yet. The sound of angry gods spills out of the Reading Room behind me, urging me on.

I have to beat Rose's orders. Make it out of here before I'm locked inside. Even invisible, it would only be a matter of time before they find me. I'm not foolish enough to believe any different, not with a nearly endless supply of relics at their disposal. Speaking of which, the staff in my hand feels *wrong*, and I wish I didn't have to carry it. I'd love nothing more than to throw it into the ocean or leave it behind in a dark closet. But I can't let go.

Behind me, it's not just the riot of gods anymore. I hear Oz again. "You can't see her!" he shouts. "Bar the doors! She could still be here!"

"Crap," I mutter, desperate to speed up, but not able to without the risk of slamming into an operative hard enough to knock the Was from my grasp.

There are too many people here. Far too many. The only hope I have is to get to the main doors. An entrance is always left open when tricksters are visiting the Jefferson.

But as I approach, I hear the unmistakable sound of it being shut. I despair. I consider falling to my knees. I search my memory for hiding places in the Jefferson that might last long enough, but if I'm stuck here it's a lost cause.

"We have to find her!" Oz shouts. "She's using Vidarr's relic."

But Oz's shouts are followed by the most blissful sound possible. "Sorry about this!" Bree calls, and I turn to see her fling herself at Oz. She puts enough effort into it to almost take him down. She throws her arms around him, hanging on, as he struggles to get loose without injuring her. "Let. Me. Go," he orders her.

"No way," Bree says. "Where is Kyra? What's she doing?"

"I wish I knew," Oz says.

Tam rushes up to them. Bree's mom isn't far behind him, a cameraman trailing her. Tam stands uncertainly beside Oz and Bree. When Nalini reaches them, she says, "Bree, he's cute, but I don't understand..."

"Tam, I could use some help here," Bree says, and to her mother, "He's trying to do something to Kyra."

"I am not," Oz says. "I'm trying to keep her from getting herself in any deeper."

Bree smiles at him. It's a brittle smile. "No one's ever been able to do that."

Tam decides to jump in after all, grabbing Oz's arm where he's pushing against Bree. The three of them grapple, and other operatives move in to separate them.

But my friends have bought me one last shot. "Thank you, Bree Norville, goddess among humans," I say and dash around the group of them – still unseen, still gripping the effing Was scepter – and trip down one more flight of stairs to the lower level.

The old tourist exit down here is not used much. But the doors are still right where they always were. The red Emergency Exit sign above them is like a beacon. I slam into the first door I reach, and the alarm blares to life, but that doesn't matter because it flies open and I'm outside. I suck in a breath of air, and take off.

This time, I stop for nothing.

CHAPTER TWENTY-TWO

I barely make it to the commuter hub before the final coach of the day leaves the city. Designed to hold ten people, it's pulled by four strong workhorses. Now that I'm here, I realize getting on board may be tricky. But I breathe easier when I spot one last paying passenger hurrying our way.

When the coachman unlatches the door, I'm right behind her. Once I'm in, I hang onto a roof strap, and only when the coach springs into motion, do I wonder – and worry – about what Bree and Tam were doing at the Jefferson.

Please let them stay out of this from here on out. Maybe I can find a pay phone and make a call to Bree later, tell her to keep her head down, that I'll be back before long. It's not as if I can embark on establishing an alternate identity with a backpack full of clothes and a hundred bucks. It's not as if I intend to, anyway.

The other passengers are academics and lawyers, not people tapped into Society intrigue. I feel almost safe. Though I still can't believe I managed to get the Was scepter. Even with my other hand wrapped around that wrong-feeling metal, the buzz I lost in the heat of the action comes roaring back.

I heisted a relic from the middle of a Tricksters' Council meeting. *Me.* I wish someone was here to give me a high-five.

Well, Bree will later. And she deserves one of her own.

I wonder if the people around me knew what I was doing, whether they'd turn me in. That's how Bronson will trick Oz into believing I am not on the side of the angels. It's easy to make people doubt their own judgment, especially when they've already been burned. Ducking my head, I look out the window and scan the twilight sky, half-expecting Anzu to be up there. Circling.

He isn't.

I really might get away. But when I rotate the Was so that the jackal head faces me, snarling, it's hard for me to believe the worst is over.

At Alexandria, I barely make it off before the coachman slams the door shut on the cabin. He's already unhooking the line of tired horses, and the other occupants of the coach scatter, off toward Old Town and safer neighborhoods.

I have some time to kill before I can get another coach to take me further, and I want to change clothes and remove the shoe. While the invisibility is nice, I don't think I can hack a long distance journey that way. Not when my eyes are increasingly heavy, and every muscle aches. My lack of sleep nips at my heels.

I'll have to come back and buy a ticket for one of the long distance coaches parked nearby, but I have to decide where to go in the meantime. Up the street, the front window of a one-story office building is painted over, identifying it as the *Hell & Co Insurance Tavern*. Opposite it is a church that gives every appearance of being well funded, a fancy blue-and-white sign deeming it the Church of Two Worlds.

The thing about religion in a world full of gods is that it gets even more complicated. All of the religions are true and none of them are. Two worlds, without a doubt.

I make my way behind the church, where I shrug off my backpack and remove Vidarr's shoe. As soon as it leaves my foot I stagger and have to press a hand against the brick church to steady myself. With the relic gone, I can barely stand. I put both hands against the wall and fight to stay up, breathing deep.

Not yet. I haven't gotten away yet.

I root through the pack and find the Ramones T-shirt. It's not exactly clean, but I want to put it on anyway. For strength, for a reminder of why I'm doing this, to feel connected to Dad. I put on my jacket, and stash the shoe.

What to do with the Was is a bigger problem, now that anyone can see it. I take one of the plain black T-shirts Ann bought me and wrap it carefully around the headpiece, knotting it at the bottom. Then I slide it through a split in my backpack strap. It should come off as a walking stick, like I'm any average traveler. I strap on the pack.

Food, then ticket, then getaway and sleep. I can do this.

In the dark inside of *Hell & Co*, people are playing pool and dancing too close together for the metal pouring out of the speakers. I choose a corner table, and the waitress who comes over wears a short denim skirt and a T-shirt knotted at her waist. She has a tattoo of a cross at her throat.

"Tourist, I take it," she says. "We have one fish sandwich left. From not far away, so it shouldn't kill you."

"Sold."

She hesitates. "You have money to pay for it?"

I give her the twenty. "Keep the difference."

Every time the front door opens, I tense, ready to run.

The table I'm at used to be a desk. There are a few cubicle walls scattered around the room, too, and more desk-tables. A couple of people are wheeling around in ex-office chairs. It's a grim scene. When the sandwich comes, I wolf it down and then leave.

The dark street is deserted now, except for the coaching stand up the street. There's a waiting carriage, the one I need, with a handful of people gathered around it, luggage being loaded onto the top. Time to go.

The ticket stand has a couple of rows of bare bulbs around its edges to make it visible, one side white and the other red. I make my way up the sidewalk to the dead traffic light, staying alert for anything out of the ordinary. At the intersection, I stop to check the street. Nothing is coming, and I step out into the crosswalk.

When I reach the middle of the street, a familiar shape wings down through the dark and lands in front of me. Anzu, and he's angry.

He growls up a storm, and his long claws scrape the asphalt as he advances on me. I should let him drive me back. The people outside the coach are calling out in alarm. They'll take off without me, or refuse to sell a ticket to me, if they decide I come standard with a monster.

"Go," I tell him, planting my feet where they are, dead center in the faded white paint.

He roars and the air from it ruffles my hair. His breath heats my face and if I had the energy, I'd be terrified. OK, I am *still* terrified.

"I don't need a guard. I'm leaving. Thanks for the effort," I try to calm him.

Anzu scrapes forward and lowers his shoulder to nudge me with it – firmly. I push back against him with everything I have left. It's not much, but I won't give up now. I won't. Not when Dad's life hangs in the balance.

"What are you *doing*?" I ask.

I'm beginning to lose ground to him. He's screwing up everything.

But when he snarls again, louder, it's not at me anymore. He takes a step back, his lion's head shaking side to side with the mightiest roar I've heard from him yet. It's a warning that puts an instant chill in me. That is the sound of a predator warning away another predator. I look around and understand. "Oh no, oh no. No, no, no."

I'm standing in the middle of an intersection. It's where the street that runs to the ticket booth hits the main highway, the one we came in here on. A crossroads.

I'd bet anything that Anzu was trying to drive me out of it. The oracles told me to avoid them, and what did I do? Stumbled blindly into one, convinced what lay on the other side was salvation.

"Is he already here?" I ask Anzu, voice shaky. "Is it too late?"

But it's a stupid question, pointless if I have to ask.

Legba's laughter is the answer, the sound of him preceding the reality of his presence. He *pops* into view. Not in the poorly lit intersection one moment, right in front of me the next. I can still be surprised, though.

Bronson is with him.

I am *so* screwed. Instinct kicks in, the need to get out of here. But Legba reaches out an impossibly fast hand and catches the back of my jacket as I bolt. He hauls me back and tosses me at Bronson. Who grabs me and holds on tight.

"Deal with her," Legba says, and turns to Anzu. He holds his hands palm up like you do with a cop or a dog, to make nice. "Old one, it doesn't have to be this way. I have no quarrel with you."

Anzu issues an ear-splitting roar, and hurls himself toward Legba. The god easily steps aside. "Oh, I see it does."

Legba blocks Anzu's next attempt with his twined walking stick. When Anzu grabs it, Legba shrugs and lets Anzu's wings carry them both off the ground.

With Legba occupied, I might be able to get away after all. I struggle against Bronson's grip and kick at him with my boots. His training kicks in, though he must not have much call for it these days. He moves his legs out of the way before I can connect.

I try pulling his hair, but he just grabs my wrists, holds me still. He stands on my boots. I can't do anything but twist my torso and rage at him.

The sounds of Legba and Anzu above us aren't comforting. Legba is still laughing. Anzu is no longer roaring.

I try to think of fights I've seen, of how people win them. But I'm a runner. I'd use whatever dirty tricks it takes, but I don't know them. Legba played Mom. He played me, too. He was in on this with Bronson the whole time. Bastard.

Just like the man holding me. I consider trying to use my stripes again, flatten my palm against his hand, but the moment I say "*Ka*" he spins me around so my back is to his chest, and slaps his hand over my mouth.

He speaks near my ear. "Stop fighting and I won't have to do what you did to Oz, something I would never let you do to me. The boy is not nearly as understanding as I am, I'm afraid. But then, he's not your family."

That Oz isn't going to forgive me isn't news.

The people across the street – the few dumb enough to stay outside – are gazing into the sky at whatever Legba and Anzu are doing. No one tries to help me. No one even seems to notice Bronson.

I'd bet anything he's wearing some kind of invisibility relic too. Vidarr's shoe can't be the only one around.

Which means no one will report anything except two gods tussling. It'll make the Skeptics' next eyewitness column. But no one will see the head of the Society in the middle of it. And no one is coming to help me.

"Kyra," Bronson says, "I'm not upset with you. I'd have done the same thing. That's obvious. But I am going to need my relic back."

That's why he and Dad are so different. Why they hate each other, I realize. Bronson's not upset with me, because he only cares about one thing. He only cares about himself.

"Good girl," Bronson says, because I have stopped struggling. There's no way to, with how he's holding me. I'm pinned, stuck, captured. "This will all be over soon enough. I have plans." He's speaking with an urgency I can't quite understand, as he pulls out a knife and cuts the Was out of the strap. He shoves me away, and removes the T-shirt from the headpiece. He stares at it reverently.

"Plans to picnic by the firelight of the world going up in flames?" I ask. "What will keep the gods from killing *you*? Have you thought about that?"

"Besides the fact I'll be their favorite person, before they start trying to burn the Society?" Bronson shrugs. Smiles. He pets the head of the staff. "Your father has a death sentence for treason already. Now I have the scepter back, and no one saw me take it. In fact, everyone saw me presiding over a meeting when it disappeared. I'll be the only Society member at the execution. It's time for me to play everyone else the way we played you, Kyra."

The way we played you. Him and Legba.

"You gave me the stripes so I'd use them," I say. "All those grandfatherly talks were bull too?"

"I gave you everything I thought you'd need. Well done on stealing my key. That I didn't even know until I got it back."

"But why does it have to be Dad?"

"Henry's the only person who wouldn't let me out of this alive. That means it has to be him. I hope you can forgive me, when this is all over. You have to understand. I need to see Gaby. To talk to her. Find out why she did it. This time, she'll stay. We'll rebuild the world."

"Blood and doom," I tell him. "That's what Mom says comes with that ritual, with Dad's death. Blood and *doom*."

"No. I'll be a hero. Believe me. As soon as I have Gaby back, I'll end this. I'll raise the walls and put them all back to sleep. You'll see. I'm not a bad man, Kyra. Everything *will* be put to rights."

Anzu falls to the ground beside us, hard. There's a red gash along his side, gushing blood. His golden eyes fight, then drift closed.

"He's not dead." Legba lands beside us. He wipes his walking stick clean with the tail of his jacket. He doesn't even appear rumpled. "Just... sleeping for a while."

Bronson narrows his eyes, as if he's concerned Legba might have heard something he said to me. I *could* tell Legba about his crazy claim he intends to "raise the walls" – whatever that means – and put the gods back to sleep, but the last part is the only sane-ish idea Bronson's had. Legba is clearly no friend of mine. Besides, how can it be true? I think this is part and parcel of Bronson's evil genius. Self-justification. He believes he can do anything. By hell *and* company, maybe he *can* turn their lights out. Who knows? So I keep quiet on the matter.

"You lied to me–" I direct that to Legba.

"Shush," Legba says, grinning, "don't talk to your grandfather that way." He must know I wasn't. "The clock's still going and we'd best be on our way."

I move over beside Anzu. His sides shift up and down in a slow rhythm that tells me Legba isn't lying about him, at least. He *will* wake up.

"I'm not going anywhere with you," I say. "You're the monsters."

"Oh, sorry, you weren't invited. I meant we, as in, the two of us." Legba gestures to himself and Bronson. "Sorry if that wasn't clear. You *are* fun to have around, but…"

Bronson gives me a sympathetic, regretful look. So easy for him to conjure those, I never should have trusted a one of them. He says, "I can't bring you back with us, because it's better if people are occupied with looking for you. You've proven yourself too resourceful. In another day, this will all be over, and I'll welcome you with open arms. In the meantime, you stay safe out here, OK?"

"Like you care," I say.

"That's the strangest thing…" Legba speaks as he puts a hand on my grandfather's elbow. "He does. We'll be seeing you, Kyra Locke. Not sooner, but later."

In another blink the two of them are gone. It's just me and my unconscious monster and a few gaping coachmen on the street. I stumble across the intersection to the ticket window, but the red and white bulbs flick out. The men shake their heads, shut doors, disappear inside buildings. I could go to the bar, but the waitress doesn't deserve *this* added to her tab. Even if she'd consider it.

I make my way back to Anzu's side. I sink to my knees beside him and bury my face in his matted mane, and I weep like my father is already dead.

He may as well be. I've already failed him.

CHAPTER TWENTY-THREE

Justin Pearson hears the front door slam and rushes out of his bedroom. He's been waiting for hours to talk to Oz, the suspicions boiling in his brain like water in a pot. Like pages from books set ablaze, edges crinkling and disappearing in the heat. Like… He *needs* to talk to Oz or he's going to come up with even worse metaphors.

What he knows – or what he believes he's discovered – has made him jittery. He pounds down the stairs, only to slow at the bottom.

Ann is at the door, her hand on Oz's arm. Oz's expression is… dark. Darker than Justin has seen it in a long time. There's a uniformed operative with him, which is even odder.

Justin found the note his friend left for Ann before she did, about how he and Henry Locke's daughter were going out for a stroll. He doubted it was true – fresh air, after all, is overrated – but couldn't imagine why a cover story would be needed. Oz isn't stupid.

Nonetheless, maybe Oz *did* something stupid.

Earlier in the evening, the phone rang and Ann picked it up. Justin lingered at the office door to listen in, beginning to worry that they hadn't made it back yet. From her troubled murmurs of response and frown of concern afterward, he picked up that Oz and Kyra were somewhere they shouldn't be. Wherever it was apparently is bad enough to get Oz sent home with an escort who isn't Bronson. For that matter, where *is* Kyra?

Justin has bitten his tongue since they met her. Oz won't listen to anything he doesn't want to. He never has. But Justin can't quite trust her.

"I'll keep him right here, under lock and key," Ann tells the operative at the door.

His name is not one Justin has ever bothered to remember. The operative narrows his eyes as if she lost Oz once and so can't be trusted. But he nods. "Good evening, ma'am," he says, and leaves them.

Ann turns Oz to face her. "What were you thinking? You could have been hurt. *Both* of you."

Oz takes the abuse, stands there and accepts it. Which Justin can't stomach.

"He's not your son," Justin informs Ann. "You don't need to mother him. Oz, can I talk to you?"

Ann drops her hands and shoots them both looks that are darker than the one Oz wears. Justin has to stop himself from apologizing to her.

"No dinner for either of you," she says. "And don't even consider sneaking out. If something happens to that poor girl…"

At that, Oz snorts. "I'm sorry if I got you in trouble, Ann. But *she* doesn't need your sympathy. She's doing fine."

Ann is troubled by this, but also softens at Oz's acknowledgment that he put her in a tough spot. "I'll bring up a snack. But no dinner."

Now Justin is almost more curious about Oz's story than sharing what he's uncovered. *Potentially* uncovered. And only *almost* more curious.

"Come with me," Justin says, and indicates the stairs.

Oz does, that blank darkness on his face lingering all the way up them. Justin peers over his shoulder to check. He lets Oz into his room, all shelves and books and a desk covered in sheets of paper. It's the only place Justin ever feels at home these days.

"Bad day?" Justin asks.

"You could say that." Oz flops onto his back on Justin's bed. "She tricked me. Let me think I was helping her and showed me up like I'm some green operative." Oz shakes his head. "I can't believe it."

"You are some green operative," Justin says.

"Not helpful."

"I know something that might be," Justin says it with care. He doesn't want to overpromise. But he realizes he might be framing it incorrectly and tries again. "It will make everything worse, though, if I'm right."

Oz is quiet for a long stretch, and Justin assumes he's considering whether he wants another problematic thing to deal with. This all started when they went along on the seizure operation for Henry Locke, at Enki House.

The sage showed Justin a book in Bronson's office, a book that Bronson was hiding there. A journal logging top secret deliberations, it turns out. Justin found it in the exact spot the vision showed Bronson stowing it, behind a collection of reference volumes for relics that rarely show up on this side of the world. In other words, where it would never be accidentally found... and where it wasn't supposed to be kept. But also not in such an obscure location that the hiding would be perceived as intentional if it were found. An oversight, a mistake. Where Bronson placed the book would make any accusation he's concealing it an easy thing to deny.

No one would be looking for it on a regular basis. These are the kinds of records that would be referred to, say, when a new Society head takes over.

Oz still hasn't made up his mind and answered. Justin will have to prod him to a decision. "Oz," he asks, "Did Kyra by any chance try to steal the relic? The Solstice Was?"

Oz sits up. He wears a grin so sharp it cuts. He's angry. "Ann told you, didn't she? I don't need the knife twisted. Trust me."

"No," Justin says. "No one told me. That's what I've been trying to tell *you*."

"She did steal it," Oz says. The grin is gone. He seems exhausted in its absence. But also still angry. "Wherever she is, she has it. And it's my fault. They might kick me out for this. They should."

Justin knows better than anyone how lost Oz would be without the Society. "No. Bronson won't do that. He'll understand."

"Maybe," Oz says. "Now, what is this mysterious thing about her that you're telling me?"

Justin considers. It might be best if he kept it to himself. He doesn't want to put Oz in a bad position. A worse one. Oz avoided saying her name just now.

Oz climbs to his feet. "Don't you dare protect me. Tell me what it is."

"OK," Justin agrees. Though he doesn't feel as sure as he did before. He pulls out his big leather notebook and hands it to Oz, holding it open to the page where he copied the text. "Read this."

Oz frowns, but takes it and scans the lines. He's still frowning when he looks up at Justin. "What does it mean?" he asks.

"Think," Justin says.

Oz shakes his head. "I'm too tired. You're the one who does that better anyway. Just tell me."

"Fine. It's a record of the deliberations among the board after the Awakening, about what emergency actions they should take."

"I gathered that much. Five people involved, right?"

"To prevent possible ties during voting," Justin says.

One of the people in the meeting was his mother. He misses her. But his dad, well, his dad has issues with a son that prefers the library to the battle. He's better off here.

"So?" Oz asks. "Everyone was in agreement, right? Seal the doors, then make a display of the most powerful god we could capture. That's what they did."

"Yes and no." Justin begins to worry he's leapt too far. If Oz doesn't see it... But he goes on. "There was one person arguing against closing the doors to the Heavens and the Afterlife. The board split in two, as you know – half of them taking care of one door, and the rest the other."

"In secret locations known only to them, for safety. Yes, I know. What am I missing? Who was arguing against it and why?"

Oz had skimmed the copied down text, instead of reading it. It would have saved some time if he'd just told Justin that. But Justin thinks of Oz waiting while he makes a mess of target practice with his bow, patiently giving Justin time to improve... some... and he pushes aside his frustration. They each have their strengths.

"William Bronson," Justin says, keeping his voice down, as if the walls can see and hear. When, if the walls could, he'd already be busted for the time he's spent rooting around in Bronson's office.

"What are you saying?" Oz asks, but Justin can tell by his tone that he's made the same jump.

"That maybe Henry Locke took the relic, but his motives were more complicated. Maybe he intended to foil a plot."

Oz asks, "Why not accuse Bronson then? And why would he take the fall after all that?"

"I don't know," Justin says. "That's the part I was hoping you could help with. You're the one who understands people."

"No, I'm not," Oz says. "What would we do about it, if you're right?"

"I don't know that either. I just... I expected you to know what we should do."

Oz closes his eyes for a long moment. Finally, he opens them. "It might not matter. Kyra has the scepter. She took off with it. Gods only know where she is by now. And she has Vidarr's shoe."

"Too powerful to keep wearing for very long," Justin observes. By the sudden lift of Oz's head, he can tell that's news to his friend. Oz really should study more. "She'd go to her friends, wouldn't she?" Justin asks.

Oz shrugs a single shoulder. "They were at the Jefferson... Maybe she arranged for them to be there, but I got the impression they didn't know where she was."

"Interesting," Justin says.

"Moderately," Oz admits, grudgingly. "What was Bronson's argument back then?"

"Now *that* is interesting. He was a proponent of the argument that we shouldn't risk antagonizing the gods. That he should be sent as an envoy to negotiate, before the emergency protocols were undertaken."

"But no one thought mediation would work," Oz says. "The gods are too powerful. We saw that immediately."

"I'm so proud," Justin holds a hand to his heart, "you *did* read something."

"Hilarious."

"The transcript is telling," Justin says, "but it's not enough. It's not proof. He might have just held a different view."

"But he knows, doesn't he? Where the Afterlife door is?"

Justin nods. "It doesn't explain why, though. Why he disagreed back then, why he'd do this now. Any clue from the trial today?"

"None," Oz says, "and I was there. All we have is a theory."

"You know what we do with a theory," Justin says, already pushing his notebook into a leather messenger bag.

"Humor me," Oz says. His tone is dry, more like normal.

Justin was right to tell him. That's a relief. Not that what's ahead of them is going to be easy. The dark might be gone for now, but that doesn't mean it's been replaced by light. In Justin's experience, the lesson of history is that darkness is never far away. And it is *never* easily dealt with.

"We prove or disprove it," Justin says.

"That's what we do," Oz agrees. Then, "How?"

CHAPTER TWENTY-FOUR

Morning finds me and Anzu sacked out a few feet apart in the alley behind the church. Sleep was fitful, not so shocking considering the arrangements. I had the presence of mind to use my backpack as a pillow, and it turns out an injured god throws off a lot of heat. A fire would have made less.

The night before, after Anzu roused, weak, I pulled myself together enough to realize we had to get out of the middle of the road. The last thing we need is pictures of a girl and her monster circulating or rumors about the same (more than there already will be). I considered putting on Vidarr's shoe, but the idea of it made me too tired to move Anzu.

And that's what had to happen. I tried helping him up by pushing under his wing. I was beyond worried about the wound, which was not healing, not even closing. But, after his golden eyes reopened from the pain of my messing around with his wing, I decided on a different strategy. I walked away from him.

I made it three steps before I looked back and found him struggling to his clawed feet. He shook his wings and his head, and came after me. He was listing to one side, but steady enough. I managed to lead him to our resting spot.

But now day has broken, and the god has yet to awaken. I stand and lean over – cautiously, because I'm under no illusion that we're suddenly best friends – to check out Anzu's side.

I experience a wave of dismay. The gash Legba left him with continues to ooze blood. The pavement beneath him is soaked a deep crimson from it, as if we completed a messy sacrifice back here during the night. The gash has pulled wide enough that the edges are visible despite the plumage that would normally hide them. Anzu's skin is not fragile baby stuff. There's no putting stitches in this guy, and he's already lost more blood than would be possible for any non-divine creature to survive.

And that's the question, isn't it? Why isn't his magic taking care of it? I'd expect a god's mutant healing factor to be off the charts. Any god's.

I am keenly aware I need to get moving, get back to the city by whatever means are available, and figure out *something* to do next. As out of it as Anzu is, slipping away from his guard duty wouldn't be so hard. The guys from the night before might not recognize me in the daylight. I could get a ticket on the first coach back in. Saturday's a light schedule, but it's a holiday. People should be chomping to go to the city for the big solstice revels on the Mall tonight. I have to hope whatever transport there is can get me there fast enough. I need to warn Mom which team Legba is on, and Dad doesn't have much time left.

I'm at a loss. I'm lost.

But.

Anzu may be a monster, *and* he may have been assigned to watch over me, *and* he may not have the best reputation among the gods. But he tried to fight off Legba *for me*. So I dig out a fresh T-shirt, and wet it down in a puddle of leftover rainwater. Then I wipe the damp cloth as gingerly as I can along Anzu's side.

A fierce growl rumbles from his throat, as he rouses at the pressure. Gold flickers to life as his heavy eyelids part.

"I'm being gentle," I say, my best attempt at a brave face for the unwilling patient. "And I promise I don't taste good."

Anzu's response is to crane his head back and snap his giant jaws together. At me. I jump back, no longer touching the slash. "I'm attempting to help you here. So, cooperate." I'd add *or else*, except I have no idea whether he understands and if he does, he'll know there is nothing to back it up.

After a tense moment with him staring at me, and me quivering back at him, he lowers his head to the pavement. He doesn't shift his wing to prevent me access to the wound. I choose to take this as an invitation. He grumbles when I touch him again, but lays prone.

"This might sting," I say. He seems to understand. At least, sometimes he does. "But I need to get a better look."

I use the T-shirt to hold back feathers and block the sun as I squint into the long bloody gash. I'm not a first aid expert, but we've all had basic training. A necessity when you live in the city, just in case. Magic aside, it strikes me as odd that the wound is behaving as if it's still fresh.

"It's almost like you were poisoned, champ." The answering rumble might be a protest at the nickname. "I mean, mighty and fearsome Anzu."

But his throat makes the noise again. A grumble this time. As if he's saying, *No stupid, not that.*

"Poison?" I ask.

A sound less like a protest issues from him, and he sighs against the pavement.

I keep talking as I move in for another look, with not a clue how I'd extract poison from his bloodstream if that's the problem. "Weird," I say. He grumbles more. "The way it's not closing at all. No anticoagulant or closure agent, I mean."

And then I spot it. Deep in the center of the seeping wound is a shard of something yellow-white that should have worked its way out by now if it's not one of his own bones. *Bone.* That's exactly what it is – and not his, either. It has to be from Legba's cane.

"I think I might know what's in there. But... I'm going to have to reach in there to get it. OK?" I smooth a nervous hand along his side above the wound. As if I'm the bosom companion of Anzu the Sumerian God, and he trusts me completely. As if anyone does.

I so wish I had an extra set of hands, and that they belonged to a nurse. Also, some food. I'm lightheaded, but it might be from the situation. I visualize his giant fangs. Immediately, my capacity to be careful and alert revives.

"You're going to have to help me out." I scoot around to Anzu's front, so he can see where I am every stage along the way. I hold the T-shirt at his lips. "Will you maybe chew this instead of my head off? I'm going to get you all fixed up… but I need my head. I have to get back to the city. Even if I probably can't fix what's going on there."

His golden gaze takes my measure and seems to find me lacking in every way. I'm a thousand years shy – at best – of anyone this guy can take seriously. But then Anzu's jaws lever open. I push the T-shirt in before I can wuss out. He bites down, shredding the fabric in one chomp.

My hand hovers over the wound, and Anzu tenses beneath me. "Easy," I say.

I reach into the blood and grab for the shard. It slips through my fingers. A louder rumble.

"One more try." I wipe my hands on my jeans, smearing blood everywhere, and find the tiny bit of bone peeking up. I imagine my fingers closing around it, lifting it out. The alley drops away. Anzu falls with it. I see only that shard I have to get out…

When I'm certain I could do this with my eyes closed, that I've memorized its precise location, I reach in…

And I get it.

I start to cheer, but Anzu's growl mutes my triumph. He stumbles and rumbles onto his feet, tossing the T-shirt to one side.

While he's doing that, I examine the shard. Big. As long as my hand, narrow and sharp. I wipe it on my dirty jeans and stick it into the top of my backpack before Anzu can demand it, the way people keep their appendix or gall bladder or some other gross part they had removed. It's my battle scar as much as his.

I'm pretty sure I just collected my first relic, though I have no idea what it does. Except make this Sumerian god far weaker than he should be.

Anzu is on his back two feet, casting a long shadow over me. His wings test the air. He's looking stronger already.

"Don't suppose you can do that handy teleporting trick like our not-friend Legba?" I ask. "I kid. You can fly instead, so who needs teleportation?" I hesitate. "If you could stay back here until I get a coach, I'd consider it a favor. See you around."

I tell myself that holier-than-thou (really) molten gold gaze is agreement. Fully aware of what a scary mess I must be, I still can't risk changing clothes and trying to clean off in front of him. Recovering animals are hungry ones. He has to be at least a million times more starving than me. Making do, I wipe the worst of the gore on my jeans off with the destroyed-forever T-shirt, put on my leather jacket, and smooth a hand through my hair. I shoulder my pack, and head out to the street without a longer goodbye.

The waitress from the night before nearly crashes into me, heading toward the church as I emerge from the alley. Across the street, *Hell & Co* is dark. She wears a long blue and white robe that shows off her cross tattoo.

She doubletakes. "Figured you'd be gone by now. You had the look of someone passing through."

"And I didn't figure you were part of this sect," I counter. "Guess we were both off."

She shrugs. That's clearly my issue, not hers. I ask, "What do you guys believe in, anyway?"

"That the apocalypse has already begun," she says, without hesitation. "But we behave as though it hasn't. Like every action matters."

"What's the difference?"

"You'll see someday," she says. "Everyone will."

"Right." They may not be far wrong. Someday may not be a luxury we get. I hope she's right about our actions mattering, though.

"Good luck," she says, and finishes her trip into the church. She stops at the door and peeks back at me.

It's my turn to shrug. "I'll need it," I call, and continue on. My destination, the ticket booth, is open… but the only carriage in front of it is another long distance one like I missed last night. Those go out from here, not into the city.

I keep my head down as I approach. The minute I look up, the guy inside starts shaking his head. The squarish beard he sports is familiar. Which means he was here last night.

"No thanks," he says. "We have the right to decline dangerous passengers."

I pull out the hundred, press it to the glass that separates us. "I just want to get back into the city. Please? You can have the extra."

He doesn't relent. In fact, he leans to the barred mouthpiece and says, "Not enough money in Alexandria. Besides, no coaches for five hours. It's Saturday."

"But it's solstice," I say. If there's a coach, maybe I can deal with its driver directly.

"Right, one coach going in tonight because of that. Usually none. But no. Way."

He yanks down the shade fixed to the inside of the glass, the word CLOSED printed on it. I bang my head gently against the window. Then I slide down the side of the booth to the ground. I pull up my knees and rest my head on my arms. My hair falls in front of my face.

I don't care who sees me sitting here, defeated. Gore girl, they'll call me in the broadsheets.

Though it's not likely they'll call me anything. No one talks about screwups that don't even make it to the same city as the showdown.

Bronson will do it. Kill my father, open the door, bring back his Gabrielle, and expect me to live with them, happily. If Mom's with them, if they get her mother to lure her, I might have to agree. While Dad's gone forever. I will spend every day of the future with the knowledge *I* was the one supposed to stop it. And that I didn't manage to.

The sound that reaches me first is people shouting warnings, "Go inside!" "Don't look at him!" But there are only a few. Alexandria sleeps in. It's not enough voices to give me reason to look up.

Then comes the roar – Anzu's maximum volume one. Nearby.

I raise my head and spot him right away.

In the middle of the street, Anzu shakes out his mane and his feathers, for all the world like a dog shaking off nerves or water. His gold gaze makes me want to flee him. But I can't quite move. He cranes his head back to the sky and roars again and again.

A sudden strong breeze whips my hair around my face. I climb to my feet. Storm clouds gather above us.

Anzu roars once more and the winds pick up strength. The storm clouds churn, thicker and darker. No rain falls.

"Nice meeting you," I say into the mouthpiece to the guy in the ticket booth. He's raised the shade so he can take in the show. "By which I mean the opposite."

Because I am almost certain Anzu is arranging us a ride. I had forgotten he's a storm god.

I walk into the street, but stop before I quite reach him – I'm afraid I've gotten it wrong.

Finally, he lowers his head and gives me a long, flat look. Then he turns his back to me. He has to be bending his monster's legs, I think, so I can reach.

Advancing slowly, I raise my arms above the feathers and begin to stretch them around the knotted mane at his neck. I give him time to pull away, if this isn't what he meant for me to do. But as soon as my hands are mostly around him, his wings beat twice and the winds grab hold of us as we rise. I get a better hold on his fur just as my feet leave the ground.

I cling tight as we sail on rough currents, through loud thunder and bright lightning, heading toward D.C.

CHAPTER TWENTY-FIVE

Anzu doesn't smell like a bird or a lion – not that I know what either of them smell like up close and personal – but instead a combination of non-human scents. Like the wet ash of a fireplace drenched in rain, a hint of stone beneath. Ancient and scary, in other words. The dried blood on my shirt is reminiscent of crumbled earth.

When we get close I realize that "city" is not a specific enough destination. He might fly us to the Houses, straight to the top of Enki's ziggurat. That's someplace I do not want to try to navigate on my own. Someplace I'm sure Society operatives would capture me – though not before Anzu injures (or worse) a few of them. My quarrel is with my grandfather, so far as I know. Not the rest.

Though at least one of them has a reason to quarrel with me. Oz.

But I probably *won't* have to face him. My hope is that he's on lockdown for a few days, a hand slap but nothing too much worse than that. Bronson might be bastard enough to risk the world for his feelings, but surely he wouldn't imprison his ward. Not for assisting me. I'm still his granddaughter. As he so kindly reminded me while taking back the relic and confirming his plans to execute my father.

"Oracle Circle," I shout over the wind, when the buildings start getting familiar. "I need to go to Oracle Circle."

We're on the outskirts of Georgetown. I concentrate on an image of the market, pushing it out on the off chance he can pick up the signal if I broadcast it at him. I'm still unsure how much of what I say he comprehends.

I breathe somewhat easier as he adjusts the angle of approach. The Circle isn't far from the Houses, but we're no longer headed *toward* them. The tall trees that cover the market come into view, and Anzu angles lower. We are about to make a very unsubtle arrival – but it's too late to do anything about that.

I brace for a jolt during the landing, but he swoops down and his wings lower us gently... right in the middle of the sidewalk. The old metro stop entrance is in front of us, the granite bowl around the top engraved with a poem. I see the words "sweet and sad," and they might be written for me. I made it back into the city, but defeated and alone. Now I have to face my mother and break bad news to her. I can't imagine she'll take it well. Not from me.

Tourists and townies alike surround us to *ooh* and *ah* at Anzu. Camera shutters go off *click click click*. Do these people not stop to consider that this is a *god* and that he *might* be hungry and recovering from a wound?

OK, probably not. I tense and wait for him to unleash a roar at them, if not something worse.

He only shrugs his feathered shoulders. When I hang on, he does it again.

I get the hint, and hop down to the concrete. As soon as he's free of my weight, he launches back into the air and settles into a lazy orbit high overhead.

That leaves the onlookers focused on me. "Who are you?" "How did you win his favor?" "Are you alright?" "She doesn't *look* alright." The barrage of questions and attention is the last thing I need. Putting my hand up to block the cameras, I inform them, "I'm no one. Promise," and stride as quickly as I can toward the market. Some follow, but most are too easily distracted. Hitting the maze of stalls, I wind through them in a pattern designed to lose anyone not familiar with the intricacies.

When I come out on the side where the street we found Mom is, I stop to verify my success. I definitely don't want to lead anyone else to her door. But no one is paying any notice to me. A glance into the sky tells me Anzu remains up there. Maybe I'm wrong. Maybe he doesn't need food at all. A disturbing thought.

How little we still know about the gods is amazing, really. But it's not as if they'll hold still for taxonomy and lab work or hand someone a book that says Secrets of Divinity Within.

Besides the fact no one's tailing me, there is one other piece of welcome news. The line of creepy oracles must be hard at work, because no doors open or curtains pull back as I head up the street. Mom's red door is ahead. The closer I get, the more I dread this. We finally had a semi-calm moment together, if under terrible circumstances. Other than that, the only way I've seen her in years is upset. My visit is going to make her that, at a minimum.

I raise my hand, figuring my knuckles won't make it to the wood. That she'll open the door again, sensing me outside. But that doesn't happen.

So I knock.

Nothing.

I knock again.

Finally, I test the knob. It slides in my palm, the door easing open. That same darkness from the other day waits within.

"Mom? It's me. Mom, you here?" I call as I go inside.

I hurry through the black of the hallway. No light glows at the end this time. The whole house is dark, and I determine as quickly as I can without light – fumbling at the wall switches does nothing, the power's out – that she isn't here. No one is. What's more, the house *feels* empty. For no reason I can quite explain I begin to suspect that she has left, not that recently, and that she never intends to return. The house has an air of utter abandonment.

But where would she go? Another oracle flophouse *or* Bronson could have her already... I should check the market again to be sure she's not working. My instincts haven't been so accurate lately. I rush back out and, after a moment's internal debate, decide to lock the door behind me. Surely Mom has a key if she *does* plan to come back. This will keep would-be squatters away in case.

I turn and stare straight at Oz.

He's about ten feet away, and he's seen me too. No doubt about that. I can't read anything in his face. He's in his full uniform, and so is Justin, behind him. They're probably on assignment to bring me in, like they were the day I met them. I do the first thing that occurs to me – I take off in the opposite direction.

"Kyra!" he shouts. "Stop!"

I check over my shoulder. He's chasing me, and that spurs me faster. This is *not* good. It also probably means Bronson *doesn't* have Mom, and so she could be anywhere. I dart into an alley, intending to make my way back to the market after I've lost them. Mom doesn't know Legba's against her and with the prophecy about Dad… I can't risk missing her because I didn't look hard enough.

Anzu gives no sign of a plan to dive down and rescue me. He stays high overhead.

"*Now* he decides to keep his distance," I mutter, hooking into another alley, and then toward the Circle. I'll go to the stall the fake fire hands woman was in, the one who told me where Mom was last time. She might be able to guide me to her again.

Running through the market would draw attention, so I walk as quickly as I can without raising alarm. I'm grateful, for once, that there's such a ragtag clientele. They probably assume my bloody jeans are some sort of solstice costume. I reach the row where the lady was, scan for her and jerk at the sound of my name.

"Kyra!" It's Oz, far too close. He barely has to raise his voice for me to hear him over the hum of conversation.

Torn, I hesitate. I need to visit that stall.

That's when Bree and Tam emerge from it. The same woman *is* there, wearing a loose white top. She has her hand on Bree's shoulder, her expression sympathetic.

And... a hand closes around my arm.

I. Am. So. Stupid. I shouldn't have let Bree and Tam being here shock me into stopping. I pull away, trying to get free. Oz is saying, "Stop fighting me," which of course makes me thrash with greater intention. His grip on my arm tightens.

"Bree!" I call. "Bree! Help me!"

Justin approaches from the same direction Oz came. He raises a hand to wave off a concerned market patron, a thin fifty-something man.

"We're LARPing," Justin says. When the man frowns, he clarifies, "Playing a game."

"No, we're not," I say.

Despite Justin and Oz's Society uniforms, the guy gives all indication of buying it.

"I have a niece who does that," he says. "Nice costumes."

"Bree," I say, because it's clear the bystander is no help. He's already leaving. "Please. Don't let them take me in. There's no time."

Bree finishes her journey to us, crosses her arms over her chest. "I should let him take you, after that stunt you pulled. And not telling me what you were up to." She sighs. "Let her go," she says.

To my amazement, Oz does.

"What is going on?" I ask.

Tam jumps in to answer. "I'm as surprised as you are, but apparently Oz and Justin may be willing to help us."

"*You*," Bree says, "willing to help *you*. Despite everything, and by 'everything' I mean a story I would like to know, because Society boy over there won't cough up the details." She pauses, and her eyes sweep down my body. Her irritation melts away. "Whose blood is that? It can't be yours, or you wouldn't be standing here. Kyra, tell me it's *not* yours."

"I had the same question," Oz says.

His inflection provides no hint of whether he's bothered by the idea it's mine in the least. I seriously can't imagine why he'd be willing to help me, after how I tricked him.

"It's not mine. It's Anzu's," I say, lifting my chin to indicate the sky. "A lot has happened in the last twenty-four hours."

"You can tell us all about it," Bree says.

But Oz shakes his head. "No," he says, lowering his voice, "we have to get her out of here. There are people here who could make a fortune off a cloth with that much divine blood on it. The gods don't take too kindly to those who try and sell it."

"OK," Bree says. "My place, then?"

Oz nods to her. To me, he says, "You can't always run from people when you have unfinished business with them."

"I don't…"

"Don't worry, we'll finish it later," he says.

Bree cuffs him. "Stop scaring her."

But it's too late, because he's right. Ours is a conversation I intended to put off forever and the promise that won't be possible frightens me more than pulling that bone fragment out of Anzu's side did.

Bree's mother turns out to be at home. The middle of the day is a prime sleeping time for her when she's on the late or early shift. Given that it's the solstice holiday *and* that there's a top secret – but leaked to people with sources as good as hers – Society execution planned for later that evening, she'll be working most of the night. Though being a workaholic ensures that she's a sound sleeper, it's for the best if she doesn't know anyone except Bree is here.

The rest of us wait around the side of the house as Bree goes to check it out, with a promise to come back to us with a report on whether the coast is clear.

Tam leans out to watch her head inside. If I'm not mistaken, something weird is going on – if not with them, then with *him*. He has barely taken his eyes off her, and isn't even trying to pick arguments with Oz and Justin. Honestly, Justin is the only one who seems to be acting normal, besides Bree. Oz is full-on grudging, not that I blame him.

Far more troubling is that my lack of sleep the night before and the excitement of the morning are catching up with me. My eyes droop, that gritty need-to-sleep feeling contained in every blink, and I find that I'm leaning on the wall for more support than I should need.

Tam squints at me. "You OK, Kyra?"

I nod. Grunt. "Uh-huh."

"She's exhausted," Oz corrects, and before I can protest, he puts his hands on my shoulders and presses down. "Go on, sit. We'll get you up when Bree comes back."

I barely have the energy to protest the suggestion. I don't have to though, because Bree returns. "What's going on here?" she asks, clearly surprised by the fact Oz is touching me.

"I wish I could explain," I say.

"She needs a shower and a nap," Oz says.

"She needs to fill us in first," Bree says.

"I agree, but I don't think she can," he counters.

"Fine," Bree says.

Oz offers me his arm in support, and I take it. "You need to know," I say, "Bronson has it. The Was. And he's working with Legba." I pause. "Yes, that's everything big. Oh, except Dad is supposed to be the subject of a prophecy. If he dies, bad things will happen. That's why I was looking for Mom."

They gape at me.

"Theory proven," Justin says.

Oz says, "We'll have plenty to do while Kyra gets her strength back. Sounds like she's going to need it."

"Why?" I ask, low.

"Why do you need your strength?" he asks.

Tam slips past us to walk beside Bree, the two of them exchanging an odd look. Justin is rattling off something about how the next things we need to figure out are the *where* of the evening's events and the elements of the ritual and...

"Why are you being nice to me, after what I did to you?" I ask Oz.

"Because what happened was my fault. First rule of being an operative: see what is really there, not what you want to," he says, one shoulder lifting in a shrug. "I should have known better than to trust you."

"Oz," I start.

"Don't," he says.

For once, I obey someone's orders. I keep quiet, but all I want is to apologize. I want him to trust me again. But I *don't* ask.

I am well aware I don't deserve it.

CHAPTER TWENTY-SIX

I don't know how many hours later, I stumble blearily out of Bree's bed. She's already done some haunting sketches of the sages that are pinned to the wall, their eyes rendered in black ink. I leave their flat gazes behind and go in search of the others.

Nalini must have left for work already, because they make no effort to keep quiet. Heading downstairs, I track the sound of overlapping voices and someone frantically flipping pages in a book. The leftover blur from my heavy sleep fades by the time I locate them in the living room.

The page turning is Justin, kneeling in front of the glass coffee table. Bree peers over his shoulder at some sort of heavy leather journal or notebook. There's another thick bound volume that could have come from my family's reliquary beside that one, and they are going back and forth between the two. Tam looms over them wearing a frown I recognize – he's thinking something over, not clear how he feels about it yet.

"The question is still *where*," Justin says. "Only a handful of people know, and they're all either a) inaccessible on this timeframe or b) not likely to tell us."

"Where what?" I ask.

Faces swivel in my direction. Bree takes me in, and says, "I'm making you some food. Justin, bring her up to speed."

Tam says, "I'll help you," and trails Bree out of the room.

I move closer to the table. There's an illustration on a page faced by tiny text. It depicts a vast plain populated by strange shapes with horns and wings and extra limbs that must be gods and their attendants, interspersed with wispier forms that must be ghosts or humans or some intersection of the two.

"What's the problem?" I pause. "Immediate problem, I mean."

Justin is quiet for a moment, peering up at me. He takes his hand off the book in front of him, and stands. "I just want you to know that I'm helping you because it's the right thing. Not because I like you."

"Well," I pretend not to be thrown by his words, "at least you're direct."

"I don't know what you did to Oz, but whatever it was… he didn't deserve it."

"I didn't have a choice."

"There's always a choice." Justin shakes his head. "The thing is, he'd probably have helped if you'd just asked him to."

I take two steps closer. "I don't blame you for sticking up for him. I'd do the same if we were talking about

Bree. But... I did it *because* of that. I was afraid he *would* help. He'd be in way more trouble then, wouldn't he?"

"Don't be stupid," he says. "Would either of us be here if staying out of trouble was our top priority? Oz isn't the type who can stand by. *I* am, maybe, maybe not. I'm not sure. But I know *he'd* never forgive himself. Bronson doesn't deserve his loyalty, but neither do you."

Ducking around him, I sink onto the couch. "I'm doing the best I can. Everything I've done, I thought was right at the time. But I've been overmatched every step of the way. Legba prodded me. Bronson too. I'm not making excuses." He gives me a look like, *Come on.* "OK. I'm not *only* making excuses. It's the truth. And... I don't see we can outsmart a god who walks through all time."

Justin turns to face me. "We can't. *But* it seems to me that he's probably playing and prodding Bronson too – at least a little. He wouldn't have bothered with you otherwise, if you were just a means to an end. Your father would have served well enough. There's something else going on here. We don't even understand why Enki was willing to be involved. Oz took a message to Set for Bronson, the other afternoon when he was being an errand boy. It's safe to assume Set and Legba are both colluding with Bronson, even if Enki isn't."

"Great." I rake a hand through my hair, slightly damp from the quick shower Bree forced me to take before I collapsed. The jackal face of the Was – Set's face – snarls in my memory. "So, immediate problem?"

Justin waves to the book that's more like a journal. "These are notes I slipped out of Bronson's study.

They're from the meeting that the Society had after the Awakening, to decide what protocols to put into action."

"I've never really understood that," I say. "How can there only be one door to the Heavens and one to the Afterlife?"

"There aren't in the natural order, but there are rituals that can make one door stand in for all the ways into and out of them. If you seal those doors, it takes away the gods' ability to resurrect. Just like us, when they die, they go into the Afterlife. There's no door needed, because death is a state of being that takes you there automatically. But gods are powerful enough to walk out of death, if there are doors to pass through. By making a single door and sealing it, we made sure no way exists for them to do that until it's reopened. It also prevents them from being able to make a new door anywhere they want. So long as that one remains sealed, the Afterlife confines any god that ends up there. Same for the Heavens, though they can't even visit there now. Even though reopening the doors isn't easy, the locations are a closely-guarded secret."

"So, on the bright side, we're only looking for one spot."

"Yes. But only the five people who were in that meeting know the locations that were used. They might be recorded somewhere, but not anyplace we're going to get into. And I am certain that the ritual tonight has to be done at the exact location of the door to the Afterlife, the underworld – whatever you want to call it. That door is the one they want to unseal, which means it's where the sacrifice has to happen."

"Hm." I know as I say it that Justin will have thought of this already, but, "It has to be nearby."

"Not really," he says. "If he has Legba's help and given some of the relics here, they could easily move your dad anywhere in the world. It would take hardly any time at all."

"That is not good news. We need an invisible door that we have no way to locate and it's" – I check the clock on the wall – "7 o'clock. Legba said solstice is midnight. That was the deadline he gave me. If he was telling the truth about it."

"I see she gets it," Bree says as she wafts back in, a long green dress flowing around her legs. I notice her shyly smile at Justin – so does Tam and he is definitely *not* smiling about it. I *will* find out what else I've missed in the last couple of days. Apparently, lots.

Justin says, "Given how rituals tend to work, he probably was. That's right at the exact moment of solstice, when the sun is at its furthest point."

Bree sits down beside me, hands me a plate with takeout Chinese on it. Nalini's rarely home to cook, and so their kitchen is always packed with half-full containers from corner groceries and the few restaurants left around the city. I begin to inhale the food. Noodles, chicken, water chestnuts. Calories. All of these things are good.

She raises an eyebrow at me.

"Starving," I say, "and it's better than *Hell & Co.*"

"I do not even want to know what that means," she says.

"It's a bar," Tam puts in.

"You just know everything," Bree says.

I can't tell if she's exercising her right to sarcasm or not.

"Not everything," Justin points out. "Or he could solve our problem."

"We're not giving up," Tam says.

Bree nods, approving, "Of course we're not."

"Five hours." I put the plate down on the floor. "Let's think about it this way. If Legba is involved and Bronson and Set – you said Set is a definite too, right?" Justin nods. I continue, as if we're not discussing disrupting the plots *of gods*. "And Dad has to be there. Are there many relics that could transport Dad and Bronson at the same time?"

"No, but a god could," Justin says.

"Point. But think about it," I say, "if you were the Society… Scratch that, you *are*. So, where would *you* put the doors?"

"We know they're far apart," Justin says.

I wind noodles around my fork. "And we know there are two of them. But we also know they wouldn't risk putting them just anywhere. They'd want them somewhere they consider a stronghold, somewhere they can protect effectively if needed."

"True," Justin says. "We could probably narrow it down to cities with a big Society presence."

"You can narrow it down further than that," the voice belongs to Oz, who lazily strides in, as if he didn't slip in the back door without alerting a single one of us.

Bree has a hand on my forearm, so she was even more startled than me. "Sorry," she says, lifting her fingers. "Jumpy."

"What do you mean?" Justin asks Oz.

"Well, Bronson has given strict instructions to every single operative on duty tonight that I believe will solve your riddle."

"How long were you out there listening?" I ask.

Oz meets my eyes. "Long enough."

I have no idea if that includes me and Justin talking about him or not. Probably not. I hope not.

Tam crosses his arms. "Care to share with the group?"

"Bronson has posted an elite force outside the Jefferson. No one's to be allowed in but the Tricksters' Council. No one is to roam inside the building tonight. He will be the only human attending the execution." He doesn't look at me, but he hesitates, and I realize it's because I'm here.

"Except for Dad," I say.

I can see no weakness in Oz, no anger. *I should have known better than to trust you.*

He nods. "Bronson will escort him alone. Everyone else is barred, assigned to be on duty elsewhere during the solstice festivities, except for those ordered to ensure no one unauthorized is admitted from outside. It has to be somewhere in the building."

I set down the plate. "The door," I say, "I know where it is."

"How?" Justin asks.

"The five people in that meeting. My dad was one of them, wasn't he?"

"Yes," Justin says.

Oz fixes on me. "What is it?"

If this wasn't so important, I'd be forced to stay quiet and leave this room to escape the weight of his gaze. The fact it isn't accusing somehow makes me feel *more* accused. But I speak. "Dad used to tell me to lay down on the sun in the Great Hall. He used to tell me it was the center of the universe, that everything revolved around it. That it could lead to *anywhere* if it needed to."

They are all quiet. I imagine them doing the same thing I am, picturing the Great Hall. The whirl of the zodiac set in marble, the four points of the compass rose marked within the big brass sun, guarded by busts and columns, inscriptions and statues. The still and grand heart of the Jefferson. Not its center, but *a* center. The center of a universe, a door that leads the way to a place where all that is mortal – if not immortal – must eventually travel. A door into the dark beyond, where a god can escape death and be reborn.

Justin shrugs. "I hate to say this, but she's probably right."

"Then," Oz says, "all we need now is a plan."

We discuss nicely and we wield sarcasm, we argue and we agree, and eventually, we do have what Oz requests: a plan, with neatly defined responsibilities. It's enough that we can pretend we have a chance of success, that any of this will end well.

But I keep hearing the echo of Mom's "blood and doom", and wondering where she is. I remember her saying the end of the world would be neater than what we can expect, if this all goes as foreseen. I think of Dad telling me to leave town, as if I'd do that.

Bree picks up my plate to take it back to the kitchen, and I get up too. Tam shoots us a look, but doesn't come with... because of something he sees in my face or in hers.

Stopping at the sink, Bree rinses off the plate.

"So," I say, "what's going on?"

Bree doesn't pretend not to know what I'm asking. "I did want to talk to you about something."

"I know," I say. "I know *you*, and I can tell. Let's do this now. Just in case."

Bree turns off the water and makes sure I see her shake her head, *no*. She says, "There is no just in case. This will work. We're going to get you your dad back."

"In case," I say, infusing it with a quiet certainty. "We're past the denial stage, Bree."

The five of us don't have much time before we split apart, each with our parts to carry out.

She starts, "OK. Well. So."

I can't help smiling. "Yes?"

She answers in a low rush. "I have a thing for Tam."

"You should have told me. For how long?"

She considers. "Long. But I understand the friend code. It doesn't matter." She lowers her voice even more. "It's just suddenly he's paying attention to me. But you should know, I'm not going to act on it."

"Don't be stupid. You should if you want." She gives me a disbelieving look and it's my turn to shake my head. "I don't own him, Bree. The two of us are friends. *Just* friends."

The perfect arches of her eyebrows lift. "But didn't you kiss the other night?"

I've almost forgotten about that kiss. I figure Tam has too. "Did he tell you about that?"

"No," she says, hesitant. "I saw it. The sages showed me."

Now that *is* a surprise. "Really?" She nods. "I wonder why they would show you *that*. Anyway, it was just the two of us confirming there's nothing more. Too bad they didn't show you the conversation afterward."

"You're sure?" she asks. "Absolutely?"

"You should be with whoever you want. You deserve that. Tam's a good person, and I couldn't have been what he needs. You could be anything to anyone. You know that, right?"

Bree swallows. "Don't you dare get yourself killed tonight," she says, pulling me into a hug. "That's all that matters to me. The rest of this will work itself out. Besides, Justin's kind of cute too."

I accept the hug, but when I push back, I say, "I want it clear, you owe me nothing. You have already done more than anyone ever has for me. Ever. You should be with whoever you want." I try to imagine her with Justin and can't quite do it. But her and Tam, I can see them together like it's already a fact.

She nods, green eyes shining with tears I don't want her to shed. So I steer us back into the living room together, only to discover one of our number is missing. "Where's Oz?" I ask.

"Went out back to get some air," Justin says, without looking up from the page he's working on.

Bree picks up a pencil and bends beside him to sketch in a shape on his diagram of the Great Hall.

Sitting down beside Tam, I lean into his ear. "I have four words for you: don't screw this up." When he feigns confusion, I tilt my head toward Bree and Justin. "No wait, four more: don't wait too long."

Tam nods. "Got it."

He rises under the guise of checking out the drawing, neatly inserting himself between Justin and Bree. Once the three of them are consumed with a conversation about the tight timing we'll be up against, I go in search of Oz.

While events like, say, the impending apocalyptic not-apocalypse might free me from the requirement to have this conversation, I need to acknowledge that the music has been playing this whole long day. The music has been waiting for me to face it. What I did to Oz can't be out there unresolved. I might not be deserving of his forgiveness, or who knows? I might. I don't expect it, but I do need to apologize. Selfish or not, I can't take Oz's help now without an attempt to fix the static between us.

I expect to find him watching as Anzu wheels around above the house. But he's *not* looking up into the darkening sky. Because Anzu has seen fit to roost in the backyard – fenced, luckily, to prevent panicked neighbors. They stare at each other, into each other, like two equals coming to an agreement.

Which is, of course, silly. Anzu is on assignment and he's a god. Oz is a boy and on a mission. Sure, there are commonalities, but not as many as it might appear. A boy and a god are as far apart as any two creatures are, when one has magic and the other has borrowed magic and only sometimes.

Because I can, and it's easier than my actual task, I walk across the lawn and past Oz, stopping at Anzu's side. He continues to stare at Oz with liquid gold eyes, as if I'm not even there.

"Let me see it," I say, and nudge Anzu's wing, where it covers the gash on his side. He grumbles, low in his throat, but it's half-hearted compared to the earlier protests. I am far more alarmed by the sound of Oz's sword singing through the air.

"Don't," I say.

He balances gleaming metal in front of him like some warrior who stepped out of the past. Before I can stop myself, I add, "Though, it is a good look."

I hear his sniff, but I'm too busy bending to check Anzu's wound. He's lifted his wing to show me the spot after all. There's hardly a trace of it left. He's healing.

"Good," I say.

He lowers his wing.

When I turn, Oz's sword is on the grass beside him. He sits, leaning on his hands with his legs sprawled out in front of him.

"What if he was going to eat me?" I ask.

"I was going to watch," he tosses back.

"Nice." I roll my eyes, and approach him. Slow, wary. I sink down sideways, my legs crossed, between Anzu and Oz. I want to be able to see both of them.

"What is this?" he asks. "Why would you need me to like you when you have a smitten monster?"

"I don't want a monster." I wish I could reel it back in. Too much truth.

"He might be more useful, given what we have in front of us."

"This isn't about that. I wanted you to know…" I stop. I don't know how to explain.

"Give me your best excuse. I'm waiting."

I glance at him. The way his head tilts back, so he can study the first few stars – or planets, I'm never sure – is maddening. He's barely listening. So I do it again. I go for too much truth. Anything else seems like a waste, at this point.

"Oz, in the past few days, I've found out everything I believe about who I am is a lie. Or most of it, anyway." I grab a handful of grass in one hand and it anchors me, because otherwise I feel like I'm hovering above my own body, that I've climbed out of my skin. I shouldn't say anything else, but I keep talking. "I still don't know what the truth is. I don't know who I really am, who I was meant to be, or who I'm going to be now. I never had anyone I could count on. Except, it turns out, Bree. But even then, I expected her to run on me. I expect everyone to, because, well, if the people who are *required* to care about you aren't able to show up, then why on earth would anyone else? So, I did what I've always done. I pulled my secrets in close and I got through these days as best I could. I know I used you, but I hated that. I want you to *know* how much I hated it."

Oz is silent. He's silent for so long I give up on any response. I put my other hand down, to press myself up to my feet. Anzu doesn't make a peep. When I look over to make sure he's still there, I find he isn't.

Oz's hand lifts, his finger pointing up at the sky. "He left, as soon as you started talking." He still doesn't look at me. "I hated it more," he says.

He gives me a grin I don't quite know him well enough to interpret, eyes a dark shine in the night as he turns toward me. My breath catches in my throat and I am certain *something* is about to happen.

"Guys," Bree calls, "better get back in here."

Neither of us moves right away. Oz does first, and I breathe out, soft to conceal my disappointment. He picks up his sword, sheathes it, and extends his hand. I let him help me to my feet. As I'm doing it, I understand I've never accepted help from anyone as willingly as I do him. Dreaded conversation over or not, he still frightens me.

"The person you can always count on," Oz says.

He could be talking about Bree or himself. I realize I should stop being surprised that he's here, or that any of them are. I should just be grateful.

CHAPTER TWENTY-SEVEN

The sound of the revels is loud enough that the muted mix of singing and laughing and fireworks reaches us before we're anywhere close to the Jefferson, the Capitol, and the Mall beyond. If we had to close our eyes, we could navigate there based on the low roar of people unaware of the danger they're in. I envy their ability to indulge in a night when magic feels close, but safe.

We each have our marching orders, and they mean that we'll only be a group – or, at least, we're only *guaranteed* to be – for a few more minutes. But we don't chatter nervously. We are all lost in our own mental preparations.

I am dressed identically to Oz and Justin, like I'm a Society girl, a good little soldier. My hair is gathered in a low ponytail. I even have my stripes on, though I've assured Oz I don't plan to use them. At least, not on him. I'd rather be wearing the T-shirt Dad left me. That feels more like armor, and I *need* armor for this. It's a battle. To pretend otherwise is a lie.

Tam and Bree also sport navy, but regular clothes instead of uniforms. No one will be fooled into thinking they are Society, except possibly from a distance. No one needs to. The only thing I feel good about, traveling through the warm summer evening toward the hardest night of my life, toward near-certain defeat, toward my father's death (*if* I don't manage to do the impossible), is that Tam and Bree's roles should keep them out of harm's way during the worst of this. The only *person* I'm willing to risk this time, really, is myself. Oz and Justin will be closer to the action, but what can happen tonight and what can't is clear in my head. I know what I can bear to let go of, and what must be protected.

Oh, how I wish I knew where my mother is.

We aren't able to access more relics before the ritual, which means we have a severe limit on resources for stopping it. There's a guard posted at Bronson's house, and another at the hall the secret passage connects to. We have to rely on ourselves and what we have on us.

The street ahead begins to clog with more not-a-worry-in-their-head people, meandering toward the revels. I am struck again with envy. I want an empty head and a calm heart. We pause at the place where the street meets another, where we have to split up.

I nod to Bree and Tam. "You guys take care," I say. "Beware of revelers."

"Good luck to you," Tam says.

"*Don't* break a leg. Or anything else," Bree says. "We'll see you soon. Very soon."

"If not, we'll have bigger trouble than broken bones," Justin adds.

He takes off first, his path between buildings obscured. Bree and Tam go in the opposite direction, toward the clamor and chaos of the revels. Once the crowd absorbs them, I take Vidarr's shoe from my backpack and slip it over my boot. With the night and the buzz of the revels, no one on the street notices when I disappear.

Or when Oz takes my hand, and does the same. His presence helps me feel slightly calmer.

The sense of something stretched out between us from earlier in the backyard lingers.

With the relic, we're able to approach the Jefferson without having to worry about anyone spotting us. When we reach the fountain, Poseidon ruling over the sidewalk, we meet a line of Society guards on horseback riding toward the Mall. They don't even blink as we make for the Jefferson's front entrance. Oz is one of the operatives assigned to a post at the main door. He will be seen, briefly, and take care of the others. Assuming all goes well, Bronson's orders that no one be let in will be quickly and quietly overthrown.

We're in a countdown now, hoping that all the pieces will end up where we want them to. But it's hard to feel confident, given that so far I've been a chess piece moved around a board I wasn't even aware I was on. Legba's pawn.

Close to the top of the stairs, I release Oz's hand. He strides out of the shadows and the rest of the way to the top, through the first of the three massive stone arches. A voice greets him. "You're late, golden boy."

I wait on the stairs below, unseen, and count.

One...
Two...
Three...
Four...

At five, Oz ducks out of the shadows and waves for me to come forward.

"That didn't take long," I say to him, finding his hand when I reach the top, so he'll be concealed again.

The two Society guards who were at their posts lay flat against the stone, unconscious. We are banking that the tricksters are inside already. That's why we left our own arrival to the party so late.

"Training," Oz says. Then, "After you," sweeping his free hand to the lone open entrance.

"I don't suppose I can talk you into going to help Justin and let me handle this part solo," I say, because it's worth a shot.

"That's not what we agreed on," Oz says. "Get used to the fact that tonight you'll have whatever you need from me. You won't have to do this alone."

"Oz, I don't know what to say. If this doesn't go well..."

"Speechless." Oz teases me. "That means I win. We didn't factor in a delay, so in we go."

He's right. There's no time for last words. We slip inside the cool, dim building, taking a turn to the left as we already agreed. We intend to approach the Great Hall slowly and from one side, toward the back of it, instead of barreling straight on ahead. While we glimpse shapes and forms within it, I stick with the strategy we planned and don't look too closely. Even though no one should sense our presence while we're protected by the relic, caution is the wisest course here. We need to know what we're walking into.

As we navigate between speckled marble walls, the pinprick electric lights and overhead fixtures wink once and die. "Power outage," I murmur.

"And there's the first thing we didn't plan for," Oz says.

There's no natural light coming in at this hour, and so we grope forward in the near dark. When we reach the agreed-upon spot, Oz whirls to face me, planting his feet to stop me from plunging ahead. The backup gaslights kick in, flickering, illuminating the scene in front of us.

"Dad!" I shout without intending to. Good thing the relic stops anyone from hearing me.

When I try to rush forward, Oz steps behind me and holds me lightly in place. "Look first," he says. "Like we agreed."

It's hard to stick with taking things slow and smart given what's before us. Dad lies prone in the middle of the zodiac, directly over the brass sun. The irony that this is the door truly hits me. The Society is *supposed* to keep the light burning to hold the dark at bay. That's why they call themselves the Society of the *Sun*. But this in front of me? This is pure darkness.

Dad isn't shackled, but thick, knotted ropes twined over each wrist and ankle bind him. They are secured beneath heavy brick-sized pieces of metal laid on top of the patterned marble. The rope and the metal are most likely relics. He stares up at the ceiling high overhead.

I whisper. "How long do we have?"

Until the clock strikes midnight, I mean. Oz gives the answer I'm afraid of, "Not very."

At least our concealment seems to be holding. That or the gods are too absorbed in waiting for the big moment to notice.

Bronson stands to one side of Dad, a leather case sitting at his feet that I'm certain contains the Was scepter. He wears his usual suit, slick and relaxed like always. Oz assured me that he wouldn't risk wearing a protective relic given what he's told the gods they're here for. He won't need one. No doubt they'll be on board when they discover the truth. It benefits them more than anyone else. I think back to my grandfather's mad insistence he will fix everything right after, raise the walls and put the gods to sleep, return us to the too-bright past just as it was.

True to what Oz heard, besides Dad and Bronson there are only members of the Tricksters' Council in attendance. They'd never miss a blood sacrifice – this is probably like the good old eons as far as they're concerned. I'm thankful Oz forced me to *look* before leaping as I take in the full scene. Even if every move we make goes exactly the way we want (which it won't), we are fighting fate. I am reminded that these beings are as old as time itself.

Set, in this up to his canine throat, is front and center, not three feet away from Bronson and Dad. On the other side of the grand space, Hermes leans against a column, as if he's lazing in his own private Grecian temple. Coyote wears his oversized animal form, sitting on his haunches beside an alcove with a bust of Thomas Jefferson inside. His face contains the same wary intelligence as always. Coyote is no one's fool. Past him, Tezcatlipoca might be a living mountain resting on marble. And Loki is half-wrapped around a feminine statue, leering at it.

Enki lingers near the entrance, not coming in and making himself at home like the others. He must have arrived right after we did. His horns are the barest inches from the tall arches above him. I'm aware how he hides his full nature, how the abzu could contain all this, plus a dozen copies of it and then some.

But he's not giving away the unconscious – and frozen by Oz's stripes – guards outside. Maybe he *will* be on our side. That's one thing we weren't able to assume. He let the Society remove Dad from Enki House, and the exact nature and limits of Anzu's dedication to guarding me remain unclear.

In fact, Anzu not showing up here doesn't surprise me as much as the fact there's no sign of Legba. He's not going to skip the show he's taken such care to orchestrate. He must be who the rest are waiting for, since no one else but Set and Bronson know what a strict schedule they have to stick to.

The frenetic pitch of the revels in the distance rises in volume. *Tick, tick, tick* until solstice…

A fake sacrifice about to happen on the Mall, a real one set for in here.

"How much faith do you have in the plan?" I ask.

"Not enough to wait for them," Oz said. "We can't."

"That's what I figured. So this is going to be interesting," I say.

"What is?" Oz asks.

In answer, I shrug off my backpack and kick off the shoe – we agreed in advance it would be more dangerous to risk the gods striking out at something without knowing *what* – then duck under Oz's arm. I stroll into the gas lit get-together like I'm holding an invitation.

None of them react right away. I have the element of surprise on my side, and I go straight for Dad. Dropping to my knees, I wince as they hit the marble, but reach for the knots on his wrist. I gasp at the burn of the rope when my fingers touch it. I'm forced to let go.

Dad blinks up at me. The cuts on his cheek from the trial are scabbed over an angry red. "Kyra... *No.*" He pours such anguish into one word. Here I thought he might be a fraction happy to see me, even if it's one last time. He closes his eyes, but then he reopens them and speaks in a rush. "You have to get out of here. You can't be here. It's not... It's unsafe for you. William, please do me one favor and get her out of here."

Bronson frowns down at us, giving every indication that he's as disturbed by my presence as Dad is. "How did you get in?" he demands.

"I brought her," Oz says.

"Osborne," Bronson grits his name. "You shouldn't have come. You shouldn't be helping her. You've betrayed your vows. I might be willing to show leniency *if* you take her outside *now*."

I rise, as Dad continues to repeat variations on, "No, Kyra, listen, you have to leave. Please. Listen to me." I move closer to Bronson, forcing him to face me down instead of barking orders at Oz. "Did you really think I'd just stay out in Virginia?" I ask him. "I'm a Locke. And I'm not going anywhere, not because you tell me to."

He tsks agreement. "You're right. I should have known better. You've proven yourself... resourceful. It's impressive." His composure is back in place, a hint of apology in his tone. He's so nimble at putting on the mask of leader, director, sympathetic grandfather.

"Only you would have the nerve to try and flatter me right now," I say. "You're not recruiting me for your team."

Set growls, and Bronson looks away from me to check the watch at his wrist. "We can talk about this later," he says.

Before I can dodge, Bronson takes my arm and shoves me at Oz. Who catches me, a reflex, rather than letting me stumble past. The brief interlude allows Set room to block us and the others from access to Dad. His angular body faces the entrance, but his canine head turns so his narrow black eyes are trained on Oz and me.

Bronson reaches down to flip open the case on the floor. In seconds, he has the Solstice Was out of it and in his hand.

All we need is to accomplish a long enough delay. We have to prevent the ritual from taking place until solstice is past and the cavalry shows – if it does.

I press aside my worry about them and dive toward Dad. My hope is to keep Bronson from being able to get to him. But Set raises a pawed hand and, with one quick swipe, sends me flying back. Oz has to catch me again.

Bronson says, "Careful."

"I will not hurt her unless forced to," Set answers.

I'm not convinced, but it's good enough for Bronson.

I've barely recovered my breath when Bronson takes the scepter and slashes the forked prongs of it across Dad's wrist above the ropes. Dad gasps in pain. He manages to speak, but it's the same refrain. "Kyra, you have to go," he pleads. "Please."

"You should have gone for the case, not your father," Bronson says, like this is some training exercise. "Though I can hardly fault a daughter who cares so much."

Set growls, but he's answered by a deep rumble beyond him from Enki. The protest is too late.

Blood wells up from Dad's wound. A faint trace of light appears around him, as if the brass sun below him is shining. I expected the door to the Afterlife to be dark. I wasn't wrong. The glow begins to grow a thick border made out of shadows.

The main details of the ritual are simple. It begins with this, the spilling of Dad's blood, and ends with his life's blood at the exact moment of solstice, when the scepter is used to kill him. To prevent the door from opening, we have to make sure he lives. That's it. If only it wasn't so impossible.

Bronson points the Was scepter toward Dad, and says to Set, "That should give you a taste for Gabrielle's blood. He is family, by marriage. You bring her to me, and everything will go as we agreed."

Set lunges at Dad, and his muzzle stops above the wound. His black and pink tongue extends to lap away the seam of blood.

Loki jumps down beside the jackal-headed god. "Not sporting to eat when others are hungry. Or to eat humans at all," Loki says. Then, "What is this, old friend? It doesn't seem like a punishment."

Set speaks, "It is a victory. Anyone who holds otherwise is a fool."

"Peace," Loki says. "I like some chaos. But the horned guy isn't a fan, and he can be a problem." He extends his thumb over his shoulder.

I look up – and up – at Enki. He's stepped into the Great Hall, and his horns seem to stretch on forever, almost to the glass far above, as if we *are* in the abzu. He might be as tall as the world. Past, present, future. The blue scales of his skin glimmer.

"You should not be here, Kyra Locke," Enki's voice rings out. "It is not what your father desires. You should go from this place."

I want to fall to my knees. Or, actually, I want to leave. The urge to do what Enki says is strong. There is a command in the words, but I fight it. "I'm staying right here."

"Kyra, go," Dad's voice is getting fuzzy around the edges. "You can't be here. This is all for you. *To save you.*"

"You can ground me, after this. I'm the one doing the saving." *At least, I'm supposed to be.* I whisper the most pressing question to Oz. "Where *are* they?"

"On their way, I hope," he answers.

I still want to know where Legba is too, but I'm smart enough to know better than to voice *that* question out loud.

Loki strides over to the line of other gods, all of them spectators now. They are interested, but not ready to get involved. He strokes his red beard. Tezcatlipoca roars with unmistakable displeasure, and Loki says, "Oh, come on. Let's see how it plays out before we decide to intervene and spoil Set's surprise."

Coyote lets out a yip of agreement. Hermes shrugs one perfect shoulder.

Set is far taller than Bronson, even with his half-canine, half-human back bowed. The god barks and it's like laughter, joyous. Bronson's not the only one getting exactly what his heart desires.

The headpiece of the Solstice Was shifts, baring its teeth, Bronson's hand curled beneath the snarl. My grandfather has his eyes closed and repeats the same word over and over. *Gabrielle. Gabrielle. Gabrielle.* As he chants, the top of the scepter strains toward Set, its true master. The pointed ends are a forked tongue of blades. I picture them slicing into Dad again.

There has to be a way to stop this. I just don't know what it is.

"Things are about to get messy," Oz says, as if he's reading my mind.

"About to?" But I see what he means.

Legba has arrived. He strolls through the entrance and past Enki's enormous form. Mom is on his arm, her elbow tucked through his like he's her escort to some unholy prom.

"Hope we didn't miss the fun part," Legba says, shark teeth gleaming.

"Kill me," Mom cries out, kohl-black tears streaming down her cheeks. "*Kill me!*"

CHAPTER TWENTY-EIGHT

Justin has already passed several operatives on horseback on their way to patrol the Mall. While he's certain Rose wasn't among them, he has to catch her before she follows. He sprints across the street toward the stables, hastily constructed behind the Adams Library after the Awakening. They have long since been upgraded into the well-appointed structure the Society's horses and carriages deserve.

He's not sure Oz should trust him with such an important duty. Bree and Tam's roles are essential too, but more in terms of the outside world. Justin's task is the only possible way they will have to counter Bronson and ensure the entire Society doesn't fall in behind him, unaware of what he's done. If the secret remains unknown within their ranks, then outside will never matter. No one will ever hear a credible word about any of this.

Justin is aware of each second of limited time ticking away, that every pounding thud of his heart brings the precise instant of solstice closer. The earth and the sun are locked in a dance that creates the potential for the most powerful of magic. It's no accident that ceremonies and rituals like this have been historically linked to seasonal changes. Justin's worry, his real and worst worry, is that Oz will sacrifice *himself*. That's the kind of person Oz is – if it comes down to him or Kyra, Justin has no doubt what decision will be made.

He does not want to live in a world without Oz. He's the only person who Justin has ever known who couldn't care less that he prefers study to swordplay, who offers no judgment about it. Oz acknowledges who Justin is. And he's counting on Justin not to let him down.

The one thing Justin has going for him is his venerable family name. His mother has always encouraged and supported Rose Greene's ascension in the ranks. "We have to stick together," he overheard his mom tell Rose one night at their family home, sitting at the kitchen table with full glasses of dark red wine, and, in response, Rose assuring her, "We do. I'll watch out for Justin in D.C." The connection may not be so solid between *him* and Rose, but he's hoping her commitment to his mother is.

There are two operatives and a stable hand outside the building, the familiar sun symbol painted above its double doors. "Rose Greene?" Justin asks them, short of breath.

"Slow down," one of them says. "She's inside saddling up."

He would be relieved, but now there's no turning back. Now he *has* to convince her.

She's leading her horse out of the stall when he nearly smashes into her. "Justin?" she asks. "What's wrong?"

He braces one hand against a stall door, the horse inside nosing over the lip of it to nudge his hand. "I need to talk to you," he says, ignoring the horse.

"OK," she says. "Get your breath first."

He says, "Bronson, he's in the Great Hall."

"I know," she frowns. "I'm sorry about Mr Locke, if that's what you're concerned about. But a verdict is a verdict."

"That's not why he's doing this," Justin says. "Bronson has the Solstice Was. He's going to use it to kill Mr Locke in the Great Hall." He lowers his voice, in case anyone else is in the stables. "I believe that's where one of the doors is, the one to the Afterlife. He's going to unseal it."

Rose blinks.

Justin knows how smart she is; he's read some of her scholarly writing. He also knows that she believes Bronson is only director because he's a man. Rose is one of the people in line for that position. She might not be one of the five who knows for certain where the door is, but she's the kind of person who makes it her business to discover information. Knowledge is power, nowhere more than in the Society. It doesn't take her long to put the situation together. "His wife. That's what this is about?"

Justin does breathe a sigh of relief now. He nods. "Yes, that's what we think."

Rose swings her leg up and onto her horse. "Get your mount," she says. "We're going in there. I'll gather operatives willing to challenge him, but we may need to clear people out of the area afterward, depending on how much of a fight he puts up." She looks down at him. "Your mother will be proud."

Justin bites down on his lip to keep from telling her he doesn't care about that. He only cares that Oz makes it out of the Great Hall in one piece and breathing. Well, and that Bronson doesn't get away with being willing to burn down the world for his own gain.

Justin heads toward the back of the stable, where his horse, Book, is.

Bree locates her mom amid a line of reporters. Cameramen are set up a few feet apart, the shining lights above their cameras aimed at infinitely poised reporters. Her mom's red lipstick sets off the white of her smile, as she waves a hand to gesture at the revels behind her. This is the kind of "news" her mom hates covering. It's not news at all, as far as she's concerned, just drunken idiots letting their drunken idiot flags fly.

As far as Bree's concerned, this is both true and beside the point. Her mom doesn't understand why people would waste a night dancing and chanting and drumming and hooking up with strangers because she finds parties a waste of time, by definition. She prefers political action, high stakes. Which means Bree is about to give her a great gift.

"Mom," Bree says, when she reaches the camera guy. She infuses it with a sense of urgency. In the near distance, the sacrificial bonfire blazes, surrounded by revelers assembled to watch a stuffed human form burn within it.

Her mom frowns, almost imperceptibly, before it smoothes away. She continues reporting – "As we approach the annual moment when we greet the summer by mimicking the way some of the ancients themselves might have…" – but glances at her.

Bree drags in a breath, and crosses her fingers that her mom will forgive her the interruption. Kyra's life is at stake. Her mom – and her camera – are needed elsewhere. Once she understands, she'll get over the fury she's about to experience at Bree, right?

Right.

So Bree steps into the frame, and says, "Mom, this can't wait."

Her mom's frown returns, not fleeting this time, but full force. She flicks a command to the cameraman, "Stop taping." She examines Bree. "You appear to have all your limbs, so I can't imagine why you would interrupt a live report."

Bree searches for the words. She had them when she came here, but has lost them. They're shocked from her, like the water of the abzu clogging her lungs. She sees a flash of the sages, and Kyra's face.

Kyra. This is for *Kyra*.

"Bree?" Her mom sounds hesitant.

"Mom, I need you to come with me. Kyra's in trouble."

"You're not supposed to be involved with her trouble. I told you," she says.

"She's my best friend," Bree says. "Besides, there's a story. A big one. A career-making one, maybe."

"My career is already made."

Bree shakes her head. To come all this way, to know that Kyra is so close, standing off against her grandfather and gods, and to fail is beyond contemplating.

"Mom, there is a huge story waiting for you up at the Jefferson. But, honestly, what is wrong with you? I am asking you for help. Do you know the last time I asked you for anything?"

Her mom's red lips part in surprise.

"Don't bother answering, because I'll tell you: never. I know what you do is important. I really do. And I don't resent the times you come in late or that you only remember to ask what I've been painting once every few months. Unlike Kyra and her parents, I always knew you loved me, and that's enough. I understand that this is the way you manage the world, by reporting on it. But you shouldn't come with me now because I'm promising you news. You should come because I need you to, because I asked. My best friend is in trouble. Not 'we snuck out' trouble, 'she could die' trouble. Now, are you coming or not?"

Her mother recoils as if Bree just threw ice-cold water on her. In a way, she did.

Bree is seconds from saying never-damn-mind and going to the Jefferson on her own, doing the best she can. But then her mom leaves her spot in the line of reporters. "Where did you say she is?" she asks.

"The Jefferson." Bree grabs her arm and pulls her along. She feels like she's floating. This is going to work. They are going to save Kyra's dad. They *have* to.

Her mom pauses, and Bree experiences a surge of panic that she's changed her mind. But it's only to toss an order over her shoulder at the camera guy. "Come on, Ed," she barks. "Don't be so slow."

Tam didn't want to split off from Bree, but once she spotted the line of reporters she insisted. They both knew where Tam's dad would be, and it wasn't there. And they have to hurry.

Because Kyra has only Oz at her side to square off against a full house of tricksters and William Bronson – who Tam has heard so many whispers and stories about at Skeptics meetings over the years that he believes the man's capable of *any*thing. It's hard to wrap his head around how many things have changed in the past several days. How much *he* has changed.

Normally, he wouldn't be anywhere near the Mall on solstice night. Not that he's disdainful of the celebration, but it's for tourists or the desperately bored. Not for people who live in this city every day. He has never felt any need to be closer to divinity or the universe or whatever it is the people around him are trying to pull in tight. But here he is, tripping down the grass toward the fake sacrifice. That's where his dad will be. The Skeptics make it a habit to show a presence there every year. Sometimes Tam's dad even volunteers to light the torch.

Such an old practice has a resonance that's accumulated over centuries, his dad says. And his mom laughs and says, no, that's not it, he just likes lighting things on fire, like any man. Tam wishes his mom was back from Chicago. He wants her here to stand beside him and convince his dad to bring the publicly critical weight of the Skeptics to bear on Bronson over this.

He locates his dad, finally, on the other side of the bonfire. There's a dummy inside the flames shaped like a human being. Gathered around the flames is a crush of cheering revelers. His father is among the "officials" presiding over the fake sacrifice, but their duties are mostly over. They're just sticking around to ensure no one tries to leap into the fire, that no one is hurt in the celebration.

His dad doesn't notice Tam right away, busy chatting, laughing, schmoozing. As soon as he does look over and see Tam, though, that's over. He excuses himself and comes forward to meet Tam. "What on earth are you doing here?" he asks.

"Can you leave?" Tam asks, and immediately kicks himself for it. He shouldn't have made it a question. His dad *has* to come. This is Tam's assignment and he *can't* leave without bringing his dad along. The reality of a situation like the one Kyra's gotten snared in is that none of them are adults. They need help from the kind of people other adults will listen to and believe.

His dad jerks a thumb back over at the cluster of men. "I have the ear of the police chief. I'd rather not," he says.

"No," Tam says, "this is important. It's about William Bronson."

"Tam," his father asks, "where is Kyra?"

"She's at the Jefferson, and we need to go there too."

His dad is troubled. "Tam… her father is being put to death tonight. It's a secret punishment. We considered trying to intervene, but the Society's justice is its own. If Henry Locke agreed to abide by their rules, we decided it wouldn't be right to insert ourselves. We have to pick our battles. Surely her grandfather will send her away, and not let her see something like that. She's welcome to stay with us until everything is figured out."

"You don't get it," Tam says.

Of course, he doesn't get it. He hasn't known the full story, and the truth is crazy. Outrageous. "You're going to *have* to be willing to intervene," Tam explains. "All those horror stories that go around about Bronson? All the times you've accused him of lying, of keeping secrets that endanger the public welfare, the belief that the tricksters aren't really on our side – you were right. And he's about to set them free."

"What do you mean?"

"I mean that he's about to give the god Set access to the underworld, and all the others with him. I mean that the status quo is about to end, and that we're going to see how right you have been all along."

His dad is already walking. "We need to get a coach. It'll be faster."

"I got this," Tam says, because he spots a carriage making as fast progress as can be through the throngs of people. A head ducks out of the window, above the station decal on the side, and Bree yells, "Move! Out! Of! The! Way!"

Tam tows his dad toward the TV station carriage. "Hey, Bree!" he calls out.

He knows she's just as tense and worried as he is. Probably even more. She's a better person, of that he has no doubt. The moment she sees him and their eyes connect, he feels a grin cut across his face. She smiles back at him, and it's as if everything stutters.

"Well, hurry up if you're coming!" she shouts to them. She disappears inside and the door swings open.

His dad climbs into the carriage with a "Hello, Nalini," and Tam follows him. He sits down beside Bree, and discovers they are still smiling at each other. He can't stop himself from reaching over, taking her hand in his. She doesn't take it back.

The carriage rattles to life, moving faster now, the driver shouting to clear the path.

Tam holds Bree's hand in both of his, and it's almost like they're alone.

"We're going to make it," Bree says, for him only. Their parents are talking over one another, comparing notes and theorizing. Tam doesn't care. He has eyes only for her. "Tell me we are," Bree says.

"We're going to make it," he says. "I promise."

Oz understood that Kyra was telling the truth about Legba being involved in all this, but he didn't fully get the enormity of that until the god arrived with her mother on his arm. He glides the rest of the way into the Great Hall like this is his party. That's because it is.

"I like to make an entrance," Legba says.

"Obviously," Kyra responds.

Oz has to stop himself from putting her behind him. That would make her angry, and he needs to figure out what Legba's plans are. So he stays where he is. Where are the others? They should be here by now. He has a moment of horrified wondering if Legba intercepted them, but nothing good can come of thoughts like that.

"Henry," Kyra's mom says, removing her arm from the god's.

"Hannah," Henry Locke says. "I'm so sorry. I failed."

Kyra's mother drifts past her prone husband to Bronson. "*Kill me*," she directs her plea to her father. "I'll do just as well. *Kill me*."

"I could never do that, Hannah," Bronson says. "I'm very sorry this is hard for you. But don't you want to see her again?"

She is trembling. "I can see her any time I like. In memory. That is the only place she would want me to find her. *Kill me*."

"Hannah," Mr Locke says, insistent, "Hannah. Kyra's *here*."

Kyra flinches as her mother's eyes land on her. They are ringed in kohl black as night, as death. "My girl," she says. "It was you all along. You we meant to protect."

"What does she mean?" Oz asks.

"I don't know," Kyra says.

Bronson hefts the scepter. They have to prevent him from winning. Oz's parents would have never appointed him Oz's guardian if they'd known what he was, what he was capable of. Part of his determination to stop

Bronson comes from that. They trusted Bronson, and so did Oz. But it's almost as if his parents have left him this important thing to accomplish. Losing them, being on his own, all of it has led him here. Kyra doesn't have to face this alone, because he's at her side. Between the two of them, they can do this, even without the others.

He's convinced of it. Kyra looks at him, and he wishes he could chase away the fear he sees in her face. It doesn't belong there. She asks, "If I distract the rest of them, can you get the Was from Bronson?"

"I can try," Oz responds. Then, "I'll get it or die trying."

"Don't," she says. "Don't die."

Kyra's mother is the real distraction, though. She takes two jerky steps toward Kyra, who seems unable to move. "It was you. You are the one whose blood spills here. You have to leave. My daughter."

"What?" Kyra asks, breathless.

Legba laughs. "It *is* funny. You can't tell someone a prophecy is about them and have them avoid it. Perhaps I miscalculated, since you are here after all, Kyra Locke. But telling you it was about your father, that he was the one who couldn't know, that was a stroke of genius. You have to admit it."

Kyra's gaze swings from Legba to her father. "*That's* supposed to be me?"

Oz wants to comfort her. He wants to kill Legba. Neither is possible at the moment.

"I could give you the twisted, clever answer, but the truth is a basic yes," Legba says. "You were the one meant to die here this evening. Your father has made a valiant effort to ensure he's the one who does instead. But here you are, and prophecies have the damnedest way of coming true. Maybe you will both die. What your mother saw, what drove her mad, was your death. The ripples from our dear William Bronson's plotting and planning led to the death of her own sweet daughter. And from there, the *kaboom*, the doom and the death. Not many mothers could live with that knowledge. Not and stay sane."

"Kill me," her mother says again, mournfully.

"No," Bronson says. "No, it can't be true."

Oz watches as Kyra absorbs this new information. She is stricken, as anyone would be. His worry kicks into a higher gear, because there *is* darkness within Kyra, the shadows she runs from, that she carries with her wherever she goes. He could detect them even from a distance, when he saw her those years before. He couldn't understand, at first, why the sages would show him that day he saw her trying to come into the Jefferson, that day she was so upset at being turned away.

But this week he's gotten to know her and witness the effect of the past on her. She's willing to put herself in danger, to risk anything, because she believes her presence here is optional, not valuable. If she can swap places with her dad? She will, in a snap, in a heartbeat, with no hesitation. Bronson might protest, but what he wants is an outcome. He's proven more than willing to make a mess to get it.

This is Oz's moment. He might not be able to fix everything, but he can get Kyra what she needs here, now.

He can ensure that the prophecy is disrupted. Nothing is set until it happens, that's what they teach in the Society, and he has to believe it's true. Otherwise there'd be no place for oracles, no reason to ever know what might come. Nothing is set until it happens. That is the truth.

He has to give Kyra the chance to see her own truth. She needs to understand that the shadows are *hers*, not the other way around.

Oz prepares to lunge for Bronson while the older man is distracted by this new revelation from Legba. While all of them are – well, almost all. Set isn't. Kyra doesn't matter to the god. She's nothing but an inconvenience. Set wants his hunting ground back. He wants to be able to move between this life and the next, to betray his fellow gods at will without death able to hold him.

As Oz moves, one of Set's hands shoots toward him, claws extended. Oz decides that maybe the prophecy should have been something else entirely. It should have been about the death of Osborne Spencer at the hand of an Egyptian god.

CHAPTER TWENTY-NINE

Everything stops – or that's how it feels. I gasp as Oz ducks to avoid Set's claws. The god is infuriated by missing Oz, and advances on him. He foolishly stands his ground.

Oz unsheathes his sword, and I know it is *only* a sword. Not a relic. Our lack of time has left us vulnerable and with nowhere near the firepower we need. I consider diving between them, but I'm not sure I can without making things worse, not with that blade out.

Around Oz, a cloud of sand appears and begins to spin. "Kyra," he chokes through it, "get out of here!"

Oz strikes out at Set despite the spinning sand – or maybe because of it – and it thickens so much I can hardly see where one of them ends and the other begins.

"Help him!" I beg Bronson.

But Bronson only says, "I'm sorry, but it's more important than ever that we end this the right way. You will be safe."

"Thank you," Dad says. "For that, if nothing else."

The obscenity of this night… Set about to kill the boy Bronson vowed to raise as his own, my father *thanking* my grandfather for killing him instead of me, my mother in her black shroud begging for her death instead... Worse, it turns out this is all about *me*, about my parents trying to avoid a prophecy no one was able to warn me about. I might have lived an entire brief life without knowing.

The racket of people entering the Hall from outside interrupts my dark line of thought. It is the best noise I've ever heard.

"Oz, hang on!" I call. "They made it!"

But he doesn't answer. Set's growling is the only thing audible in the cloud of whirling sand.

Rose is at the front of a large group of operatives, a bow strung tight in her arms. "William Bronson, stop and face charges of your own treason," she says.

"I can't," Bronson responds. "It is not for you to censure me. Stay where you are." He raises his voice, "Set, it's time. Keep them back."

The grains of sand fall to the marble, and Set shoves Oz away from him. Oz has a nasty gash on his neck, and the cloth of one sand-coated arm of his uniform is ripped, but he appears to be breathing, and mainly unhurt.

As if Bronson's command is Set's wish, the god sets his sights on the invading operatives. He stalks forward, then flinches at the shock of the bright light of a camera flashing on. I find Bree, right behind her mother, directing the cameraman to film everything, like we agreed.

Rose glances over and frowns, but the man keeps filming. Tam and his dad are right beside them. Everyone is here, just like the plan dictates, but I know in my bones we've run out of time. Solstice is here too, and Bronson raises the scepter.

Before it can come down on Dad, Oz is in motion. He flies forward and grabs it, his hands on either side of Bronson's, forcing it up instead of toward its target. Bronson holds on, saying, "Let go, stupid boy."

"You did this. Now fix it," I tell Legba, figuring it's worth a shot. "Or you'll be out of Lockes to kick around."

"Not my place." Legba lifts his hands to signal he isn't going to intervene.

"Since when?" I ask.

But it doesn't matter. He's brought us all here for his amusement or some other reason he's not inclined to share. Enki continues to hang back, not getting involved either. There's no voice in my mind offering advice, and no Anzu. We are on our own.

Set turns away from the operatives, his attention back on Oz and Bronson. "Oz, heads up!" I shout, but Set is faster…

If not quite fast enough. He releases a high-pitched yelp as an arrow sinks deep into his shoulder. I look over, expecting to see Rose reloading, but Justin holds a bow beside her and it was clearly his shot. The arrows must be the relics, because he takes another one from the quiver slung over Rose's shoulder, reloads to shoot again.

The entire Great Hall seems to crawl forward in slow motion. Mom sinks to Dad's side, stroking his cheek, sobbing quietly. Bronson keeps fighting with Oz, and he's managing to angle the Was down and into position. He's going to pierce Dad's chest with it. I understand that Oz won't be able to stop him.

Like that, I know what I have to do.

If this is where I'm meant to die, I have to be sure that Dad will live, and that Bronson won't get his way. I have to know that the world will make it through, even if I don't.

I jump between Bronson and Dad, Mom well behind me. I land in a crouch, and the Was scepter points straight at *my* heart.

Bronson's hand falters, the scepter dipping as he meets my eyes. I am not sure whether he'll kill me or not. I don't think he knows either.

"No," Oz says, through gritted teeth. He gives one last wrench and, helped by Bronson's hesitation, yanks the Was scepter from his hands.

"He *has* to die so she can live," Bronson hits on a last-ditch argument, pleading. "You heard what Legba said. There's a prophecy. We have no other option."

Oz says, "That's not an option."

But Bronson reaches inside his jacket, and when his hand emerges something shines in it. A knife. He brought a backup weapon. Relic, not a relic, it won't matter. He could still kill my father with it.

It won't finish the ritual and open the door, but I understand his desperation. He wants to salvage something, be a hero. He's bought into the prophecy, and thinks he can trade a life for a life. Dad's for mine. But it won't end here, tonight. That won't be enough for him.

Bronson will *never* give up the search for his Gabrielle. Not after the things he's already done.

If he uses the knife to kill Dad, he'll be able to claim he executed the traitor for treason, as decreed. Even with Rose here, he'll get away with everything. He can blame Set for the reappearance of the Solstice Was, or maybe Legba. But he'll never stop trying to bring back his wife, no matter the cost.

"You understand what it means to want someone back," Bronson says, bargaining with me. He sweeps his gaze to Mom, who weeps, inconsolable. "We are alike, Kyra. You and me. We could be a family. With Gabrielle here, and me, your mother... We could be a family again."

"Oz," I say, "give me the scepter."

He understands. In one move, he's at my side and placing the Was in my hands. Set, wounded, pivots toward us, but is distracted by another arrow. I'm sure it came from Justin.

Mom holds up splayed fingers, an inadequate shield for Dad as Bronson lowers the knife. "William, don't do this. It doesn't have to be this way," Dad says.

Legba's grin gleams, his laughter ringing out around us.

In my mind, I hear Enki's voice. Finally. He says: *Yes. You do right.*

There is only one way to end this. I grip the Was scepter and I feel as if I'm holding a spear in some long ago village from the first time of the gods. Before I can change my mind, I shove it forward.

The forked blades cut through Bronson's chest so easily. The sensation of the weapon sliding into him, through skin and between bones, is sickening in its easiness. It's as if the scepter craves his death. Maybe it does. Death is its purpose, and so it slips through him.

I don't have any illusions about what I've done. The relic might like taking life, but it didn't make the decision. I did.

Bronson drops the knife and it clatters onto the marble. He clutches at the metal buried deep within him. I aimed for the heart. It's what made him like this. His broken heart brought us here.

He lifts his head and looks at me. He drops his hands, stops fighting.

"I hope she forgives you," I say. "Now you can be together."

"Gabrielle," he says, the word soft, a whisper. I can't read his expression. Pain, fear, hope... Maybe all of them pass over his features, and then he falls. In that instant, the glow around Dad disappears.

Legba claps. "Well done. But oops." He takes flight and lands halfway up the stairs.

"Kyra!" Bree shouts, and Oz echoes it.

But my attention is stuck on the reason. Set has someone to blame for not getting what *he* wanted, and that someone is me. He rips the second arrow from the round bulge of his shoulder, and comes at me, snarling. The scepter might be enough to save me, a weapon wielded against its creator. But it's in Bronson.

Oz pushes in front of me, but Set bats him out of the way and Oz hits the marble hard. Set's sharp teeth snap in my face and his clawed hand grabs the back of my neck and pulls me to him. I wonder how he will kill me. Are those teeth going to close on my throat? The claws sink through my skin? Am I really destined to die here, tonight?

In that moment, I am aware how much I want to live. My blood sings with the need to survive.

A layer of ice sprays over Set, freezing him in place. But not for long – cracks appear almost immediately as he thrashes against the coating. But, in the flurry of motion, he releases me and I scramble away from him. Set's attention is no longer on me, but on Enki, striding forward. He sends another wave of ice through the air, and Set counters with a wave of sand.

The operatives are calling out to each other, not sure whether they should get in the middle of this or not. Enki bellows displeasure, and Set lashes out. Shadows like snapping jackals emerge from his hand, and latch onto Enki's scaled arm.

"Bravo!" Legba calls and jumps back into the thick of things.

He lands next to Enki and Set. He brings the bottom of his walking stick down on the marble, hard. The floor shakes with its force. His voice booms out, echoing through the Great Hall. "So, you're probably wondering why I brought you all here this evening."

Maybe it wasn't the floor trembling. It might just be me.

Oz gets back up, sword in one hand, and reaches for me with the other. I make it to his side, and we lean into each other. He holds the sword in front of us. Any protection is better than none.

"Chin up, girl, you made it," Legba says. "I didn't know if you would."

Hermes called out from the column where he still lounges. "This is quite a mess you've made, so if you *would* care to explain…"

Legba swings his cane in a circle. He makes a circuit, not quite wandering to where the Society operatives wait, unmoving, and the TV camera films on. Nalini has her hand on Bree's shoulder, holding her in place. Ben has a similar posture by Tam. Justin lingers beside Rose, bow lowered.

"I like to walk through time," Legba continues. "Some while back, it occurred to me that it was an awfully big coincidence that all we gods went to sleep at the same time… and then woke up that way. I don't know about my brothers and sisters here, but I wasn't even feeling tired when it happened. I didn't recall that right away. When we first woke up, the world was new, and there was so much to see. I barely remembered lying down for a nap."

"The point, please, before you put us back to sleep," Hermes says, with a stagey yawn.

Enki's massive body swivels to face Legba.

"No hard feelings," Legba says to Enki. The next he directs to the other gods. "But it seems our Sumerian friend here had a crush – love, really, though never consummated, alas – on a human woman, who just happened to be an early member of this Society that wanted humanity to be on top. She convinced him that humans deserved a time of their own, that it cost the gods nothing to take a little sleep. He helped her do it, achieve her dream of us all dreaming."

Tezcatlipoca extends one blocky hand and knocks the statue of the woman with the globe raised above her head across the hall. The light from the TV camera zigzags as Nalini and Bree dodge it. The statue skids to a stop on its side with a crash.

"I'm not done yet," Legba says. "I followed the lines of this action forward, into the future, and what did I see? I saw William Bronson – R.I.P. – waking us up, but not because he had any great love of the gods. No, he wanted his wife back, but it didn't work. All he got was us. And his action created still more lines, one to his own granddaughter, who it seemed was *also* a descendent – on her father's side – of the very same woman who charmed Enki into putting us into a sweet slumber for thousands of years. But, you know, it wasn't her fault. So I thought I'd give the girl a fighting chance. And I was right, she didn't disappoint. It is your life, girl, but this is a big world. And here's the thing."

"Yes?" I ask. Because it's clear that he's talking to me now.

"There's part of me that admires your ancestor. She was human, and she wanted to protect her people. You humans now, you've only made us upset. The way I figure, the only way to push you humans to be better is to give you no choice but to try harder. Hannah, can you tell us what you saw, all those years ago? What you've seen so many times since?"

Dad strains against the ropes, but Legba stares at Mom. She wafts to her feet, swaying like a flower in a breeze. She says, "I saw the great gods warring, the start of the end of everything, and it began here. I saw blood and doom, riot and ruin. The end of our days, but not of yours. I saw my daughter bleeding on the marble, the ritual complete, the door open..." She hesitates, lost. "But that has not come to pass, so maybe none of it will?"

"Shhh," Legba says. "No, some conflict is just the thing to get the blood flowing." He sweeps his arms out. "After all, I'm the only one who got what I wanted: the truth out in the open. I can't imagine there won't be hard feelings among my old friends here. It'll be interesting to see who stands with you, Enki, or if those loyalties evaporate like dreams in harsh morning light. To you, girl, and humanity, I say good luck." He whirls, the tails of his suit jacket flying, and he's gone.

The gods who are left stare at Enki, who twists his horns as he bellows. The floor trembles. The walls shake. He's not apologizing or making nice. He's offering a challenge. Operatives skitter out of the way as he turns and leaves.

STAY HERE. His words are bell-clear in my head.

Set is the first to go after Enki, shadows pouring from his claws. But he isn't alone. The battle is beginning, and as Legba predicted, sides being chosen. Operatives move aside to let them out, because what else *can* they do?

Bree and Tam rush over as soon as the gods make their exit. The screams of the revelers get louder. The operatives peer after the gods, as if they aren't sure what to do. Rose calls out, "We'll have to go out there. Try to get as many civilians off the Mall as possible." She's already heading out the door, uniformed men and women behind her.

Bree asks, "Kyra, are you OK? That was…"

"I will be. I think," I say, which is a better answer than *I don't know*.

None of us look at Bronson's body, only a few steps away. Mom is rocking beside Dad saying, "This is where it ends, this is where it ends…"

"What do we do now?" Tam asks.

"Good question," I say.

A sound reaches us that might be the Capitol building collapsing in one loud crash. We stopped the ritual, but it might have been for nothing.

"Once they're done fighting each other, they'll remember this is where the door is," Oz says.

Justin is nodding. "You're right. They'll come back and find some other way to open it. They won't have to fear death anymore then."

I ask, "Can't we… I don't know, move it?"

"Not that quickly," Dad adds.

Bronson claimed to have a way to get rid of the gods after his precious ceremony was complete. Apparently he *had* known they were put to sleep, and how to wake them. He must have been telling the truth. What was it he said? That he'd raise the walls, *then* put them to sleep.

I drop beside Dad. "The walls, Dad – are they real? Can I put them up? Bronson told me he was going to after the ritual. Would that help?"

"Yes," Dad says, blinking up at me. "Yes, do it. The walls will protect us until we can regroup, strategize. It will keep them out of here."

"How do I do it?" I prod.

Oz taps my shoulder. "I know how. Every operative does, in case of something like this. They're our last defense. You sure, Mr Locke?"

"Yes," Dad says again. "If there are negative consequences, I'll accept them."

I don't want him in danger again, not anytime soon. "Should we find Rose and ask her?"

Oz shakes his head. "Only the board can order the walls up, because the rest of the world doesn't know about them. The gods don't know about them. If we're doing this, we have to do it alone. We can't wait to see if everyone agrees."

Another loud crash sounds outside. "Go," Dad says. "Be quick."

The few operatives who stayed behind are closing the doors, barricading the Jefferson against the fighting.

"We'll need a horse to have any chance of making it down there in the crush," Oz says.

"Book's tethered outside. Take her," Justin says.

"Down where?" Bree asks.

"The Washington Monument," Oz says, and I don't have to ask if he's kidding. He isn't. "There are pieces from the walls of Asgard embedded at the top. The city was designed with this feature in mind. Their original purpose was to safeguard the Norse gods when they were in residence at Asgard. But once we activate them, they should do the opposite. They should force the gods out, and protect the city."

Tam cues in on the same word I do. "Should?"

"It's never been tested. Because how could we?"

Mom lies down beside Dad, tucks her head in below his chin. He can't put his arm around her and she's careful not to touch the ropes. Dad closes his eyes, and they look almost cozy.

"The ropes burned me," I say to Justin.

"We'll get him free while you're gone," he says.

Oz claps a hand on Justin's shoulder. "Nice shooting. Guess you won't be able to complain about all the hours of practice anymore."

Justin can't seem to manage a quip back, and Oz lets him off the hook. He says to me, "Ready?"

"Be careful, Kyra," Dad adds. "We don't want to lose you now."

"We'll do our best," I say, hardly able to believe we're all alive. We might make it through this night. "Oz, let's go raise some walls."

CHAPTER THIRTY

We speed down the stairs and through the ground floor exit. Once we make it outside, I have to press down the impulse to run back in and hide. Steady streams of people are flooding toward us, attempting to flee the madness behind them. Some stumble, drunk, and a few of the women are half-dressed at best. Two men have skulls painted over their features, the greasepaint bones blurred from tears.

The crash we heard wasn't the full collapse of the Capitol, but the perfect white dome is partially missing. A black hole with jagged edges gapes on one side. The solstice revels turned gods' battle is an all-too-close roar on the other side of it.

I have never thought of myself as a hero, as the type of person who rushes into something like this. I'd never have believed I could be the kind of person able to do anything about it. Sometimes a hero is whoever is available, doing whatever is possible.

Having outlived my supposed fate makes me bolder. I really don't want to die. Neither do any of these people, or others having quiet evenings at home in the city. We may not be able to protect the entire world, not tonight, but we can try to protect this place, and keep the door safe.

Oz guides us to a hitching post at the edge of the street. There's one lone horse tethered there, a large, brownish-black mare.

A Society operative gapes at the Capitol, though there's nothing to be seen except flashes of light above it. He looks at us. "Is it true the director's dead?"

I nod. "Is that as bad as it sounds?"

"Worse," he says.

"They could use your help inside," Oz says to the operative, who rushes away, all too glad for an excuse to leave the fray.

Oz strokes his hand along the mare's side. The horse's shoulders move like liquid as he unwinds the reins from the post and leads her to me. "Unlike that guy, Book doesn't spook at anything," Oz says.

He gracefully mounts, then holds out his hand to help me up. I grab his hand, manage to put my foot in the stirrup, and awkwardly swing on behind him.

"That was… you'll need riding lessons," he says.

"Shut up," I say. "We're in a hurry, remember."

He holds the reins in one hand, and a jounce of his foot to Book's side sets us moving. I put my arms around him and hold on.

The night is warm, and though a few pinpoint stars are visible, an eerily large pale moon dominates the sky, poised on the horizon as if it might fall the rest of the way to earth and take out a national landmark or two.

Or a warring god or two.

Oz spurs the horse forward through the press of people. The solstice revels are always well attended, and this year is no exception. Book's hooves land hard on the pavement, giving no sign of alarm at the roars and shouts and booms ahead. When we round the damaged dome, the reflecting pool in front of the Capitol is on fire.

The effect turns out to be a trick of distance and darkness. Gods are lobbing the fire – reflecting in the pool – at each other. Other members of the pantheons have been summoned by the fighting. Gods swarm the air, some touch down on the ground for a moment, others race along it. Everywhere there are brilliant, burning colors, broken up by dark, shadowy blacks.

We pass our first few casualties, and I'm grateful they are facedown – except for a brown-haired girl who might be in college, staring sightless, revealed by an angry red flare.

"Keep your head down," Oz says.

He navigates Book over to the sidewalk in front of the museums along the left-hand side of the Mall. Smart. He's keeping us out of the grassy area in the middle where the worst of the conflict is taking place.

The old-fashioned carousel usually in front of the Smithsonian soars in a high arc, smacking into a large god with bat wings. I make out Enki's horns high above the middle of the green. The area beside him is a great absence of light with rippling edges. It has to be Set, growing more shadows.

The obelisk of the Washington Monument is visible in the distance, but it feels so far away. Oz urges Book forward at a faster pace. "We'll make it," Oz says. Maybe he's reassuring himself.

I'll never forget the things we pass. It feels wrong, riding on instead of stopping to help people. I remind myself: *You are going to help them.* I close my eyes, but Bronson's face waits for me there. I open them immediately.

There are a few operatives riding along the middle, attempting to get the crush of people out of harm's way. One of their horses stumbles, screaming as a god's elongated hand wraps around its front legs and tugs it down.

The fake sacrificial bonfire smolders, deserted, across from the Smithsonian castle, wreathed in wilting flowers. Where the carousel used to be is nothing but churned earth, spilling over the ground. Ahead of us, a blaze of flame licks through the sky. The ground shakes. There is another flare of light. And another. The screaming only gets louder.

Oz and Book stay calm, focused. We trot along at a fair clip, as far as we can be from the Mall while still riding along it, and Book's dark coat and our uniforms help to hide us. Except for flashes of fire, the power outage has taken out the streetlights that normally make this a well-lit area. Sticking to the shadows, we make decent progress. Not that I could say how long has passed. Seconds, minutes, hours. Decades.

To get to the Washington Monument itself, we have to leave our relative safety. Book trots onto the grassy slope around it, and my arms tighten around Oz as a large shape lowers into our way.

The god straightens to his full height. It's Mehen.

Oz trains Book to the left to go around him, but Mehen's head coils back, his hood flaring on either side of it.

A familiar lion's snarl accompanies Anzu's dive from above. He rams into Mehen, cutting off his path to us.

"I have never been so happy to see a monster in my life," I say.

"Thank him for me later," Oz agrees.

He spurs Book into a gallop across the open ground. There are no people up here – the Monument itself has been off limits to the public since the Awakening – but spears of light flicker above.

There is a Society guard posted at the base of the monument, the stone shooting high above us. It is surprisingly enormous this close up. In the distance, it seems slender, the sky around it so much larger. Oz greets the guard with, "The board has ordered us to raise the walls."

Oz urges me down first, and the guard helps catch me. After Oz dismounts, the guard accepts Book's reins. Apparently watching the mayhem unfold in front of him is enough to sell the story. "Godspeed," he says to us, without a shred of irony.

We make it into the lobby, where we're greeted by a bronze statue of George Washington. Oz doesn't pause on the way to the elevator.

"The power's out," I remind him. I point to a crumbly set of roped off steps that will take *much* longer.

"Not here." Oz nods at an electric light fixture I hadn't noticed. But, sure enough, it's on. "The building was hardened with its own supply, for that reason." He pushes the call button, and the door pings open. I follow him inside.

The doors close, and we are quiet as we begin to speed upward.

"I killed my grandfather," I say.

Oz makes sure I meet his eyes. "It was the right thing to do."

"Do they tell you that?" I ask, jealous that maybe I wouldn't feel this way if I'd grown up training for nights like this. "Do they prepare you for what it feels like after you have to…?"

Oz says, "Yes, but I haven't had to put it in practice yet. I don't think what they tell us would make it much different at all. It should be hard to make a decision like that. But you did the right thing."

"I feel sick when I think about it. It was over so fast."

"It was the right thing to do," he repeats.

"I know." And I do. Oz's lack of judgment reinforces it.

I want to believe that Bronson has gotten what he wanted, that he and his Gabrielle are together, that she met him at the threshold of death and told him the drowning was an accident, and that they can make a happy death together. It's not much of a fairy tale ending, but I want it for him, despite what he did.

The elevator lumbers to a stop and we exit onto the observation deck. It has a dark floor, and stone walls covered by glass. Two rectangular windows with thick glass are positioned in the center of the wall in front of us.

"What do we do now?" I ask.

Oz says, "It'll be here somewhere." He examines the walls. On his second circuit, he stops in front of a stone with a crack at the side, or maybe just a thicker join. There's a small hollow circle above it. "Stand back." He bashes the glass in front of it once with his elbow, then again, and it breaks. The larger fragments drop at our feet, and he brushes the shards clinging to the frame aside.

"Where are you…?" he says, reaching into the hollow spot with two fingers. I watch as he presses down with his weight, and worry he'll break a bone in his hand. But stone scrapes stone, and he removes a large rectangular piece from the wall.

"We have to strike inside this area with a weapon, so that the wall repels the attack. That's all – in theory." He removes a short blade hidden inside his boot.

I recognize the knife. It's the one that Bronson used to threaten my father, his backup weapon. Oz offers the grip to me, and I accept it. How fitting.

Through the broad window nearby, more flames are visible. There is a *boom* like the loudest thunder I've ever heard.

Oz says, "Do the honors."

I lift the knife and insert my arm into the hollow stone opening. I scratch the knife along the stone as I withdraw it. My skin buzzes at the contact of knife and stone. But…

Nothing. More. Happens.

The sensation fades as soon as I remove the blade from the empty space.

I frown. "What am I doing wrong?"

"Try striking harder," he says. "It needs to mimic an attack. But be care–"

There's no more room for over-cautiousness here. I gather my strength and punch forward with the knife. The opening swallows my hand, and the blade hits the back of the stone within with a crunch. My knuckles vibrate with the impact, my skin stinging and scraped by the rough surface.

But it works.

A deep bass echo and invisible... *force*... pitch me back against the glass protecting the opposite wall. From the hollow comes a deep reverberation, sound made tangible as a shock wave, followed by bright light. At the observation window, Anzu snaps and snarls, angry instead of an ally now. But then he tumbles back and away.

I still have the knife in my hand as we move to the window to watch the walls rise.

They are nearly transparent, but not quite, emanating out from the Monument into the sky in an arc that must end at the edges of the city. The gods are being pushed out en masse, flung beyond the borders like the walls stand between this world and another one. The sound finally dies, but the forcefield – because that's what the walls are – holds.

The streetlights below come on all at once, showing the destruction left behind. The eerie calm lasts for a single long moment. The first emergency sirens fill it, blaring from speakers mounted around the city.

"We did it," Oz says.

"We did." I study the boundary, and wish I could know for certain whether it will be enough to save us. "We postponed the end of the world."

CHAPTER THIRTY-ONE

We ride back up the Mall, the streetlights showing every battered body and smashed national landmark, every response worker trying to help those who hang onto life. Oz rides to the stables, and goes in with Book to make sure he is settled. The stablemen are already spinning stories about the night, and one of them says, "Never thought they'd raise the walls in my lifetime."

I listen, and wait for Oz to come back out.

A large group of people is gathered around the Jefferson, waiting for something – an explanation, probably. They pay no attention to us. As we approach the less-used ground floor entrance of the Jefferson together, I discover I'm nervous about seeing Mom... and Dad. About seeing what the future will hold now that we have one. Legba made it sound as if this game isn't ending anytime soon.

Oz stops at the door, puts his back to it and faces me. We stand close, chest to chest. "What is it?" I ask.

But his serious expression tells me. It takes me back to that moment in the yard, when something was going to happen between us until Bree interrupted. The connection between us never left, not during any of this.

I'm still afraid of it. "Oz," I say, before I can convince myself not to, "it's better if we stay friends. I'm not... I can't... Ask Tam. It won't end well."

He continues to look at me. Though the shadows around us hide the blue-gray of his eyes, I know them so well by now that I can imagine it.

"Kyra?" he asks.

Before I can give more excuses, he leans in and kisses me. I'm confused at first. Has this night really happened? Is *this* really happening?

Oz's hand slides to the back of my neck, and his fingers pull my ponytail loose and tangle in my hair. I wrap my arms around him, press close to him, because I want more of this. This feels... new, like I expected a first kiss to feel before I had one.

Someone knocking on the other side of the door makes us separate. His palm drifts down my cheek. I'm not sure how to act after that, and I try for casual. "Kissing at the end of the world," I say, tone light.

"No better time," Oz says. "But before you give me a speech about why that can't happen again, you should know that it will. Kyra, don't freak out. I'm not asking for your hand in marriage."

"Gah," I say. "I can't believe you even said that."

"I know you think you're not relationship material," he says. My shock must be plain, because he says, "Bree told me."

"I'm not." But I'm less sure of it than I ever have been.

"No matter what happens, we have gone through all of this together," Oz says. "And we *will* be friends, because of that. So, why not see where the rest goes?"

Because that way lies pain. Because that ways lies danger.

He's right. I know he's right. My internal protests are weakness. There will always be pain and danger and risk. But on the other side of those things might be something worth braving them for.

"You make a compelling argument," I say.

That earns me a devilishly attractive grin.

The person on the other side of the door bangs on it with greater force, and Oz finally steps aside. It swings open. "Sorry," Oz says, "we had some unfinished business."

Two Society guards give us the eyeball, annoyed. But then they recognize us. "You two," one of them says. The other adds, "You're wanted upstairs by the acting director." "Acting *directors*," the first corrects him.

Oz and I exchange a look. We shrug in tandem. "Then that's where we're headed," he says.

Upstairs, we find Society operatives everywhere, going in and out, up and down stairs, with loud chatter. In the Great Hall, my grandfather's body has been removed and Dad is no longer tied down to the sun. The toppled statue still lays on its side, the marble below it cracked.

Rose clicks across the floor, her uniform exchanged for a sedate dove gray suit. Her black bob is neat and her makeup perfect. Right behind her is my father, also cleaned up and in a fresh uniform. I stop.

"You OK?" Oz asks.

"We saved him," I say, and he must get how overwhelmed I am at realizing that, at seeing Dad in front of me alive and well, because he only nods.

Rose spots us before Dad does, and signals him so they meet us. I expect Dad to, I don't know, thank me or fold me into a hug or tear up, but he greets me with, "Good to see you made it back unharmed."

"Where's Mom?" I ask.

"Nearby. I'll take you to her as soon as we're done here," he says.

I didn't realize we were *doing* something here, but fine. I can wait.

"Are you aware, Osborne," Rose asks, "that the board is the only entity that can decide to raise the city walls?"

Oz turns to Dad. "Mr Locke said–"

"I know, and it was quick thinking on your part. Good job," Rose tells him.

"That wasn't nice," I say.

The freckles on Rose's cheeks lift as she smiles at me. "You did OK too, especially for someone with no training. Don't you agree, Henry?"

"She made me proud."

"Please, stop," I say, and mean it. I think I may be blushing. Oz's grin is back and it makes me want to punch his arm. Or pull him into a dark corner.

The levity doesn't last. Rose sighs, says, "After all, you couldn't have known we needed Bronson alive."

"We didn't," Dad says. "We're better off without him. I'm sorry, Oz, but there are better guardians for you."

"He broke his vows," Oz says. "And worse."

It can't be that simple for Oz. But I know he'll get through this new loss and deal with the strange circumstances of it, whether it brings more nightmares or not.

Rose lifts one shoulder. "It's a little inconvenient. We haven't found a single note he left about how to put the gods back to sleep, no matter what he claimed, and I don't expect that we will. We lost the only person who had the knowledge to truly protect us from the gods. Now we have to come up with a plan B, figure out how to move this door."

"Which we will," Dad says, confident.

Another group of people enter the Great Hall, and I am beyond glad that Tam and Bree are among them. Justin, Nalini and her cameraman are too – even Ben. He's wearing a suit that doesn't look like one he'd own.

I go to meet them, and Oz sticks with me. "What's going on?" I ask.

"You'll see," Tam says.

"We live in bizarro world now," Bree adds. "Everybody getting along, cooperating. It's freakish."

Rose calls, "Are we all set? You understand what we'll be doing?"

Ben nods, the picture of solemnity. Bree's mother says, "We would like to keep the footage for archive purposes–"

Dad interrupts. "National security. I'm sorry, Nalini."

She lowers her chin in agreement. "You stand here then," she says to Rose.

"Are you guys OK?" Bree asks Oz and me.

"We are," I say.

I notice Tam and Bree are holding hands. Excellent. I give Tam a nod, and I can tell he's walking on the air somewhere around cloud nine.

It's time for Rose's show. Dad makes his way over to watch with the rest of us. He's never liked spotlights. Rose may as well have been born in one, though.

She positions herself so that the downed statue is visible behind her, torch hand thrusting up. The cameraman and Nalini stand opposite her. Nalini says, "I'm here with one of the two new acting directors of the Society, who have taken over after Director William Bronson was slain earlier this evening. The Tricksters' Council is consumed by violent infighting, and the Society has put special security measures in place to formulate a response. Rose Greene, what can you tell the world this evening?"

Rose begins to talk, weaving a story about the secret precaution that could force the gods from D.C., about the massive response the Society would be mounting worldwide, urging calm in the face of what were sure to be anxious days ahead... At the end, Nalini turns the microphone to Ben and asks for comment. He says, "I know I have been the Society's harshest critic, but I urge you all to trust them on this. I... I believe they are working to restore peace."

"Wow," I say.

"Yeah," Tam says. "Never thought you'd hear that, did you?"

"Never," I agree.

The interview over, Dad turns to me. "You ready to see your mom?"

"Can we make a stop at our reliquary first?" I ask.

"Sure. It's on the way," he says.

I can tell he wants to find out why, just like I want to ask on the way to where, but neither of us says anything more. "See you guys a little later," I tell the others, mouthing "Mom" to them, so they'll understand.

I accompany Dad downstairs, and he raises his eyebrows when I make it clear I don't need direction to the gaslight fixture that leads to the network of secret hallways. When we get to the House Locke reliquary, I take the blue eye from my pocket and insert it. The door zips open.

Dad coughs. "I'll be needing that back. And my stripes."

So it *is* his. "But–"

"You'll get ones of your own. Kyra, if you've taken to this like it appears, we'll get you more training. You could take your vows before you know it. Maybe in two years."

I scoff, "It won't take that long. Trust me."

He laughs, and I try to remember the last time I heard him do that. "So... you like the Ramones?" I ask. "You know this means I have to embrace country and western, right?"

He winces. "What about classic country? Johnny Cash would be good."

"Not even. I'm going to pick something you loathe."

He laughs again as we go inside. I walk along the hunter's map and then toward the case that's my destination.

"Why are we here anyway?" he asks, trailing me.

"Oh no," I say. "I completely forgot. I left Vidarr's shoe upstairs."

He shakes his head. "I noticed. Someone put it away for safekeeping. I figured I'd return it later."

"Oh, good," I say. I hope they found my backpack too, so his Ramones shirt isn't lost either. Or my jacket. But I see no need to mention that right now. "Because losing a major relic seems like the kind of thing that would be a black mark on my record."

"I think you'll find the record you're building speaks for itself."

I'm still me, and so I work to keep my expression neutral, rather than basking in an actual compliment from my father. Reaching deep into my pocket, I remove the shard from Legba's cane and unwrap the tissue I put around it. I open the glass door and place it beside the white and black cap of chaos.

"And that is?" he asks.

I close the case. "It's a bone fragment from Legba's cane that I had to remove from Anzu. It kept him from healing. Don't know what it'll do as a relic, though."

"Make that your record will *more* than speak for itself." He puts his hand on my shoulder. I turn to him. We aren't yelling at each other yet. It's a record. "Kyra, I'm sorry I handled the past few years the way I did. I just worried about you all the time, and that meant rules you couldn't handle, and so much distance between us..."

"I know." Still no yelling. "You were being an idiot."

"Watch it. I *am* your father."

"You don't know how grateful I am for that."

I know we will never go back to that terrible place where we can't talk to each other. We may still shout at each other occasionally, because old habits and strong opinions don't always mix. But anger won't be our constant state of being.

"Mom?" I ask.

"Mom," he says. "Let's go see her."

We start toward the door. "You didn't let her go wandering around?" I ask.

"No, she's with the Pythias, her sisters in spirit. They should be able to stabilize her some."

He means those women from the hall. I don't ask any more questions, curious to see if she will be better. Legba could bring clarity to Mom – maybe they can do it without tricking her afterward.

We stop at a door like a waterfall, made of a thousand mirror shards. Inside, Mom sits between the two women Oz and I saw. She wears her black dress, kohl smeared around her eyes, a spot of darkness between the pale white dresses of the others. But all of them are beaming as if they emit light.

Dad folds an arm around my shoulders, and Mom wears a broad smile as she rises. She floats toward us. "My daughter," she says, "who changed her fate."

Dad brings us both into a hug, and we stand there

with our arms around each other for a long time. It's still not quite long enough to recapture the years we lost.

Mom eventually pushes back. "I want to see it, the wall, the barrier, the light that keeps the dark out," she says.

Dad's disapproval threatens to return, but I say, "Me too. Let's go look at the walls. Together."

"Fine," he agrees.

I think it was the together that got him.

Dad holds Mom's hand as we navigate the halls back upstairs. I know the turns at this point, so I lead. When we reach the Great Hall, there's no one left in it. We head over to the guard at the line of massive doors.

"We're going out," Dad says.

The guard grumbles a little as he moves aside from the open one. "You and every single person not on duty."

The front porch and steps of the Jefferson are covered with operatives, a civilian crowd massed on the sidewalks below. I spot my friends near the top of the stairs. We make our way to them. Dad keeps one hand on Mom's shoulder, and his other on mine.

Oz and I lock gazes, but I break away to look up, where everyone else is. The boundary is a slight sheen, arcing high above.

There are no gods visible outside it, not here. But somewhere nearby, at the edge of the city, there will be. The walls might have forced the gods from D.C., but they are out there, and the rest of the world will witness their anger.

I close my eyes, and see my grandfather's face again. I

have to find out what he knew about putting the gods to sleep. The woman who charmed Enki so long ago is also part of our family's history. I feel the thread between the past and the present. The link may be fragile, but I am certain I can follow it. I can discover its secrets. I have to.

Radiant fire races along the outside edge of the translucent wall above, and the operatives around us gasp. But Dad doesn't, and neither do I. It only confirms what I already assume.

The world is burning. We won't have much time to smother the flames.

ACKNOWLEDGMENTS

This has been a maddening trickster of a book to write, one that's been rattling around my brain and word processors for several years and reincarnations. Which means there's a small army of people who have offered insight and assistance on it. For comments on early versions of this story, I offer thanks to: Karen Joy Fowler (who kept asking about it), Karen Meisner, Justine Larbalestier, the insanely helpful workshoppers at the 2009 Rio Hondo and Blue Heaven workshops, and Stacy Whitman. I'm indebted beyond measure to the friends who listened to me whine, brainstormed worldbuilding, and kept me from jumping off a cliff in Mexico while I was writing this version. This book simply would not exist without my wonderful agent, Jennifer Laughran (without who I would be lost), and the patient belief of my editor, Amanda Rutter. To my husband, Christopher Rowe; once again I couldn't do any of this without you, because I'd starve and fall into despair.

And, of course, my eternal gratitude to: the booksellers, librarians, bloggers, and friends who have been so supportive; my publisher, Angry Robot, and the sales team at Random House; each and every one of my readers.

Finally, I'm indebted to one of my favorite non-fiction works, Lewis Hyde's *Trickster Makes This World: Mischief, Myth, and Art*. I couldn't – or wouldn't – have written this book without it. My thanks to Neil Gaiman, who put it into my hands many years ago.

Any mistakes and shortcomings here are, as always, my own.

EXPERIMENTING WITH YOUR IMAGINATION

"Exciting, funny, clever, scary, captivating, and – most importantly – really, really awesome."
James Smythe, author of The Testimony

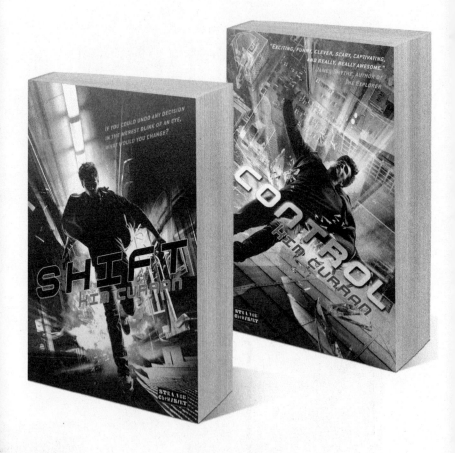

EXPERIMENTING WITH YOUR IMAGINATION

"With a whip-smart, instantly likeable characters and a gothic small-town setting, Bond weaves a dark and gorgeous tapestry from America's oldest mystery"
Scott Westerfield

EXPERIMENTING WITH YOUR IMAGINATION

Whoever said being a teenage witch
would be easy?